LOVE IN SLOW MOTION

B. RANDALL

Haunted Hearts Publishing

ISBN: 978-1-965794-00-5

Cover by Paper or Pixels Covers

Proofread by Gennifer Rulmen

brandallromance.com

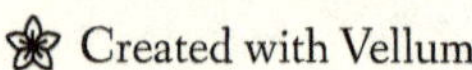 Created with Vellum

*For all the women
still searching for themselves*

AUTHOR'S NOTE

Dear Reader,

More than anything, this is a story about a woman trying to find herself after losing her identity in a toxic relationship. It touches on a lot of heavy subjects, and I hope that you will take care of your mental health as you move forward. To help, I've included a list of possible triggers below.

Cheating (not main couple), divorce, mentions of body dysmorphia, fatphobic comments, emotional abuse, cancer (not main couple), death of a family member, mentions of homicide and domestic abuse, discussions of pregnancy complications and miscarriage (no miscarriages on page), mentions of sexual harassment (not seen on page), degradation kink (consensual), very light BDSM (belt use).

LOVE IN SLOW MOTION

1 QUINN

Someone once told me that getting divorced is often harder for people on a psychological level than losing your spouse to actual death. Something about the sheer rejection of losing someone you thought would always love you, I suppose.

Not for me. As I walk out of the mediator's office one husband lighter, I feel like someone unlocked the door to the cage I've been in. I can see the sunshine. I can feel my body unfurling. I can breathe.

"Quinn! Wait!"

My shoulders slump, and I come to a halt in the mediator's lobby. The doors to freedom are right there. I can practically smell the Boston smog on the other side. I turn and face my ex-husband. Looking at him and thinking that word—ex-husband—has a shiver going through me, even though it won't be final for a little while.

For the past three months, while we've dealt with the mediation and moved our lives around, none of it has really felt real. I kept feeling like I was waiting for life to go back to normal.

But there's no such thing as normal anymore. Normal now looks like living alone in a big, empty house, job hunting, eating dinner at a reasonable hour instead of waiting around all the time for Chase to get home from work.

Or home from fucking one of his many mistresses, as the case may be.

"What do you want, Chase?" All things considered, Chase has been a pretty good sport through this whole divorce thing. He could have fought me over the house; he could have tried to get me to call the whole thing off; he could have found a way to screw me out of money that I don't have. But instead, he paid for the mediator, gave me the house, and is mostly letting me out of this arrangement free and clear.

Which just goes to show how invested he was in the marriage to begin with.

Chase, dressed in one of the gray, pin-striped suits he usually wears to work, comes to a stop in front of me. Behind him, the woman sitting at the reception desk isn't even trying to hide the fact that she's watching us. I'm sure she gets soon-to-be ex-spouses fighting in front of her desk all the time.

But Chase doesn't look like he's about to pick a fight. He's got that expression on his face that has afforded him an entire lifetime of forgiveness from everyone around him. His eyebrows curve in, and his big eyes are perfectly round. He looks like a puppy at a shelter, begging me to take him home.

"Listen," he says, his hands up between us like he might have to fend off an attack. And if he doesn't let me leave pretty quickly, he might be right. I might be tempted to stab him with my new Quincy Bay Mediation Group pen. "I know you hate me right now, and of course I get it, but I need a favor."

I scoff. "You're kidding, right?"

His hands drop to his sides with a soft *smack*. When someone has to politely squeeze by us to get to the front desk,

Chase motions at me to follow him out onto the sidewalk. The sidewalk where I was supposed to be free. Instead, I'm still somehow shackled to Chase and his puppy dog eyes.

"I know you don't owe me anything," Chase goes on, speaking louder now that he's having to yell over the traffic on the street. It's rush hour in downtown Boston, which I'm hoping will be enough to get him to get on with whatever he's asking me to do. Not only am I late for dinner with my best friend, but I'm starting to sweat in my sensible black heels. "But I really need your help."

I roll my eyes. "Would you just spit it out? I'm late."

He scowls, all trace of the *please sir, can I have some more?* facial expression gone. "Late for what? A date?"

"Jesus Christ," I growl, glancing over at a homeless man crouched against the pink marble building so I don't have to look at Chase's face, a face I've spent the last five years staring at, a face I hardly recognize anymore. "I'm not going on a date fifteen minutes after my divorce mediation, not that it's any of your business. Unlike you, I figured I would at least wait until the divorce is final."

He flinches like I stepped on his toe. "Yeah, I get it. I won't keep you. But here's the deal. I talked to my mother yesterday. I called to tell her we wouldn't be going out to the lake house this year, and she was pretty bummed about it. I guess Sabrina doesn't want to go this year either, and you know Reed never goes. So, Mom said she would up the price."

Up the price. Every summer, my mother-in-law (at least, until the divorce is final) hands each of her children a $100,000 check if they show up for the family vacation at her lake house in Wolfeboro, New Hampshire. Madison Lynch has had the words "independently wealthy" attached to her name since she was my age, but spoiling her kids was never a concept that seemed particularly interesting to her, so the only time she willingly gives them money is for showing up to the lake house.

While Chase and I were married, Madison gave us $100,000 each, a hundred grand for me and a hundred grand for Chase. If anyone else in the family found it unfair, they never said so. Of course, the only person around to complain was Sabrina, Chase's sister, who hardly cared about the money anyway.

And Reed...well...Reed never goes to the lake house. Everyone says he used to go, but for as long as I've known the Lynch family, he's never shown his face in New Hampshire.

When I don't respond, Chase continues. "Since nobody was planning to show up this year, she's only upping the price if all the kids come: me, Sabrina, and Reed. $500,000 a piece if we all show."

The amount almost makes me choke. It might not seem like all that much to the Lynches, but I didn't grow up with that kind of wealth, and I never really got used to it while I was married to Chase.

"I don't understand what that has to do with me," I say, beginning to feel antsy. Brooke is sometimes late to dinner, and if I don't hurry up, we might not get a table at our favorite place. "I'm not part of this family anymore, remember?" I gesture toward the building behind him. The sun is spearing off the gold lettering beside the door, blinding me.

Chase sighs. "Well, as far as my mother knows, you are."

His words echo in my head, swirling around in my brain along with the noise of honking cars and people on the sidewalk muttering into their cell phones. Does he mean what I think he means?

"Chase, please tell me you told your mother that we're getting divorced." His mouth falls open in a guilty look, and I groan, my hand going up to my hair. Better to grab my bangs than his neck. "Chase! What the fuck is wrong with you!" I turn and start down the sidewalk. I cannot be that close to him anymore. I can't stand to look at him, can't stand the sound of his voice, can't stand the never-ending idiocy that I used to be able to overlook and no longer can.

"Quinn, please." Chase catches up to me at the crosswalk, and in that moment, I hate that I'm the kind of person who lawfully waits for the sign to change. Everyone else would just wait for the break in traffic least likely to leave them flattened. "You know my mother adores you. I didn't want to break her heart. It's not like I wasn't going to tell her *ever*; I just didn't want to tell her right then, over the phone, when she was already upset about nobody going out to the lake."

The little person appears on the crosswalk sign, and I hurry away from Chase. But he's not wearing heels and is able to easily keep up with me. "Again, I ask, what the hell does any of this have to do with me, Chase?"

He wraps a hand around my elbow, pulling me to a stop once we reach the other side of the street. Once we're eye-to-eye again, the rest of the foot traffic seamlessly parting around us, he sighs and says, "She won't give any of us the money unless we're all there. Including you."

I yank my elbow out of his grip. "Well, then I guess you should have thought about that before you cheated on me. Why don't you share *that* with your mother?" Ignoring his heart-broken expression, I turn and rush down the sidewalk.

TO MY SURPRISE, BROOKE IS ALREADY SEATED AND waiting for me when I get to the little Italian bistro we like, Michelangelo's. She waves at me from a two-person table beside the far window, and I head over, feeling the stress start to seep out of my pores at the sight of her. When I'm with Brooke, it's like stress has lost my address.

I fall into my chair with a sigh and immediately catch a whiff of the massive pizza that Brooke has ordered for us. Margherita. My favorite. The cheese on top is about three inches thick, and my stomach growls at the sight.

"How do you feel?" Brooke asks with the brightest smile on her face. "Was it everything you ever dreamed of?" She makes it sound like I just came back from a trip to Disneyland.

"Divorced at twenty-five isn't exactly ideal, but sure, I'm happy it's over."

"Me, too," she says, offering the pizza a conspiratorial look. Brooke was never Chase's biggest fan. I guess I should be grateful that she hasn't said anything along the lines of *I told you so* since we found out that Chase was cheating. She *has* offered to murder him several times. After I tested positive for chlamydia, confirming Chase's extramarital activities, Brooke may have almost run him over with her car, but by that point, I was teetering over to the side of violence as well.

"You'll never believe what Chase did."

Brooke's eyebrows shoot up. She picks up a slice of pizza from the tray, the melted cheese stretching as she plops it down on the paper plate in front of me. "Is it worse than having multiple sexual partners that aren't his wife and then giving you an STI?" She takes a slice of pizza for herself and nods toward mine, silently urging me to eat.

"I guess *worse* isn't the correct way to look at it. It just *is*. And what it is, is moronic." I hold up one finger. "First, he didn't tell his family about the divorce. Except Reed. Reed definitely knows. He told me months ago that he was sleeping on Reed's couch, so I just assumed he had told his whole family. My mistake." I put up a second finger. "Second, he followed me for like six blocks to talk to me after the mediation." Third finger. "And third, he asked me for a *favor.*"

Brooke emits a laugh so loud and sharp that the couple at the next table startle, their shoulders going up around their ears as they look at her. I send them an apologetic smile, even as Brooke continues to laugh. "Is he kidding?" she demands. "I swear, the fucking *balls* on that guy."

"I know." I finally take a bite of my pizza, closing my eyes at the greasy, cheesy goodness. I moan quietly, and when I open my eyes, Brooke is smirking at me.

"Geez, I didn't realize you were so hard up that all it would take is a slice of margherita to get you off." The startled couple sends Brooke another scathing glare. Brooke doesn't notice, of course. Brooke has no interest in other people's opinions. It's one of the things I love most about her. Where I stress about the way I'm perceived by everyone, Brooke is who she is, no matter who's looking.

"So, what was it?"

"Hmmm?" The soda in my hand is almost halfway gone, and I manage to pull myself away long enough to say, "What was what?"

Brooke blinks at me like I'm an idiot. "The favor. What was the favor that Chase asked you to do?"

"Oh, jeez." I shake my head and roll my eyes. I can't even believe it's a thing that really happened, that he even had the audacity to ask me such a thing in the first place. "Madison is upping the summer allowance if everyone shows up at the lake house this year. $500,000. And since Chase never got around to telling her that we're getting divorced, I'm included in the *everyone* of it all."

Brooke's disbelieving look makes me feel especially justified about the whole thing. "How would that even work? What, you pretend to still be married? Or do you show up and say, 'oh hey,

I'm not your daughter-in-law anymore, but I'll take that half a million if you don't mind'?"

"Hell if I know. I didn't exactly consider the logistics. It's not as if it's going to happen."

Brooke gets a far-off look in her eyes. She watches the traffic go by outside. I know that look, and I don't particularly like it. It means she's thinking about doing something impulsive, like trying to run over my ex-husband. The last time she got that look on her face where I could see it, she almost violently attacked her next-door neighbor, who, oddly enough, is now her boyfriend.

"What?" I ask her, wiping my mouth and staring longingly at the pizza between us. She got the whole thing, all eight slices, like we haven't in a very long time. I want another piece, but I know I shouldn't.

Her eyes travel back over to me. "Nothing. It's just...half a million dollars is a lot of money."

A humorless laugh bursts out of me. "Are you kidding? Stop it. Do not even get that thought in your head. There's no way I'm going to that lake house. I'm done with Chase and his entire family, okay? I am no longer a Lynch." When I say the words out loud, my chest gets tight and my stomach lurches. But that's the reality of it. It's time to move on.

"Right. Yes. Of course. You're totally right." She shakes her head, like she's trying to banish the thought from her mind, and then she puts another slice of pizza on my plate.

"Oh, I shouldn't," I say, pushing my plate away, even as my mouth waters.

Brooke's lips twist. "And why shouldn't you?"

I meet her eyes. I can feel her disappointment across the expanse of the table. I sigh. "Come on, Brooke. You know how many calories are in a slice of pizza like this."

Brooke's jaw tightens, and her mouth forms a line. "Quinn, do you want the pizza?"

I hold her stare for a long time because we already know the answer, and I already know what she'll say once I admit the truth. "Yeah, I want the pizza."

She shoves my plate closer to me. "Then eat the damn pizza. He doesn't get to tell you what you're allowed to eat and not eat anymore." She winks at me. "I love you."

I laugh and pick up the slice as she starts telling me about her latest shenanigans at work. Brooke used to live in Boston, just like me, but when she broke up with her boyfriend, who she was sharing an apartment with, she had to move to Belmont. Even though Belmont is only half an hour away from Boston, it was hard for me when she moved. I used to be able to bike to her place, and now I have to wade through awful Boston traffic to get to her new apartment. Not to mention the fact that since she started dating Clay, she hasn't been calling as much.

I know it's not her fault, but when you're used to having your husband and your best friend around all the time, it's tough to find yourself alone most hours out of the day. These days, I'm lucky if I speak to another human being in the span of twenty-four hours.

"How's the job search going?" Brooke asks when the pizza is mostly gone and I'm on my second soda refill.

"Going about as well as my marriage, I guess."

Brooke grimaces. "I'm so sorry. I could easily get you a job at the bar, but it's a long commute, not to mention that it wouldn't exactly put that marketing degree to good use."

I look down at the empty pizza tray between us. "I'll figure something out," I say, even though I couldn't feel less confident about the validity of those words.

2 QUINN

At first, winning the house in the divorce seemed
like a good thing. After all, I've spent countless hours cleaning,
decorating, and hosting parties at this house. I'm the one who
made it a home. But the reality is, when you get the house in a
divorce, you have to live in it alone, you have to pay the mortgage on it alone, and you have to constantly face the memories
that cage you in every time you sleep in the bed you once
shared with your spouse or shower where you used to shower
together. The couch where we used to fall asleep during
movies, the table where we used to have dinner on nights when
Chase made it home at a reasonable hour, the garage where he
used to drink beer and pretend like he was going to teach
himself to fix things.

I fought to keep the house, but now I don't want it. I just
didn't want to have to find a new place to live, on top of trying
to find a job after letting Chase support me for the last three
years.

Walking through the empty house, I start to undress,

leaving my shoes and the clothes I wore to the mediation scattered across the floor the way that used to earn me a comment from Chase when he got home.

"Come on, Quinn. You don't have time to take your clothes to the laundry basket? It's like living with a teenage boy."

Sometimes you just want to leave your clothes splayed out across the couch. Well, now there's no one around to tell me I can't. There's also no one around to criticize me for stopping at the market down the street to buy a giant slice of cake that's probably meant to be shared by two people.

I've just settled onto the couch, slice of cake in one hand and the TV remote in the other, when my phone *dings* to let me know I have a message. I toss the remote onto the coffee table and grab my phone. It's probably Brooke, letting me know that she made it back to Belmont, and her boyfriend's loving arms, safely. I roll my eyes. Those two are so in love it's sickening.

Was I ever that in love, even in the early days, with Chase?

Now that all is said and done, I can't remember.

The notification on my phone is an email, and when I see that it's from the marketing firm that I interviewed at last week, I stop breathing. I've been to countless interviews. I've smiled until my cheeks hurt, and I've come up with more bogus interview answers than I ever thought I would in my life.

But every single job has rejected me and all for the same reason: because as soon as I got my marketing degree, I married Chase, and we agreed that I didn't have to work. Between the lake house allowance and Chase's executive job, we had more than enough to get by. And because of that, I have no experience and a huge employment gap. My last job was at the Suffolk University campus bookstore, for God's sake.

I open the email, and my eyes go straight to the greeting.

Dear Mrs. Lynch...

I try not to cringe at the name. I haven't had a chance to change it, but I put a trip to the tax office at the top of my mental to-do list. I do *not* want to be a Lynch any longer, at least not if it means being married to Chase.

> *We were happy to get to meet you last week, and while we found you to be very professional, competent, and personable, we unfortunately are looking for someone with experience in the field. Thank you for interviewing with us, and we wish you the best of luck in your professional endeavors.*

I drop my phone into my lap and burrow down into the couch. What the hell am I supposed to do? I've sent so many applications, been on so many interviews. Should I just go get a job at the nearest Starbucks? Or at the bar where Brooke works? Even if the thought of that was at all appealing, it's not like it would be enough to pay the bills. The mortgage on this house is astronomical, and I'm not going to be able to pay it on a barista's salary.

My eyes find the shape of me in the TV's reflection. I stare at myself, the way my hair has gotten too long and my skin has gone sallow. How did I get here? How did I go from a person who was married and had her entire life put together to a person who can't even afford to keep a roof over her own head? This is what happens when you don't fight for alimony. It's my own damn fault. I just wanted the whole thing to be over and done with, and I figured that as long as I got the house, I would be fine.

But now it's been months, the money I have in the bank account is running out, and I don't know what to do.

Maybe I could get a roommate, or three. We have four bedrooms. That would get me through for a little while at least. Or maybe I could rent them out on AirBnB or something. I could learn to cook and make breakfast for people looking to stay in Boston on vacation.

I feel the weight of my phone in my lap, like someone set a medicine ball on my thighs. I could call Chase. I could ask him for a little more money to get me by until I can get a good, paying job. He wouldn't fight me. I know he wouldn't. He knows I need the money. Of course he does. Otherwise, why would he have cornered me outside the mediation office and asked me for that absolutely ridiculous favor?

But then...he wouldn't have asked if he didn't need the money, too. He can't be paying that much for a live-in hotel or an apartment, if he's gotten one already, especially since he spent some time after our break-up sleeping on Reed's couch. So why does he need half a million dollars so bad? Maybe it's just contingency.

There's another option, of course.

The option that is so bizarre and out of the realm of anything I would even consider.

The option of spending a week at the lake house in New Hampshire. On the one hand, I would make $500,000 and get to spend one last hurrah with Madison and Sabrina and Reed.

My stomach clenches at the thought. Through this entire process, I've done a really good job of refusing to think about the fact that Chase's family will no longer be my family. I love the Lynch family, and the knowledge that I might never see any of them again feels like someone standing over me with a hacksaw, getting ready to amputate my arm.

But if I were to agree to go to the lake house, I would have to pretend to still be married to Chase. I don't know if I could do that. PDA? Calling each other "sweetheart"? Is that the sort of thing I could stomach for half a million dollars?

I don't think any of this even matters. There's no way that anyone is getting Reed to the lake house. As long as I've known the Lynch family, the only person who has never shown up for summer vacation is Reed. So even if I agreed to go, would he?

I pick up my phone and dial Chase's number.

3 REED

As soon as I open the door and see Chase on the other side, I slam it again.

"Reed!" he shouts from the other side. "Come on! I know you're mad at me, but I need your help."

Mad at him. He thinks I'm mad at him. I imagine "mad" as a subatomic particle, the tiniest piece of matter that exists in the universe. What I feel toward my brother is an atomic bomb. If detonated, it could destroy entire towns. "Mad" is laughable.

I stare at the door and sip my coffee. "You must have me mistaken for a person who gives a shit. Have you tried calling Sabrina?"

"Yes, actually," he says through the door. "And she agreed to help me. But I need everybody in on this one."

I continue to stare at the door. It doesn't have a peephole, thank God. I don't want to see my brother's little rat face all distorted through the glass. He's clown enough without all that spectacle piled on top.

"I'm not helping you with anything, Chase. Go home." I turn away from the door. I've spent too much of my life trying to help my brother, bending over backward to make sure he had everything he wanted, and what did he do?

He threw away a marriage to the best person in the world. He had everything he could have ever wanted in life, and he fucked around until he lost everything. And I don't feel bad for him. Play stupid games, win stupid prizes.

Leaving my door chain firmly intact, I head into my bedroom and get ready for my meeting. Standing in the mirror, I roll up my sleeves. I can't keep my eyes from wandering over to the picture frame on my wall. The entire Lynch family, all together for Thanksgiving five years ago. College-aged Quinn and Chase smile back at me, so happy, so optimistic about life.

I wonder how she is, if I should reach out. I've started a text to her at least three hundred times since Chase told me they were splitting up. But what would I even say? *Sorry, my brother is a piece of shit. I don't suppose you want to run away with me instead?*

I run my fingers through my short hair and stick my wallet in my back pocket on my way to the door. A glance at the clock tells me I'm going to get there right on time, which sort of irks me. I like to arrive early. I like the moments before the storm.

With that lovely thought in my mind, I open my door to leave and trip over something.

"Fuck!" a voice that isn't mine says as I stumble and smack into the wall across the hall. Chase is sitting on the ground in front of my door, cross-legged like he's getting ready to recite his alphabet in a kindergarten class. He glares up at me. "You can't look before you step out your door?"

"What the hell are you still doing here? Go the fuck home, Chase."

He scrambles to his feet, and I push past him to lock my door. The last thing I need is him squatting in my apartment while I'm at work. I head down the hallway to the elevators, but I can hear his footsteps behind me.

"Reed, you can't ignore me forever. I'm your family."

I spin around, and he smashes into my chest. I hold firm, and he bounces off of me. Chase might be a smidge taller than I am, but he's a lot scrawnier. "Quinn was your family, okay?"

Chase stands to his full height, crossing his arms. "Look, I get that you're pissed, but what's the big deal? It's *my* life I ruined, *my* wife I lost. What does any of it even have to do with you? People cheat on their wives all the time."

If he thinks he's making a case for himself, he's sorely mistaken. I don't answer him, mostly because I think he sounds like an idiot, but also because if I keep fighting him on this, he's going to figure out that I've been in love with his wife for five years.

Ex-wife.

I put the date on my phone calendar. They completed their mediation today. All they have to do is wait for the ink to dry, and they're done.

I continue to the elevator. But while I'm waiting for it, Chase hovers around me like a fly. "Would you hear me out?"

"No."

I step into the elevator, but much to my chagrin, he steps in with me. When the doors close, I see the smug expression on his face in the reflection off the elevator door. He glances over at where the button for the lobby is lit up. He's clearly calculating how much time he has before the doors open again and I can escape.

"Here's the thing," Chase says, "Mom has upped the price if we go to the lake house. $500,000. I know you don't care about the money, but I really need it. Mom says she'll only give me the money if I convince *everyone* to go. That means you and

Sabrina. I know you hate me, and I know you have no reason to do anything for me, but I'm your brother, and I'm *begging* you."

"Absolutely not." I'm not about to go stay at the lake house with him just to make him even richer than he already is. Mom had to have known there was no way I was going to show up. I don't know what she thought she was going to accomplish with this, but it doesn't matter. Because I'm not going.

The elevator doors slide open, and I take a step out, but Chase appears in front of me, blocking my way. "What do you want from me, Reed? I'll do anything, I swear."

I shove past him, out into the lobby where I send Jackson at the front desk a dirty look. It's his job to keep people like Chase away from our doors. Just because Chase is my family doesn't mean Jackson can sleep on the job.

"If you won't do it for me, will you do it for Quinn?"

I slow to a stop, feet from the door to the street. On the other side, people walk by on the sidewalk. Without turning around, I say, "What does Quinn have to do with this?"

He knows he's got me. I can feel it in the way the air shifts, can hear it in the slow, measured way that he approaches me now that he knows I'm not going anywhere. He steps up beside me. "Mom and Sabrina think we're still married. You're the only person I told about the divorce. If we want the money, everybody has to come to the lake house, even Quinn."

I'm the only person he told about the divorce. It wasn't by choice. He didn't have anywhere to stay that first night after Quinn kicked him out of their house and he showed up on my doorstep, asking if he could sleep on my couch.

I let him stay a week, but only because I didn't know why Quinn kicked him out. It wasn't until I caught him sending nudes to some random woman in the middle of the night that I put two and two together and left his shit in the hallway while he was out.

"And Quinn agreed to this?" There's no way Quinn thought this was a good idea. It's true that she's always enjoyed going to the lake house in the summer—which I only know because Sabrina always texted me when she got back to the city to tell me what a great time I missed out on. But there's no way Quinn would put herself through that.

Chase shrugs. "She went from having a man providing for her 24-7 to having no source of income. I know how much that house costs. She needs the money." He says it with a tilt to his mouth, like he's bragging.

Look, I love my brother, but ever since I found out he was fucking around on Quinn, I've sort of wanted him dead.

And then his words sink in.

Quinn already agreed. Quinn is going to the lake house. And she won't be married to my brother anymore.

"Okay, I'll go."

Chase's face changes, lighting up like I told him he won the lottery. This certainly does seem like a lot of work on his part for half a million dollars. But at the end of the day, I don't care why he needs the money. All I care about is getting to that lake house and seeing Quinn.

And this time, I'm not leaving without her.

4 QUINN

Oh, my God. What the hell am I doing here?

I pull my car into the huge driveway of the Lynch family's lake house and turn it off. The lake house is mostly glass and wood, with the shimmer of the lake just beyond it. I've always loved the lake house. It's nicer than any place I've ever been in my entire life, the kind of place that has two kitchens and three living rooms, more space than any family has any business needing.

I have so many good memories of this place: nights spent around the fire, late morning breakfasts after walking through the shops the night before, enough hiking trails that it seems unlikely that anyone has ever traveled the same one twice. When all of this is over, it's not Chase I'll miss. It's his family. It's his family's houses. Madison has several, and they're all as big and grand as this place.

As I'm grabbing my bags out of the backseat, the door of the lake house opens, and two women rush out, heading straight for me.

"Quinn!" Madison shouts, the way she always does when

she sees me, acting like it's been a lifetime since the last time we were together. Behind her, Sabrina is moving toward me at a much slower pace, a half-smile on her mouth and a shawl draped lazily over her shoulders as if it isn't positively balmy outside. But that's Sabrina, ever the cool one.

When Madison reaches me, she wraps her arms around me, and for a second, I close my eyes and let myself enjoy it. Madison is one of those mothers everybody wants. She asks you about your life and actually cares about the answer; she gives hugs and strokes your hair and pats you on the back gently as she walks by; she protects her kids, even though they're grown adults who don't need her to anymore; and she smells like lilacs.

"It's so good to see you," she says in my ear, and for some reason, it makes a lump form in my throat. I saw her at Christmas, but at Christmas, I didn't know about Chase's affairs. I didn't know how soon they would be slipping away from me. I fist my hands in the back of Madison's shirt and squeeze her tight.

"Mom, would you let her go? You're going to break all her ribs."

My blood runs cold at the sound of Chase's voice. Madison does relinquish me, stepping back to hold me at arm's length, and out of the corner of my eye, I see Chase coming from the side of the house. He's shirtless, chest glistening, and I focus on keeping my eyes averted. My attraction to Chase was never the issue in this relationship, just his attraction to every other woman in the Boston area and his inability to keep his hands off them.

Madison doesn't look over at him. She's still smiling at me. She tucks a strand of hair behind my ear and says, "I'm so glad you were okay to drive yourself here. I know it's a long trip for you, and to do it all alone because of Chase's little business trip must have been exhausting."

My eyes shoot to Chase. He holds my gaze. I raise an eyebrow at him. *Business trip?* He gives the tiniest, almost imperceptible shrug. I guess that was the only excuse he could come up with for why we didn't drive in together. A week ago, he asked if I would be willing to make the trip together, since everyone would be expecting the happily married couple to be arriving in the same car, but I told him no. It's bad enough that I have to be here with him. I wasn't about to deal with him for the entire two-hour drive from Boston on top of it.

"It was no problem," I tell Madison.

"Right," she says, linking her arm through mine and turning me toward the house. "Well, we decided to forgo a big dinner since I figured everyone would be too tired to do anything as formal as sitting around the table, but Lydia put out a little charcuterie on the bar, so you just help yourself while you're unpacking and settling in."

"Oh, Lydia is here?" I should have seen that one coming. Lydia is Madison's righthand woman. She cooks and cleans for Madison, on top of anything else she needs her to do. Anytime I would visit Madison's home in New York, Lydia would hover around like a soldier in chainmail, ready to swoop in and take your trash from you, your bags, your empty plates. And yet somehow, she was always halfway invisible, able to disappear as soon as you turned around.

"Of course," Madison says, "but don't worry. She's agreed to sleep in the basement."

We approach Sabrina, who smiles at me and reaches out to squeeze my elbow before falling into step with me and her mother. "Don't put her in the basement," Sabrina says to her mother. "There's an empty room upstairs. She might as well take it. You know Reed isn't going to show."

I trip over a loose board on the porch and stumble. Madison, her arm still looped through mine, manages to keep me from falling, and when I've right myself, I smile reassuringly at her, even though a storm has begun to brew in my stomach. Why did Sabrina say that Reed isn't going to show? Reed *has* to show. All of us have to be here in order for Madison to give us the money. That was the agreement.

But I can't ask. I don't want Madison to know I'm just here for the money. It's bad enough that she has to bribe her kids to spend time with her (well, really just Reed and Chase. Sabrina and her mother are inseparable). All the summers Chase and I have spent here at the lake house, even before we were married, were never about the money for me.

We step into the lake house, and the smell of it makes all the stress evaporate from my body. It's so familiar, like coconut and fresh linen. We step down into the living room and then my eyes meet my favorite sight: the lake. The living room is encased in glass windows, and outside of them, the lake stretches from one side to the other, seemingly never-ending. The sun is low in the sky, casting pink and orange light across the water.

I sigh. "I missed this."

Madison smiles and unhooks her arm from mine, stepping into the living room and sitting delicately on the white couch.

Chase, now with a t-shirt firmly in place, collapses onto the couch beside her. "It looks exactly the same as it did last year," he says, dismissively, leaning back and putting his feet up on the glass coffee table.

Madison swats his legs away, and he groans, setting his feet back on the ground. "God forbid your wife appreciate the view that I paid millions for."

Your wife. Oh, God. It just sank in what this week is going to look like. I have to pretend to be Chase's wife. In theory, I fully understood what that meant, but now that we're here, it's really hitting me. Will we have to kiss? Sit next to each other at every meal? Share a room?

Panic starts to brew in the center of my chest, and I back away from the couch. "I actually think I'm going to go get settled in my room. I'll be back in a bit."

"Take your time," Madison says without looking at me.

I turn toward the direction of the hallway, where all but the master and basement bedrooms are, and almost run right into Sabrina. She was standing behind me this whole time. Her eyes scan over my face, and her smile falls a little.

"*Sorry*," I whisper, moving to go around her. Shit. Well, maybe she'll think I'm sick or something, and not sick at the idea that I have to be in close proximity for the next week with a man who is supposed to be my loving husband. I think I might puke.

And all for nothing. If Reed doesn't show up, I won't even have the money to show for this absolutely brainless endeavor.

I try to walk at a steady pace down the long hallway that houses the three guest bedrooms. I walk straight to the one that I've shared with Chase for the last five years. I step inside, shut the door, and lean against it, trying to catch my breath.

Don't panic. Don't panic. I knew what I was getting myself into. I knew this was going to be hard.

On the king-sized bed, Chase's large gray duffel bag is nestled in beside my suitcase that Chase must have carried in. I'm going to have to sleep in that bed every night beside a man who spent a large portion of our marriage having sex with people who weren't me...while also having sex with me.

A shudder runs through me at the thought. I gave everything I had to that marriage, made sacrifices and looked away from my unhappiness in order to convince myself to stay. And for what?

The door behind me opens, smacking me in the back. I roll my eyes and step out of the way to let Chase in. He shuts the door behind him, and then we stand there, looking at each other.

He smiles. "This is gonna be cozy."

I grit my teeth and walk over to the bed, opening my suitcase to pull out my things. "I thought you said you talked Reed into coming."

Chase's amused expression fades. "I thought I did. When I left his place, he assured me that he would be here. I don't know what happened." He walks over to the other side of the bed and jumps on, making the whole mattress bounce. "But that's Reed for you. Always way more focused on himself than anyone else."

Anger whips through me. I can't believe he has the audacity to talk about Reed after everything he's done. Sure, Reed is a bit of a no-show, and he almost never spends time with his family, even though he lives in Boston, just like us. He never calls, never texts, but that's his business. He has a busy life, and it's not like Chase is a perfect family man either. He was trying to call out of this trip too before Madison offered him all that money.

"I'm not staying if he's not coming."

Chase sits up, leaning back against the massive wood headboard. "What are you talking about? You have to stay."

I snort. "No, I don't. I came here for the money. If Reed doesn't show, the money doesn't happen. I'm not just sticking around for a good time. So, if he's not here by morning, I'm out of here."

I pull out all of my toiletries and walk into the bathroom to line them up across the counter. Even if I don't end up staying, I'll need them in the morning. Behind me, the massive garden tub sparkles, strategically placed in front of the floor-to-ceiling window that looks out on the lake. How many times have Chase and I had sex in that tub? How many times was he finishing inside me just to get out and text one of his many women?

I grab onto the edge of the sink and take a deep breath. I can't let this anger consume me the entire time I'm here. I'll never be a believable wife if all I can think about is the cheating. I'll just have to do my best to put distance between Chase and me when I can. It's not like we were climbing all over each other in front of the family at our other vacations and holidays. Hand holding, the occasional kiss. Nothing too intimate. I can manage that.

When I walk back into the bedroom, Chase is standing by the window, watching the last dregs of the sunset with his hands in his pockets. He doesn't turn to look at me when he speaks. "I don't want you to leave."

I stop in the middle of the room, watching him.

He finally turns away from the window, and I'm shocked by the genuine sadness in his eyes. He's kidding, right? All the anger that I just managed to push down comes springing back.

"Chase, what the hell are you doing?"

He takes his hands from his pockets and walks toward me, arms outstretched. "I miss you, Quinn. Big time. Look, we don't have to do this. We don't have to go through with the divorce. I can change. I can be faithful—"

Before his fingertips can graze my skin, I lunge out of his reach. He stumbles, jarred by my sudden movement. He has the audacity to look hurt by my rejection. Carefully keeping my voice low, I walk over to the door, setting my hand on the knob.

"Chase, you admittedly fucked over a dozen women in the course of our short marriage. I'm not convinced you *ever* loved me. This trip is not some kind of shot at reconciliation. The divorce might not be final yet, but we're done, and if you come anywhere near me while we're alone, I will remove every single one of your fingers with a cheese knife."

I move out into the hallway and let the door fall closed behind me. I center myself before going out into the living room. Madison and Sabrina are still on the couch, speaking quietly amongst themselves, so I wander into the kitchen. The bar is full to bursting with plates of cheese, meats, fruits, and crackers. I'm starving. I slice some gouda with one of the expensive cheese knives I just threatened Chase with and set it on a cracker. If left alone with this charcuterie board long enough, I will eat the entire thing, especially with all of this stress that's rushing through my body with the force of a tsunami.

"Hello, Mrs. Lynch."

I almost choke on my gouda. I cover my mouth with my hand so I don't accidentally spit any food out. "Hi, Lydia. I didn't see you."

Lydia, only a few years older than me and absolutely gorgeous, with long dark hair and a perfect smile, sets a small plate beside me that I'm clearly meant to use. If it was anyone else, I would feel chastised, but I know Lydia isn't trying to be rude. "I'm very glad to see you. Madison was beside herself when she thought no one would be coming for the summer. You know how she looks forward to these trips."

I swallow my cracker. "I do. It's just been kind of a busy year, you know?"

Lydia waves me off, stepping around to the other side of the massive marble-topped island. "Of course. And Madison understands that she has four wonderfully busy and successful children. She just misses all of you when you aren't around."

Four children. Not three. Four. She's including me in that count. How am I going to break all of these people's hearts when the week is over? How long should Chase and I wait after the trip to tell everyone we split up? Will Madison want her money back?

I open my mouth to answer, but Lydia has vanished, off to magically appear somewhere else she's needed. When I first met Chase, Lydia hadn't been hired yet, but by the time that first summer here came around, it was like she had always been there, always anticipating everyone's needs at all times. I wish I could tell her that I'm trying to get through this trip with as little contact with Chase as possible. I bet she could help me manage it. But I also know her loyalty to Madison. She can't be trusted.

With my little plate full of goodies, I go back to the living room, where now only Madison sits. And as if she was waiting for me, she sighs and stands. "Sabrina has gone to bed," she tells me. "You know, she had that long flight from Paris. And I'm feeling quite exhausted myself. I think I'm going to turn in early. But please, stay up, enjoy the food, and I'll see you at breakfast."

She squeezes my elbow, and then I'm alone, feeling miniscule in the vastness of the house. When I hear Chase moving around, I make a run for it, going out the side door, out to where the giant infinity pool and hot tub are both covered. I can only assume that come morning, Lydia will have unveiled them both.

I take a seat on one of the pool chairs and eat my cheese and crackers. As I watch the last remaining rays of sunlight disappear over the water, I tell myself I can survive this trip if the whole thing is just like this.

5 QUINN

I wake up in the pool chair, stiff and chilled. My plate is on the ground beside me, and I pick it up and go back inside. A glance at the clock on the stove tells me it's almost midnight. The house is quiet, undisturbed, like no one has moved in hours. Setting my plate in the sink, I tiptoe down the hallway to mine and Chase's room.

Chase is asleep, still dressed, lying on top of the comforter. It's like he was waiting for me to come back, like he wanted to participate in the nightly routine we used to have: talking while we scrubbed faces, brushed teeth, changed clothes.

I can't even look at him. I don't want to get into that bed beside him. I don't want to lie next to him, risk rolling over and touching him in the night.

There are five rooms in this house. Three in this hallway, with Sabrina and Lydia already in the other two. Madison is in the master bedroom on the other side of the house. But there's an entire basement downstairs. Nobody likes the basement. There's a second kitchen down there, an extra bathroom, a second living room, and a bedroom. But instead of a gorgeous view of the lake, there's just walls. High on the walls, little rectangular windows face out onto the front of the house, where all of our cars are parked. But that's it. No sunsets. No beautiful view.

Empty.

I grab a set of clothes from my suitcase as I go back out as quietly as I came in. The stairs down to the basement are behind the kitchen, and the house remains perfectly still as I move through the shadows. Lydia must have turned the lights out when she thought everyone was in bed. Somehow, she didn't see me out there by the pool.

As I descend into the basement, I get a little chill. It's much colder down here, and the dark is impenetrable. I don't bother to flip on the light in the main room. I keep moving to the bedroom, feeling my way in what little moonlight makes it in through the small, high windows.

I've only been down here a few times, mostly during the big 4th of July party at the end of the trip. Every year, Madison throws a huge 4th of July party and invites everyone from the surrounding neighborhoods to attend. And almost every year, Chase and I would end up down here, fucking on the couch. Nobody who isn't a Lynch knows about the basement, so it seemed like a good place to have fun.

I erase the memories of heavy breathing and strawberry daquiris from my mind and open the door to the bedroom. The bed isn't a king. This one is smaller than the one upstairs, but that's fine because I don't have to share it with anyone. I shut the door and feel the first real peace I've felt since I got here. All I have to do is make it through this night, sneak back upstairs in the morning before everyone is awake, and then I can go home.

I slip into my pajamas, sweatpants and an old t-shirt, and

slide into the bed. The sheets are cold, and the mattress is far softer than what we have at home. Chase likes a hard mattress, even though I don't, so the bed at home is firmer than I'd like. As soon as I have the money, I'll replace it.

I hope that king-sized upstairs has a mattress so soft that Chase wakes up with a backache.

Now that I'm here, I realize I'm not really that tired anymore. I slept on that pool chair for almost three hours, so now I'm wide awake. There's no cell service out here, so I can't scroll around on my phone. I decide to just let myself be. In the dark, in the quiet. It's like being at home, but here, I'm not alone.

I don't know how long I lay like that before I feel myself starting to drift.

And then I hear a sound.

It's not outside. These windows are so thick that hearing what's going on out on the lake is almost impossible. No, it's definitely inside the house. And if I can hear it, that means it's down in the basement.

I can hear the quiet shifting of fabric. I sit up quickly. What if it's a rat or something? There are all kinds of wild animals on the lake. Oh, fuck. What if it's a snake?

I hold my breath, trying not to make any noise as I listen, the covers pulled up around my chin.

The doorknob to my room turns, and I squeak, pushing myself back against the headboard.

Snakes can't turn doorknobs. Who the fuck is trying to get into this room right now? Is it someone who waited for everyone to go to bed, someone peeking in through the windows who saw that I went down to the basement, where I'm alone and isolated?

The door opens silently, and a dark figure stands in the doorway, big, broad-shouldered, obviously male. I should probably scream, right? Alert the house to an intruder? But I can't seem to get my mouth to open.

And then the man steps into the moonlight, and every muscle in my body goes slack.

Reed smiles. "Hey, Quinn."

6 QUINN

Brooke is already making out with someone. I swear, I don't know how she does that. She walks into a room, decides who she wants, and has them begging in half an hour or less. I haven't left the space by the door of the dorm room. It's one of those suites that has four rooms and a living room, only for the upperclassmen. I don't even know whose room it is. Brooke just walked into our dorm last week and said, "Buy a cool Halloween costume because the parties are going to be lit!"

I guess this is what she meant, although it feels like a normal party to me. Everyone wearing cheap costumes, getting drunk, wandering off in pairs, probably to their own rooms.

I don't mind that Brooke has already found someone more interesting than me to hang out with. I mean, if I had the magical powers she has to be able to get a guy to pay attention to me, I would be making out with someone right now, too. Brooke isn't the only one who would very much like to meet a guy tonight. She's just the only one, out of the two of us, who isn't still a virgin. And at the rate I'm going, I'm going to be a virgin forever, seeing as how I'm pressed up against the wall, dressed like a skeleton, and trying not to bump into anyone. Isn't the point of these parties *to* bump into people? Preferably very attractive boys who will rid me of my V-card and also my loneliness.

When I realize that absolutely nobody is going to notice, I start to inch my way out into the brightly lit hallway. Out here, the music is still perfectly loud, the bass so intense that the floor is vibrating with each *thump*, but it feels less suffocating. I press myself to the wall and try to decide if I want to head back to our room. It's on the other side of campus, and I don't really want to walk alone, but Brooke is probably not coming back tonight, so it doesn't exactly make sense to wait around.

While I'm still trying to decide, a very large boy bursts out of the dorm room and throws himself against the wall beside me. I watch, shocked, as he sets his head against the wall and breathes out a long sigh. I watch the bob of his Adam's apple, let my eyes wander down the tattooed length of his arm, where the sleeve of his black t-shirt ends. He's not in a costume as far as I can tell, just a t-shirt and jeans, and his hair is a mess around his head, like he just rolled out of bed to come to this party.

His eyes open, and then his face whips in my direction, and he jumps. When he sees me full-on, he laughs. "Shit. You scared me."

I huff a little, turning away from him to watch what's happening inside the party. "Yeah, that happens a lot."

He nods. "I bet, with a costume like that. You totally blend in with the wall." He takes the long sleeve of my white skeleton costume between his thumb and forefinger and gently pins it to the wall beside me. He's right. It's basically the same color.

I laugh. "Right. I actually meant because people tend to forget I exist. I guess it was about time I literally blended in with the wallpaper."

He makes a quiet snorting noise and rolls his eyes. "Right. I believe you," he says sarcastically.

I turn fully toward him now. "Excuse me?"

He sticks his hands in his pockets, still leaning against the wall, but he's looking in at the party, clearly refusing to look my way. "Don't pretend you're a piece of furniture when you're that pretty. I don't believe for a second that people forget about you."

I put one hand on my hip. "Oh, yeah? Did you know that we had a class together last semester?" Because I remember. I remember all too well. This guy standing next to me, who's so gorgeous it makes my stomach hurt, sat in the row in front of me for the entire semester, but he never once made eye contact with me.

His dark eyes slowly slide over to me, and I have to hold back the smug *told you so* smile. "Shit," is all he says.

I sniff and lean against the wall. "Told you. I might as well not exist."

I fully expect him to leave at that point. I figure he came out here for a breather, and now he's probably ready to head back in and find a much more interesting girl to take home. In the two years that I've been going to Suffolk, I've seen this guy with at least a dozen different girls on his arm, maybe more. When we were in Intro to Psychology together, he was always flirting with the girl he sat by, putting his arm around her shoulder and whispering in her ear through class.

But he doesn't leave. He just keeps standing beside me until I start to feel self-conscious. Should *I* leave?

"I'm Reed," he says finally, putting out his hand for me to shake. He's got a leather chord on his wrist, all wrapped up in a silver bracelet that sort of looks like a bike chain. My palms immediately start to sweat at the thought of making contact with his skin.

"Quinn." I shake his hand quickly, like it's a business transaction, and then drop it.

Reed laughs, his eyes all lit up like it's his birthday. "So, why are you hovering outside the party instead of, you know, joining it?"

I shrug. "Some things are easier for me to experience from the outside."

He nods, looking off into the distance. And once again, I'm waiting for him to walk away. I'm so bad at social situations, and I can't tell whether or not this conversation is awkward, but it has to be, right? This guy has to be getting bored of standing beside me quietly while I try to figure out what else to say. As if to prove my point, he says, "I appreciate that you went the anatomical route with your costume." He tilts his chin toward me and uses his index finger to trace my costume in the air. "No black outline for contrast."

I look down at my all-white body suit, hanging off of me a little bit, with thick black lines outlining each visible bone. "Right, well, I wanted to be authentic."

His lips spread into a smile. "Dedication. I like it."

"Oh, you haven't seen the whole thing yet." I reach up for the mask that's perched on top of my head, pulling it down to cover my face.

He lets out a joyous laugh that makes my stomach spin. "Perfection," he says, the word slightly distorted because he's smiling so big. Have I ever made a boy laugh like this? I'm not even trying to be funny. I'm just trying to have a conversation.

And then it dawns on me, the reason why he's out here with me instead of inside the party with his friends.

"Look, I'm not going to sleep with you," I blurt out, the words echoing loudly behind my thick plastic skeleton mask.

His smile fades. "What?"

"I bet you think that because I'm out here, I'm lonely and that I would go back to your room or whatever because you're cute and friendly, but I'm not going to sleep with you."

For a moment, his face is blank, and then his eyes seem to change, like he's smiling with them and them alone. "Listen, Quinn. I'm not going to lie to you. If you asked me to have sex with you, I would. You're beautiful and funny and interesting, but I'm so drunk right now that I don't think I'd be able to get it up, even for you."

I roll my eyes and collapse back against the wall. "Well, that's charming."

He smiles and shrugs. "Just being honest." We go quiet, our heads turned awkwardly in each other's direction, and then he turns his body toward me, pressing his shoulder into the wall. He reaches out and lifts my mask, just enough for him to actually see my eyes and not just the suggestion of them through the mask's eye holes. He's standing close enough to me that I can see that his eyes are brown, his jawline a little round. He has a sweet face, contrasted by the dark tattoo crawling up his neck. He smiles, like he just caught me during a game of Hide and Seek.

My stomach does something weird, like anxiety but in a pleasant way, sharp and sudden.

"Don't worry," he says, his voice low, "my mother taught me right."

"I don't know if bringing up your mom is really the best flirting material."

I reach up to take off the mask, our fingers brushing. When it's gone, he takes a step back, like he could only be that close to me when I was in hiding.

He shrugs. "Eh. Well, my mom always finds her way into every conversation, so I've started just throwing it out there to save time."

I send him an are-you-crazy look. "Why does your mom come up in every conversation?"

His face is blank, like he's waiting to see if I'll make a joke. "I thought you said you knew who I was."

"I said we had a class together. I've seen you around campus, that's all. Why? Who's your mom? Is she, like, a mayor or something? My knowledge of local politics is ghastly."

His smile is back, spreading slowly across his mouth, and I can't seem to tear my eyes from it. "No. She's not a mayor. It's not important."

He seems to find this amusing, but I don't know why. I lace my hands behind my back and duck my head. He can't honestly find me interesting, right? "The only thing I really know is what's right in front of me right now."

"And that is?" I can hear the hesitation in his voice. I do know about his reputation, and I know he probably thinks I'm going to call him out on it. Instead, I smile up at him and say, "A guy who's drunk and clearly can't handle the indignity that comes with dressing up for Halloween as an adult."

He laughs. "Oh, but you can?"

I motion at my skeleton costume. "Obviously. I grew up in a small town in Minnesota, so I didn't have much dignity to begin with."

He looks like he's going to protest. His jaw clenches for a second, but then his eyes go soft. "Hey, why don't I get you a drink, skele-girl?"

"I don't accept drinks from strangers."

He purses his lips. "That's entirely fair. But you can watch me the whole time. See?" He wraps his hands around my upper arms and very gently pulls me toward him, positioning me so that I'm standing in front of him, my back to his chest, facing the open door of the party. It's jarring, the way the darkness seems to creep out of the dorm room compared to the blinding florescent lights in the hallway.

I feel him shift behind me, and then his voice is in my ear, sending a shiver through me that I just barely suppress. He extends his hand, pointing with two fingers and his thumb like a gun into the room. And he's right. There's a straight line of visibility from the doorway to the counter where drinks are being poured.

"Or I could go in with you," I say, keeping my back to him.

"You could, but I like you out here, in the light, where I can see you." He steps away from me, heading for the party. "Be right back, skele-girl."

As soon as he's gone, swallowed by the mass of bodies inside the dorm room, I press myself back against the wall and suck in a deep breath. I will *not* have sex with a boy I just met. I will *not* go back to this boy's room and let him touch me everywhere. Nope. Nope. Nope.

In the dim lighting of the party, I see him appear in the kitchen, standing at the counter, exactly where he said he would be. He has a red plastic cup in his hand. His eyes find mine across the expanse and he turns the cup upside down, shaking it out to show me there's nothing in it. He sets it down on the counter and then lifts his hands, showing me the fronts and the backs.

I fight back a laugh. The situation itself is definitely not funny. He just looks really cute trying to reassure me. He starts to pour something from a very large jug into the red plastic cup, but he hasn't quite finished when a girl approaches him. Dark-skinned and long-haired, all I can see of her is her mouth. The rest of her face is covered in glittery face paint in the shape of a butterfly. I guess that's her costume as she's otherwise just wearing a sweater and a denim skirt.

Reed has seemingly forgotten about my drink. He smiles down at the girl and then immediately begins what looks like a very friendly conversation with her. She says something and he laughs, his hand pressed to his stomach.

Another girl appears on his other side. She's dressed like a pirate, complete with vintage leather hat. She goes up on her toes to hug him, and he warmly reciprocates the embrace.

I feel like such an idiot. He isn't really interested in me. I was just...available. Someone for him to talk to until he found someone better, just like I thought. He caught me with my guard down. Well...that's just fine.

"Have a nice night," I say to the empty hallway, and then I turn and smash right into someone.

I feel the warmth of the coffee seeping down the front of my costume before I process what it is. The strong smell fills my nose as I take in the guy in front of me, the one with his mouth hanging open and a mostly empty coffee cup in his hand.

I look down at the brown liquid, watch it as it spreads across my stomach, quietly staining my fabric rib cage and spinal column. "Well, there goes any hope I had of recycling this costume," I mutter, pulling the wet fabric away from the clothes I'm wearing under it. Don't need those stained, too. Luckily, the costume is quite loose on me and is very thick.

"There goes any hope *I* had of cramming for this exam." The boy I bumped into grimaces and looks down into his coffee cup. He has a stack of books tucked under his other arm and a look of despair on his face. He sighs heavily and finally meets my eye.

Sheesh. Is every guy in this dorm hall offensively beautiful?

Where Reed is dark—his hair, his clothes, his eyes—this guy

is light, with caramel-colored hair, light brown eyes, and a general glow around him that seems to come from nowhere and everywhere.

"Sorry," I say, because technically the collision was my fault. I should have been paying more attention, but I was a bit distracted by the fact that I was just ghosted by a total hottie.

The guy in front of me, tall and slim and gorgeous, shrugs. "That's okay. I was gonna fail the test, no matter what, but I thought I would get a little higher up on the *failed horribly* scale. Seems there's no use now." He stretches and tosses his coffee cup into a nearby trash can. And then his eyes go straight to the stain on my costume.

"Geez. You look like you have bone rot." He nods in the direction of the hallway behind me, ignoring the loud thumping of the party, like it's not even there. "My room is at the end of the hall. You could come and soak that if you wanted to."

It sounds like a pick-up line, but he doesn't look like he's trying to flirt. He looks like a guy who needs coffee or maybe some sleep. And he looks like a guy who's very, very cute. "You don't mind?"

He shrugs. "Nah. I could use the company. I'm trying not to party for the rest of the semester, so with that racket going on..." His eyes shoot to the party that's still happening over my shoulder. "...it would be nice to have someone to keep me distracted." He looks so sincere, it's almost funny.

I reach behind me and pull down the zipper on the back of my skeleton costume. It parts around my shoulders and sags to my waist. "Why are you avoiding parties?"

His eyes follow the drop of the costume and then take in the shorts and tank top I'm wearing underneath. Apparently, something about what I'm wearing is amusing because one side of his mouth tips up. "Because when I go to parties, I tend to get in trouble, and I need to stay on the up and up, or I'm going to get kicked out."

I step out of my costume and hand it to him. "Your door stays open the entire time."

He smiles fully then, taking the costume from me. We have to pass right by the party in order to get to his dorm. I duck my head, wrapping my arms around myself and hurrying past the door, just in case Brooke sees me. I don't want her to know I'm going to a boy's dorm room alone because she'll freak out. And I would freak out too if our places were reversed, but I'm on high alert.

The guy unlocks the door to his room and holds it open for me. "I'm Chase, by the way."

I smile at him over my shoulder. "Quinn."

7 REED

There have been times in my life where I really felt like I got the shit end of the deal. I'm the oldest, so I was always expected to mature quicker than Chase or Sabrina; I'm not very good at following rules, so I've always been the one who was in trouble for something; and I have a bad habit of disappearing where my family is concerned, so I'm pretty sure no one cares if I ever come around.

But today, I'm certain I'm God's favorite, because after an excruciatingly long day of meetings, followed by a miserably long drive out to the lake house, I've tiptoed down to my room in the basement to find Quinn in my bed. And God, she looks incredible, with her blonde hair wild around her face and her cheeks flushed in the moonlight. I want to crawl into that bed, cover her with my body, and make her forget she was ever married to my brother.

But as soon as I let that thought cross my mind, I realize how awful it sounds. If I want this thing with Quinn to work, I've got to go slow, move at her pace. And I only have a week to make this work.

"Hey, Quinn."

Her tense shoulders seem to relax, which makes my stomach go warm. "Reed. God, you scared the shit out of me."

I set my bag down by the door and step all the way into the room. "Sorry. I figured nobody would be in the basement. Everybody hates the basement."

"Right. Well..." She looks nervous, like she doesn't want to say something, but then she sighs, her hands going up into her hair. "I couldn't be upstairs with Chase. I couldn't share a bed with him after..." She shakes her head, throwing the blanket off herself and swinging her legs over the side of the bed. She's in sweatpants and a shirt so big it swallows her. "I can take the couch out in the living room."

I look over my shoulder, where I have a clear view of the couch in the downstairs living room. It's barely even a loveseat. It's a tiny little thing, really more for show than anything else. I can't let her sleep there.

"No way," I say, turning back to her. She's already halfway to me, and when she stops, it's close enough for me to touch. "I'll take the couch."

She scoffs. "Reed, you're massive. There's no way I'm going to make you curl up on that tiny couch. You'd probably slip a disc or something." She starts to move past me, but I wrap a hand around her upper arm to stop her. I can feel the faint pulse of her in the bend of her elbow.

She looks at me and then her eyes sweep down my arm, where my tattoos are visible past the sleeve of my shirt, all the way to my hand wrapped around her. When she looks up again, it feels like she's looking for the first time. Like before this moment, she was too distracted and now she can really see me. "You look different," she says.

I know what she means. The last time we saw each other, my hair was the longest it's ever been, always brushing the collars of my work shirts. But now it's the shortest it's ever been, buzzed close to my scalp, and I have dark scruff on my jaw, which I've never really had before.

She doesn't look different. She looks the same. The same beautiful woman she's always been. The same long hair, the same bright green eyes, the same sad tilt to her mouth. There's some comfort in the fact that she hasn't changed, but I can't help but wonder if it bothers her.

"I'm sorry." It comes out of my mouth before I have a chance to think about it.

Her brow furrows. "Why are you sorry?"

I take a deep breath. This guilt has been eating at me for a while, and I can't even explain to her why without scaring her off. "I should have called. I should have reached out after Chase did what he did."

Her face shifts, and I recognize the expression well. It's the face of a person who's been getting *are you okay?* comments because her ex-husband is an asshole and now everyone knows it. "You don't have to apologize for what he did. You don't owe me anything."

At that, I finally let my hand drop away from her. I don't want to hold her in place. I want her to stay because she wants to. "We're friends. I should have made sure you were okay." But I didn't let myself. I knew what would happen if I did. I want her too much. I would have made a move, and it would have been the wrong time, and she never would have forgiven me.

Her eyes fall away. "He told you everything?"

She already knew I knew about the divorce, or she would have been more embarrassed to be caught outside of Chase's bed. But I guess she doesn't know the full extent of it.

"Yeah. When you kicked him out, he came to my place, asked to sleep on my couch. But once I found out the whole story, I told him to go to hell."

She smiles, and I almost crumble. How can she not see what she does to me? How can she not see how I feel about her? "He's your brother."

"Doesn't matter. He hurt you, and he shouldn't be rewarded for that."

Her smile fades, her eyes going soft in the moonlight. "It went on for so long." Her voice breaks on the words, and before I can stop myself, I've stepped forward and pulled her into my arms. I know I shouldn't. I need to keep my distance if I'm going to keep her from running away, but when she buries her face in my chest and sighs, nothing has ever felt so right.

After a minute, she takes a step back, letting out this odd little watery laugh. "Jesus, I'm sorry." She wipes at the wet spot on my shirt, and I try to slow the racing of my heart. Can she feel it?

"Don't worry about it," I say as her hands drop down to her side.

She twists, her eyes going back to the bed over her shoulder. "Maybe you could stay in here with me?" she asks, and even though there's nothing even remotely suggestive in her voice, my mind immediately begins to race, imagining her spread out on the bed, my lips finding every inch of her.

I smile and walk over to the bed, swiping one of the pillows and dropping it onto the floor at my feet.

"Oh, that's not what I meant. You don't have to—"

I put up a hand to stop her. "Trust me, this is going to be more comfortable than the couch out there." I kick off my shoes and watch her take in everything before shutting the door.

My heart starts to pound in my head again. How many times have I imagined this? The two of us alone together behind a closed door?

She climbs into the bed, and I have to look away from the shape she makes as she crawls up toward the pillows. She throws the blanket over herself as I settle onto the rug. Luckily, my mother insists on those insanely thick rugs that always have you levitating half a foot off the ground.

Quinn shifts on the bed, and her face appears over the edge, her long hair curtaining around her head. "Goodnight, Reed," she whispers, and then she disappears again, and I'm left to lie awake for a long time.

8   QUINN

I wake to the sound of violin music, very confused
for a minute before my brain wiggles back into place and I
realize I'm in the basement of the Lynches' lake house. The
room is still dark, but my alarm is reminding me that I need to
get up to the ground floor before anybody wakes up and realizes I didn't sleep with the man they all think is my husband.

I scramble out of the bed, and then I see Reed on the floor. I
forgot he was there. He hasn't shifted at all, clearly not bothered by the sound of my alarm or my moving around.

For a second, I just stand there, looking at him. I can't
believe how different he looks with his short hair and all his
stubble. Reed has always been devastatingly gorgeous, but in a
different way than Chase. They have different fathers, Reed
being the odd one out of the siblings, and it shows. Where
Chase's features are small, delicate, and perfect, Reed's are
bigger, with thicker lips and a larger nose. But something about
Reed has always been softer to look at.

I tear my gaze away from his peaceful form, one hand
splayed across his chest in sleep, his chin tilted to the side so

that I can see the curve of his throat, and carefully step around him to go upstairs.

The house is undisturbed, the floor cold under my feet and the air still around me. I rush down the hallway, careful not to make any noise as I move through the living room and into the room I'm supposed to be sharing with Chase. I quietly close the door behind me and turn to find Chase already sitting up in bed. He's still wearing his clothes from yesterday. He clearly fell asleep the second he laid down and never got back up.

His golden hair is a mess, and his clothes are wrinkled. The sun has begun to rise outside the window behind him. There are no curtains, lest the view of the lake be sullied, so as soon as the sun comes up, the whole house will be awake. In the gray light, Chase watches me cross to the bathroom.

"Where were you?" he asks, his voice hard.

I spin around, my hand already on the bathroom doorknob. I want to tell him that it's none of his business, but I can't afford to antagonize him right now. I need everything to go right this week. I don't want to rock the boat in any way and risk that money that I so desperately need.

"I slept on the couch," I tell him.

He immediately frowns, and I'm startled again by how different his and Reed's faces are. I'm not even sure Reed would be capable of a frown like that. "Someone's going to see you. You don't think anyone would find it odd if they caught you sleeping on the couch?"

"I'm being careful."

He hasn't moved, his face turned at an awkward angle to look over at me. He looks like something out of a sci-fi movie, an immovable robot. "You slept next to me for five years. You can't manage one more week?"

Anger burns under my skin. I can't believe he has the audacity to ask me that. "For those five years, I didn't know you were screwing around on me. Now I do." I slam the door between us.

I LAY BACK ON MY POOL CHAIR AND TURN MY HEAD AWAY from the sun. But that turns my face toward Chase, lying on the deck chair beside me. I roll my eyes and turn the other way. The chair beside me is empty, but on the other side of the yard, Reed is rocking slowly in the hammock, reading a book. When he sees me, he smiles.

"Well, this seems a little bit silly," Madison says, walking by us with her purse tucked into the crook of her arm. She shields her eyes from the sun and points out past the boundaries of the yard, toward the lake. "Why are you all sitting around the pool when you could be in the lake?" she asks, as if she wasn't the one who had the pool installed.

Sabrina takes the pool chair beside me, her white skin blinding in the sun. Seeing as how she and Chase are both relatively fair-haired, I don't think they'll be sunbathing for long. "Because," Sabrina says, taking a sip from the margarita in her hand, a chunky yellow thing, "lakes have parasites."

Madison lovingly rolls her eyes. "When I was a kid, my parents took me to the lake every summer, and we always went into the water. Nobody got parasites."

Sabrina adjusts the giant, wide-brimmed hat she's wearing. "Your generation is positively riddled with parasites."

Madison scoffs and waves Sabrina off. "I'm going to run into town for the day. I've made reservations for dinner at the Crescent at six tonight, so please everyone, meet me there." She wiggles her fingers in a wave and heads for the front of the house, where the cars are parked. Sabrina watches her go.

As soon as she's gone, Chase groans. "God, I forgot how boring the lake house is."

I roll my eyes, glad I put on sunglasses so Sabrina won't get an unobstructed view of my utter exhaustion with Chase. "It's not boring. It's relaxing. You're just not used to it."

Out of the corner of my eye, I see Reed glance up at me and then back down at his book. I want to know what he's reading, if he thinks it's good or not, but it feels like the kind of thing Chase will criticize him for if I draw attention to it.

With a groan, Chase gets up and stomps past my seat. When he slams the back door of the house closed, Sabrina's head whips toward me. "God, what's his problem?"

I shrug. "He's just cranky. You know how addicts are when they can't get their fix." I know Sabrina will think I mean Chase's work addiction, but I'm mostly talking about sex or women, whatever made it impossible for him to stay loyal to me. I'm sure it's killing him that he's going to go this whole week without getting laid.

Sabrina nods knowingly. "Right. Mom's whole 'no Wi-Fi' thing." She scoots closer to me until she's sitting all the way at the edge of her reclining pool chair. She produces her cell phone from the pocket of her knit shawl. In a very quiet voice, she says, "Don't tell Chase because he definitely needs to unplug a little bit, but I have a hotspot on my phone." She pushes a few buttons and then turns the screen toward me to show me that she has full wi-fi access.

"No way," I whisper back, scrambling for my phone, which I remember is all the way in my bedroom.

"I'll write down the log in for you," she says, stashing her phone away. With her this close to me, I can smell her coconut sunscreen and make out the tiny flowers on her orange bikini. It's much more revealing than anything I could ever bring myself to wear, but that's Sabrina, so confident. "So what's going on with you?" she asks, scooting back into place on her seat. She adjusts her sunglasses. "How's Boston?"

Lonely, I want to say, but I don't. "It's good," I say instead. Classic stock answer.

"You still volunteering?"

My stomach sinks. "Not so much anymore. Life got... complicated."

She raises an eyebrow in my direction, but thanks to the sunglasses, I can't exactly read her expression. "I totally get you," she says, arching her neck for the sun. "Sometimes you give and give and give, and you wake up one morning, and you realize you don't have anything left."

Yes. That's exactly it. I was always giving to Chase, to my mother, to school, anything to make myself useful, but now that's all over.

"Sometimes, you have to *take*." Sabrina says this in a low voice, barely more than an exhale.

I sit back on my chair. What does it even mean to *take*? If I had any money at all, I'd pay Sabrina to be my life coach. "What about you? How's New York?"

She shrugs. "You know how it is. Boston, New York, they're all the same. Loud. Crowded. Insufferable." She smiles over at me. "I love it. I just spent a week in Paris, too, for a small job. A glorious city like the rest of them."

"Seeing anyone?"

"Nope. Hey, is your friend Brooke still single?"

I laugh. "Sorry, but she just met this great guy a few months ago. Pretty sure this is it for her."

Sabrina gives an impolite groan. "Oh, well. Probably for the best. There's no way I'm relocating to Boston for a *woman*, you know what I mean?"

I smile. "You'll find someone."

She nods, not looking at me.

Just then, Chase re-appears, stomping by my chair again, like a petulant child. He drops down into his seat and hands me a plate. It's piled high with green grapes. I take the plate, about to thank him, when I get a look at the plate he brought back for himself. It has a very large slice of strawberry cake on it.

"Are you serious?"

Chase spears his fork into his slice of cake before looking over at me. "What?"

My mouth pulls into a line. I know I'm supposed to be playing this off like we're the happiest of couples, but even happy couples get into arguments, right? "You brought yourself a slice of cake, but you brought me a bushel of *grapes?*"

I don't know why I'm surprised. This is classic Chase. A perfect wife should have his idea of a perfect body. That's always how it's been. A perfect wife eats salad, cleans the house, waits by the door like a puppy to greet him when he comes home by offering him a blowjob. Never stray from the path.

Chase is looking at me like he doesn't recognize me, like I'm some stranger who just trespassed and is here by mistake. "But you love grapes."

I set the grapes on the concrete beside my chair. The birds will enjoy them later, I'm sure. "I do love grapes. But I love strawberry cake more. Why do *you* get cake, but I get fruit?"

He shrugs. "Because I go to the gym more than you do."

On my other side, Sabrina makes a choking noise. "God, Chase, you are such a dick."

"I'm not a dick!" he insists, leaning around me to see Sabrina. "Quinn is watching her weight. She always has."

Sabrina narrows her eyes at him, and I'm glad she's here, saying all the things I wish I could. All the Lynch siblings have always gotten along, at least from what I've always been able to tell, but when Chase is acting like an asshole, I'm glad Sabrina can recognize it.

"Quinn is watching her weight, or you're watching it for her?"

Chase opens his mouth, clearly intending to double down, when a shadow suddenly blocks out the sun. Before I can look up, a hand appears in my vision—a veined hand, with a silver ring on the thumb and a small raincloud tattoo on the fleshy part between the thumb and the index finger. The hand holds out a giant slice of strawberry cake toward me.

Taking the plate, I look up into Reed's shadowed face. "Thank you."

He doesn't say anything, just nods and goes back to his spot in the hammock. I watch him settle, stretching out his long tattoo-covered torso before going back to his book.

9 REED

The Crescent looks exactly like it did when I was a kid, spending summers at the lake house before I had an excuse to stop showing up. White, cloth-covered tables are stacked three deep, twinkle lights lining the counters and serving stations. It's the kind of place that wants to convince you it's top quality so they can charge outrageous prices, when really, it's just the only place around that serves wine.

We all shuffle in, half-burnt from being out in the sun and the kind of exhausted you can only be after a day of doing absolutely nothing. Mom is already sitting at the end of a long table, waiting for us. She smiles as we all file in, awkwardly trying to decide where to sit. I instinctively move in to sit next to Quinn, but when Chase gives me a confused look, I step out of the way and move around to the other side of the table to sit beside Sabrina.

Quinn sits across from me, and as they take their seats, Chase leans over and kisses her cheek. Her entire body stiffens, and if our mom was paying any attention, she would have seen it. Quinn's eyes meet mine. Even here, in the middle of it all, I see the way she relaxes a little. She knows I'm on her side. If she can't keep it together for the week, if she isn't sure she's going to make it out of this alive, I'll be here to make sure she does.

I try to tell her with my eyes that she doesn't have to deal with Chase alone, but she looks away from me, her smile focused on my mom. A waitress appears with appetizers that my mother must have ordered, placing two plates in the center of the table.

Mom smiles out at all of us and clasps her hands beneath her chin. "I wasn't so sure I would ever see all of you here together again," she says, her eyes glowing in the dim lights. "I'm so glad you're all here."

My stomach turns. Because I know that Chase and Quinn are only here for the money, not that Quinn can be blamed. She shouldn't be here at all. But this certainly isn't the lovely daydream that my mother seems to think it is.

We order food and drinks and settle into comfortable conversation. That is, until my mother turns her attention to Quinn. "Quinn, my love, how's your family?"

Quinn, who just put a bite of scallop in her mouth, covers her lips long enough to chew. Once she swallows, she says, "I couldn't tell you. I haven't spoken to any of them in a while."

My mother's eyebrows curve in with that pitying look that I know she doesn't give to be hurtful. But I also know that Quinn won't be able to avoid the pain that comes from that look. "I'm sorry to hear that."

Quinn's eyes fall to the table. "It is what it is."

I have to end this. "Mom, what do you have planned for the 4th of July party this year?"

My mother's attention is immediately caught, like I hoped it would be. Her eyes light up. "The works! I want this year to be particularly big. I invited everyone on our side of the lake and even a few people from New York. You're all welcome to invite anyone that you think would come. I want this year to be huge, the biggest year yet."

Chase, his mouth full of food, says, "What's the big deal about this year?"

When my mother doesn't immediately answer, the table falls silent. She has a small smile frozen on her face, and she seems to look at all of us before landing on Sabrina. Sabrina, who's looking down at her hands like she can't bear to make eye contact with anyone.

I can hear my heartbeat in my ears. "What's going on?"

My mother takes a deep breath and says, "I didn't want to do this here. I wanted to wait until the trip was over so that nobody felt—"

"Mom," I cut her off. "Just tell us. What is it?"

"I have breast cancer."

Across the table, Quinn makes a small noise of distress, and I look over at her because I'm not sure what else to do. I feel like if I don't look at her, I'll float away.

My mother has breast cancer.

My mother has breast cancer.

I turn to Sabrina, who still has her head ducked. "You knew about this?"

She clenches her jaw, and whether she intended to answer or not, our mother speaks instead. "Sabrina moved in with me six months ago. She's been helping me to get to and from my chemo appointments."

"*Six months?*" Chase demands. I almost forgot he was here. His face has gone all red, his eyes wide. "You've known for six months, and you didn't say anything?"

"What was I supposed to say, Chase?" My mother's voice is quiet. She's always had more patience than she had any right to. "There was no point in scaring all of you with this.

The chemo treatments are going well, and it'll all be over soon."

Quietly, almost so low that I don't hear it, Sabrina sniffles. I reach out to pat her on the back, but my hands are numb. My mother has breast cancer. Is she going to die?

Before anyone else can ask any more questions, Quinn pushes her chair back. "I'm so sorry," she says and rushes off in the direction of the bathroom.

I expect Chase to go after her. After all, he's still her husband, as far as this crowd is concerned, but he just gets an exasperated look on his face. "Jesus," he says under his breath. "She has to make everything about her."

I see red. Slamming my chair back, I stand. "Her mother died four years ago, you fucking asshole. She's allowed to be upset." I turn to my mother, checking to make sure it's okay that I leave the table. When she nods, I follow the path that Quinn took and find the hallway back to the bathrooms.

It's much brighter back here, the walls a stark white. I lean against the wall opposite the women's bathroom and wait. Inside, I hear the water running. Then there's silence for a long time before the door opens and Quinn walks out. As soon as she seems me, she stops. Her face is red and splotchy, wet like she tried to cool it off with cold water.

When I don't move, she leans back against the wall beside the bathroom door.

"You okay?" I ask.

She lets out a humorless laugh. "Is everyone mad at me?"

There's no way I'm going to tell her about Chase's reaction. She doesn't deserve that bullshit. I just shake my head. "Of course not. You're allowed to have your emotions."

She sighs and sets her head back against the wall. "She's *your* mother."

"I'm aware."

"So I should be comforting *you*."

I take a deep breath. It's not as if I've had even a moment to let any of this sink in. I don't know how to feel. "She didn't say she was dying. A lot of women survive breast cancer. It's highly treatable."

She seems to be processing my words, her throat working and her eyes falling closed. "You're right. I'm sorry. I don't mean to be so dramatic."

"Stop apologizing." When she opens her eyes, I say, "I know this must be hard for you."

Her eyes shift, going over my shoulder, and I turn my head to find Chase coming down the hallway, his eyes glued to Quinn. When he gets to us, he nudges me with his elbow in this companionable way that makes me angry. We're not friends. We're not buddies. And I don't want to leave him alone in this hallway with Quinn. He should have been the first one back here.

But Quinn's looking back at him, and I can't deny them their chance to talk, even if the thought of leaving them alone makes a metallic taste form in my mouth.

I turn and head down the hallway, back to the table.

10 QUINN

Chase takes my hand in the car, stops my fingers from trembling. "You're overthinking this," he says as we pull up to the high-rise in New York where his mother lives. I crane my neck to look up at the building as we wait for valet. I grew up in Minnesota and then went straight to Boston for school. This is my first time in New York.

"Easy for you to say," I tell him.

He smiles over at me and pushes his door open, handing his keys to the valet. "Come on. Mom is going to love you. They're all going to love you."

I climb out of his car and fix my skirt, making sure it's fluttering perfectly around my knees. I spent a week picking out this dress, forcing Brooke to go with me to a dozen different stores. I've never met a boy's family before.

Chase takes my hand and pulls me into the building. Nobody at the front desk stops us, instead waving Chase through, clearly familiar with him. My eyes are pulled in all directions, caught on the lights and the shiny surfaces and the way that everything seems to *sparkle*.

When we get into the elevator, there's a person already in there, and when I step forward, fully intending to press the button up to the floor—the tenth, Chase has already told me—the man that was here before us pushes it for me without my having to ask. He's dressed in a suit, and when I look from the lit-up tenth-floor button to his face, he smiles.

"Happy Thanksgiving, Miss Porter," he says. I step back into Chase's embrace, feeling like an idiot. A shocked idiot. Chase didn't prepare me for this. I knew that his family came from a different world than mine, seeing as how they all call New York City homebase, while I'm vaguely tied to a little house in suburban Minnesota.

Beside me, Chase chuckles. When I tilt my chin toward him, watching his smile in the reflection of the elevator doors, he says, "You just have to roll with it. I didn't realize how fucking *dystopian* my life was until I left it for a little while."

I'm not totally sure what he means until the elevator doors slide open, and my feet won't move. It's the penthouse. The elevator opens directly into a white marble, geometric penthouse, beyond which huge glass windows display what feels like the entirety of New York City.

"Holy shit," I whisper.

Chase ushers me out of the elevator, almost against my will. My body is physically rejecting this entire scenario. Not only because I don't generally approve of such intense wealth, but because I *do not* belong here. I had absolutely no idea. Sure, Chase dresses nice, usually in polos and designer jeans, but we go to school in the city. Everybody dresses nicer in the city than they do on a normal day in the suburbs, even if they're not wearing designer clothes. And I've always felt out of the place *there*.

This. This is something else entirely.

I'm so busy taking in my surroundings that I don't even realize there are other people in the room until a woman steps forward, her arms out in front of her like she's going to hug me. "Hello and welcome!" She has a huge smile, the kind that can only be sincere because if it wasn't, it would break her face. "You must be Quinn."

I try to get my mind to focus instead of winding out in all directions. I let this woman who smells like expensive perfume hug me, and when she has her arms around me, I see the massive framed magazine cover on the wall. It's an issue of TIME magazine, and the woman currently squeezing me is on it in a white suit against the black background. "Madison Lynch Is On Top" the headline reads.

I still have my eyes on it when Chase's mother lets me go. At least, I'm assuming she's Chase's mother. Otherwise, this whole thing is very uncomfortable.

"It's nice to meet you, Mrs. Lynch."

She scoffs and waves me off. "None of that. I'm Madison, you're Quinn, and I'm so happy you're here. Come on in." She pulls me further into the apartment, and the pieces of it start to slot together. There's a massive kitchen, open to the rest of the room, and a huge living room that would probably be perfect for a party of a hundred people.

"Everyone else is in the dining room. They're anxious to get to dinner because it smells so amazing. Spencer really outdid himself this year." At her words, a man steps into the kitchen with a very large white ceramic platter in his hands. He smiles up at us and then immediately goes back to his work.

"It does smell lovely," I say as Madison squeezes my hand.

"Who all is here?" Chase asks, coming up beside me. To his

credit, he hasn't complained about the fact that his mother has ignored him. His eyes shoot over her shoulder to the doorway I'm assuming leads into the dining room.

"Just your brother and sister. Just us family this year."

My stomach drops. Did Chase invite me when he wasn't supposed to? "Oh, I'm so sorry if I'm intruding—"

"Of course not!" Madison tugs me in the direction of the doorway. "I *begged* Chase to bring you. I wanted to meet the girl he's been talking so much about. In the past, we've often invited acquaintances and neighbors, but I really wanted it to be the five of us this year."

She ushers me through the doorway and into what feels like a glass elevator. It's a floor-to-ceiling glass room with a table so long that it looks like it would fit at least twenty people. And it's full of food. Down at the far end, two people are seated, a beautiful girl with long, straight hair and...

My feet skitter to a stop. My eyes meet Chase's brother's. Eyes I've thought about an embarrassing number of times since the Halloween party. Seeing him sitting at the table is like waking up from a dream about a stranger and then bumping into them on the street. Round face, dark hair, bright eyes.

"This is Sabrina," Madison says, motioning toward the girl. She smiles and waves. She has to be the youngest of the siblings. She looks like a teenager. "And you know Reed," Madison continues.

The shock of her words makes my chin jolt back, like I've been hit. So, that's it? Chase's brother is the guy from the Halloween party, and everybody knows that we met at that party and flirted and that I wanted to lose my virginity to him but ended up losing it to Chase a week later instead?

Reed stands, reaching across the table to hold his hand out for me to shake. My mind reels back to the Halloween party, when he did the exact same thing.

"No, we haven't met," he says, his eyes steady on me. He's still waiting for me to shake his hand, but I can't seem to get my limbs to move.

He doesn't remember. He was so drunk that night that he can't remember that we met, that we flirted, that we *clicked*. Maybe that's a good thing. Maybe it's for the best. Nobody in this room ever has to know that he tried to get with me, if that was what happened. One girl in a long line of them.

"Oh!" Madison's voice is like a bullet. It knocks me out of my reverie, and I finally shake Reed's hand. "I just assumed you two would have bumped into each other at some point on campus."

Reed takes his hand back, straightening and putting them both in his pockets. "Nah. Chase has been hiding her away." His eyes shoot sideways to his brother. Chase shrugs. Is that what he was doing? Hiding me away? "He didn't even want to drive up together."

"We wanted to spend our break on campus," Chase says, defensive. What he means is that we decided to stick around for a few extra days since it meant that Chase's roommate would be gone and we could have sex whenever we wanted without being in anyone's way. I lost my virginity three weeks ago, and in that time, I've discovered that I very, very much like sex, even if it's a little...tamer...than I thought it would be. I keep waiting for Chase to be less gentle with me, but it never happens.

"We actually had a class together last semester." My comment takes everyone by surprise, even myself. Reed's eyes shoot to me, and I'm not sure if this is what I meant to do, offering him a piece of what I told him at the party in hopes that he'll remember.

Reed's eyes narrow a little bit, like he's examining my face for clues of familiarity, and then his head tilts. "Sorry, I don't remember."

Of course he doesn't.

Everyone seems to move on after that, getting into place at the table, even as my mind is settled heavily on the situation I've found myself in. Serving dishes get passed from one person to the other, but when Chase should pass the bowls of mashed potatoes and cranberry sauce to me, instead, he serves me, giving me reasonable portions before passing the dishes on to Sabrina across the table.

Spencer sweeps into the room, the massive platter with the turkey on it held aloft in his hands. He rushes to the head of the table and presents the perfectly golden turkey as if he shot and killed it himself. Everyone at the table applauds kindly, so I do as well. Spencer places the platter in front of Madison, but when he picks up the carving knife, Reed shoots up out of his seat.

"Hey, man, let me do it."

Spencer gives Reed a devious smile, as if he's used to this kind of behavior. He happily hands over the carving knife and disappears. Reed brandishes the knife, smiling over at his mother, who looks up at him adoringly.

Chase tilts his face toward me and rolls his eyes. "Oldest child gets all the attention," he whispers, but his comment is loud enough that everyone at the table can hear. Reed doesn't acknowledge the comment, but Madison looks over, her face blank.

I smile politely at Chase and watch Reed carve the turkey. He's wearing a short-sleeved shirt, not terribly unlike the one he was wearing the night we met, and I can see so many of his tattoos. Some of them are words, intertwining with images. A bundle of flowers, a bird with wings spread, a very intricate sun. My eyes travel over all of it, caught on the slice of muscle just above the angle of his elbow that flexes and smooths as he cuts and serves and cuts and serves.

I'm so attracted to Chase. So, so attracted to him.

But Reed is something else entirely. He's dark where Chase is light, hard where Chase is soft. By the time I realize Madison is talking to me, I've lost track of how long I've been watching the curve of Reed's arm.

My eyes shoot to his mother, her smile bright. "I'm so sorry, say again?"

"You're not a vegetarian, are you?"

"No."

"Oh, good. I mean, of course it's fine to be a vegetarian, but we're a family that's rather fond of meat. Please let me know should you ever change your mind."

I hold back a smile at her words. *If you ever change your mind.* She's talking like I'll be around for a very long time, and the thought makes me warm in the chest.

When I look back at Reed, his big brown eyes are on me, and I feel the heat rush up my neck at his gaze. I focus on the very dainty-looking china plate in front of me. It looks like it would crumble under my touch. As I'm thinking that, Chase grabs the plate and hands it up to Reed, who drops some meat onto it.

As we all finally start to eat, Sabrina looks across the table at me. The sun shines bright in her eyes. "So, Quinn. Your family isn't big on Thanksgiving?"

My family isn't big on being a family. "Not really. All of my siblings have sort of scattered around the country, so getting everyone together can be hard."

"Big family?" Madison asks, taking a sip of the wine Spencer has just poured her. When he comes around to my side of the table, I start to shake my head no, seeing as I'm not of age yet, but Madison nods to Spencer who tips some wine into my glass.

"Yes. I'm the youngest of eight."

The same thing happens now that happens every time I tell someone I have seven brothers and sisters. They all stop eating and look up at me with wide eyes, everyone but Chase, who already knows this about me. When I told him that I haven't spoken to any of my siblings in a long time, he invited me to spend Thanksgiving here. Even with just the five of us, it's far cozier than anything I would have gotten back in Mendota Heights.

"Eight," Sabrina says. "That's pretty wild, but it actually sounds nice."

With a fork full of corn, I can't seem to stop myself from blurting, "Yeah, it's really nice until your dad picks up and leaves and your siblings start vanishing the moment they turn eighteen, until it's just you and your mom left in a town where everyone has their eyes on you."

And just like that, I've made it worse. It's so quiet that I can hear everything Spencer is doing in the kitchen outside the open doorway. He's putting away silverware, each piece making a *clink clink clink* noise as he settles them into their spots.

"This turkey's fucking delicious," Chase says. And when he reaches over, grabs the back of my chair, and slides it over until my hip is touching his, a laugh bubbles up in my throat. I smile over at him, happy to be here with his family, and lean in to kiss him on the cheek.

When I settle back in my chair, my eye meets Reed's, sitting across the table from me now that he's done carving and serving the turkey.

There's an odd look on his face, like he's suddenly woken up somewhere he doesn't recognize. He blinks and then, like someone has ripped the words out of him, he says, "Me and Oscar got a place."

I have no idea what that means, but Madison's eyes go bright and her fork clatters to her plate, so that must mean it's a good thing.

"Oh, sweetheart, that's wonderful. You're going to love being a business owner."

"A business owner?" I can't stop the question from coming out of my mouth.

Reed looks over at me, but when I think he'll answer, Sabrina answers instead, smiling at me from her spot beside him. "Reed is going to have his own restaurant in downtown Boston after he graduates next year."

"Oh! Are you a chef?" I didn't know our school had degrees in culinary art. Or maybe he's getting a business degree. How exactly does a person become a chef anyway? I can barely boil water.

Beside me, Chase says, "Well, sort of. He's a dessert chef."

Reed raises an eyebrow. "I'm a *pastry* chef."

"Right. Yep. Pastry chef," Chase says, and the way he says it makes me giggle. He smiles over at me, his cheek bulging with whatever he just put in his mouth. "He makes these fancy as fuck desserts that I can never pronounce. What's the one you made us eat last week? The custard thing."

"Zabaglione." Reed's amused eyes shift from his brother to me. "What's your favorite dessert?"

My face flushes at having his attention so fully focused no me. "Oh. I'm not sure I—"

"You might as well tell him," Madison chimes in. "He does this with everyone, and he won't let up until you tell him."

As if to punctuate Madison's point, Reed stubbornly crosses his arms and leans back, raising his eyebrows at me in a way that makes my stomach flip. I feel like someone turned up the heat several degrees.

I tell myself to look away from him, but I can't. He watches me, and I want to give him a good answer, but I don't know any fancy deserts like that Italian thing he just said, and I already feel like I'm not making a very good first impression.

But when Reed has been watching me for what feels like an eternity, I say, "It's not exciting."

Reed's face changes. That smug guy that his mother said would never stop seems to vanish, replaced by someone softer. Someone who settles his elbows on the table and leans toward me, like he's going to whisper. Like we're the only two at the table, even though everyone is watching.

In my mind, I see him lift the corner of my skeleton mask in that dorm hallway and smile down at me.

"Dessert doesn't need to be fancy," he says in this voice that's almost nothing but breath. I'm watching his mouth move as he says it, the shape of his lips.

Chase's elbow bumps mine, forcing clarity back into my brain, and it finally jolts the truth out of my mouth. "Chocolate chip cookies."

For a beat, it's like the world stops turning. How stupid do I sound, choosing chocolate chip cookies over something like crème brulé or whatever?

Reed's face spreads into smile. "Noted."

11 QUINN

Chase and I lay in bed, staring up at the ceiling in the dark. Neither of us have said anything or even really moved since we got in bed, shoulder-to-shoulder. I can hear him breathing.

Finally, when I can bring myself to speak, I say, "I'm sorry about Madison."

When he found me near the bathrooms, neither of us could find the words to say. Yes, I feel bad for him, but I also feel bad for myself, and I could see on his face that he was frustrated that I was so upset. That's Chase. Everyone has to earn their right to everything except him. He just gets what he wants, no matter what.

But I know this isn't what he wanted. Chase might be a jackass, but I know he would trade every cent his mother has ever made to undo what we just found out tonight.

"She's going to be okay," he says up at the ceiling. "She has to be."

I find a certain comfort in the timbre of his voice. So famil-iar. How many times did we lay just like this in our bed back in

Boston, talking about stuff that happened during the day, making arrangements for who would take care of what things the following day—grocery shopping, gassing up cars, sending texts to mutual friends about some social event or another.

"She will be," I whisper, but I don't know if I believe it. When we got back to the table, Madison and Sabrina explained it all to us: the chemo treatments, the stages, the likelihoods and percentages. And according to it all, Madison is going to make a full recovery, look back on this years in the future and know that it was just one more challenge in her life that she bested. But that doesn't make any of it easier, because I know how fast life can steal someone away from you, and there's nothing keeping it from taking Madison now.

The silence resettles and then Chase shifts, and his hand brushes mine. At first, I think it's an accident, but then he shifts again and his fingers attempt to curl around mine.

I rip my hand away and push the covers off me, sitting up on the edge of the bed. The floor is cold under my feet, and it's exactly what I need to force myself to stand. I was waiting for the house to be asleep for a while before I moved to the basement, but if I don't get out now, I might fall apart.

I stand and turn back to the bed. Chase hasn't moved, his body still prone, the blankets on his side of the bed undisturbed. "Look, I'm truly sorry about Madison. I know that your family is about to go through a lot of stress and hardship. But I can't be there to comfort you. We're not married anymore. I'm not part of this family anymore." My voice shakes when I say it. Because I *want* to be part of this family. These people, Madison and Sabrina and Reed, they mean something to me. I *want* to be here with Madison while she goes through this thing that is going to be so traumatic for this family.

But I can't. It's over.

I reach for the door, and Chase finally sits up, finally speaks. "Where are you going?"

"I'm going to sleep on the couch."

He frowns. "Someone will see you." Same argument he used this morning, now with more desperation.

"The couch in the basement," I specify. I wasn't planning on sharing that part of it, but I get the feeling it'll quell some of his fear.

His frown was nervous before but it quickly becomes something else, maybe angry. "Down there with Reed?"

Anger spikes through me, manifesting in a flush that crawls up my neck. "There will be a door between us," I growl, "and unlike you, Reed knows how to keep his hands to himself." I yank the door open, step into the hallway, and quietly shut it behind me, even though I want to slam it closed. I don't know why I said that. Surely, Chase wasn't worried about whether or not Reed could control himself. He can't possibly think anything would happen between us.

I wait for a moment, listening for anyone still up. Down the hall, I can hear Sabrina talking to someone in her room, the shift of her walking around, like maybe she's pacing. Maybe a video call with one of her friends, since there's no way she has cell service. Her voice is low, her words muffled enough that I can't make them out. Lydia's room is silent.

I move carefully through the house, around the kitchen to the stairs leading to the basement. I'm not really sure what to expect. It's not like Reed and I had a conversation about where I would sleep for the rest of the trip. But I *know* I'm not sleeping next to Chase, even if that means I have to sleep in my car.

When I hear noise down in the basement, I stop. What if it's not just Reed down there? What if Madison is down there for some reason? How would I explain to her why I was sneaking out of my room and into Reed's space?

I wait for a second, not sure if I should turn around or take my chances, but then Reed's voice travels softly up the stairs. "You coming down, Quinn?"

I guess I didn't really know until that moment how much I was relying on the solace of the basement to get me through. A relieved sigh rushes out of me and my shoulders sink. I move down the stairs and find Reed standing in the basement kitchen, drinking something out of a coffee mug. When he sees me, he leans back against the stainless-steel fridge and sticks one hand in the pocket of his gray sweatpants. He hasn't turned on any of the lights, so only the moonlight through those high prison windows guides my feet across the basement to the kitchen.

"I hope that's decaf." I lean against the kitchen island, feeling...I don't even know what. I guess I thought it would be weird if I asked Reed if I could sleep down here for the duration of the trip. I mean, who does that? Who stays with their brother-in-law (still, I guess) instead of just sucking it up and sleeping in the same bed as their soon-to-be ex-husband?

But well...it isn't weird. It never has been with me and Reed. And maybe that's because he doesn't remember that first night that we met. But I think it's because Reed is so easy to be around. He's never asked anything of me and has always offered me kindness in return.

It's going to hurt to leave that behind.

"It's bourbon, actually. Want some?"

A laugh bubbles out of me. "Sure."

He pulls another mug out of the cabinet over his shoulder and pours me a healthy serving. I've never been one for straight liquor, but desperate times and all that...

I take a long pull, coughing a little around the burn in my

throat. I wait a second and then gulp down half the glass. I'm going to need a lot more than this to get through this week. Maybe if I was drunk off my ass the whole time, that would be enough.

"Whoa, there. Not too fast. You're going to get dizzy."

Maybe I want to be dizzy, I think as I gulp some more. All that's left is a golden ring at the bottom of the mug.

"He tried to hold my hand." The words burst out of me, mostly because, out here in the middle of nowhere, I have nobody to talk to. There's basically no cell reception and Madison's whole no-wifi thing. However, there *is* a guy I've been friends with for five years, even if he's the immediate family of the person causing me so much discomfort.

Reed's eyebrows raise over the lip of his mug. When he pulls it away, he says, "Seriously?"

I slam my mug down on the counter, feeling encouraged by his reaction and emboldened by the warmth that the whiskey has put in my stomach. "I know he's going through something right now, but does he really think I'm here in any way, shape, or form to help *him?* I came here because it turns out that owning a house in Boston is fucking expensive when you don't have a husband who earns six figures. Because I..."

I cover my face with my hands and take a deep breath before dropping them again. Reed stays firmly on his side of the kitchen, not offering me comfort this time, just his presence. "I'm not qualified for any jobs. I graduated with a Bachelor's degree and then basically spent three years doing *nothing* because Chase thought it would be hot to have a stay-at-home wife, when what he really wanted was a wife who looked the other way while he went out and fucked other people. I've been trying to get a job for three months, and I can barely even get an interview. And when I *do* get an interview, they discover that I'm a miserable wretch and don't want to hire me."

"Hey." His voice is a vicious bark and that startles me out of my rant. I'm surprised at the angry lines on his face. "That's my friend you're talking about. I'm not going to let you call yourself names. You're not a miserable wretch. You're an incredible woman who put up with a lot of bullshit. You'll find a job. Of course you will."

A knob forms in my throat, and I swallow hard. Have I ever been called an incredible woman in my entire life? I shake his words off, but that makes my head go fuzzy. I anticipate that I have about ten minutes before all that bourbon goes sour and I can't stand up straight.

"Could I tell you something?" His voice is soft, almost like he's hoping I won't hear him.

"Of course."

"I lost the restaurant."

His words are gibberish at first, my hazy brain trying to put them in the right order, the right context, to make sense. And then I remember Aeronaut, Reed's downtown Boston restaurant, the one he sunk every penny to his name into as soon as he graduated. The last time I was there, a year ago, it was a hot spot, *the* place to be.

"I don't understand," I sputter, my tongue starting to feel useless in my mouth. "What do you mean, you *lost* it?"

He sighs, leaning back on his palms, resting on the marble countertop. "I mean that Oscar, my business partner, got himself into some financial trouble. He put the place up as collateral. When he couldn't pay his debts, we lost it."

My mouth falls open. "But that's bullshit!" I shout.

Reed's eyes shoot to the ceiling, both of us falling quiet, listening for shifting or footsteps. When there's nothing, Reed says, "I know. But that's what happens when you go into business with someone. I could pay his debts off for him, buy his half of the restaurant, but I'm not equipped for that right now."

"So you're here because $500,000 could get you your restaurant back?"

"I don't think I want Aeronaut back. But I can start fresh. On my own this time. No partner to drag me down."

In the shadows, I can just barely make out the darkness of his eyes. "I'm sorry that happened to you, Reed. You deserve better than that."

"Yeah, well...I haven't told anyone."

Something spears through me. He hasn't told anyone. Except he told me. He knows my secret, and I know his. But his doesn't have the potential to bomb this entire week. This entire family.

"Your secret is safe with me." I set my mug down on the counter and realize there's a sticky note pressed to the top of it that I didn't see until my eyes adjusted to the dark. Bright pink. I gasp. "Is this Sabrina's wi-fi log in?" I already have my phone out.

"Yeah. She gave it to me and told me to give it to you when I was done with it. I'm sure it won't take Mom long to figure out we all have access."

As soon as I'm connected, my phone starts to vibrate in my hand with notifications. One of them catches my eye, and I click on it, opening up my email. I read through what came in, surprised by the nerves in my stomach. "Well..." I say, "...that's that."

Reed comes over to me, glancing down at my phone. "What is it?"

"An email from the mediator." I look up at him, feeling the zing of alcohol in my blood when I find him towering over me in the dark. "Chase and I are officially divorced."

I'm not sure what kind of reaction I was expecting from him. But Reed gives none. He just nods. "You okay?"

"Good fucking riddance." I hiccup, and he grins. "Come on. Let's get you to bed before the world starts to spin, yeah?"

"I'm fine," I say, but he's already started to steer me in the direction of the bedroom. "Nope," I say, ducking under his arm and knocking into a corner of the wall when I attempt a ninja spin to face him. "I'm sleeping on the couch."

He sighs. "We doing this again?"

I back toward the couch. "Just let me sleep on the couch, and we won't have to do it ever again."

"I'm not letting you—"

I stick my fingers in my ears. "La la la," I sing quietly. "I can't hear your protest. La la la."

I don't realize I've closed my eyes until I feel his hands wrap around my wrists and yank my fingers out of my ears. "Okay, crazy lady. If you insist on me taking the bed, then I insist on you sharing it."

I blink up at him. "Share the bed?"

He shrugs. "Sure. It's big enough. We wouldn't have to have any contact. We can even put a pillow wall between us."

Something about the way he says it makes me snort with laughter. "It's really ironic when the idea of sharing a bed with my brother-in-law sounds way better than sharing one with my husband. I mean, ex-husband." I burst into a fit of giggles.

"You can trust me."

His words immediately kill the laughter in my stomach. My brain has finally caught up with my ears, processing what Reed has suggested. That we share the bed. Sleep in it together. The thought makes my entire body start to go hot, like I've broken into a fever.

"I know. I do." I trust him far more than I can trust Chase right now. If I went back up there, would he even make it a whole night without trying to get me to have sex with him again? That kind of makes me want to gag. "Yeah. Okay. We can do that. 'S a big bed."

He's clearly holding back a smile, which I sort of wish he wouldn't do. He has a great smile. A smile that could launch a thousand ships. And probably already has. I would fully believe that a minimum of a thousand girls have been obsessed with Reed over the course of his lifetime.

"Let's go, kid," he says, taking me by the wrist and leading me into the bedroom.

I shut the door behind us. "You know, you have some nerve calling me 'kid.' You're only two years older than me."

"That's two whole years of life experience." He throws back the blanket on the bed, and I suddenly get very nervous. I know I agreed to this whole thing, and I really would rather share a bed with Reed than with Chase right now, but it's still *Reed*. We've never shared a bed before, never even really spent this much time together before, day after day like this.

He settles onto the mattress, and I'm still standing beside the bed, trying to get my limbs to move. I've never slept beside anyone but Chase.

Okay. This is silly. It's just Reed. It would be like sharing a bed with one of my brothers. I just need to pretend he's Marshall or Lance or Sammy. Except that when he's laying down the way he is, the blanket at his waist, I can see the shape of every muscle under his shirt, the ridges of his abs and the swell of his chest. *Definitely* not like sharing a bed with one of my brothers.

I push back the comforter and climb in beside him. He doesn't make a move to put a pillow wall between us, so I don't say anything about it.

We lay there, the lights from the lamps shining down on us, both of us breathing quietly and saying nothing. I turn my head look at him, and he turns his to look back. Heat rushes up to my cheeks.

"I feel like I'm at a sleepover," I say to break the silence, a snort of laughter bursting out of me. "You better not fall asleep first. I'll draw a mustache on your face with a Sharpie." When he raises his eyebrows at me, I burst into even louder laughter. "Oh! You already have a mustache!" At that, I laugh until my stomach hurts.

When I've finally settled down, it's to find Reed quietly watching me with a small smile on his face. "I think someone's a little tipsy."

I settle my arms above my head, feeling content and comfortable for the first time since getting to New Hampshire. "I almost never drink." I lick my lips, tasting the honey flavor of the bourbon on my mouth. "I'm very warm."

He chuckles. "Yeah, that'll happen when you've shot-gunned that much bourbon."

"Hey," I whisper to him, "do you want to watch a scary movie?"

His eyes flicker to the TV mounted on the wall. "Sure. It won't make it hard for you to sleep?"

"Ha! Nothing scares me. Except maybe misogyny and not being able to trust the things we always thought we could." Not sure where that came from.

Reed, the remote already in his hand, blinks at me. "There might be a few movies we need to avoid then."

12   REED

Quinn makes it about four minutes into the movie before she falls asleep and about twenty-four minutes before she rolls over and cuddles up against me. My breath stutters out of me when her small, delicate hand settles against my chest, first just lying there gently and then curling into the fabric of my shirt, like she's trying to keep me from leaving.

As if I ever could.

Texas Chainsaw Massacre is still playing on the TV, but my eyes are glued to Quinn. Her hair cascades around both of us, and even though I absolutely know that I shouldn't, I reach up and run my fingertip down the curve of her ear. Her earlobe is so soft, soft enough that I can't stop there. I have to trace the jut of her cheekbone and the sharp line of her jaw. She smells like vanilla. Good enough to eat.

She makes a humming noise in the back of her throat, and something stabs me in the gut. This is instinctual for her. Does she—or at least, the version of her in her sleep—think I'm Chase? Is she casually pressing her body all along the length of mine because she thinks I'm my brother, the man she's slept next to all these years?

But even more than that, I have to wonder if I truly care. Or does it not matter who she thinks I am as long as she continues to burrow deeper into me? When she throws her leg over my knees, the delicious shape of her calf cradled against me, do I care that she probably feels this comfortable with me because she thinks I'm someone I'm not?

Or do I just want to let this happen...?

Let her hold me as tight as she wants to so that she can find some sort of peace through this entire stressful experience? I can't even imagine what's going on in her head, how truly abhorrent it must feel to have someone betray your trust so spectacularly and then have to be locked in a house with them for a whole week.

I take a lock of her hair between my thumb and forefinger, testing the texture and weight of it.

I'll do anything to protect her from Chase. I'll do anything to make sure she doesn't get hurt again, that he doesn't get a chance to rub salt into the wound. She deserves better than that, and I'll do what I have to in order to make her feel safe and comfortable.

And so, I turn off the TV and the lamp that I can reach without disturbing her. I leave the other on, the golden light shining down onto her hair, and fall asleep with her wrapped around me like she's never going disentangle our two bodies.

13 QUINN

4 Years Ago

"Miss Porter, I'm so sorry to have to ask this, but someone will have to come down to identify the body."

I try to open my mouth to respond, but I can't. It's like I'm choking, like something thick and hard is caught in my throat. I suck in a breath but end up coughing instead.

"Miss Porter, I understand this is a very difficult time. Why don't I give you a moment to settle things with your family? I'll call you back in the morning."

I nod, even though the man on the other end of the line can't see me.

But he clearly understands because he simply says, "Goodnight, Miss Porter."

I set the phone on the table and am finally able to gulp in a full breath. *Settle things with your family...*

What is there to settle? There's a reason they called me. There's a reason I have to be the one to drive back to Minnesota to identify my mother's body after they fished her out of Lake Michigan.

I have to be the one to do it because all of my other siblings are gone. Every single one of them, as soon as they graduated, left town and never looked back. And it's not like I can blame them. But what about me? What about Mom? It's not her fault Dad left, and it's not her fault we were made out to be circus freaks in town just because my parents weren't terribly strict on the birth control.

There goes another Porter kid. How many is that, fifteen?

And in the end, for the last few years since Mindy moved out, it's been Mom and me. Yes, I picked up and moved away, too, but I didn't abandon her. I didn't stop answering her calls or stop coming to visit the way everyone else did.

They said they arrested her boyfriend. They said she was dead before she went into the lake.

That he most likely killed her.

I sob into my hands, wet tears spilling all over my little kitchen table, the one I eat breakfast at every morning with Chase. I wish he was here now. I can't believe I'm at home alone with this news, sitting on the table in front of me while the world keeps turning.

Once I've cried so much that I start to feel sick, I pick my phone back up. I have to call someone. I have to let someone know. One of my siblings. *All* of my siblings. My father.

I don't want to call any of them. Not yet. I don't think I can bring myself to talk about it until the identification is over. Maybe I'll feel like I can talk to all of those people once I've seen her with my own eyes. Once it really feels real. But until then...

I scroll to Chase's name in my phone. It doesn't even actually say *Chase*. It says *boyfriend*. I thought it was cute at the time, but looking at it now, I don't know. It makes my heart race, and not in a romantic way. It's sort of making me panic, like the walls of this apartment that we share together are getting closer and closer. I can't breathe.

I scroll past *boyfriend* to *Brooke.* But I can't. It's the day after Christmas. I can't do that to her. She's staying with her family this week, and even though I know she'll be mad at me when this over, mad that I didn't call her immediately just to spare her feelings, I scroll by her name too, a sob rising up in my chest when I realize I don't have anyone to call. Anyone I *want* to call.

I don't have to call anyone right now. I can deal with this on my own. Chase will be home from his night out with his brother soon anyway.

My eyes land on my phone screen again. I scroll to the bottom of my contacts list, where Reed's name is listed. I don't even know why I have his phone number. It's one of those things that just happens. You end up in a group chat with someone, or you decide you're all going to meet up at the same restaurant, and suddenly, you have someone's number that you never speak to, "just in case."

I stare at his name. I can't even put words to what's going on in my head. It's just this *knowing* that Reed will know the right things to say. There are just those people, the ones that make you feel...safe. That give off this vibe like they would stand between you and anything that tried to hurt you. Like maybe you could hide yourself away in them. That's what Reed is like.

And it's inappropriate for me to even be thinking about him that way. Who the hell has thoughts like that about their boyfriend's brother and not their actual fucking boyfriend?

And yet, here I am, still considering it. Still wondering, what's the worst that could happen if I call Reed? If I listen to the sound of his soothing voice, just for a second, until my heart stops hammering and my hands stop trembling.

Without another thought, I select his name, and the screen changes, showing me that it's calling him. I put my phone to my ear, listen to the gentle buzzing of it as I wait for Reed to answer.

It rings twice, and then I rip my phone away from my ear. God, what the hell am I doing? Reed and Chase are *together*. If I call Reed, Chase is going to know. And even though it's completely innocent, I can't let Chase know that it was my first instinct to call Reed for comfort before him.

God, that's so messed up.

I'm so messed up.

Even though I'm not sure it's what I want, I try Chase next, my heart pounding at the thought of him picking up, of me having to tell him what happened. But he doesn't answer.

I set my head on the table and cry because my mom is dead and I'm alone in the world.

But then my phone rings. I sit up quickly, thinking it has to be Reed calling back, but when I look at the screen, I see it's Chase. "Hello?" I know I'm not going to be able to hide anything. My voice is thick with tears, my nose running, making me sniffle almost as soon as I answer.

"Baby, what's wrong?"

I immediately start sobbing, crying and crying into the phone until I'm sick to my stomach. When I've finally settled down, am finally able to catch my breath, I hear human noises, the quiet hum of a crowded bar in my ear.

"I'm coming, baby," he says. "Just hang on. I'm on my way to you."

And in that moment, I feel so much relief that I have Chase, that I'm finally able to stop crying. "Hurry."

"Quinn, it's time to get up."

I'm not sure if it's the voice or the rumble of said voice under my cheek that wakes me. My eyes slide open, immediately finding the gray sky in the sliver of window high up on the wall. I process it all slowly, the light, the feel of the cold sheets, and the hard chest under my head.

I shoot up, my hand going to my mouth as my eyes meet Reed's. He hasn't moved, his body relaxed and open, his eyes watching me take in what must have happened. Sometime in the night, I snuggled up to him, my body acting on the instinct of being married for several years and sleeping next to a man who didn't mind cuddling. Muscle memory. That's what this is.

"I'm so sorry," I whisper, the air feeling like it shouldn't be disturbed before the sun is all the way up.

Reed's expression doesn't change. The blankets pool around his hips, wrapping around my legs as well. "Hey, it's no big deal."

"It *is* a big deal." I throw the blankets off of me and climb off the bed. "You don't deserve to be mauled by your sister-in-law. You trusted me, and I broke that trust. I'll sleep upstairs with Chase tonight." It kills me to say it, but it's all true. He should have been able to count on me, but I was tipsy and emotional and exhausted, and look what happened.

"Hey," he says, sitting up and draping his hands over his knees. "Nobody here feels mauled, okay? You were just doing what your body is used to. No harm, no foul."

He's being far too blasé about this. "You were harmed."

"I can assure you, I wasn't."

I want him to stop arguing with me. I want him to hold me accountable. "Reed, stop trying to—"

"No." His voice is firm, heavy with finality. His eyes meet mine, and they're steady. "I told you that you're safe with me, Quinn, and I meant it."

I can't find words. It's not just about the cuddling. I think...I think I want him to criticize me because he deserves better than being used as some kind of stand-in for Chase. He deserves better than being in this house with the two of us, being the only one who knows the truth.

I want to apologize again, for everything, but instead, I open the door, walk quietly out into the basement, and close the door between us.

15 REED

Quinn is freaked out. She's been putting as much space between us as possible all morning, and I can't really blame her. I came on too strong. I didn't want her to apologize for touching me, for sleeping half on top of me. Because I liked it. I liked it so much that long before I woke her up, I had to focus on a lot of very un-sexy things to get rid of the morning wood that was pressing against her leg.

But all she wanted me to do was punish her. Because that's the kind of shit Chase used to do, punish her for being less than perfect. Less than *his* idea of perfect. To me, nothing could make her anything but absolutely perfect.

We're sitting in the breakfast nook with Sabrina, trying to pretend nothing happened between us this morning while Sabrina and Lydia discuss the correct way to make Eggs Benedict. My eyes meet Quinn's across the table, and she looks away quick. I don't want her to be uncomfortable. I'm starting to rethink this whole thing. It's too soon. She and Chase are still too fresh. The divorce just became final *last night*. But...

But if I have to leave here without her, I'll be sick.

When Lydia moves into the kitchen, I lean across the table toward Sabrina. "Does Lydia know about Mom?"

Sabrina sends me that *you're a fucking idiot* face that she does so well, even this early in the morning. "Of course, Lydia knows. Lydia's been taking good care of Mom back in the city. Mom would be totally lost without her."

I shrug. "I thought that's why *you* were living with Mom."

Sabrina rolls her eyes. "Come on. I'm just emotional support. I'm useless when it comes to anything that's actually useful."

"Hey," Quinn barks. Her eyebrows are curved in, her mouth turned down in a frown. "Don't talk about yourself that way. You're not useless. You're helping Madison fight cancer, for God's sake."

Sabrina's eyes go glassy, and she looks down at the wood grain of the table, brushed a gentle yellow color. "The chemo makes her so sick, and there's *nothing* I can do to help her."

Quinn's arm flexes, and I know that she's taken Sabrina's hand under the table. "I bet Madison is so happy to have you with her. She loves you so much."

Sabrina sniffles and nods. "I know. I love her, too." Her voice breaks, and I'm about to stand, to move around the table to her, when Chase comes stomping into the room.

"Hey, man. Did you know you have an oil leak?"

We all stare at him. It's like having someone throw a bucket of ice water on you when you're half-awake.

And then I realize Chase's eyes are on me. He's *talking* to *me.*

"What?" I ask, my brain still in an emotional fog.

Chase points over his shoulder, toward the front door of the house. "Your bike. It has an oil leak. Looks like it's been going for a while."

"Shit." It *has* been going for a while. I turn and look at

Sabrina, who no longer looks like she's going to cry. Her face is back to normal, no sign of upset at all. I don't know whether to be impressed or concerned that she can put herself back together so quickly. She shouldn't have to do that. I open my mouth, intending to offer to stay with her, but she makes a shooing motion at me, so I turn for the door.

But when my eyes catch the hallway that leads to our mom's room, a thought hits me, and I turn back to the breakfast nook. "Mom never sleeps in," I say, aware of how stupid the comment sounds as it comes out of my mouth. Of course she's tired. She has cancer, for fuck's sake, but it's not just that. "When she said she was going out with friends in town yesterday, did she go to a doctor?"

Quinn's lips part, and her eyes slide over to Sabrina, clearly seeing the logic that I just did.

Sabrina nods. "Her doctor wouldn't let her travel unless she saw someone else while she was here. She had some treatments. Nothing like the chemo though."

I just nod. I don't know what to do with that information, what to do with any of it, how to process the fact that my mother is in the other room sick, and we're all supposed to go on with life as if everything is normal.

16 QUINN

Sabrina sighs. "I think I'm going to go for a walk."

And just like that, I'm alone with Chase. Without a word, he takes the seat that Reed vacated, picking up the last piece of toast Reed left behind and buttering it.

I watch him, unable to look away. It's amazing how you can be so into someone and think they're the most attractive person you've ever known, and then it's like you see inside them and you wonder how you overlooked how ugly they were the whole time. I'm disgusted by Chase's sharp cheekbones, the jut of his chin, and the way his hair is messy when it's normally perfectly styled for his executive job. He looks like a child to me, some sixteen-year-old kid who can't control his sexual urges.

I hate him.

And as if he knows that, as if he can feel the waves of hate coming off me, he leans back in his chair and says, "We need to talk."

I burst out of my seat. "I'm going to go help Reed with his oil leak."

Chase throws up his hands. "I sincerely doubt he needs

your help with that hunk of junk," he says. "You can't just run away forever."

"I can do whatever I want," I throw over my shoulder, and when I spin back around, it's to find Lydia in my path. I almost don't stop in time, nearly slamming right into her. She smiles up at me, that soft, sweet smile of hers, and my stomach churns. Did she hear what Chase said? Is it obvious that we're not together anymore? Or do normal married couples fight the way we are? Why can't I remember? Why didn't it matter enough to me? Did Chase and I ever fight? Or did I just let Chase call all the shots without ever arguing?

Lydia's eyes lock onto mine, and I get the distinct feeling that she's...trying to save me from Chase. Or at least, from the argument we're having. "Can I get you anything, Mrs. Lynch?" she asks, her voice small and quiet. "Some iced tea or some fruit?"

"No, thank you, Lydia. I appreciate it. But maybe you could prepare a little treat for Sabrina for when she gets back? A hot bath or something?"

Lydia ducks her head. Is she...blushing? What is that all about? "Absolutely," she whispers before stepping out of my way.

I throw open the front door and close it behind me, leaning against it for a second to take in a long, deep breath of fresh air. It has that twinge to it, the smell of lake water, and I find it comforting.

"Doing okay?"

I open my eyes to find Reed at the bottom of the stairs, a wrench in his hand and a concerned tilt to his features. He has the sleeves of his Henley rolled up so that I can see the tattoos covering both of his forearms.

"I'm fine," I say to him, making my way down the stairs, suddenly feeling unsure if this is any better than hanging out with Chase. I still can't believe I cuddled up to Reed in my sleep. I know he said it didn't bother him, but I mean...I had my leg thrown over him like I was getting ready to dry-hump him. And he smelled so good that when I woke up, I was so disoriented because...well...he didn't smell like Chase. And for a second there, that was so comforting. I knew it wasn't Chase, but my subconscious knew it was some big, strong man, ready to watch over me while I slept.

My cheeks flush. I was humiliated. I don't need Reed getting the impression that I'm so hard up for companionship or I miss Chase so much that I would crawl into bed with any guy, especially my soon-to-be ex-husband's brother, for God's sake. How embarrassing.

"Just didn't want to stay in there with him," I say. I get to the bottom of the stairs and follow Reed over to where his bike is propped up on its kickstand on the decomposed granite road leading from the house down to the lake. He crouches down by the bike, and I hop up onto one of the flat-topped wood plank posts that surrounds the house.

"You know," he says with a grunt as he loosens something with his wrench, "you're going to have to spend time with him eventually, or the whole family is going to know that something's up."

I shrug, even though I don't feel very casual about the whole thing. I'm actually feeling a little panicked about what Lydia heard. "Couples fight. I'm pretty sure Lydia got wind of something, but she probably thinks we're in an argument. Easy to believe when someone is married to such a bull-headed jerk."

One side of Reed's mouth curls up in a smile. "I'm sure she thought nothing of it." He nods in the direction of his bike. "Want to help me with this crush gasket?"

"Sure, if you tell me what a crush gasket is."

He chuckles. "I don't actually need your help with it. It's a pretty easy fix. But there's something up with my exhaust that's making me go through these gaskets faster than I should. So, I keep a few spares." He steps over to me, his shoes crunching on the ground, and holds out his fist to me, palm down. When I just stare at him, he nods at my hand.

I reach out to take whatever he has, but before he lets me have it, his eyes meet mine. "It's kinda greasy. My hands are..." He lifts his other hand so that I can see the grease coating the ends of his fingers.

"I don't mind," I find myself saying, my eyes on his hands, on the little storm cloud he has in the fleshy part between his thumb and index finger. He opens his hand and the silver gasket falls into my palm. It's light and round, sized perfectly to circle the lines on the center of my palm. I'm still looking at it when Reed turns back to his bike.

He crouches again, and I watch as he settles another silver gasket into a hole that's perfectly shaped for it toward the front of his bike. His long, lithe fingers press into the curve of the metal piece, gently fitting it into place. And then he swirls his thumb along the circumference of the gasket, and I watch, transfixed at the shape of his hands, the way the tendons flex and stretch as he settles them over the hole.

"Hand me that screwdriver?"

I look away, clearing my throat. I hop off the post and pick up the screwdriver he left on the ground by the grass. There are a few other tools there, ones that are small enough to fit in the storage compartment on the side of his bike.

"Ever been on a bike?" Reed asks when I hand him the screwdriver. He wraps his hand around the hot metal, his fingers engulfing it, and I let go quickly, taking a step back.

"No. Chase always says motorcycles are for adrenaline junkies." I sort of regret it as soon as it comes out of my mouth.

I'm not trying to be the thing that comes between these brothers, but all I've done on this entire trip is shit talk Chase.

But Reed smiles, like I paid him a compliment. "Maybe he's right. But is that so bad?"

My stomach feels like I'm in a free fall, like being dropped out of an airplane. I squeeze the gasket in my hand so hard that it bites into my skin. "You know what?" I say, dropping the extra gasket on the ground at Reed's feet. "I actually need to go."

"Go?" His smile falls.

"Yeah, I, uh..."

Out of the corner of my eye, I spot Sabrina. She's doing something on her phone, coming off the hiking trail that leads from the lake house up into the woods on the hill. She still looks sad, her mouth turned down at the corners.

"I need to talk to Sabrina," I say, moving in her direction. I give a nervous laugh.

Before I say anything I'll regret, I make a run for it.

17 REED

If I was feeling a bit roguish, I would keep Quinn from leaving, make her explain why she needs to get away so fast. I know it's because she's thinking dirty thoughts about me. I know it because she was staring at me like I was covered in whipped cream and she wanted to lick it all off.

And God, does that feel amazing.

But I just got an email, felt my phone buzz in my pocket, and I need to read it.

So I let Quinn go, even though I want to do anything but.

Pulling my phone out of my back pocket, I open the email before I remember that my hands are covered in grease. Oh, well. It's not the first time I've gotten grease all over my phone and my clothes.

Reed, I'm in. I'm thinking 50k. Sound good?
—Jack

My stomach flips. Before I made the choice to disappear for a week to come here, I contacted investors all over Boston and

New York that I knew from my years in the business to find out if they wanted to invest in my new restaurant. I don't have a building or a chef or any idea how I'm going to do this thing on my own, but I know I *am* going to do it on my own.

My eyes lift to find Quinn and Sabrina by the side of the house. They're over there talking, Sabrina finally looking more like herself while she and Quinn laugh about something. I want to tell Quinn about the restaurant. I want her to be proud of me, like she always is when something amazing happens in my life, sending me little *Congrats!* texts that I save in a special folder so they can move from phone to phone with me.

But I can't tell Quinn that I have investors lined up because I kind of, sort of made Quinn believe that I came here for Mom's money. And sure, having that $500k would definitely be a big leg up for me. It would mean the difference between a small storefront restaurant with a struggling staff for a year or two and a gorgeous, classy restaurant in a high-rise with enough staff for everyone to be comfortable.

But that's not why I came here. I would have come with or without my mother's money as an incentive.

I came here for Quinn.

Like she's reading my mind, her eyes travel the length of the driveway and find mine. She looks away quick, but Sabrina twists her head and motions for me to come over. I wipe my hands on a rag as I head over to them, and as soon as I'm close enough to hear, Sabrina says, "Hey, we're going to take the boat out on the lake. Want to come?"

"Sure. Sounds good."

"Go inside and tell Chase," Sabrina says, and if she wasn't looking down at her phone, she wouldn't have missed the look that Quinn and I shoot each other. She grimaces and I roll my eyes.

We really have to stop this. Quinn has to pretend that

everything is absolutely perfect with Chase or Mom is going to catch wind of it.

"I'll go in and see if Mom feels up to coming." Sabrina turns for the house, and I lean around Quinn to see that Chase is lounging by the pool.

"Guess I'll go let him know," I say, nodding toward Chase.

Quinn just nods, her head bowed. I want to know what she's thinking, but I don't think this is the best time to ask. I step around her and head for the pool. When he sees me coming, Chase puts a hand up to block the sun.

"The girls want to take the boat out."

He chuckles. "And they need the men to set it up for them?"

I just stare at him, my hands in my pockets so I'm not tempted to knock him one. "Sabrina's been taking the boat out by herself since she was old enough to reach the lock on the boathouse. I don't think anybody's inviting you to come along because of your rippling biceps."

I clearly said the magic word. Chase sits up on his lounge chair and pushes up the sleeve of his unbuttoned Hawaiian shirt. "Are you really going to deny that I have rippling biceps?"

Luckily, I don't have to answer. The door of the house opens and the women trail out. I'm glad to see my mother in the back of the pack, putting on a pair of sunglasses and settling her big hat on her head. She's always loved being on the lake. According to legend, she was a rower back when she was in college and then bought this lake house with her first million so that she could row on it whenever she wanted. Her rowing days were mostly behind her by the time I was old enough to have memories.

Chase heads for the boat house, but I wait for Quinn to catch up to me before turning to head down the trail to it, Mom and Sabrina following behind us.

It's like muscle memory, pulling open the big door to the boat house and untying the skiff. I check to make sure we have life jackets, even though we won't use them, and that the boat has enough gas. My mom's old canoe is up on the wall, with the oars criss-crossed in front of it. It shines in the light reflecting off the water, like it's brand new.

We all pile into the boat, Chase helping our mom into it, and then we rocket out of the big opening of the boat house and onto the lake. Once we're far from the house, Chase lets the engine die, and we float through the center of the lake.

"Should have brought the fishing gear," Chase says, but our mother waves him off.

"Isn't it nice every once in a while, not having any distractions? No cell phones. No social media. No mile-long to-do list. Just a boat full of people you care about, floating on a lake far from civilization." She leans back on her seat and tilts her head up toward the sun. I smile as I watch her. For someone who has built their entire career off monetizing the internet, she's really good at disconnecting from it all.

I feel the heat of someone's eyes and glance over at Quinn, pressed into the seat beside Chase. She smiles at me, and it's so strangely peaceful and uninhibited that my heart gives a lethal *thump* in my chest.

"I don't feel like I know what to do next with my life." The words come from Sabrina, and we all look to her in tandem. I know that everyone is thinking exactly what I am. We all feel the same way. When she realizes she's the center of attention, Sabrina shrugs, pulling her legs up onto the seat with her and wrapping her arms around them. "I've accomplished so much already, and I'm proud of that, but I don't know what I really want to *do*. I can't keep up with this lifestyle forever."

Mom, sitting beside Sabrina, puts her arm around her

shoulders. "You can do anything you want to. You have all the power inside yourself."

Sabrina throws her hands up. "I get that, but I don't know what I *want*. I didn't go to school like you guys did." She motions to the three of us. "I don't have an empire like you," she says to our mom. "I've just been following opportunities as they arise, but what happens when the invitations stop coming?"

Our mother sits up straighter, pulling her shoulders back, turning into Madison Lynch. "When the invitations stop coming is when the real fun begins. When people stop expecting things from you, you start to listen to yourself more. You start to understand your own desires. Sabrina, my love, you're twenty-two. It's okay to have not a single clue what you want to do. No one should be expected to have it all figured out by twenty-two."

"You did." Sabrina looks around the boat. "You all did."

I look to Chase, and he shrugs back at me. She's not wrong. We both knew exactly what we wanted by the time we left Suffolk.

"I didn't," Quinn's voice pipes in, quiet like she's hoping no one will hear her. But we all do. She looks around at all of us and then focuses on Sabrina. "I still have no clue what I want to do with my life." I can see the way she's choosing her words wisely, trying not to give away that she's now a single woman, rebuilding her life after a divorce. "I keep hoping that I'll wake up one day and have it all figured out, but maybe that's not the point. Maybe what you *do* isn't the point. Maybe you just need to focus on who you *are*."

My heart races for her. She looks so beautiful in the late morning sun. The light curves along the length of her eyelashes and the jut of her collarbone. I love her, and I'm certain, the way I can be certain that the sun rises in the east and sets in the west, that I'll never love anyone else this way.

And like he's somehow thinking the same thing, Chase puts an arm around her shoulders, pulling her close and smiling at her. "You know who you are, Quinn," he says, and I think he genuinely meant it to be comforting, but Quinn clasps her hands together and meets my eye. She looks like Chase spit on her.

"I wonder how fast I can swim back to the boat house." The words pop out of my mouth. If I was any dumber, I'd have the IQ of a piece of lake moss. But once everyone is looking at me, I know I have to follow through with my idiotic comment. And I will, for Quinn.

I stand on the edge of the skiff and strip my shirt off over my head. I can't keep myself from glancing at Quinn, feeling mighty proud of myself when her eyes rake over my bare chest. I want it to be her hands. Her mouth.

"No one's going to challenge me?"

I fully expected Chase to make a play for it. I thought his competitive streak would take over, and I would be able to get him off this boat and away from Quinn. But he doesn't move. He keeps his arm wrapped around Quinn and watches me. It's like he has her imprisoned.

I look to Sabrina, thinking that if she joins in, Chase will for sure, but she's still got her knees pulled up to her chest. When she finally glances up at me, she shakes her head. "I didn't put on my suit."

"Neither did I," Quinn says, but she stands, finally pulling away from Chase. Her foot comes up onto the edge of the boat, and she's over the side before I know it, still wearing her shorts and tank top.

I don't hesitate. I catapult myself into the water, even as I hear Chase shout, "What the hell!"

When I come up to the surface, it's to see Quinn already

swimming toward the house. I start in after her, and back in the boat, Chase shouts, "What are we, twelve?"

Contentment settles in the center of my chest. This is how it should always be, me and Quinn against the world.

I overtake her easily, and hear her little grunt of disapproval as I pull ahead. She couldn't have been expecting to win this. She's half a foot shorter than me, and I used to swim in high school. I push hard and swim straight into the opening of the boat house, turning in the shadow of the overhang and watching Quinn dive under the water and take the rest of the way under the surface.

She comes up out of the water, wiping it out of her eyes and off her face. Her cheeks are flushed, her mouth pulled into a smile. "Think he'll follow us?"

I roll my eyes, pressing my back against the wooden slat behind me. "What do you think that was, a quarter mile? There's no way Muscles back there followed. He's a terrible swimmer. He knows there's no way he'd win."

She's grinning up at me, bobbing in the water, her hair all stuck around her face, and she's fucking glowing. "I clearly didn't stand a chance against you. Probably because you have the wingspan of a pterodactyl." As if to punctuate her point, she reaches for my arm below the water, her fingers dragging against my stomach as she tries to find my wrist. She's clearly having too much fun to worry about whether or not she's accidentally touching my bare skin.

She raises my arm over her head, her face full of joy.

"I only won because Sabrina didn't come. She's the fastest swimmer I know."

She drops my arm, and it makes a huge splash that makes her giggle. She wipes her hand down her face. "Don't be modest. You're a fast swimmer. How long were you waiting here for me?"

I shrug. "Not long." I lean my head back against the wall, my eyes going up to the rafters over our heads. "Jesus, I haven't been in this boat house in ages." I lower my eyes, find her watching me. "I loved this lake house as a kid. It was one of the few times all the money didn't bother me."

"Why did you stop coming?"

Because I hated seeing you with him.

"Life just got in the way. I was working all the time and trying to make something of myself and—" I cut myself off.

"And trying to prove you were worthy of it all."

My eyes shoot to hers. Water clings to the lines of her face, dripping gracefully from the point of her chin. She's always seen through me. That's the real problem. That's why coming here and spending a week or more in this house with her every summer was never an option. Because every time I'm with this girl, she finds a way to break me open and look right into my chest.

I have to look away from her, down at the murky water. I can see the distorted shape of her beneath the surface. She's swimming so close to me that her knees keep bumping into mine. I could move away so she's not touching me, but I would rather die. "It's hard being part of this family sometimes. We're all just trying to live up to the incomparable Madison Lynch."

"You don't have to live up to anyone." She floats closer to me, until the front of her body brushes the front of mine. I hold my breath. I can't allow myself to move or I'll pull her against me and beg her to be mine. She tilts her face up to me. "You're perfect the way you are."

I can feel her breath on my lips, the puff of it, wet and heavy. Her eyes fall to my mouth, and I hold very still, like she's a bird that I might startle away from her perch if I so much as twitch.

She grabs hold of my arms, pulls herself up my body, and kisses me.

It's quick, a simple press of her lips to mine. But when she pulls away, breathing against my mouth, I can't stop myself. I take her face in my hands and dive back into her.

It's like breathing for the first time. I haul her up against me, and she doesn't protest. Her mouth opens under mine, and I get my first taste of her. She tastes like good memories and summer sunshine and everything I've ever wanted in my life. I swipe my tongue into her mouth, and she moans, meeting me like we've done this a hundred times.

But we haven't, and we're both starving. Five years I've starved for her. Has she been starving just as long?

One of her legs comes up to wrap around my waist, and I know she can feel that I'm hard for her. I can feel her stomach pressing against me, and as she wraps her arms around my neck, opening her mouth on mine like she's going to swallow me whole, her body gently rocks once against mine.

I'm about to reach for her ass, pull her up against me and get a rhythm going, when Chase's voice sounds from nearby.

"Where the hell are they?"

Quinn jerks away from me, ripping her mouth off of mine. I don't want to let her go, want to tighten my arms around her so she can't get away, not when it's finally *finally* happening. But I let her float away from me, her hands reaching up to cover her mouth like she just realized I'm actually a serial killer.

"Quinn," I say, but she's already swimming away from me, moving out of the cover of the boat house and waving as the skiff appears on the horizon.

I stay where I am, my back pressed to the wall, trying to slow the erratic pulsing of my heart.

18 QUINN

Oh my God. Oh my God. Oh my God. What the fuck did I just do?

What the fuck did I just *do*?

I help Sabrina get the boat back into the boat house and tied off, but as soon as it's secure, I make an excuse and take off for the house, my phone already out by the time I reach Chase's bedroom. I lock the door and then close and lock the closet door behind me, too. I can't let anybody hear the phone call I'm about to make.

There's no cell service, but thanks to Sabrina's brilliance, I can video call Brooke through the wi-fi.

When she answers, she's all smiles, the way she always is these days. Brooke has always been the sunny, optimistic one, but since she started getting railed regularly by the guy across the hall, she's been downright perky.

"Hey, buttercup!" she says as she stirs whatever she's making herself for lunch. "What's going on?" She finally focuses on the phone and she squints at me. "Why are you soaking wet? Did you get caught in a storm?"

"The lake," I say, and I realize I'm out of breath. That's how fast I booked it up the hill to the house.

"Did you forget your bathing suit?"

"Would you just—" I lower my voice, realizing that *shrill* is probably more likely to be heard in other rooms. "Look, I did something really, really stupid, and now I don't know what do."

She stops tending to what she's cooking and takes the phone with both hands. "Oh, God. Did you murder Chase? Did you hold his head under the water at the lake? I'm not gonna lie, ever since you said you were going to that house, I've been thinking maybe it's not such a bad idea. Do you need help weighing down the body?"

It takes me a second to find words. "Jesus Christ, Brooke. No, I didn't kill Chase. I *kissed* Reed." She's silent for a second, and I can hear whatever she's cooking sizzling away on the stovetop. I point over her shoulder. "Is that going to burn?"

She spins around and shoves the pan off the burner. She flips the burner switch off and then spins back to me. "Oh, my God. Okay. Tell me everything."

I shrug. "It's sort of a long story, but the short version is that Reed and I have been sharing the bed downstairs in the basement so that I don't have to sleep in the same room as Chase. And, I don't know, things have felt...different. Anyway, we were in the lake today, and he started being sweet and looking really good, and I had a moment of temporary insanity, and I kissed him."

Her mouth is hanging open. "Holy fucking shit. Okay, and then what happened?"

"And then *nothing* happened! The rest of the family showed up, and I ran in here to call you."

"Geez." She leans back against her counter. "Good for you, Quinn."

Now *my* mouth falls open. "What the hell do you mean, *good for you*? I can't be kissing my ex-husband's brother."

Brooke's face twists. "Why the hell not? You and Chase are divorced."

"That is so not the point. Whether we're divorced or not, it's still a betrayal."

Her face twists even more. "Who gives a fuck if you betray Chase? The man cheated on you. He betrayed you first. And it's definitely *not* a betrayal if you guys aren't married anymore."

"But it's a betrayal to his mom and his sister."

At this, Brooke finally falls quiet. "Yeah, I could see how you could make that argument. But I gotta say, babe, I fully disagree on this one. Reed is just a guy, and it's not like you're proposing to him. You *kissed* him. Once." She pauses, her eyebrows raising. "Unless...you know...you wanna kiss him again. Nobody could blame you. Reed Lynch is so many different categories of yummy."

"I do *not* want to kiss him again."

"Then why did you kiss him in the first place?"

I push myself back against the wall, shoving Chase's shoes out of the way and resting my head back to think. "I don't know. My brain is all confused. I mean, I've always liked Reed. We've been friends a long time. And I guess...you know, this whole trip is super stressful and Reed has been super support-ive, so, I don't know, it was just instinct."

Brooke nods. "Well, maybe you should let that instinct lead you to a very satisfying dicking down."

My head snaps up, almost smacking right into the shelf above me. "What? No. That's not an option. And it's not some-thing I want either."

Lies, a voice whispers in my head. *So many lies. If you*

didn't want him that way, why haven't you been able to keep your eyes off him for the last two days? I ignore it.

"Listen, bestie," Brooke says, setting me down on her counter and bending over to rest her chin on her downturned hands. "There is nobody who deserves good dick more than you right now. And there's no way Reed is not serving up some top-notch dick."

"Can you please stop talking about Reed's dick?" I whisper, barely even able to get it out of my mouth.

"No," she responds, point blank. "You're about to disappear from these people's lives. You might as well get a few good orgasms out of it before you peace out. Having sex with someone you know and trust is always way better than a stranger. You don't want to have to wait until you get back to Boston to meet some guy on Tinder in order to get your jollies."

"Even if I'm about to never see any of them again, I couldn't do that to Madison and Sabrina. I just couldn't."

Brooke gets a thoughtful look on her face. "I understand. You're too nice for your own damn good. Maybe we need to teach you how to care a little less about other people's feelings."

19 QUINN

"Quinn?" Chase bangs on the bedroom door, and I sigh. Why can't Chase just disappear? Like a magic trick. *Abracadabra*.

"What?" I shout through the door. It's been locked all afternoon, and absolutely nobody has come looking for me, not while I showered, not when I didn't show up for lunch, and not as they apparently watched a movie in the living room, which I heard the majority of through the wall.

Because I've been lying on this bed all day, trying to figure out what the hell I'm supposed to do now. This is definitely a *don't shit where you eat* situation. I have to be in this house with these people for the rest of the week, and on the third day here, I made a total tit of myself coming on to the one person in the house I definitely *should not* be coming on to.

I mean, I guess it wouldn't have been any better if I came onto Sabrina or Madison, but my point still stands.

"What do you mean, what?" Chase's muffled voice asks through the door. "The door is locked."

"Yep."

There's a beat of silence, and for a moment, I think he's actually going to leave. Maybe I shouldn't have answered at all, and then he could have imagined me in here dead. Death by mortification.

"Can you let me in, please?"

I don't exactly have an option. It's his room, after all. But if it's his room, then that means I don't have any space to run and hide anymore. I can't hide away in the basement now that I've fucked everything up. So this is where I'll have to spend the week, in this room and in this bed...with Chase.

I grumble and roll off the bed, throwing open the door and immediately turning back the other way. When I hear Chase shut the door behind him, I sigh.

"We're starting a bonfire," he says, whipping his shirt off over his head and moving to the dresser against the wall to get a fresh one. "You might want to make an appearance. You can't sit in here all day. What's your problem, anyway?"

He has to be kidding. Even if he doesn't know about the whole Reed situation, he can't honestly think I'm having the time of my life on this trip.

"My problem is that pretending to still be married to you is eating away at my soul."

He slams the top drawer of his dresser closed and turns angry eyes on me. "You know what, Quinn? Could you at least try to make this trip a little less miserable? I didn't just bring you here so I could have that money. I brought you here because I know *you* need the money, too. I'm not stupid. I know how expensive that house is, and I know you've got to be struggling to find a job. I'm trying to help. And all you've done is act like a spoiled teenager who hasn't gotten her way. I don't want to be here any more than you do, but if you don't start acting like you don't hate my fucking guts, Mom and Sabrina are going to start asking questions."

Uncomfortable silence settles between us. I feel so exposed, standing here in the middle of the room, having my first open conversation with Chase since that night so many months ago, after I came back from the doctor with a chlamydia diagnosis and Chase told me he was sleeping with the sister of one of his college buddies.

"Yeah, you're right," I finally say, the words coming out sour. I hate saying them, but Chase isn't wrong. I have to find a way to get myself on emotionally neutral ground so that I don't fuck this up for everyone. Chase *did* bring me here so that I could have a cut of the money, too. That has to be worth something, right? "Let's go out to the fire."

His face loses all traces of anger, and I'm struck by how much he looks like that guy I met in a dorm hallway five years ago. That night when he took me to his dorm room and treated the coffee stain on my stupid skeleton costume and we talked about our favorite movies and the bands we'd seen in concert and the classes we loved and the ones we hated. He kissed me that night, holding the skeleton costume out between us and then leaning forward to brush his lips over mine.

I wanted him to be that person forever. But I'm not convinced he ever actually was that guy, the sweet one who wanted to help out a strange girl. Chase is far too cunning for all that. And he was never that guy again.

THE SKY IS DARK AND THE BONFIRE IS IN FULL BLAZE BY the time we get out to the fire pit. Sabrina and Lydia are laughing about something and Madison is quietly watching the fire, her face ablaze in its light. The pit is sunken into the stone deck, one long cushioned seat moving around it in a circle. I walk down the cold steps and settle at the seat closest to the stairs.

Chase, much to my discomfort, takes the seat right beside me.

Across the fire, sitting between Sabrina and Madison, Reed watches us. His eyes are bright in the light of the fire and they drop to where Chase's hip is positioned firmly against mine. It's not as if I can help it. Chase was right about what he said. We have to pretend to still be a couple.

A tray of hot dogs is passed around, and Chase takes one for himself before offering me one. Once I take one, he sets the tray on the stone wall beside me.

"How's the job searching going?" he asks before stuffing the hot dog into his mouth. He looks at me, waiting for me to respond. And maybe this isn't so bad. Sure, he was a shitty husband. But maybe I was a shitty wife, too. And maybe it was never meant to be, so who even cares if he cheated and gave me an STI? We were only married for three years, and so much of those three years was spent trying to figure out how to be adults together.

Maybe we just never figured it out.

"Not great," I tell him, quietly enough that nobody else can hear. The fire pit is big enough that I can hear Lydia and Sabrina's voices on the other side, but I can't quite make out what they're saying. If I wanted to speak to them, I'd have to shout. The fire crackles loudly in the center. "Nobody wants to hire someone with no experience for a job that would actually pay a decent salary. And it's not like I could blame them. Maybe I should just get a job at Trader Joe's or something so that I've got something to put on my resume other than a Bachelor's degree."

"Or maybe you should hold out for something you really like."

"I don't know if I have that luxury."

His hand settles on my knee, and I work hard not to flinch. My eyes immediately shoot to Reed, and I can tell he's clocked it, too, his eyes glued to Chase's sweaty palm. Chase clearly hasn't thought twice about it though. His thumb moves back and forth across my skin as he takes another bite of his hot dog, leaving a smear of mustard in the corner of his mouth.

"I could talk to some people. I have a lot of contacts at—"

"I don't need your help."

His mouth clamps shut, his cheek protruding with food.

I sigh. I hate the way he makes me feel guilty for how I feel. Hate that he can do it with one glance at me. I shake my head and gently brush his hand off my leg. "I'm going to go talk to your mother."

Madison and I haven't had a ton of alone time in the few days we've been here, so I stand and move down the bench, taking the seat beside Madison. From here, I can only kind of see Reed, just half of him, the angle of his broad shoulder and his hands, hanging over his knees. Big and veined.

"Hello, sweetie," Madison says, slinging her arm around me.

"I wanted to make sure you're feeling okay."

She smiles at me. "I'm fine. This is exactly why I kept the secret so long. I didn't want anyone worrying about me."

I lean against her a little, meet Reed's eye over her shoulder. "Sometimes it helps to worry about people. I wish I had gotten some time to worry about my mother before she was gone."

Madison presses her forehead into mine, and I feel so certain that I could never do anything to hurt this family, to hurt *her*. Someday, she'll get over the fact that Chase and I got a divorce, but I don't know if she'd ever forgive me if she knew that I'd kissed Reed, too. And right under her nose. I'm embarrassed that it happened.

I know I can never let it happen again.

20 REED

I CAN SMELL THE RAIN. IT ROLLED IN AS WE SAT AROUND
the fire, forcing all of us inside and into our beds. It's been an
hour since we all grumbled and decided that we didn't want to
watch another movie and that there wasn't much else to do for
the day. We went our separate ways.

I watch the water hit the small window high on the wall,
watch it run down in rivulets.

She's not coming.

I've been laying here in the dark, my ears trained on any
sound of movement in the house. But it's been still and silent
and now it's pushing midnight. She's not coming. She's going to
sleep upstairs with Chase because she thinks it's a better idea
than potentially finding herself in a compromising position
with me again.

And maybe she's not wrong. Maybe it's batshit crazy to be
making a move on my brother's ex-wife while he's in the same
house, while everyone is watching all the time. It would be way
smarter to wait until we're back in the city, after she's had some
space.

That was the plan originally. I was counting down the days until I could knock on her door and try to wiggle my way back into her life. But then Chase showed up, and I saw an opportunity.

But I blew it. Even if I wasn't the one to initiate that kiss, I certainly didn't stop it. I couldn't have if I had fucking wanted to. And God knows I didn't.

I throw the covers off me and go out into the basement kitchen. I can't fucking lay in bed anymore, thinking about her curled up next to Chase. I spent countless nights before the divorce trying not to think about everything Chase had that I wanted. I spent all those years trying to stop wanting her. Sleeping with other women and going on dates and joining dating apps. But it never worked.

Nothing will ever fucking work.

Because I've only ever been in love with one woman.

And she's the one woman I can never have.

I open the fridge and find all the basics. Flour, butter, milk. I find a bag of chocolate chips stuffed in the back of the pantry. Who knows what they were purchased for. Probably for Lydia to make chocolate chip pancakes or something. Too bad.

Baking, working with my hands, it quiets my mind. It always has.

To help me focus, I stick my earbuds in and put on some quiet music.

This is how I've always been. It's like my mind is going all the time, and the only way I can get it to turn off is if I'm doing something with my hands that doesn't also require my brain. The whole time I was at Suffolk, I worked in the records room at the library, spending all day listening to crime podcasts and filing paperwork. It was amazing.

And then I discovered baking. By the time I started my last year at Suffolk, I was ready to go into business for myself, and six months before graduation, I found the building for Aeronaut. I'm not going to pretend like my mother's money didn't help me get where I needed to go, but I put my own blood, sweat, and tears into that place.

I can't bring myself to tell her it's gone. All because Oscar and his goddamn pill problem.

I lean down and open the stove, pulling out the first batch of cookies that I put in ten minutes ago. They're perfect, soft all the way around with no crunch, just the way Quinn likes them. I turn to put them on the counter and jump.

Quinn is standing in the doorway to the staircase, watching me. My heart immediately starts to pound in my chest. I set the pan down and rip the earbuds out of my ears.

"What are you doing?" she asks quietly.

"Baking you cookies. Three dozen, to be exact. Once I started, I couldn't stop."

She comes over to the island, picking up one of the cookies that came out of the oven a while ago that's already plated. It's gotta be nearing two in the morning. Has she been awake this whole time like I have, just trying to decide what she was going to do about *us?*

She takes a bite of the cookie and gets a very confusing wrinkle between her eyebrows. Did I fuck them up? I've probably made a thousand cookies in my lifetime, so I don't know what I could have done wrong, unless I mistook some salt for the sugar.

But when she opens her mouth, it's not to critique me on the cookies. "I owe you an apology."

I lean on my palms on the kitchen island. "Please stop apologizing to me."

"No, I just—"

"Quinn." My voice comes out much more stern than I intend for it to.

This seems to startle her enough to stop her arguments, but she doesn't say anything, just holding the cookie between us, a bite taken out.

"Let's forget about it, okay? You're going through a hard time right now. I understand that." I push the plate toward her, the sound of it scraping against the marble countertop settling into the gaps between my teeth. "Eat as many cookies as you want. I'll sleep on the couch tonight if it'll make you feel better." It makes my stomach hurt to make the offer, but if that's what she needs, then that's what she needs.

She shakes her head. "I don't want you to do that. Maybe I should just spend the rest of the week with Chase. I think we've found some kind of...I don't know...middle ground."

The pain in my stomach intensifies, my gut twisting. "For what it's worth, I *want* you down here."

Her eyes lift to mine. "You do?"

I can't tell her it's because having her near is the only thing that stops the pain in my chest that started five years ago, but I can tell her a little piece of the truth. "I know how I come off to you guys. I know I'm always on the outskirts of things, and it probably looks like I enjoy being there. But the truth is that I'm lonely. And having you here—a person who I care about and who I'm pretty sure cares about me—it helps."

"I know the feeling," she says, "and I do care about you."

She cares about me. She doesn't love me. For now, that's enough.

I jerk awake when Quinn makes a noise I've never heard her make before. She's not cuddled up to me like she was last night—probably because she's not half-drunk now—and across the expanse of the bed, I see the sheen of sweat on her skin. As I watch, her mouth opens on a tiny sound, a gasp, and I immediately reach out for her.

"Quinn, wake up."

She does, startling awake and turning her face toward mine immediately. She's wearing an expression I can't explain, her eyes wide and her mouth parted.

"Were you having a nightmare?" I ask her, feeling the racing of her pulse under my fingers where they're wrapped around her wrist.

She stares at the ceiling, her chest rising and falling with her heavy breaths. And then she bites her lip and shakes her head. "No. It's okay. Go back to sleep."

She's got to be kidding. "I'm not going back to sleep. Are you sick?"

She squeezes her eyes shut, and for a second, I think she's going to cry. "No, I'm not sick, okay? It's just really embarrassing."

I sit up, moving closer to her. I'm worried now. Is there... some chance she could be pregnant? Is that what's happening right now? Maybe she's embarrassed that she and Chase were still sleeping together while he was cheating on her with another woman. Or maybe they had sex *after* she found out. People do that. Have sex with their exes. "You don't have to feel embarrassed with me."

I see the moment her embarrassment turns to resolve. Her jaw tightens, and she closes her eyes again like she can't say what she needs to with them open. "I haven't been fucked in months."

My brain shorts out. It takes me far too long to make the connection between what she just said and what we were talking about before she said it. And then it all starts to fit together like puzzle pieces. She had a wet dream. She woke up horny. She was embarrassed. She and Chase definitely haven't had sex recently.

I have to sit with all of that information. And when I finally put it all together, everything below the waistband of my pants goes tight. Quinn is in bed with me and she's horny, and she's *telling* me she's horny, and even though I know it's not the right time and not the right thing to do in this moment, I find myself spitting out a response anyway. "I could help you out."

"What?" Her eyes go wide, and she pushes herself up so her back is against the intricately-carved headboard. "Why would you even— We're friends, Reed."

I shrug, trying to play this off like I am much more cool in this situation than I actually am. Everything in my head is going off like fireworks and meteor showers. "You've never had a friend offer you a helping hand?"

Her cheeks go pink, so pink that I can see it happen in the moonlight. She looks away from me, lets out a little sigh. "No. I've only been with Chase."

Too much information is coming at me really quickly. "Really?"

"He was my first, and then we got married. No friends with helping hands."

I inch closer to her. "People help out their friends because it's a safe space. You choose someone you're comfortable with. You let them help you with something you need. Like asking someone to help you move." God, I sound like a complete moron.

A smile creeps up her face. "Are you comparing getting a hand job to someone helping you move?"

I sigh out a laugh. "Yeah, I guess I am. I'm sorry. I'm just trying to make you feel comfortable. You know...if you need something that I'm able to help you with."

She looks down at the blanket, pulled up to her chest, like

she's trying to keep herself covered, even though she's fully clothed. "Why would you want to do that for me?"

"Why would I want to put my head between your legs and lick you until you come?"

She shivers, and pride spears through my chest. That kiss yesterday might have been some weird instinctual thing, but she's definitely attracted to me. "Yes," she whispers, so quietly that I barely hear her.

"Because we may be friends and you may be my sister-in-law, but that doesn't mean I don't think you're sexy as fuck." I might be coming on too strong. I'm saying a lot of things that I wouldn't normally say to a girl until we were already naked and getting ready to go at it. But based on the flush she's wearing that's so prominent I can even see it in the dark, I don't think she's bothered.

Her eyes trail down to my lips, and her fists tighten in the blanket she has around her. I want her to say yes. I want her to let me do this for her. Even if that's all it is, a chance to make her feel better when she's been without for so long.

"Tell me you've never thought about it."

She licks her lips. She's not going to say it. And the knowledge that she *has* thought about it sends fire through my blood. I'm so hard that if she pulled the blanket back right now, she would find a steel pipe in my pants.

For a long moment, there's nothing but the sound of our breathing.

And then she sinks a little into the bed before reaching for my hand. I give it to her, not entirely sure what she's going to do with it. She guides my hand under the blanket, down across her belly and straight into the waistband of her shorts. Her eyes hold mine as she leaves my hand there, her own retreating, even as I start to rub against the fabric of her underwear.

The *wet* fabric.

I bite back a groan. We have to be quiet, which is truly unfair. If this is the only time I ever get to do something like this with her, I want to hear all her sounds. Memorize them to play in my head over and over for the rest of my life.

Fuck. I was ruined before, but now I know I'll never be able to touch another woman without comparing it to this moment. Quinn has always been the baseline, and she always will be.

When I reposition, finding my way under the band of her underwear and down onto her bare wetness, her mouth falls open and her eyes glaze over. I shiver, sliding my fingers up and down her slippery flesh. I'm not even doing it to make her feel good. I just want to feel her, touch every part of her that she'll let me, know every single inch of her body.

When I find her clit, feel it hard under my fingers, I draw circles around it, watching intently at the way her eyes fall closed and her head falls back with a *thunk* against the headboard.

"Is this what you wanted?" I whisper to her.

She nods without opening her eyes.

"Do you want my hand or my mouth?" I want to give her a choice, but I also want to beg her to let me use my mouth. I want to taste her. I've imagined it so many times, stroked myself with my eyes closed thinking about her legs thrown over my shoulders, her moans muffled by her thighs against my ears.

Her eyes open and meet mine. I can feel her hesitation in the way her body pauses its trembling, the way she stops rocking against my fingers. "Your mouth," she finally says. "Is that okay?"

Is that okay? I can't get the blanket thrown off her fast enough. I slide her shorts and her underwear down her legs, and it isn't until her knees come together, blocking me, that it occurs to me that she might be nervous about me seeing her naked. I've seen her in a bikini and in her pajamas, of course, but we've never been in any state of undress around each other.

I meet her eye. "Are you sure you want to do this?"

She bites her lip and nods, slowly letting her legs fall open. I have to hold in a groan, but I can't stop the way my breath starts to thunder out of my lungs at the sight of her. Her long, shapely legs, leading up to the most beautiful pussy I've ever seen. And I know I'm pretty damn biased. I feel like I'm in a dream, looking down at Quinn with her legs open for me.

With my eyes on her to make sure she's okay, I move onto my stomach between her legs, pressing kisses up the inside of her thigh in an attempt to make her feel calmer. It's a big thing, asking someone to do something like this for you, especially when you don't know that that person has been fantasizing about doing this very thing for the last five years.

When I slide my tongue up the center of her, she gasps and covers her mouth with her hand.

"You're perfect," I whisper, but I don't know if she hears me. All I know is the taste of her and the way her legs are trembling on either side of my head. I open my mouth over her clit, suck at her slowly and deliberately, taking my time.

I clutch her thighs in my hand, trying to convince myself this is real, until she lets out a squeak, and I realize that I've grabbed her too hard. I look up to apologize, but she rips her hand away from her mouth.

"Please, don't stop. Oh God, please. I'm so close."

My heart deflates. She's close. She's going to come and then there's no excuse to keep going. The whole point of this was to get her off. As soon as she's done, I'll have to stop touching her, stop tasting her, stop feeling the luxurious silk of her on my tongue.

So when she starts to gasp, starts to pant, I pull away, watching her drop and come back from the edge.

"Reed," she hisses. "Why did you stop?"

I don't say anything. I'm not about to tell her that I'm trying to draw it out. That I'm trying to keep it from being over so that I can eat her all night. I go back to sucking, using my fingers to stroke the flesh on either side of my tongue until her back is bowing off the bed. I rip my mouth away again.

Her hands fist in the covers, and I smile, listening to her breath puff in and out of her. I know I'm not going to be able to draw it out much longer. She's going to reach the point of no return, and I would hate for her to come without my tongue on her. I suck hard on her clit and then stop to lap at it, until she's rocking against my mouth, trying to find her release. I feel her muscles seize up under my hands and push her a little harder.

She must think I'm going to pull away again because she fists her hands in my hair to hold me in place, even though I have every intention of sucking on her until she sees stars. When she grips me harder and starts panting like she's suffocating, I look up at her. But I can't see her face. God, I would give anything to see the face she makes when she comes.

But feeling her cunt tremble under my lips will have to be enough. Her toes curl underneath her, and her hips pitch up desperately. I taste it when she finishes, feel the wetness of her on my tongue as I keep lapping at her. I need to memorize this taste, the texture of her, the quiver of her skin.

"Oh, God, you have to stop," she says, now pulling at my hair instead of using it to hold me in place. "I'm too sensitive."

I don't want to stop. I'm like a child eating Halloween candy until they have a stomach ache. I want to lick her until I've starved to death.

"Reed," she whispers, and I force myself to pull away, but now my eyes are caught on the place between her legs. Now that it's red and swollen and dripping. That's fucking art.

She immediately closes her legs, and then her eyes meet

mine, and pride bursts in my chest. She looks like someone who just fell to pieces. Her hair is wild, her bottom lip swollen, her cheeks pink. I've dreamed of seeing her this way, of being the one to make her look this way.

Her eyes drop to the front of my pants. I don't have to look down to know I've become a spectacle. I've never been this hard in my life. I don't have an ounce of blood left anywhere else in my body, and I'm fine with it.

She bites that already swollen lip. "Let me help you."

I sigh, realizing I'm having just as hard a time catching my breath as she is. "I'm good. This was just for you."

A crease appears between her eyebrows. "But...friends and helping hands and all that."

I smile at her. Am I going to regret this later when I can't get this raging boner to go away? Probably. But making her come was more satisfactory than anything I've ever felt in my life, and in this moment, that's all I want. I want her to know she's safe with me, that she can ask me for this without me expecting something in return. I just...want her to feel good.

"I promise, I'm good." Even if a certain part of my anatomy would beg to differ. I collapse onto the bed beside her, pulling the blanket up over both of us. It's wild to look at her now, knowing that I ate her out without ever having kissed her in the process. I want to kiss her now, but I don't want to scare her.

"Reed?"

"Mmm?"

"Thank you."

I turn my head and meet her eye. She's gripping the sheet around her, and I realize she never took her shirt off. I take a second to mourn that fact. If I never get to see this woman without her clothes again, I'll regret not seeing what I assume are absolutely perfect breasts. "Anytime, Quinn. I'm always here if you need it. I know what it's like, needing it and having to go looking for strangers."

Her mouth twists uncomfortably. "I don't think sex with strangers is my thing "

"I get that. It's not for everyone. That's what friends are for."

She laughs, throwing her arm over her eyes. "I think you have a slightly skewed image of friendship, Reed."

21 QUINN

3 YEARS AGO

THERE'S BLOOD SPEWING OUT OF MY HAND. BEFORE I CAN
stop it, it drips onto my dress. "Fuck!" I half-whisper, half-
scream, rushing down the hallway. I can't remember where the
damn bathroom is in this massive castle of a church. So I go for
the next best thing.

I throw open the door under the glowing EXIT sign and
hold my hand out in front of myself, letting it bleed out onto the
concrete at the side of the church. I need to put pressure on it,
but I absolutely cannot get another dot of blood on my wedding
dress. The damn thing is Vera fucking Wang, courtesy of the
woman who is about to be my mother-in-law.

"Holy shit, Quinn. What happened?"

Reed appears out of nowhere. That's what he's good at,
after all. Popping into my life when I least expect it. He takes
my hand in his and wraps a long piece of fabric around it,

which I quickly realize is his tie. Instinctively, my eyes go to his bare throat, where the top button of his dress shirt is open. They travel from there to where his sleeves are rolled up just below his elbows.

His voice snaps me out of it. "Do you think you need stitches? I can take you to the emergency room."

I'm already shaking my head, pulling my hand away from his and cradling it against my body, now that there's not blood free-flowing. "No, I just..." I don't know what I'm going to say. I look down at the splatter of blood on my dress. There's so much tulle that the blood is almost hidden in the folds of it.

Reed is looking, too. His eyes scan down my dress and then back up. When he sees that I'm watching him, he shakes his head in this really confusing way. "You look beautiful," he says.

I swear something inside me cracks. Because I cut my hand on a pair of scissors that I was going to use to cut myself out of my dress. It laces up in the back and no one was around to help me out of it. But instead...I cut myself. And now I'm here, realizing how insane it is to be worried about getting blood on the dress when I was just ready to rip it to shreds. I grip my hand in a tight fist.

"What is it?"

I'm tempted to turn my back to him. Two years I've known Reed now, and more than anyone else, he always sees right through me. He can read me like a book he wrote himself. Turning my back will do no good. Nothing will. He's already seen the doubt all over my face. "I don't know what I'm doing," I whisper, halfway hoping that the words get swept away on the humid summer breeze.

Reed watches me, clearly trying to digest what I just said. This isn't the time or place to have this conversation. We're outside the far wing of the church, but someone is bound to come looking for us eventually. When I glance to my left, I can see the parking lot, can see my car. An escape.

"You're having second thoughts." It's not a question. Of course it isn't. Because Reed never has to question anything, it seems. He just always knows.

My face flushes. "I'm sorry. I shouldn't have brought you into this. You're his brother, for God's sake." I start to turn, not even sure where I intend to go, when Reed reaches out to touch my arm. His hand is a million degrees, his fingers on fire as he lets them slide from my upper arm, leaving tingles in their wake.

"Look," he says when I've turned around to face him, "you can talk to me. Yeah, he's my brother, but..." He sticks his hands in his pockets and looks down at the concrete, baking in the sun. "I think it's normal to be freaked out on your wedding day."

I let out a laugh that has no humor to it. "I don't know about all that. I should be excited. And I am. I mean, this is the start of a whole new life for me, but..."

His bright eyes meet mine, so sincere, waiting to see what I'm going to say. There's only one way through this: forward.

"I don't know. We're so young. And I'm worried that we're going to regret this. I feel like...if my mom were here, she would tell me to wait. But if I call it off now, Chase will never forgive me." That's the first time I've said any of that out loud. Saying it makes it feel particularly true.

He's silent for a moment, his eyes flickering over my shoulder. He takes a deep breath. "Quinn, you and my brother are great together. Everybody says so. You're like puzzle pieces, fitting together perfectly."

Yeah. Lives that make sense together, everything so perfect and logical and scientifically built to last.

"And not everybody waits until they're thirty or whatever to get married. Some people just know they've found the One when they're young." He pauses, his eyes meeting mine. "Sometimes, you meet the right person, and everybody is telling you that you have to play the field and date a bunch of people, but you just *know* that the person you're with is the right one for you."

A lump forms in my throat. I think about that night, when I found out about my mom and called Chase. He was half-drunk, but he held me all night while I cried, fed me in the morning, took care of me for weeks after. Such a good guy. And he would make such a good husband. I don't need Reed to convince me of that.

He takes a step toward me in this sideways fashion, so that we're shoulder-to-shoulder, him facing the church and me facing the parking lot. "You've always known exactly what you wanted, Quinn. My brother loves you, and I know you love him. Don't throw it away because you got scared."

I turn my head to look at him, and he turns his head to look at me.

And I know he's right.

I made the right decision, and I know that if I do something impulsive now, I'll regret it forever. Impulsivity and I have never gotten along.

"Thanks, Reed," I say. I look down at my wrapped hand. "I guess I need to figure out what to do with this. I'm guessing you don't want your tie back."

One corner of his mouth turns up in a smile. "That's okay. Keep it. Something to remember this day by."

I laugh and turn for the door. As I move past him, I pat Reed on the shoulder. "You look better without it." I'm not even sure why I said it, but with my hand on his shoulder like this, I can feel the heat of him under his shirt, and my eyes get caught again on where his top button is undone.

"They're probably looking for you," he says, his voice low. My eyes travel up to his mouth and something in my stomach rumbles a little bit. It's just nerves. Just weird, achy, uncomfortable nerves.

"See you at the altar," I say.

22 QUINN

There are at least three million books on divorce. They'll tell you how to navigate everything from custody hearings to properly splitting up your silverware.

But none of the books I read cover what to do when you let you brother-in-law go down on you because you had a sex dream about him and couldn't bring yourself to reject his offer. They also don't tell you what to do when you have to pretend to be married to your ex in front of his family while the brother-in-law that went down on you is in the same room.

"Smile!"

I try to force my face into a natural, happy expression, but we've been doing this for almost an hour and the muscles of my mouth feel like they're going to go into spasm at any moment.

"Got it," the photographer says, pulling her camera away from her eye and smiling at all of us.

Apparently, as soon as Madison heard that all the kids would be at the lake house at the same time, she hired a photographer to get family pictures done.

"Because when are we ever in the same room?" she said

when we all met in the living room this morning. And then we all immediately had to go back to our rooms to get ready. Which now seems a bit silly. All that makeup and hair product, and we're all sweating through our clothes. I'm not sure the pictures are going to come out that great, but I'm glad I packed at least one nice sundress. Most of my clothes are shorts and tank tops because I know how much Chase likes me in a sundress, and the thought of him finding me physically attractive makes me feel ill.

But when I came out of our bedroom wearing my favorite sundress with the little purple flowers on it, Reed's eyes ate me up from across the room, and it made me *very* glad to have packed it, a feeling which immediately led to crippling guilt.

"Okay, now just the kids," Madison says, stepping away from us to stand by the photographer. I start to inch away too, but Madison shakes her head and steps forward to push me back into the photo. My heart skips a little because by the time Madison gets these photos back, everyone will know about the divorce and the photos will be useless.

God, am I terrible person?

"If you'll tilt this way a little bit," the photographer says, spreading her arms wide like she's encompassing all of us. "I want to get as much of the lake as I can behind you." I can see our reflection in the windows of the house, the four of us standing awkwardly in front of the lake. The photographer must see the same awkwardness I do because she says, "Get closer together. Act like you love each other." She laughs, but it's the furthest thing from funny.

I'm standing between Chase and Reed, and at the same time, they both move in until I have the heat of them all along my body. Reed puts a hand against my back at the same time that Chase puts his arm around my waist, his hand settling with familiarity on my hip.

I can hear Reed's gentle breathing beside me, feel the very subtle way his fingers dig into the skin of my back. I feel like everyone can see. Can they see? Will the camera pick something up and months from now, when Madison is looking back on the photos, will she think to herself, *why do Reed and Quinn look so cozy?* I try to remember if Reed has ever touched me like this before. It's the way someone touches an acquaintance. It's not sexual by any stretch of the imagination. But nobody knows his hand is there, pressed into the fabric between my shoulder blades, except for me. Nobody can see the way Reed's index finger draws circles on my spine.

I try to smile. Does it look normal? Is this how I normally smile? I can't even remember right now, my brain is so fuzzy.

And then the photographer says, "Alright, got it." She sets her camera against her chest, hanging from its sturdy strap, like she's all done, and I breathe a sigh of relief.

Reed pulls his hand from me, his fingers brushing along the length of my back as he extracts himself. I shiver, goosebumps covering me, and before Chase has a chance to notice, I pull away from him, pretending by fanning myself that I did it because I'm so hot.

"Could we just get one more?" Madison asks, rushing back over to the photographer. "I'd love a few with our little married lovebirds." She grins big, and I realize she means Chase and me. I glance sideways at him, and he has a blank look on his face. I can't tell if he's enjoying this or if he's as miserable as I am. I guess I have to give him brownie points for his poker face.

"Mom, come on, we're hot," Chase says, and for the first time in a very long time, I want to thank him.

But it's a useless sentiment because Madison frowns. "Is it really too much to ask for you to take pictures with your wife? The only framed photos I have of the two of you are from your wedding. Just a couple, come on."

"I'm going inside then," Sabrina says, whipping off the stylish sunhat she's wearing to cover her blonde hair. She disappears inside the lake house, and I glance over at Reed, feeling panic settle in my stomach. I don't want him to leave. I don't want to be left here with Chase, who is going to have to put his hands all over me.

But Reed doesn't move toward the house. He stands there, still as a statue, in his dark sweater and his dark scruff. And when Chase steps up beside me, wrapping his hand around my waist again, Reed's eyes go straight there. He watches Chase's fingers curl around the jut of my hip. Even with the space of the back courtyard between us, I see his jaw tighten.

"Smile, darling," Chase says in my ear, and I do, hoping it looks like something real and not manufactured.

My mind spins all the way back to last night, to Reed's mouth between my legs, the salt on my skin as I bit down on my arm not to scream in ecstasy.

I feel the nape of Chase's neck under my hand, where I have it thrown over his shoulders. His hair tickles the tips of my fingers, and I'm so repulsed at the feel of it that a shudder moves through me. Chase twists his face toward me, a sly smile on his mouth. "Is it getting you going, being this close to me?"

He thinks I'm turned on, when really I'm trying not to wrench myself out of his embrace.

"No."

"Ah, come on," he whispers, pressing his lips against my ear. "You miss this. I know I do."

I can hear the click of the photographer's camera over and over. She thinks she's capturing a sweet moment between husband and wife. I smile at the camera and then turn my face toward Chase's, our cheeks brushing as I say quietly, "You could have had *this* all you wanted. I'm not the one who gave it to someone else."

He stiffens against me, and my eyes meet Reed's. He's watching us so closely, his hands balled into fists. Is he...jealous? He spent years watching Chase and me together, but I guess it's different now. We've been in bed together. He's made me come. I wish I was pressed to him right now instead of Chase.

"That's perfect!" the photographer calls. "Now a kiss."

Reed's hands drop to his sides, and his eyes slam over to the photographer before sliding back to find me. I'm the only one who sees him. While Madison applauds the photographer for her romantic idea, Chase takes my hips in both his hands, turning me toward him.

"You heard the woman," he says, the words smothered in smarm. One of his hands snakes up between us, and he takes my chin between his thumb and forefinger. My eyes dart to Reed, watching us so closely, like he's trying to stop Chase's downward descent toward my mouth with his mind. And then Chase's lips find mine, and I shut my eyes.

He bends me back slightly in a romantic gesture, and I hear Madison say, "Awww," even as I have to focus on breathing. Just a couple of pictures and then this will be over.

Maybe I should still be feeling something for Chase. Maybe it's telling that I moved from affection to revulsion so quickly. But I don't think it was just the cheating. Chase and I stopped having a fulfilling sex life a long time ago. Every time we slept together, it was in a rush. Chase wanted to get off quick, and if I also got to finish, that was an added bonus. But if I couldn't find my orgasm in seven minutes or less, I was shit out of luck, and I would go to bed still throbbing between my legs.

It just started to feel like one more thing on my to-do list. Do the dishes, start the laundry, satisfy Chase, meet Brooke for lunch. It was like I wasn't there. I was just the nearest plaything. I wanted him to want me so bad that he ached. But instead, he found someone else he could use as a plaything, and he stopped wanting me altogether.

I can't quite pinpoint when it was exactly that I stopped wanting him in return.

Chase opens his mouth over mine, and I know he's going to try to deepen the kiss, try to take something that doesn't belong to him anymore, so I fake a laugh and turn my face, knowing it'll make a good picture and get me fully off the hook.

Chase finally lets me go, and I straighten my skirt before smiling at everyone and excusing myself. I rush past Reed, feel his eyes follow me all the way inside the house, and slam the door behind me. I know they can all still see me through the big windows, whoever might still be looking, so I take it slow through the living room. But once I'm in the hallway, where I can't be seen anymore, I run to the bathroom, lock myself in, and throw up.

I sit on the edge of the bathtub, my heart racing. I feel ridiculous at being so stirred up by kissing a man that I kissed every day for five years, but I know it's not just that. It's everything. Being here, sneaking around, kissing Chase, pretending to *be* with Chase, Madison's cancer. It's all bearing down on me.

I wash my hands and go back out into the hall, wiping away the sweat that's still beading up on my forehead. Somewhere down the hall, I hear quiet voices. Curiosity gets the better of me, and I walk quietly down to where Sabrina and Lydia's rooms are across from each other.

Sabrina and Lydia are sitting on Sabrina's bed, their heads together, speaking low. When I step into the room, they both look up at me quick, like I caught them doing something awful, and then Lydia hops off the bed. She keeps her eyes on the floor as she walks by me, and I feel like I walked into a movie halfway through it.

"Did I miss something?" I ask, turning back to Sabrina and realizing she's turned her face from me and is wiping something away. "Hey," I say, moving to take Lydia's place on the bed. "What's wrong?"

Sabrina sighs, finally turning her face back to me so that I can see the streaks of makeup down her cheeks. I reach for the nightstand, for the box of tissues there, and gently wipe at her skin. "It's just this whole thing," she says, a stutter in her voice. "All of this one-last-time shit with my mom. One last trip. One last photo shoot. I'm starting to worry that she's more sick than she's letting on."

I let the tissue fall to my lap, the bile threatening to rise again in my throat. "You think she would lie to you about that?" I believe she would lie to *us*, but she's much closer with Sabrina than she is with us.

Sabrina hesitates, her eyes lowered. Then she nods. "I think she would do it to protect our feelings."

For Sabrina's sake, I hope she's wrong.

23 REED

Mom and the photographer seem pretty pre-occupied, so I take the chance to walk over to Chase. He's got his hands tucked into his pockets, staring out at the lake like some kind of old man on a postcard.

"If you keep pushing her, she's going to leave."

Chase doesn't even turn his head. He knew I was still here. He knew I would come over to talk to him. "She's not going to leave. She needs the money."

"She doesn't need it enough to put up with your bullshit. You should play nice. She is." I take a deep breath, reminding myself to keep my cool. I have to pretend that watching Chase put his hands all over Quinn didn't make me want to pummel him, that watching him go in for a deeper kiss didn't make me want to drag him by his hair into the lake and drown him.

Chase scoffs. "I'm being nice."

"No, you're being rape-y."

He turns to me in a huff. "She's my wife. I hardly think it's rape-y if I kiss her."

My eyes shoot over to where Mom and the photographer

are still deep in conversation, now slowly walking toward the front of the house, where the photographer's car is parked. I don't think Chase is speaking loud enough for them to hear.

Chase doesn't seem to care. His jaw is tight with anger, and his hands are no longer in his pockets. Instead, they're curled at his sides. I've ruined his perfect little postcard afternoon.

"She's not your wife anymore, Chase," I say calmly, and all of his anger seems to dissipate, just like mine has. Chase has already lost Quinn. He's not going to get her back, not that I necessarily think he wants to. But that display today, her turning her face away and pretending to laugh so that she didn't have to kiss him? It's over between them. If it wasn't clear last night, when she let me put my head between her legs, it's clear now.

"I need to ask you an honest question." I try to dig deep and see the brother I've always loved and protected. The brother I grew up with, who used to talk to me about things he cared about and take my advice. The brother I once respected and trusted, just like Quinn did. "Why did you cheat on her?" What I really want to ask is, *how* do you cheat on someone like her? How do you have the perfect person in your grasp and then do the worst thing you can to them?

He looks out at the lake again, takes a deep breath, and lets it out. "You want to paint me out as the bad guy, but it never felt like she really wanted to be there either."

A shot of anger goes through me again. "You don't get to blame her."

He whips his head around to face me. "I'm not blaming her, but we weren't perfect for a long time."

"So that means you get to fuck around on her? Just because things weren't perfect after a few years?" I can't push down the anger anymore. And I know I started this, but I can't stop it.

Something seems to burst inside him. "I was fucking around on her the whole time. Since the very beginning."

As soon as the words are out of his mouth, I can tell he regrets them. His shoulders slump and his head falls forward, like it's too heavy for his neck. Even after everything, I always thought Chase and I would find our way back to each other. Brothers until the end. But I feel the wall go up between us. It's made of steel, and there's no breaking it down now.

I can feel him waiting, poised on the edge. "What, you want to yell at me now?"

"Yeah, I do. But I won't." All the years I spent keeping my distance, advocating for them and their relationship, thinking he deserved her more than I did. It was all a lie, even more than I thought it was.

He sighs. "I'm not very good at telling myself no. Quinn was hard work, and random women who didn't want anything more from me than my dick weren't."

I intend to put in the work. I'll work for Quinn until my hands bleed.

I take a step back, nod. "I hope it was worth it."

After my conversation with Chase, I'm feeling raw. I have these moments sometimes. I don't even know how to explain it. It's like I've stepped outside of my body. I don't feel like myself, more like I'm just observing my shell as it goes through the motions of life.

That's what it felt like to hear what Chase did, to hear my brother speak about someone he's supposed to care about as if she was just something to be tossed aside to make way for his instant gratification. Because the only way to cope with the knowledge that someone you once trusted and respected so fully is actually utter shit is to watch it happen like a TV show.

I float through an afternoon at the pool, then dinner, and then an action-adventure movie that Mom picks, until she decides she wants to go to bed early, and Sabrina raises a knowing eyebrow at me.

"Wanna shoot pool?" she says, her toned arms spread along the back of the couch. She taps her manicured nails along the fabric. I know that agreeing to play a game of pool with Sabrina is a death sentence. The only truly annoying thing about Sabrina is the fact that she's good at everything, including pool.

I groan. "I don't know if I feel like getting my ass kicked tonight."

Sabrina's arms drop to her sides. "Aw, come on, Reed. We'll play teams. I'll take Quinn."

Quinn scowls. "Hey!"

Sabrina sends her an innocent smile. "Sorry, babe, but you know how it is."

I bite back a smile. I've never played pool with Quinn, but I'm guessing Sabrina has in the past, and I'm also guessing she's not very good at it. I would gladly have Quinn on my team, but I know it'll be easier for her to team up with Sabrina.

"Okay," I tell Sabrina, and she squeals and jumps to her feet. We all follow her down to the basement, where the pool table is pushed into one corner of the living room. I move straight to the rack and grab a cue stick in each hand. When I feel someone come up behind me, I reach behind me to hand them a cue stick. Soft, warm fingers brush against mine, and I turn my head in time to see Quinn watch her hand engulf mine. She takes the cue stick, her cheeks turning pink, her hand sliding away slowly.

My God, I want her.

Chase appears over her shoulder, and I turn quickly, taking a deep breath as I grab another cue stick for Sabrina.

"Not gonna lie," Quinn says, sounding much more normal than I feel at the moment, "I might need someone to remind me of the rules."

Chase laughs. "Geez. This is going to be an easy win."

I roll my eyes and turn back to the table. Over in the corner, Chase and Sabrina are bickering about something, so I set the table, racking the balls. Quinn joins me, picking balls out of the pockets and bringing them to me.

"I'm really, really bad at pool," she says, quiet enough that I can tell she doesn't want the others to hear.

She glances sideways at me, and the sound of Chase and Sabrina arguing dies away when I see the question in her eyes. We haven't gotten to talk all day, at least not in any meaningful way, haven't gotten to talk about what happened between us last night. I glance over to make sure Chase is preoccupied and then let my eyes fall down Quinn's body, over the curves of her in her cute little sundress. I have to fight away the image that forms in my head of me bending her over this table, lifting the skirt, and fucking her senseless.

When my eyes find hers again, she's blushing, her eyes quickly dropping to my mouth and back up. We haven't had a discussion about what we are, what we're doing, what last night meant. We both just know it happened, and I don't know about her, but I want it to happen again.

"Just make sure you have a strong stance and that you line your body up with the shot. Confidence is key. Don't let Chase bully you."

I pull the rack away from the balls and send her a wink. When she smiles at me, I know that even if nothing else ever happens between us, Quinn and I will be okay. I don't want to be without her ever again for the rest of my life, but if I can even just have her as a friend, that'll be enough.

"Okay, let's get this party started," Chase says, coming around the side of the table while Sabrina stays where she is, her arms crossed in irritation. If there was ever someone Chase was unable to charm, it's Sabrina.

I move around the table, putting space between Quinn and me just as Chase saddles up to her. He stands so close to her that there's no space between their bodies. They're pressed from shoulder to hip and Chase puts his arm around her, settling his fingers on her waist.

"Did Reed remind you how to play?" he asks her.

"Yep!" she lies, casually moving away from him to the other side of the table. "Who breaks?"

Halfway to empty on the table, it becomes pretty clear that Sabrina has made a huge mistake bringing Quinn onto her team. Chase and I together are mediocre at best, but the two of us are enough to put the girls to shame because Quinn can't hit a ball to save her life.

I'm loving it because watching Quinn bend over, driving me absolutely mad in her little sundress and then flying right past a ball that should have been an easy hit, is making this day easier to bear. She's sexy as fuck and also absolutely adorable.

Chase is also loving it because he also can't seem to keep his eyes off Quinn, a fact that I've had to ignore because I can't very well pummel him for looking at his own wife, or at least as far as Sabrina is concerned. He's also gloating like a fucking twit over the fact that we're winning.

Sabrina, however, looks like she's being strapped in for brain surgery. Sabrina hates to lose, mostly because she's not used to it.

And it's just as Chase is lining up his next shot, a shot that's going to perfectly sink two balls if he can manage to do it just right, his arm cocked back, that a loud, long, highly erotic moan rips through the mostly quiet room.

Chase's elbow jerks, the stick goes left, and he misses the shot entirely.

The sound vanishes.

All eyes go to Sabrina, who's tapping away at her phone. The sound of the moan seems to still be echoing in the air even as she smiles and puts her phone into her back pocket. She cocks her head and looks right at Chase. "What?" she says innocently.

"What the hell was that?" Chase stomps over to her and

tries to snatch her phone out of her back pocket, but she dodges him and presses her back to the wall.

"It's nothing."

Chase scowls. "I thought you were above resorting to cheating."

Sabrina smiles. "Well, you were wrong."

While Chase's back is still turned, Quinn lines up a shot. I reach over and adjust her arm so that she's straight, pulling her elbow back quickly, even as Sabrina's eyes travel over Chase's shoulder to catch me.

Quinn shoots and sinks one.

At the sound, Chase spins around, making a choking noise. Sabrina steps around him, quickly lines up a shot, and sinks it.

"That's not fair!" Chase says, sounding like an actual six-year-old.

Sabrina grins at Quinn, motioning for her to take her spot at the table. Quinn's eyes meet mine, and I see the hesitation in them. She doesn't know what I did earlier to fix her posture, so she doesn't know how to recreate it. I smile back at her and shrug.

Chase scoffs. "Who's fucking team are you on, Reed?"

Planting her cue stick on the ground like she just left her flag at the top of Everest, Sabrina says, "Chase, would you like me to get you a drink? It might help you unclench a little bit."

It's such an obvious ploy to get Chase to overdo it, but Chase doesn't seem to care. He's practically sniffing the air as Sabrina walks over to the small, self-serve bar in the corner and pulls out two glasses.

Quinn shoots. She's all twisted in the wrong shape and sends a ball spinning to the right that should have gone straight. She grimaces and straightens away from the table.

"Better luck next time," I say to her, and she narrows her eyes at me, moving out of the way so that I can take my shot. I lean over the table and line it up. I'm just about to slip the cue stick forward when something bumps it hard, knocking it completely out of whack.

I shoot up and spin around. Quinn leans against the wall behind me, a smirk on her face as she examines her nails.

"Oh, I didn't realize we were playing it that way," I say to her, biting back a smile.

She shrugs, her eyes lifting to mine. "I don't know what you're talking about."

"Are we fucking playing or not?" Chase asks. I look over at him in time to see him toss back at least three fingers of whiskey.

"Jesus," I say. "Are you going to be able to tell all the balls apart?"

Chase scoffs. "Are you so much of a lightweight that one drink would double your vision?"

I raise my eyebrows at him as he turns to fix himself another drink. I look over at Sabrina, and she just snickers, getting ready to take her turn. With her attention diverted, I turn back to Quinn. She's watching me quietly, her dark eyes giving nothing away.

"Drink?" I ask her.

She shakes her head.

I turn to the bar, and as I pass Quinn, with my heart racing, I put my hand out and let my fingers slowly trail along the bare skin of her thigh just below the hem of her dress. I hear the quiet intake of her breath but keep moving. I keep my back to her as I pour myself a drink, the tips of my fingers buzzing from the thrill of getting to caress her skin.

I want her to know that she can have whatever she wants from me. I want her to know that I want her, that I want more, and that I'll be waiting for her tonight if she wants more, too.

I turn and lean against the wall beside the bar. Sabrina is

still making quick work of the pool table, Chase is watching her with a sour expression, and Quinn's eyes are glued to me. I hold her gaze over the rim of my glass as I take a drink, loving the look of her as I taste the sweet whiskey sliding down my throat. The air between us crackles, like the air before lightning strikes, and only we can feel it.

"There it is, ladies and gentlemen," Sabrina says after she pockets the 8-ball. She plants a hand on her hip and grins at the three of us. Honestly, she might be just as bad as Chase is when it comes to gloating over pool, even when she and Quinn blatantly cheated.

"Doesn't even count," Chase says.

Sabrina rolls her eyes and leaves her cue stick in the middle of the table, ever accustomed to having someone clean up after her. "Don't be such a sore loser," she says, turning toward the stairs.

"I'm not a sore loser; you're just a cheater." Chase follows her to the stairs, and then the two of them wait at the bottom, both of them still going on about whether or not the girls cheated as Quinn starts to tidy up.

"Leave it," I say, walking toward her.

She pulls her hands away from the pool table quickly, like she got caught doing something she shouldn't.

Without another word, I down the rest of my whiskey and brush past her, letting my hand graze hers for a split second. I watch from the open door of my bedroom as Quinn joins Sabrina and Chase, glancing over at me one last time before the three of them go upstairs.

25 QUINN

I close Chase's bedroom door behind me and go barefoot down the hall to the basement. I half-expect Reed to be in the kitchen like he was when I stumbled on him last night, but he isn't and when I turn to the bedroom, a spear of golden light shining through the crack under the door, I'm suddenly unable to move.

Because I know I shouldn't go in there. A layer of goose-bumps has covered my skin, and my chest has gone all hot, like I'm sick with a fever. I know what will happen if I go in there. I know what I *want* to happen. I've had this feeling all day, this soreness under my skin, like if I don't touch Reed, if I don't get as close to him as I can while everyone's backs are turned, I might just wither and die.

My need for him feels *urgent*. It's felt urgent all day, made all the more urgent by his proximity. Always close, but not close enough to touch. Always in the room, but in the way a ghost is in the room, abstract and invisible. I didn't know what it felt like to sit across a table from someone and have to pretend that you don't care they're there. Just another face.

I push forward, throwing open the bedroom door without knocking and closing it behind me, leaning up against it like I ran all the way here and need a breather.

Reed stands beside the bed, still dressed from the day, just like I am. It's like the planet stops moving for a little while, like we lose our places on the surface of it.

My eyes meet his across the room, holding like our lives depend on it. He looks like a portrait someone would put on a wall, some post-modern thing, in his sweater in the middle of summer, the dark scruff on his jaw creating a sharp cut. His eyes watching me like he knows every thought that has ever gone through my head.

I push off the door, walk across the room, dig my hands into the short strands of his hair, and kiss him. He doesn't need time to catch up. His hands cradle my jaw, his mouth opening over mine. When our tongues meet, he groans into my mouth, and I press myself fully to him, needing every inch of my skin to touch every inch of his.

This, here, this is the best I've felt in months. Maybe even years.

Just this. Not even the orgasm last night or what I know is coming as soon as we can convince ourselves to part long enough to take our clothes off. No, just the kiss. Just the feel of him holding me and kissing me so deep and so slow, like this is all he's ever wanted. No hurry. No pressure.

Reed nudges me back toward the bed until I've toppled backward onto it, our mouths somehow never disconnecting. His hands grasp onto my thighs, sliding up under the hem of my dress, and I make a sound in the back of my throat, something horny and surprised and needy.

Reed rips his mouth from mine. "Hey, you okay?"

Part of me wishes I could stop everything right here. Just let this be enough. Reed on top of me, his strong grip holding me and his face in my hands. I don't even know how to explain what I feel with him. Comfortable. Visible. Wanted. And just those things are enough for me not to care about anything else because when was the last time a man looked at me like this, like I'm something precious, something real?

Possibly not since that night in the hallway, when it was twenty-two-year-old Reed, with his hair wild and alcohol on his breath.

"I'm good," I tell him. "I really want to do this with you."

He lowers his head, close enough that I can feel his breath on my lips. "You have no idea."

My breath stutters out of me at his words. It's not like I couldn't tell he was sexually attracted to me. He's hard against my thigh, and last night, after he was done with me, he was sticking up in his pants like a flagpole. But Reed has always been a little more reckless than Chase. Is he reckless enough to sleep with his brother's ex-wife just because she was around and available and in his bed?

His hand slides higher on my thigh until he tugs at the waistband of my underwear, and I shiver. I shove my hands up under the hem of his shirt, losing track of everything when I feel his muscled, hairy chest under my hands. "Take this off," I say into his mouth, and he smiles.

When he goes up on his knees to rip his shirt over his head, I use the opportunity to unzip my dress and wiggle out of it. I settle back onto the blanket and look up at him. He's still hovering over me on his knees, and I forget the English language when I see him.

I knew he had to have new tattoos, and I'd gotten a glimpse of them on the boat yesterday. But now I let my eyes hungrily take in all the new ink, a bird over his heart, something in

French up the length of his ribs, a skeleton peeking out of the waistband of his jeans. And all of it dusted with a fine layer of dark hair.

My God, he's so beautiful.

Reed grins and bends over me, planting kisses along my jaw. "You're pretty fucking gorgeous yourself," he says in my ear, and I realize I said that last part out loud. To even the score, I settle my hand over the ridge of his cock through his pants and rub.

Reed gasps, immediately removing my hand and pinning it to the bed. "Not so fast," he says, eyes meeting mine in the almost-dark. He's golden in the light of the bedside lamp, and my brain tries to reconcile this moment with every other memory I have that's tinted in that familiar gold light. This is not something I could have ever imagined, not something that even feels like it's really happening.

Holding my hands in place against the mattress, Reed trails the back of his other hand down my chest, watching with clear satisfaction as my nipple puckers up under my lace bra. I sigh, and Reed's eyes meet mine, like he's taking in every one of my reactions. "You're so soft," he says, gently digging his fingers into my stomach and then my hip. It's like he's trying to memorize me.

"You're so hard," I whisper in retaliation, my eyes still on that bulge in his pants.

He laughs, his eyes full of light. "Yes, I am," he says, his voice rough. He shifts, settling his body on top of mine, and the weight of him is so good that my eyes roll back in my head, falling closed. Sometimes I think it wasn't the sex with Chase that I wanted, just the weight of him on top of me, the way he would press me into the mattress. It feels so good.

But when Reed rocks his hips against mine, I immediately take it back because his weight feels good, but his hard dick against my clit feels even better. I immediately start to move to his rhythm, knowing if he wanted to finish me off like this, it would still be enough. Anything he wanted to give me right now, when I feel raw and split open, would be a comfort.

"I want to be inside you." He says the words against my throat before running his tongue along my skin. "Is that okay?"

"Yes. Yes, absolutely, yes. Please."

He sits up at that, tugging the belt of his jeans open and then getting off the bed to step out of his pants. I watch, even as I reach behind me and remove my bra. Maybe it would be sexier to let him do it, but all I care about is being naked so that he can fuck me. I slip my underwear down my legs and look up just in time to see him to push his own underwear down, letting his dick spring free.

My mouth goes dry. Holy shit. I know it's not right to compare, especially when you're morbidly comparing brothers, but Reed's dick is bigger than Chase's, and it's...more beautiful? Is that a thing with genitalia? Can dicks be beautiful? Because if they can, then Reed's is. Long and uncut, the foreskin just barely covering the head because he's so hard.

And all I can think is that I can't believe Reed is about to put his dick in me. Reed, my friend. Reed, my brother-in-law. Reed, the first guy who ever looked my way when I was twenty and a virgin.

"You sure about this?" he says, and there might have been some chance that I could have said no about fifteen seconds ago, before I saw his dick and started imagining how good it would feel inside me. But we've definitely passed the point of no return now.

"I'm sure, if you are. I don't want to talk you into anything you don't want to do."

One side of his mouth quirks up, and he gestures at his erection. "Do I *look* like I don't want to do this?"

In any other situation, maybe his joke would be funny, but we're in a whole other reality right now. "Physical consent is the not the same as emotional consent, Reed. Just because you're hard doesn't mean you want to go through with it."

His smile fades, his head tilting to one side. It feels bizarre to be having this conversation at all, much less both completely naked. "Quinn, I want to fuck you. Do you want to fuck me?"

I nod enthusiastically.

"Should I wear a condom?"

Jesus, a condom didn't even occur to me. I haven't worn one since about two months into my relationship with Chase. But things are different now, aren't they? I don't have a condom, though. It's not like I thought this was going to happen. Does he have a condom? Did he think *he* was going to be getting laid on this trip?

"I'm still on birth control," I tell him, resisting the urge to cover myself while we discuss this. "But..."

He raises an eyebrow, waits for me to finish.

"But Chase gave me chlamydia. I've been treated, and I'm all clear, but if you're worried—"

"I'm not. If you say you're good, I'm good too. I, uh, I don't usually go without a condom, and I was tested not too long ago."

There's something about the way he says it that makes me realize that Reed knows my entire sexual history, and I don't have the faintest clue about his. I never even asked him if he was seeing anyone. I'm sure he has a long list of women back in Boston who are waiting for him to return and booty call them.

"I don't even have one with me," I say.

"What do you want to bet Mom keeps them stocked in the bathrooms?"

I cover my face with my hands. "Oh, my God. I can't think about Madison buying us condoms right now."

Reed chuckles. The bed shifts, and when I pull my hands away from my face, it's to find him crawling on top of me. He lowers himself, his hard cock brushing my stomach, and I'm halfway through a moan when he covers his mouth with mine. He kisses me slow, like we're starting all the way at the beginning, even though we're both naked and ready to go.

Without taking his mouth from mine, he reaches between us, lining himself up against my entrance and then pushing inside. I immediately pull my mouth away, gasping for breath. It feels so good I could die. I close my eyes, lost in the sensation of him pushing and pushing and pushing, until we both exhale when he fits all the way in.

"How's that?" he says against my ear, and it's the first time that it's really occurred to me that if anyone hears us, we're fucked. I didn't lock the door, and I don't know how quiet I've been or how much can be heard through the walls and ceiling. All I know is that when I'm down here, I can't hear anything from above.

"It's perfect," I whisper back.

And then he pulls back and thrusts into me.

"Oh, fuck," I breathe out against his neck. He has his face tucked into my shoulder, but I feel his lips curve against my skin in a smile.

He stays there, his arms wrapped tight around me, and then starts to thrust...hard.

My whole body seizes up. I wrap my arms around his shoulders and my legs around his hips, trying to get as close to him as I can. Every inch of my body is touching every inch of his, and when he starts to tilt his hips in a completely unfamiliar way, my eyes roll into the back of my head.

With every thrust, he's rubbing all his weight against my clit and after a few minutes, I can't remember my own name.

He goes up on his elbows, and I whimper a little, trying to

pull him back down. I want him touching me completely. The contact feels so good. But he just presses his forehead to mine, his eyes boring into me. We're silent, only the sound of our breathing loud in the room. I've got him in a vise grip, terrified that it's going to end before I'm done.

This is where Chase always checked out. He wasn't terrible at the foreplay, and he was good at getting me going. But about half the time, before I could make it across the finish line, he would be gone, having already made it where he needed to be.

"I need to come," I say, holding Reed's gaze. "Please make me come." I was always too embarrassed to ask Chase for what I needed, but this is why Reed and I are here, right? This is about needs. About both of us getting what we can only get from each other in this house. So, I should ask. Because I didn't go through all of this—fighting the morality of sleeping with my ex's brother, sneaking away from his entire family upstairs, finally finding the courage to go for it—just to make it out of the arrangement with nary a single orgasm.

Reed huffs and then his hips pick up speed, his hands coming up to grip my hair. My eyes start to close, but Reed growls, "Look at me."

His eyes are so dark they look black, and there's something in them that I've never seen before. He's looking at me like he plans to never look away. Like he would hold me here and make me stare into his eyes forever. Like he's controlling me with his gaze, making it impossible for me to break it.

I can feel my orgasm rising. I can't hold his gaze anymore. I physically cannot keep my eyes open as the sensation builds and builds and then starts to break. I throw my head back and open my mouth to scream, but Reed's hand clamps over my lips, even as he continues to thrust and thrust and thrust.

I whimper and moan and cry out into his hand, my fingernails biting into the skin of his shoulders, until he uncovers my mouth, slams his lips down on mine, and moans while he bursts inside me.

In the aftermath, I'm dazed. My whole body is heavy, my brain like white static, and I realize that sex has never felt quite like that before.

Quinn is eating a cookie like nothing happened. Like she didn't just rip me to pieces and then put me back together.

I watch her, bare shoulders and blanket tucked under her arms. She looks...relaxed. She doesn't look like someone who had to kiss her ex for their mother today. Her hair is tousled. No, she looks like someone who came so hard their entire body shook. I felt that orgasm in my soul.

I want to give her another one.

"What are you going to name your new restaurant?"

I can't believe she's asking me that. I feel like the entire universe exploded into a million pieces and then regenerated, but now everything is more colorful, more beautiful. The air is cleaner, the stars brighter as they shine down through the window. I reach for a cookie.

"I'm not sure. I haven't thought about it too much."

She chews, considers. "I never really liked Aeronaut. It sounded sort of..."

"Pretentious?"

"Yeah. Sorry."

"No, it's okay. The name wasn't my idea." It was my partner's idea. He thought it would represent our "roles as trailblazers of the industry." As if we were doing something important. As if we were special. Not special enough not to get mixed up with the wrong crowd and lose a shit ton of money. By that point, I had sunk every penny of the money I had saved over the years into the restaurant. There was no way to keep it from sinking.

"Have you ever thought about opening a bakery instead? Do it all on your own?"

"Sure. But the vibe is just different. People walk into a bakery, they take their stuff, and they go, you know? They might have a coffee, but that's about it. I always liked the idea of people coming and sitting down with their friends, having a drink, ordering a delicious dinner, and then realizing there's a dessert menu. And not just a dessert menu that has cheesecake and chocolate cake. A dessert menu that has fresh eclairs, homemade limoncello ice cream, and custard-filled sopapillas."

She smiles over at me. It's so easy to talk to her. That's always been the problem, hasn't it? I've never had to hide from Quinn. Never had to play it cool, or bury my thoughts, or hold in responses. Everything I think and feel is safe with her.

"Now, imagine all of those things, but it's a mom and her teenage daughter on a Saturday afternoon, walking through the city and going to bookstores and seeing a movie and then stopping when the scent of vanilla meets them on the sidewalk." She turns her head to find my eyes. "Sometimes, I worry that you've all been in this world for so long that you've forgotten about everyone else. Those swanky restaurants are nice, but Minnesota Quinn never would have been able to afford to eat there. It breaks my heart to think that there are people out there who'll never get to taste your perfect chocolate chip cookies because they couldn't afford to eat at a five-star restaurant." She shrugs. "I don't think I'll ever be that caliber again, you know? It's going to be Hostess snacks and box cakes for me for the rest of my life."

"Jesus, don't say that. You're breaking my heart."

She finishes the rest of her cookie and then burrows deep into the covers. When she meets my eye, all that joy and pride I found in them a moment ago is gone. "Did we do something bad, Reed?"

I set my half-eaten cookie back into the Tupperware container I put them in last night. "After everything, I don't really know what's good and bad or right and wrong. And I don't know that it matters, either. There are no innocent parties here."

I could feel bad for having sex with Quinn. But at the end of the day, Chase and Quinn are not really married anymore and Chase cheated on her. We kept our distance for five years. I respected the Bro Code or whatever. It's not my fault Chase made the biggest mistake of his life.

All I know is that what just happened between Quinn and me wasn't a mistake. This is the way it should have been all along.

27 QUINN

"Are you even looking at these dresses?"

I blink, snapping out of my hazy daydream. Is it a daydream if you're dreaming of something that really happened? All I can think about is Reed and how hard he made me come last night. Which, of course, is a terrible thing to be thinking about while you're out shopping with your sister-in-law, who thinks you spent the night with her *other* brother.

"Yeah, I'm looking," I lie, examining the skirt of the dress she picked out for me. It's a long, pleated silk skirt that would probably make her look like a fashion icon, but I would just look like an old lady in a night gown. "I don't think so."

Sabrina makes a sad face and puts the dress back. When I told everyone I was going to go shopping for a 4th of July dress on my own, Sabrina protested, saying there was no way I could shop by myself without someone around to tell me what looked good and what didn't, and she's not wrong. She has a much better eye for these things than I do.

"What kind of dress do you think you want?" she asks, eyes scanning over the racks around us of colorful cocktail dresses.

What I want to say is *a cheap one*, but as far as Sabrina is concerned, I'm still married to a man that makes six figures and would have no reason to be concerned about the price tag of a dress. "Something blue."

Sabrina levels me with an unkind look. "I guess that's a start, but you have to give me a little more than that."

A dress that Reed could get me out of easily when the party is over.

I immediately brush the thought away. What happened last night with Reed is definitely not happening again. It's bad enough that it happened once. What the hell would we even do if his family found out? It would destroy everything. I could never do that to them. It was just a little fun.

"How about something tea length?" I ask. "I've always loved that Old Hollywood look."

Sabrina snaps. "Yes. Absolutely. That's what I'm talking about."

Like a heat-seeking missile, she immediately locates a navy-blue dress with sequins sewn into the bodice. "What about this one?"

IT TAKES ME HALF AN HOUR TO FIND A DRESS, AND THEN Sabrina and I are walking through the shopping center on the lake when she comes to a stop outside a lingerie store.

"Oh, let's poke in here," she says, holding the door open for me without giving me a chance to protest. I don't guess I really would have. Sabrina is hard to say no to, and I don't have a legitimate reason for avoiding a lingerie boutique. She doesn't know that the sight of very lacy things reminds me of Reed and the way he ran his fingers down the curve of my breast last night.

I follow her into the little shop, my eyes scanning the

collection of underwear. Body suits and garter belts and push-up bras. When I stumble onto a display in the very back of crotchless panties, I turn away quickly, my pulse speeding up. I immediately picture the dress I bought, wearing a pair of those underneath and letting Reed slip his fingers right into my—

"See anything good?" Sabrina steps up beside me. Her eyes go to the crotchless underwear, and instead of making a disgusted face like I sort of thought she would because I'm her sister-in-law and would therefore be wearing these things for her brother, she says, "Ooooh. Those are cute." She walks straight to the display and picks up a pair of violet panties. "Crotchless can sometimes be a little strange, but these are pretty cute." She shuffles through a few of them, and I decide to leave her to it. I can only imagine the sex life she has back in New York. Someone who looks like Sabrina would have her pick of the eligible bachelors.

I wonder, suddenly, if it's hard for her, being in the city and being the daughter of Madison Lynch. Everyone knows she's rich and powerful, and I can only imagine that means being pursued by people who want to use your name. I pretend to be looking at some see-through bras and glance back at Sabrina. Even though I've known her for five years and think she's amazing, we haven't spent a ton of time getting to know each other on a personal level.

I know that Sabrina is one of those people who has made her money doing a little bit of everything. She was modeling when we met, when she was still in high school, and not long after that, she was the face of Dior. Now, she's mostly famous for a TikTok series she did where she would travel the world and only stay in small family-owned bed-and-breakfasts instead of five-star hotels. Everyone knew she had money so people thought she would find something wrong with the little B&Bs.

But she ended up boosting dozens of small businesses and helping a lot of failing Mom-and-Pops.

I remember reading the comments on those videos and being so surprised that people were upset that she was so nice. After a while, people assumed her kindness was fake and the videos ended. I'm not entirely sure what she's doing these days, other than living with Madison.

She turns and catches my eye, smiling big. She seems a lot better today, her mother's potential diagnosis no longer on her mind. "Need my help picking something?" She already has an armful of things. She steps over to me and holds up a bodysuit. It's black, a lacy, half-cup bra and thong, connected by parallel silk ribbons that would stripe down the wearer's body. A silk belt around the middle holds it all together, giving it shape. It's sexy and elegant and not like something I've ever worn in my life.

Something starts to simmer under my skin. When Chase and I first started dating, I wanted to have sex with him so bad. I'd been holding onto my virginity for a long time, wanting to save it for the perfect person, and when I met Chase, I knew he was the right one. I knew he would be gentle with me and caring.

And he was.

And then the gentle and caring went on and on. Long past our second time or fifth time or hundredth time, and I kept wondering when there would be *more*. I had spent a year rooming with Brooke, and I knew that she was into guys who were a little more demanding in bed. She would talk about a guy who wanted to spank her or wrap his hand around her throat or go at her so hard that she would be sore the next day. And she loved it. She would tell me about these encounters with a dreamy look in her eye.

I would think about it when Chase pushed inside me,

wondering what would happen if I flipped us over and rode him the way I imagined sometimes. Or if I bit him or asked him to fuck me hard, so hard it would hurt to sit down for a few days.

Then one day, when I could tell he was close but I was barely creeping toward the finish line, I whispered in his ear that I wanted him to be rough with me. It was a simple request. One that, in hindsight, doesn't seem all that scandalous. But that wasn't what *we* did. That wasn't the people we were, picture perfect Chase and Quinn.

He didn't say anything. His hips paused, barely a stutter, and then he continued on as if I had said nothing at all, bucking away until he spilled inside me.

"Could I ask you an honest question?"

Sabrina lets the lingerie she was still holding up for my inspection fall to her side. Her head tilts a little, and there's something behind her dark eyes—eyes that, I realize now, are the same color as Reed's—that I can't quite place, but I think it's trepidation. "Of course."

"Would you say you're sexually adventurous?"

She looks like she's really considering my question. She finally leans one hip against a display. "I think it depends on your perspective. I think some people would think I'm sexually adventurous, but I think some people might say I'm boring. Why? Are you and Chase having problems?"

My stomach lurches. This feels so deceptive, like I'm outright lying. And I don't want to lie to Sabrina. I want to tell her everything that's going on between Reed and me in that basement. But I can't.

"I wouldn't say *problems*. I just...think maybe we don't want the same things."

"You mean anal?"

A nervous giggle pops out of me. "No, nothing like that."

My eyes meet her sincere ones. "Not that I have a problem with it. I've just never...done that." I couldn't even get Chase to fuck me on the kitchen table—which I hesitantly suggested once and then laughed off as a joke when he started to lecture me about how gross it was to have sex at a table that other people sat at occasionally—much less get him to have anal sex with me, which I'm not positive I'm even into.

"Do you want to tell me what it is?"

No. I don't. I've just had these...thoughts for a long time, things I've heard of other women doing that I sometimes thought might be hot, but I know that I could never outright tell Sabrina—or anyone else—about them. The only reason I'm bringing it up is because she brought me into this shop.

"Not really. I guess I'm just curious about, I don't know, where to start when you want to try something different."

Sabrina's mouth spreads into a smile and she holds up the piece of lingerie again. "This is a good place to start. Walk in wearing this, and he won't know what hit him."

I try to imagine what Reed would say if I showed up in the basement bedroom in that stringy, lacy bit of fabric. But all I can imagine is Chase, looking at me like I've done something wrong and then leaving me standing there, mostly naked, without another word.

What if Reed is just like Chase? Yes, the sex we had last night was good. It was intense and felt incredible, and Reed made sure I came. But it was good without being all that different from what Chase and I used to do together. What if I ask for more, and Reed is disgusted with me for even suggesting it?

But what if Reed is into it? What if...?

I reach out and take the lingerie from Sabrina. "But how do I get him to try something we've never done before?" I have to stare down at the fabric in my hands. I can't meet her eye, even though I know she's not judging me right now. I never had the guts to ask Brooke if there was something wrong with me, if I was the problem in my sex life with Chase, but the stakes feel so much smaller with Sabrina.

"You ask."

The laugh that sneaks out of me then is bitter. "You make it sound so easy."

She's quiet for a long moment, and when I look up, she's giving me this face like I've asked her a particularly difficult math question. Finally, she says, "He's your husband. You should feel comfortable asking for what you want."

She's right. I *should* have felt comfortable asking Chase for what I wanted.

But I never did.

And now, what if I ask Reed for what I want and I scare him away? Maybe it doesn't really matter in the end if I scare him away or not. This whole arrangement—this thing that we're doing that we haven't fully discussed—is temporary. He's going to walk away from it in a few days anyway.

And maybe the risk is worth it if I get something I really need.

28 QUINN

1 Year Ago

"Absolutely not," I say to Brooke, low under my breath. "Just because he's my brother-in-law doesn't mean we can drop his name to get a table at his restaurant."

Brooke ignores me. She's got a hold on my wrist, dragging me down the busy Saturday night streets of Boston toward Aeronaut. This whole situation is her fault anyway. We agreed to meet downtown for a nice bestie dinner while Chase is out of town, and Brooke's job was to pick the restaurant.

And she did. But she didn't make a reservation, and neither of us is willing to wait an hour for dinner.

"It's our only chance to get food that isn't McDonald's tonight," she says. "And *good* food, too." She stops abruptly, and I slam into her back. She doesn't react. "Hey, his food will be good, right? I mean, he's not the chef. What if we get there and it's all oysters and caviar?" Brooke shudders. She's not much for high-end anything, and I certainly don't blame her. The only reason she agreed to meet me downtown is because I told her I would pay. If she had to pay for her own dinner, it definitely wouldn't be at the expensive restaurants in downtown Boston.

"It doesn't matter," I say, using the opportunity to yank my wrist out of her hold. "We can't take advantage of him like that."

Brooke crosses her arms and glares at me. "What's the point of having fancy in-laws if you're not going to take advantage of it? I mean, you already refuse to tell people you're Madison Lynch's daughter-in-law. Haven't you done your part for the meek and modest?"

She actually kind of has a point there. But it's been a while since I last saw Reed. Since we both live in Boston, it isn't unheard of for us to spot each other on the street while I'm out running errands and he's out on business. We usually spend a minute catching up and then go our opposite ways.

My friendship with Reed has always felt very real, very tangible, and yet somehow a figment of my imagination. I feel like we're only friends in my head. It's always felt just different enough from every other friendship I've ever had to be uncomfortable.

Maybe he won't even be here. We can go in and name-drop and then leave and no one will be the wiser. McDonald's for dinner it is.

We step into the dark restaurant, and I immediately wish we hadn't. There's just something about Aeronaut. Everything feels so *perfect*. The floors gleam and the lights twinkle, and everybody knows how to order the French entrees *in* French and which wine to pair them with.

I grew up in Minnesota, and not even five years being with Chase has really taught me how to fit in with his lifestyle.

Brooke, however, takes to it immediately. She steps up to the maître d's station, a smile on her face, pretending she can't even see the people lounging in the bar area, clearly waiting for tables of their own. "Hi! A table for two, please."

The maître d', a man wearing a vest and a bowtie, raises one eyebrow at her. "And what name is your reservation under?"

Brooke looks like she's been waiting her whole life to be asked that question. "Oh, we don't have a reservation, but we know the owner, Reed Lynch. Maybe you could go get him for us?" She leans around the man, peeking into the main dining area, where nobody is paying us any attention.

The maître d's eyes flicker over to me, and I paste on a smile. If Brooke wants to be the one to go through with this, then I'm fine with her taking the lead.

"Ladies, Mr. Lynch is very busy. So, I'm afraid that without a reservation—"

"Quinn?"

I turn. Reed has appeared as if from nowhere, but I see now that there's a door behind him, hiding in the shadows beyond the host's station. He lets it fall closed and then his mouth stretches into a smile. "What are you doing here?"

I've never seen him like this, with a blazer on the color of molten metal and his hair slicked back. He *looks* like a guy who owns a fancy restaurant and not the guy I've seen time and time again across a dinner table in New York.

"Oh." I suddenly remember why we're here, that Brooke dragged me so that we could use Reed's good name to get some dinner. Guilt slices through me. "We were in the area, and Brooke wanted to see the restaurant. She's never been."

Reed seems to find Brooke then, like he didn't see her standing right beside me until now. They met at the wedding, of course, and I'm sure they crossed paths at Suffolk, but I don't know how much contact they've actually had. He smiles at her, and she plants her hands on her hips.

"Hey, Brooke," he says politely.

"Hey, fancy cake maker."

She has her flirty voice on. I watch them smile at each other and feel a heaviness in my chest. Brooke has a boyfriend, but what if they...hit it off? Would she break up with him for Reed? I try to imagine the two of them sitting beside each other at family dinners, holding hands beneath the table, sneaking off to kiss in dark corners—

"Okay, well, it was nice seeing you, but I think it's time for us to go." The words burst out of me far too loud, and the maître d' twists to look at us, grimacing like I just appeared with a crying baby.

Brooke's mouth falls open—because we obviously came here to get something out of Reed, and now that Reed is here, I'm ready to run the other direction—and Reed's smile falls.

"You're not going to have dinner?" he asks.

"Well...I mean...the place is pretty busy..."

Reed doesn't let me finish. He turns to the maître d'. "Marcus, is there a table in the back by the kitchen?"

The maître d' hesitates. He obviously doesn't want to have to tell Reed the truth right now. "Yes, sir. One is being cleared, but—"

"Great. Take Brooke and Quinn over, please."

Brooke does a little happy dance as Reed walks away, but I just stare at the width of his shoulders as he goes, heading in the direction of the kitchen.

"See?" Brooke says as the maître d' leads us to a table that's as far from the front of the restaurant as we could possibly be. "He wasn't offended. He *wants* to get us a table. You're his family."

That weight settles on my chest again. There's something about the way she says it that gets under my skin.

We take a seat at a small two-person table and Brooke immediately snatches up her menu. I'm too distracted by the soft piano music coming from the corner and the real roses in the center of the table. The place really is nice. I saw it when it first opened, when Reed invited everyone for a big party before the official grand opening, but it's different to see it when it's actually full of people, with a piano actually being played by a real person, with the delectable smell of expensive food wafting through the air.

WE DON'T SEE REED AGAIN AS WE ORDER WINE AND FISH and then contemplate dessert.

Brooke has her menu up between us, but mine is folded on the table.

"You can't skip dessert," she says, her eyes scanning. "Reed would be so heartbroken if you skipped it."

I resist the urge to say, *maybe he would only be heartbroken if* you *skipped it.* "I'm just trying not to go so heavy on the bread and sugar lately."

She sends me a dirty look over the top of her menu, and I look away. I know that Brooke hates it that I work so hard to be the woman that Chase wants me to be, but she doesn't understand. Chase takes care of me. He's the one with the high-paying job, the one who works hard for our lifestyle. The least I can do is make sure he has the wife he wants on his arm.

"Uh, Quinn?"

"Look, I don't need dessert, okay? It doesn't even sound that great. The fish really filled me up." It's not a lie, but the idea of having a dessert made by Reed is definitely a temptation. I know from past experience that his desserts are to die for. He's always making things I've never heard of before and that I think about for weeks after.

"No, it's just..." Brooke pauses.

"What?"

Her eyes meet mine over the top of her menu, and then she lays the tall paper menu on the table between us. "There's a dessert on this menu that's named after you."

I scoff, thinking she's trying to tell me a joke, like *this dessert has your name written all over it*. "It's not named after me."

She shoves the menu toward me, until I'm forced to look down at it because it's poking me in the stomach. "Are you sure? Because it's called 'The Quinn,' and it's perfectly baked chocolate chip cookies and absolutely nothing else."

I lean over the menu, eyes scanning the words until I find the dessert section at the very bottom. *Champagne cake, peach shortcake trifle, lemon cakes with lavender glaze, baby chocolate bourbon bombes, chocolate-coconut pavlova cake.* And at the very bottom, something that's simply called *The Quinn*.

Perfectly baked chocolate chip cookies, just like Brooke said.

I open my mouth, even though I have no clue what to say to that, when Reed's voice startles me.

"Everything to your liking, ladies?"

I slam the menu closed and smile up at him. He has his hands behind his back, like he's a butler who's going to use his feather duster on every surface the moment this conversation is over.

"Of course," I say, craning my neck to look up at him. The edge of one of his tattoos peeks out above the collar of his shirt. "The swordfish was delicious."

He grins. "Great. Hey, you wanna come back and meet Oscar?"

Oscar, the partner. The one who presumably is responsible for the swordfish. "Sure."

"Oh, I'm actually going to go use the bathroom," Brooke says, shooing us off. "I'll meet you back here for dessert." She gives me a knowing look, but I don't actually know what she *knows*. I have no idea what it means that there's a dessert named after me. Probably nothing. Probably just that someone who helped create the menu also knows someone named Quinn...who also loves chocolate chip cookies...

When I stand from the table, Reed leads me to the side of the restaurant and down a hallway that's momentarily quiet until a big silver door swings open right in front of me. Inside, the kitchen is chaos, dishes clanging and people yelling. When I stop walking, suddenly feeling like I'm definitely not supposed to be back here, Reed smiles and settles his hand at my back, giving me a little push.

"Don't worry," he bends to say into my ear. "It's always like this. It's part of the kitchen experience." He opens the door for me and ushers me in.

Standing in the doorway, unsure where to go, I turn my head to look at him. His face is close to mine, his eyes the exact same color as the chips in chocolate chip cookies. His smile falters, and his eyes scan my face.

"Reed, get the fuck out of the way," someone barks, and then Reed yanks me out of the path of someone with a whole tray full of white dishes with picturesque food on them. The person slides by us, kicking open the door and disappearing into the hallway.

"Sorry," Reed says with a laugh in his voice. "These guys don't know how to play nice." He nods at someone, and a guy with a severely straight mustache wearing chef whites comes over, wiping his hand on a towel.

"Who's this?" the guy asks, eyes running down to my feet and back up. I look away, fidget, suddenly feel five years old again, unable to speak for myself.

"This is Quinn," Reed says, and the tone of his voice makes

me look up at him. He sounds...proud, like someone showing off what they brought to Show-and-Tell.

"Ah," the guy says, nodding. "The elusive Quinn. Happy to finally meet you." He holds out his hand, and I shake it, but not because I want to. I don't know what he means by *the elusive Quinn*. When Reed brought us all to the restaurant before it opened, Oscar was there, but I distinctly remember him refusing to leave the kitchen because he was having some kind of a breakdown over a lost shipment of truffles.

"Yeah, that's me," I say because I have no idea what else *to* say. "The swordfish was lovely."

The silver door swings in and the maître d'—the one from before that clearly still dislikes me from the way he glances at me, rolls his eyes, and then looks away—sticks his head in. "Mr. Lynch, you're needed up front."

"Oh, sure," Reed says, like this happens all the time. He holds the door open for me and we step back out of the kitchen. "I'll see you later, Quinn, okay? Don't forget to order dessert." And then he's gone, and I'm left standing in the hallway.

When a waitress attempts to squeeze by me with a tray of bite-sized cakes, I press myself to the wall, trying to become as small as possible. When she still can't quite get by, I duck into an open doorway beside me to let her pass.

After she's gone, I stay where I am. I'm in a dimly lit office, with two desks that face opposite walls, every surface seemingly covered in papers and receipts and handwritten notes. My eyes immediately catch a family photo, sitting in a brown frame beside a computer. I quietly step over to it and pick it up. Reed, Chase, Sabrina, and Madison smile back at me, huddled together in a boat on the lake. I've been to the lake house a few summers now, and just looking at it, I can feel the heat of the sun on my skin.

Reed has never been there with us though, not as long as

I've been going. He's always here, running his business, while we're fishing and sunbathing and riding jet skis.

I put the frame down and pick up the next one. He has several. I smile when I recognize a younger Madison Lynch. She's holding a baby in her arms that I can only imagine is Reed, wrapped in a blue baby blanket. I'm moving to put that frame down when my eyes catch on the next one, and I freeze.

My hand shakes as I pick up the frame. A picture I recognize because a much bigger version of it hangs in my own house. Me in my wedding dress. I have my back to the camera, my chin tilted just enough so that the photographer could get my profile, earring and hair hanging down gracefully.

Why does he have this?

Footsteps sound in the hallway, and I put down the frame and exit the office in time to find Brooke coming to meet me. "We should probably go," I tell her as soon as she makes it to me. "I'm going to pay. It's getting late."

"They said Reed paid." She's watching me closely, and I'm reminded about the cookies on the menu.

And the picture of me in his office.

And I've forgotten where I am and what life I'm living and whether or not I should be here at all.

"Let's go," I tell her, and we slip into the night without seeing Reed again.

29 QUINN

THE HOUSE IS QUIET WHEN WE GET BACK FROM THE SHOPS. The back door is open, and Reed, Chase, and Madison are all lounging on pool chairs, laughing about something.

I set my bags on the kitchen island and watch Reed, the gentle way his shoulders move as he laughs, the way his sunglasses are barely even a shade darker than the dark hair on his face and head. Madison seems to be telling a story in sweeping movements of her arms, and Reed is enjoying it.

Sabrina starts to take things out of her bags. We stopped at a small corner market on the way in so she could buy her favorite smoothies. But when she opens the fridge, she pauses. There's a whole row of smoothies that look just like the one in her hand lined up in the door. "Oh," she squeaks. "Lydia must have gotten me more. I didn't even know she left."

"She's looking out for you," I say, only half paying attention to her as I fiddle with the handle on the bag in front of me, the bag from the lingerie store. I don't know why I bought the outfit. I don't even know how I'm going to keep Chase from seeing it. This was a terrible idea.

"Who's looking out for you?"

I jump, startled by the sound of Reed's voice. He's halfway through the living room, making his way to the kitchen. He goes to stand beside Sabrina, reaching into the fridge that she still has open and pulling out a bottle of Fiji water. He keeps his eyes on me as he uncaps it and takes a pull. I watch his Adam's apple bob.

"Lydia stocked up on my smoothies," Sabrina says, knocking me out of my reverie.

"That Lydia's pretty great," he says, leaning back against the counter. He nods in my direction, playing casual so well. "What did you get?"

I pull out my dress for the 4th of July party and step around the island so he can see the entire length of it up against my body. There's a smile in his eyes as he looks at it and then at me.

"It's nice. I'm sure it looks great on you."

I bite my lip, feeling a blush travel up my neck.

"Speaking of things that are going to look good on her," Sabrina says in a sly voice. She reaches into my other bag. I lunge forward to stop her, but she has the piece of lingerie out of my bag before I can stop her. She whips out the lace under-wear I bought, the thing with all the strings and the barely-there thong. She holds it up with a cheeky look on her face that I know she's only wearing because she thinks this is innocent. She doesn't know what's been happening in the basement every night. She doesn't know that I bought that slip of fabric with Reed in mind.

Reed has just enough time to see it, enough time to process that I bought it for him, before the sound of someone's bare feet come slapping into the house. I jump the rest of the way to Sabrina, snatch the garment out of her hand, and shove it under the bar as Chase comes into the room.

The three of us are behind the bar, smiling innocently.

Chase stops in his tracks and scowls. "What the hell are you all doing?"

I CAN'T DO THIS. I DEFINITELY CANNOT DO THIS.

After dinner, Sabrina announced that she wanted to hang out in the hot tub, and Chase immediately jumped at the idea. At first, an evening in the hot tub sounded great. But now that I'm here, pressed shoulder to hip with Chase, I'm not so sure.

Sabrina keeps making weird faces at me, and I know it's because she thinks tonight's the night I'm going to ask Chase to do things to me that he doesn't even know I want. And of course, she's wrong. But she isn't wrong about the fact that I'm going to ask *someone* to do things to me they don't even know I want tonight.

Reed has been pretty talkative, he and Sabrina comparing the many differences between New York, Boston, and Paris. All the while, Chase is pressed up against me, getting drunker by the moment.

"You look fucking hot in that bikini," he says to me now, his voice low.

I resist the urge to shove him away from me. "You can't say things like that to me," I say quietly. Reed and Sabrina don't seem to be paying attention to what's going on over here, but I kind of wish they would. Maybe then Sabrina would make some joke about PDA and Reed would be on my side and insist that Chase not try to proposition me in the hot tub.

Instead, he's kept his eyes steadily off of me, making me second guess everything I was planning for tonight. Now that we've had sex, has he gotten over it? Maybe he just wanted to know what it would be like to fuck me. Now that he knows, he can move on with his life. I thought there would be more, but maybe he doesn't want that.

Chase shrugs at my brush off. "Just because you're not going to be my wife anymore doesn't mean you stop looking hot when you're half-naked."

I ignore him, burrowing deeper down into the steaming water so that not so much of me is in direct contact with him. "Let's just sit here quietly," I whisper, setting my head back against the lip of the hot tub and closing my eyes. It's a relatively cool night, all things considered, and I focus on the way the bubbling water tries to pull me down and then lift me up, over and over again, like ocean waves.

Chase shifts beside me and then I hear the splash of him getting out of the water. I open my eyes and watch him wrap his towel around his waist. "I need another beer," he says to no one in particular and then disappears inside the house.

Sabrina and Reed's conversation trails off. Sabrina relaxes back into the water, eyes closing, and Reed very quietly and very gently crosses the diameter of the large hot tub. He sits beside me, not looking at me, just staring straight ahead.

Low under his breath, barely audible over the bubbling of the water, he says, "Did you buy it for him or for me?"

My breath catches in my throat, heat moving through me like molten lava. I don't have to ask him what he's talking about. I know he means the lingerie. "For you," I say quietly, knowing that Sabrina can't hear us from the other side of the hot tub, not with the jets splashing as loud as they are.

Out of the corner of my eye, I see the way his jaw hardens, like he's holding himself back from saying something.

Something brushes my leg, and I have to suck my lips between my teeth to keep from making a sound. Reed's fingers trail slowly up my leg, curving around the inside of my thigh, so close to the juncture between my legs that I have to grit my teeth.

I keep my eyes firmly glued to Sabrina. If she so much as moves, I'll have to pull away from Reed. I try to control my breathing as his fingers inch higher, brushing the fabric of my bikini bottom.

"I was thinking about taking the jet skis out tomorrow," he says without looking at me.

My mouth falls open, an answer right on the tip of my tongue as he shoves the fabric of my bikini aside and rubs one thick finger against my clit. My mouth snaps closed, and I grit my teeth not to let out a sound.

"Mom said one of them needs a little work, but I'm feeling pretty confident I can get it running. What do you think?"

God, why is he doing this to me? He knows that if I don't answer, it'll be suspicious. But if I try to answer, I have no idea what kind of sound is going to come out of my mouth. Reed presses my clit harder and I manage to squeak out, "Are jet skis and motorcycles similar in design?"

He smiles and turns his face toward me to answer, but from somewhere behind us, Chase says, "Jet skis are way more like 4-wheelers than motorcycles."

I jump, but instead of whipping his hand away from me, Reed moves slowly, shifting only what's under the water, until his hand has left me completely. "Yeah, but some things are the same, no matter what vehicle it is. I can fix most things." He's not even saying this to me. He's saying it to Chase, carrying on a conversation with him as if he wasn't just fingering me.

"Right, Mr. Fix-It," Chase says, climbing back into the hot tub and settling beside me, a beer in one hand. "If you were so good at fixing things, why couldn't you figure out what was wrong with the Mini Coop?"

Reed grimaces. "I did. It needed a new transmission. Some things aren't worth taking the time to fix."

Chase nods in this condescending way, like Reed is lying.

I'm starting to feel feverish. It was bad enough that hot tubs are always a little uncomfortable to me, but between what Reed can do with his hands and the anger that's always simmering beneath the surface toward Chase, I'm starting feel queasy.

"I'm going to head in," I say over the boys' brewing argument. They can argue all they want, but I'm not going sit here while they do it. Who cares what kinds of cars Reed can and can't fix, for God's sake?

"I'll see you in there," Chase says, raising the bottle to his mouth as I try to gracefully step out of the hot tub. Sabrina's eyes are still closed, and with Chase's back to me, I smile at Reed and turn, bending over to snatch my towel off a nearby pool chair, giving Reed a show.

If he wants to drive me crazy when I can't do anything about it, two can play at that game. When I straighten up to wrap my towel around myself, Reed's eyes aren't on me. They're glued to Chase. But where Reed's arm are thrown across the edge of the hot tub, I see that his hand is curled into a tight fist.

While I'm in the kitchen grabbing a bottle of water, I hear the very distinct sound of someone vomiting. My eyes immediately go to the window. Outside, I can see Sabrina, Reed, and Chase, all still sitting in the hot tub, their wet skin shimmering in the moonlight. I close the refrigerator and step toward the hallway that leads to the basement and to Madison's bedroom.

There's the sound again.

I move down the hallway, my wet feet slapping against the hardwood floor. The door to Madison's bedroom is open, and I peek around the corner just in time to see her wash her hands in her ensuite bathroom. She runs her wet hands down on her face and turns off the faucet. When she turns, she sees me in the doorway and sighs.

"I'm sorry. I thought that was closed. Was I too loud?"

My stomach twists. I can't believe she's apologizing to me right now when she's the one who's sick. I think about what Sabrina said, that maybe she's lying about *how* sick she is. Could that be true?

"It's okay," I tell her, wrapping my towel tighter around me. "Do you want me to go get Sabrina? She's just—"

"No, no," she says, sitting down on the edge of her bed. It didn't really process until this moment how much bigger her bedroom is than the one Chase is sleeping in. Three times the size of the one in the basement. It's like a queen's chambers. "It's perfectly normal. It's the chemo. It makes me feel icky. But everything is fine." I start to protest, but she holds up a hand. "Quinn, I promise that everything is fine. I know Sabrina is worried, but I'm going to recover from this."

I nod. I'm not really sure what else to do. When Madison tells you to do something, you do it, so I'm not about to sit here and argue with her. "Can I get you some water or something to eat?"

She waves me off. "That's what I pay Lydia a small fortune for. Come sit with me." She pats the bed beside her.

"Oh, I'm wet."

She waves me off again. "Sheets can be washed. Come here."

I smile and perch beside her on the edge of the bed. It's so tall, so soft and fluffy, that my feet almost don't touch the ground.

Madison turns to me, and I see for the first time the crow's feet on either side of her eyes, the tells that she's exhausted and fighting and maybe a little anxious. She reaches out and tucks a strand of my wet hair behind my ear. "Quinn, you're so beautiful."

A lump forms in my throat. Something about the way she says it reminds me so intensely of my mother, who always used to say that I was the prettiest girl in every room, even when I knew it wasn't true. "Thank you."

"Sometimes I think my son has forgotten how lucky he is."

I fight to keep my face straight. He definitely forgot how lucky he was.

"Quinn, darling, tell me you have everything you could ever want in life."

"What?" I feel like she asked me to spell my name in Swahili.

She takes one of my hands in hers. "I know that what Chase wants is for you to be the woman at home waiting for him. He wants to be the breadwinner and the one to handle everything, but that kind of lifestyle only works if it's what *you* want, too. But you went to school with the intention of having a career, and please forgive me if I'm overstepping my bounds, but I just want to make sure you feel fulfilled with the life you've chosen."

I can't find any words. When Chase and I were together, I was the furthest from being fulfilled with our lifestyle as I could possibly be. Chase wanted to prove to the world that he was all I needed...all while he was getting what he needed somewhere else.

And in this moment, I don't know whether to be honest

with her and tell her that the life Chase wanted for me was not one I wanted for myself, one that I let him force me into because I thought I loved him, or if I should just keep my mouth shut. Nod my head. Keep the peace.

Because in a few days, what will it even matter?

I'll be gone, and Madison will forget I was ever once a part of this family.

"I'm okay where I'm at," I say, because I guess it's true enough. I need a job, yes, but after this week, I'll at least have enough money to make sure the house is taken care of so that the pressure isn't so intense. That will give me the time and energy to job hunt, to go out and network, all that good stuff.

Madison sighs, looking off into the distance. "Life should be more than just 'okay.' I know some people don't have the luxury of going after what they want, but *you do*. Don't let my son take the reins. Make your own choices. Go after what you want."

What I want.

It's so simple for her to say. Madison Lynch knew what she wanted as soon as she turned thirteen. I read the TIME article on her, the one that she has framed on her wall back in New York. She knew the kind of woman she wanted to be and kept her focus until her life looked exactly the way she wanted.

Chase never talked about his dad while we were married, but I know that he and Madison were married and that she divorced him because "his ego got so big that I realized he was trying to sabotage my career. Can you imagine a man with so little dignity?" She spoke about him in the TIME article, but not Reed's dad. I can only imagine a young Madison Lynch, in love with a man but being forced to choose between him and a career.

She chose her career, and can I even blame her for it? I chose the man and look how that turned out.

"What if I don't know what I want?"

I expect Madison to begin another soliloquy, another motivational speech, the likes of which made her famous. But instead, she just says, "What a beautiful thing to have the freedom to figure it out."

30 QUINN

I CAN'T REMEMBER THE LAST TIME I CURLED MY HAIR. IT seems a little odd to be doing it now when I'm hoping that Reed is about to mess it all the way up, but I want to look like someone different, just for tonight. I stare at myself in the mirror. I've put on the lingerie that I'll have to cover and hope I don't accidentally wake Chase. If he sees that I've done my hair, he'll know something is up.

Am I completely fucked for getting ready to spend the night with Reed when his brother, my ex-husband, is on the other side of this bathroom door?

Yes. Probably. Fuck. I don't know.

All I know is that Madison told me to go after what I want. I may not know what I want to do with the rest of my life now that it's just me in it, but I know I want to go downstairs and face my fears and ask Reed to do to me what I've always fantasized about.

I turn off the bathroom light before slowly opening the door. Chase is a pretty heavy sleeper, so I'm not worried necessarily, but I'm not about to lose out on everything now because I decided I no longer needed to be cautious. I watch him as I quickly cross the room, the moon beaming in through the curtainless window, painting him in blue light.

His eyes stay firmly closed as I open the door to the hallway, step out, and close the door behind me. I decided to go the robe route instead of having to struggle my way out of my clothes with the lingerie on under them. If I had a trench coat, I would have worn it. I creep down the hallway wearing not much more than a bathrobe and pray the mightiest prayer I can muster that nobody will come out of their rooms. It's almost two in the morning. Isn't that what the legends call the witching hour?

I get a thrill in my stomach knowing that I don't have to knock when I get to the bedroom in the basement. Reed is expecting me, waiting for me, hoping to finish what we started in the hot tub. I just know it.

I can't even believe we started *anything* in the hot tub. When I close the bedroom door behind me, the nerves threaten to choke me. This could backfire. Everything I feel about Reed — that he's the kind of person who will be okay with what I have planned—could be wrong. Sure, I've known him for a long time, but if I added up all the hours we've spent together in the last five years, could I even get a full day out of it?

"I thought you were never going to come," he says from the bed. He's lying there, the book he was reading a few days ago laying open on his stomach, tragically obstructing my view of his perfect body. What is the equivalent of lingerie for men? Tattoos? A blanket thrown over the pelvis? That look in his eye that's telling me he's waiting for me to disrobe?

"Should I leave?" I have to keep myself from smiling because I know exactly what he's going to say.

"Is that a serious question?" He pushes the book off his chest and lets it fall beside the bed with a clatter. He comes to meet me by the door. "If you leave now," he says, lowering his mouth until his lips are brushing my cheek, "I'll never recover."

I smile up at him, feeling like a teenager flirting for the first time. I can't remember ever being so nervous before. "Sure, you will. You must have a harem back in Boston to comfort you."

His hands reach for the tie of the robe. "Is that what you think? That I have a revolving door of women?" The tie comes undone, the cold air immediately sneaking inside the fabric.

"Don't you?" His fingertips find my stomach, and I shiver.

He doesn't answer, just reaches up to slip the robe off my shoulders, letting it slide to the floor. Somehow, I feel more naked in this lingerie than I did when I was actually naked in front of him last night. He steps back, letting his eyes move down my body, all the places where strings are wrapped around my skin.

He huffs out a breath. "I want to lick every single inch of your body."

I bite my lip. I know that now is the time. If I'm going to do this, ask him for the thing I want, I have to do it now, before I lose my nerve and run right back upstairs. Before I find an excuse to ditch altogether and go back to Boston.

"Will you do something for me?"

His eyes lose a little bit of the heat that was brewing there. Who knows what he thinks I'm going to ask him at a time like this.

I take a deep breath, feeling like I'm about to plunge my head into a bucket of ice water. "Will you be rough with me?"

I watch him process my words, fighting not to look away from him, even though I want to hide. I want to bury my head in the sand and pretend I never did this. Instead, I wait to see what he'll say, how he'll react, what he'll do. After a long moment, he takes a step toward me, forcing my back to hit the door, and I'm trapped.

"Why do you look so scared?" he asks, his voice low, dark. "Are you worried I'll say no?"

So much worse than that. I'm afraid he'll think I'm disgusting. My sex life with Chase was complicated at best. I put myself in a little box so that he wouldn't think there was something wrong with me. And in two nights, Reed has made me want to break out of it. The problem was never that Chase didn't want to do the things I did.

The problem was how he made me feel about wanting to do them in the first place.

"You can," I finally bring myself to say. "Say no, I mean. If that's not what—"

He grabs my wrist in a tight hold. "You want to see what it does to me when you ask me to be rough with you?" He presses my palm to the front of his sweats, and I feel the thick, hard ridge of him behind the fabric. "Tell me what you want," he growls against my mouth. There's no more air left in the room, but I'm trying to find it, sucking in short breaths.

"I want it hard," I say, my lips brushing his. "I want you to bruise me. And—" I cut myself off, some of my courage slithering away.

His hand comes around my throat, pressing just enough to hurt. "Say it."

"I want you to call me names," I choke out.

His hand leaves my throat, and he cages me in against the door with both arms. He lowers his mouth to my ear. "You want to be my little slut, is that what you're saying?"

Something snaps inside me. I attach my mouth to his neck, sucking at the skin there at the same time that I start to shove his pants down. I've never wanted anyone more than I want him right now. If he doesn't get inside me, I'm going to die. Every inch of my skin aches.

He pulls me away from the door, turns me toward the bed,

and bends me over it, my face in the mattress and my ass in the air. I almost have the wherewithal to feel embarrassed, but I'm too turned on. I grip the covers in both hands, waiting patiently for what's to come.

Reed settles his weight on top of me, his bare chest against my mostly bare back. His hips fit right against my ass, the length of him pressing into me. "You better stay quiet," he says in my ear. "I don't need everyone in this house knowing what a filthy slut you are."

I'm trembling. My mouth hangs open as I try to breathe. I feel like I've been tipped into some other universe, some place where this is allowed to happen between Reed and me. There are so many reasons why it shouldn't, but at this moment, I don't care about any of them. I want this so bad that my fingers are prickling, I have goosebumps along my arms, and I'm bucking against the mattress. He licks me, all the way from the base of my spine to the back of my neck.

I have become a wanton animal. I guess that's what happens when you let someone out of their cage.

"Is this what you wanted, Quinn?" Reed shifts, and I realize he's pushing his pants down. The weight of his cock slaps against my back, and I lose all grasp on reality. All I am is blood and bone and need. "Is this what you need?" He pulls aside the G-string and what little lace covers me and then dips two fingers into me. "Already wet as fuck."

I surpassed wet long ago. I am dripping.

He wraps a hand in my hair and uses it to tilt my face to the side. Pressing his forehead to mine, he says in a small voice, "Okay?"

I can't find words, but I nod. I need this more than I need food or air or a beating heart.

He slams into me, and I bite my lip so hard to keep from screaming that I taste blood. I claw at the sheets as he stands at the edge of the bed, my hips in his hands, and drills into me mercilessly.

Yes. This is what I wanted. This is what I couldn't ask Chase for. This is what I have never imagined I would get to have. It's not something I could bring myself to ask a stranger for. But with Reed...

He uses the hand wrapped in my hair to yank my head back so far that I'm staring at the ceiling as he pounds into me. I reach between my legs, desperate for orgasm, but Reed shoves my hand away, pinning it behind my back.

"Not yet," he says, letting go of my hair, and then somehow manages to pick up speed. I bury my face in the covers, terrified that I'm going to let out wild animal sounds and someone will come running. At this point, do I care? Let Chase see what Reed does to me. Let him see how Reed makes me feel. How free I am with him.

I've reached a point of pleasure that I didn't know existed, where I'm dangling from the edge but can't go over. My nerves are screaming at me, my whole body at the point of going numb from sensory overload. I'm silent now, nothing coming out of me, not even gasps. All I can do is hold my breath and feel, feel him moving in and out of me, feel his hand wrapping around my hair again. Feel the power of him over and behind me.

"You like to be fucked, don't you?" Reed says. He's pulled my head so far back that he can speak directly into my ear. The pain feels incredible, like a salve to a wound. "All that gentleness I showed you, and you wanted to be fucked like a whore."

Everything inside me squeezes tight, and I know all he would have to do is swipe one finger over my clit, and I would be gone. "Please," I finally find the breath to whisper.

"Please? Please, what? Ask me nicely."

I sob, something like joy and pleasure and defeat. He has complete control over me. "Please, make me come."

"You think you can be quiet?"

I try to nod, but his hold on my hair is too tight. "Yes."

"You sure?"

I want to smile at the way that he slips just a little bit back into the Reed I've aways known. You sure you don't want another piece of pie? You sure you don't want the best seat in the house? You sure you can spend a week pretending to be someone you're not?

The answer to that last one is yes. I can pretend to be something I'm not because I get to be *this* as soon as everyone goes to bed.

"Yes," I gasp out. "I'll be quiet. I promise."

Out of the corner of my eye, I see him smile. He lets go of my arms, freeing me to fall forward onto the bed, and then he reaches between my legs, puts his fingers right over my clit, and rubs in a tight circle.

The whole universe dissolves. I put both hands over my mouth and slam my face into the mattress to keep from screaming. The world goes black and then white and then all that's left is my limbs shaking so hard it's like I have hypothermia.

When my ears stop ringing, and I'm able to focus again, it's to find Reed on the bed beside me, gasping for air like he just ran a marathon. His dick is still mostly hard, wet from me and laying heavy against his belly. He looks up at me where I've pushed up onto my hands and knees.

And then I start crying.

It all wells up inside me, like holding a balloon closed with your fingers and then letting all the air out at once. I collapse onto the bed, crying into my hands.

"Hey," Reed's voice comes from beside me. The bed shifts, and he's pulling my hands away from my face so that I have to look at him. "Hey, did I hurt you? Did I go too far?"

I shake my head, but I can't speak yet, my throat

constricted. He pulls me onto his chest, and I turn my wet face into it, making his skin as wet as mine.

When I can finally get a breath of fresh air, I say, "No. It was so good. It was so, so good. I'm sorry. I'm being so stupid."

He puts a finger under my chin and lifts it so that I have to look at him. He doesn't ask why I'm crying, but I can see the question there in his eyes. If he didn't hurt me, then why am I freaking out?

"I never could do this with Chase. What we just had was..." *More intimate*, I think, but I can't bring myself to say it. "I always knew this is what I wanted but I didn't feel like I could ask. I always thought that if I asked, he would laugh at me. Or think I was disgusting."

"You're not disgusting."

"You don't think I'm fucked up?"

His eyebrow furrows, his mouth pulling into a line. "Of course not. I'll give you whatever you want. Whatever you need."

Something about the way he says it doesn't feel comforting. Like he would give it to me even if he didn't want to. That's not what I want. I want to experience this with someone who wants to experience it with me. Asking him this is almost as hard as asking for the act in the first place. "Did you like it?"

His mouth pulls slowly into a smile. "Fuck, yes. I like you being my little fuck toy."

My whole body convulses, something compulsive and uncontrollable.

He grins fully at me. "Is that your way of telling me you want some more?"

31 REED

I'VE JUST BARELY SHOT MYSELF INSIDE QUINN A SECOND time before she passes out. I sit beside her on the bed, untangling what's left of that little scrap of lingerie from around her ankle. It didn't survive the second round.

I toss the thing to the floor and watch her sleep. She's a mess, her hair tangled around her shoulders and her skin slick with sweat. The most beautiful thing I've ever seen.

When she walked in here and told me to be rough with her, to call her names, I thought I was dreaming. These kinds of things only happen to me in my fantasies. And here I am, one step closer to everything I've ever wanted. It's not that I've always dreamed of throwing Quinn down on a bed and pulling her hair while I fucked her. I mean, sure, a good animalistic marathon fuck is always a good image. But it's not something I ever saw myself needing from her.

But knowing that's what she wants... That she never felt like she could tell Chase about it... That she trusted me enough to tell me... This can't be reality.

My phone beeps with an email, right on time. I go out into the kitchen in my sweats and shut the door quietly behind me. When you're doing business with a guy that works the night shift at a restaurant, it means business at all hours.

I pull up the email my guy sent me just as he video calls. I glance at the bedroom door. I don't want to wake Quinn, so I head up the stairs and sit in the main living room with nothing but the light of the moon coming through the back windows.

When I answer, Jack is walking down the street in the dark. "Hey, man," he says, looking beyond the phone for a second and then concentrating again. "I found a place."

"I see that." I've pulled up the listing for a storefront that he sent me. "I think it looks great. Where's it at?"

"Freedom and Hanover. On the opposite block from that café with the really good arugula salad."

This is how we communicate, in menu items. "I like that corner. It's busy though. Should we go for something quieter?"

On the screen, Jack blinks at me. "Reed, you're really throwing me for a loop here. First you want a restaurant downtown, someplace so upscale that you're in the running for a Michelin star, and now you want, what, a bakery in the suburbs?"

I think about what Quinn told me, that I should give people a chance to try my food that aren't rich. It makes sense. I know that Quinn didn't come from money. And now she's back to not having any money. She can't respect a lifestyle that can disappear so quickly. And she's right. What about the people who can't pay fifty dollars for a plate of calamari the width of a tennis ball?

"I just think it's time to try something new," I tell Jack. "I think it's worth looking into every avenue. Isn't that what it means to be good at business?"

His jaw tightens and he levels me with an exasperated look.

"If you want to be good at business, open a restaurant that will pay your bills."

"A dessert house in Boston will pay the bills." An idea occurs to me and my eyes slide back down the hallway, to the stairs that lead down to Quinn. "And actually, maybe it wouldn't hurt to look at places outside of Boston. What about Chicago? Or New York?"

If I asked Quinn to leave Boston with me, would she? Hell, if I asked her to leave this lake house with me, would she? How attached is she to her life in Boston? What if I could sweep her away to someplace new, someplace that doesn't have Chase written all over every surface? Am I insane for even considering it?

All I know is that the life I've always wanted is within my grasp. If I could have a place to make desserts and Quinn on my arm, I would never ask God for anything else ever again. There's no improving on perfection.

"Chicago?" Jack screeches, and I quickly turn down the volume on my phone. "New York? Are you kidding? You are not leaving Boston."

I shrug. "Maybe it's time for a new life."

Jack sighs. "Alright. I'll look at other places, but New York is going to be expensive. Might as well check out Seattle while we're at it." He rolls his eyes. "I'll get back to you in a few days. But hey," he says, his voice serious now, "the investors aren't going to be happy with the building downgrade, especially if you're thinking of leaving Boston."

That, I did think about. I didn't come to the lake house for the money, like I told Quinn. The money for a new place was basically already in the bag with all the investors I contacted. But if they start to pull out, my mother's money could definitely be useful, even if a small bakery outside of the city would cost me far less than a restaurant.

"I've got this figured out," I tell him, feeling rather smug. I hang up with him and go back downstairs. I stand in the doorway of the bedroom and watch Quinn sleep, naked except for the blanket pulled up around her body.

We were meant to be. I just need her to remember.

32 REED

5 YEARS AGO

I GLANCE OVER THE DRESSED-UP HEADS OF ALL THE partygoers to make sure that Quinn is still right where I left her. She's watching me, leaning up against the wall in her little skeleton costume.

She's cute as shit.

I know she's nervous about flirting with a guy at a party—as she should be—so when I grab a cup, I meet her eye and turn it over to shake it out. *I promise I'm not slipping you anything,* I want to say, but it's my first instinct to make it a joke. I don't even know why. I want her to trust me. I would never hurt this girl—or any girl—but I know she doesn't know that. I show her my hands, knowing full well that she's putting a lot of faith in me. She can't see everything I'm doing from way over there. She has to trust I wouldn't take advantage.

When she smiles, my stomach goes all bubbly. She has a beautiful smile, and it's making me nervous.

My hands shake as I pour her a drink. I can't remember the last time a girl made me nervous. As shitty as it sounds, I figured out pretty young that I have something girls want. I get that I look good by most people's standards. "Classically handsome," my mother always says. I've never had to fight to get a girl to kiss me or go on a date with me or sleep with me. College has pretty much offered me a smorgasbord.

But that's definitely done something to my head, the knowledge that if one girl doesn't want me, I can just go for another. And it's never really bothered me. I've always liked the girls I've gone for, and I might have even been in love with a girl I dated in high school, the girl I lost my virginity to.

But it's been a while since I worried so much about whether or not a girl *liked* me. Not just wanted me. I know tons of girls at this party who would let me take them back to my room, but it would just be for a night, and most of them wouldn't care if I was a good guy or a bad guy, if I was funny or kind or any of that. Just that I look good and could make a girl come.

Which I do and I can.

"Hey, Reed." I'm not sure when Mariana approached, her face painted like a butterfly. I smile at her because Mariana is nice and because she loaned me her Econ notes when I had to miss class because I had the flu.

"Hey, Mariana. Love the face paint."

"Thanks. I was going to come as a boring, straight white guy, but then I heard you'd already planned your costume, and I didn't want to step on any toes."

I laugh, throwing my head back. Mariana has always been funny and fully not interested in my shit. I open my mouth to answer, but just then, someone else approaches on my other side.

"Reed, pour me a drink?"

"Cass, hey." I bend down to hug Cassie, who I slept with once last year and who has since become a good friend. She's dressed like a pirate, the costume hugging her curves in a way that tells me she's not planning on leaving this party alone. "Doing okay?"

"Sure. Hey, do you know that guy who sits in front of me in Humanities?"

I screw off the top of a bottle of vodka, knowing that screwdrivers are Cassie's thing. "I think his name is Mark?"

She leans against the counter and grins up at me. "Think you could put in a good word for me?"

I chuckle. "Oh, I see. You've moved on to greener pastures. What is he, like, six-three?"

"Six-four," Mariana whispers from my other side.

They start talking about how good they've heard Mark is in bed, and I snatch up my two cups, ready to return to that pretty girl in the hall that's turned my skin inside out.

"If you'll excuse me, ladies," I say to them and then duck out from between them. Mariana immediately moves closer to Cassie, and I turn to make my way through the shifting bodies of partygoers.

But when I catch sight of the hallway, it's empty.

Panic bursts through my stomach. Where did she go? Where's Quinn? Did she get tired of waiting for me and take off? Did one of her friends have some kind of emergency, and she had to leave to take care of it?

While I'm still standing there, in the center of a mass of writhing bodies, Quinn suddenly reappears. Only she's not wearing her skeleton costume anymore. She's in shorts and a tank top, so much of her skin showing that my brain stutters to a halt.

And then I process the rest of the scene. Chase. My brother. The one who refused to come to this party because he didn't want to be hungover for an exam he has tomorrow. He's talking to Quinn. And he's...holding her skeleton outfit. He says something to her that makes her laugh, and then they walk away...in the direction of Chase's room.

I watch them go, still holding Quinn's drink in one hand and mine in the other, because what else am I supposed to do? The hallway empties, and I can't seem to stop staring at the spot against the wall where we stood talking, where she made me laugh and forget how much being at this party has made me feel numb, how much I've been trying to keep my head above water these last few months, between trying to finish school and figure out how to do something with my life that will make me worthy of my last name.

For a few minutes, she made me feel good. She made me feel like I was worth more than my dick or my good grades or all the plans I have for a restaurant taped to my wall.

But I guess that's over.

33 REED

THE SUN SEEMS BRIGHTER TODAY. WE'RE ALL LOUNGING IN the living room, and I swear, Quinn is glowing. She's wearing this tiny pair of shorts that are driving me crazy and reading the book I brought with me, a sci-fi novel that I stuck in my bag last minute before heading here. My bookmark is still sticking out of it at the halfway point, her hands wrapped around the spine, and even though it wasn't a book I was particularly loving, I know I'll never get rid of it now. She looks like a woman in a Victorian painting...if women in Victorian paintings wore shorts so short you could see the curve of their asses. She's turned sideways on the couch, her bare legs stretching out toward me but not quite reaching.

"I was thinking I might go for a hike today," Sabrina says in an absent-minded way. She turns her face away from the window, towards us. "It's a really beautiful day, and I'm starting to feel a little antsy."

Beside her on the couch, Mom chuckles. "I swear. People your age can't sit still, can they?"

Sabrina rolls her eyes. "Isn't that a good thing? I'm a hard worker; I like to keep busy."

Mom brushes a strand of Sabrina's hair behind her ear. If I didn't know perfectly well that my mother doesn't pick favorites, I would think she likes Sabrina better than me and my brother. But I know it's not true. "It's a good thing to have a work ethic, but if you don't slow down every once in a while, you're going to wreck your health."

Sabrina sighs dramatically. "I'm pretty sure the experts would agree that a hike in the fresh air could only *improve* my health."

As she says this, Chase comes into the room and plops down on the couch between Quinn and me. Quinn scrambles to get her legs out of the way in time and then glowers at Chase. I don't think anyone but me notices.

Sabrina stands, stretching out her long limbs. She's the tallest of the three of us, with arms and legs that go on for days. "Anybody want to join me?"

Chase stretches his arm out along the back of the couch, his fingers dangling into Quinn's space. They brush the curve of her shoulder, and she flinches, almost imperceptible. I grind my teeth together. I get it; he wants to make sure everyone thinks they're still a couple, but how is putting his hands on her when virtually nobody is going to notice helpful in any way?

"Join you where?" he asks, tilting his head back to look up at our sister.

"Hike," she responds, already halfway out of the room. "I'll wait for anyone who wants to come, but I want to go before it gets too hot."

"That seems really nice," Mom says, pushing up off the couch. "Anyone else want to come? Chase?"

I'm not sure why she singles him out, but he looks at her

with his eyebrows raised. "Huh? Me? Nah. I actually need to go into town to do a little bit of work. Have some phone calls to make. You guys have fun."

Quinn watches him go, and I can't quite make out her expression. Does she *want* him to come with us? I would have thought having him gone for the afternoon would be a good thing.

Mom shrugs and then smiles at both of us. "You two coming?"

I SHOULD HAVE STAYED BACK AT THE LAKE HOUSE. WITH Quinn walking up the hiking trail in front of me in a pair of athletic shorts that's tight against the shape of her ass, I'm having a really hard time convincing my dick not to stand up and salute.

"You seem awfully distracted today," my mom says, walking beside me. I can see the house past her shoulder, down the slope that leads to the lake. At first, I think she's caught me salivating over Quinn's ass, but then she says, "Is it because you had to leave the restaurant for the week? I know how nervous that makes you."

She's right. It did used to make me nervous to leave the restaurant. That's because it always felt like if I wasn't there to chase everyone around and make sure they were doing what they were supposed to that things would start to fall apart. And maybe my fears weren't so unwarranted, considering I turned my back for a second and my partner tanked the entire thing.

But if I had kept any closer of an eye on the place, I would have had to live in the backroom.

"I'm actually doing okay," I tell her, guilt gnawing at me for lying to her. But I don't think anyone understands how hard it is to live in the shadow of Madison Lynch. If she finds out that I let someone else put the restaurant under their name, that I gave someone else control over something that I should have been watching like a hawk, I'm afraid she'll tell me I'm a terrible businessman. And she would probably be right. Yes, I have a business degree, but I'm a pastry chef first and a businessperson second. An overly-trustful, idiotic pushover third.

As I think this, Quinn glances over her shoulder at me, and my stomach dips.

She doesn't think I'm an idiot. She believes in me. And that knowledge is enough to keep me going.

In the break of our conversation, I hear Sabrina up ahead ask Quinn, "How did he like the outfit?"

Oh, fuck. This is definitely not going to help me not pop a boner. I have to avoid imagining Quinn in that little string and lace thing she wore for me last night—*bought* for me—and focus again on my mom, who looks like she might be getting a little winded.

"I've been keeping up with things," she says. "I saw that you got a few big celebrities in there a few months ago. That's certainly good for business."

I trip over my own Nikes. Mom is "keeping up" with Aeronaut? That means it's just a matter of time before she finds out that it no longer exists. It's a good thing she doesn't believe in wi-fi at the lake house. By the time this trip is over and she gets back home, I'll have a new place secured, and it won't matter if she knows about the restaurant closing because there will be a new one set to open. I have to time this right, but I know that Jack is going to find me something today, if he hasn't already. He's the best. That's why I called him to begin with.

By the time this week is over, I'll have a space to start fresh.

My eyes travel up to Quinn again. Hopefully, a space that she wants to share with me.

"Yeah," I tell Mom. "We've made a lot of big changes. Once I get back, I think we'll have a lot of things sorted that we've been meaning to take care of." I don't even have to lie. All of that is true. "You'll have to come out when everything is done." Another not-lie. When I have the new place open, the first thing I'll want to do is have my mom there. And Quinn. The two people whose opinions I care about the most.

Quinn's voice carries back to us on the wind as we head up a steep pass. "...never done that before. What are your favorite places in the city?"

I bite back a smile, even as worry settles in my stomach. When this is all over, and I ask Quinn to be with me when we leave here, what will Sabrina think? What will our mom think? Is it too much for me to hope that maybe life can go on like it always has, but with Quinn being mine?

Jesus, just thinking about it like that, I know there's no way it's going to be that easy. Maybe Quinn and I will have to keep it a secret for a little while. Maybe we'll have to figure out how our life is going to work together before we can tell anyone else. I don't want to lose my family, but I know I can't lose Quinn either. If they can't handle the fact that I want Quinn, that I've always wanted Quinn, then maybe they aren't the people I always thought they were.

Beside me, Mom starts to huff a little.

I turn to her quickly, reaching out to pull her to a stop. "Hey, are you okay?" Her face is red and sweaty, her breath blowing out of her in billows.

"I'm okay," she says. "I just haven't done a lot of exercising these last few months. This might have been a little bit more than I could handle."

Holding onto her arms, I lead her over to a big rock beside the path and lower her down onto it.

"Mom?" Sabrina rushes over, worry etched on her face. "Are you okay?"

Mom waves her off, bending over her knees to catch her breath.

Quinn stands off behind us, watching with her hands clutched to her chest.

"She's going to be fine," I tell her, looking around Sabrina, who's producing a bottle of water from a very small backpack that she's unslung from her shoulders. "She just overdid it."

Quinn doesn't say anything, but her sad, worried eyes meet mine. I try to smile. I don't want her to worry. I know my mother. She's strong and resilient. Everything she's going through right now with the chemo and the treatments and the doctors, it's all just a passing thing. In a few years, we'll look back on this and be proud that she made it through.

"I'm going to take her back," Sabrina says, helping my mother to her feet.

"We'll come with you," I say, but Sabrina puts up a hand to stop me.

"No way. You guys have been just as cooped up in that house as I have. Enjoy the hiking trails. We'll see you back for lunch."

I don't argue with her. As much as I wish it was under different circumstances, I'm excited at the idea of getting to be alone with Quinn. Really alone. And in a place that means so much to me.

I move out of the way to let Sabrina and our mom pass, moving a lot slower back down the hill than we did climbing it. As soon as they're out of sight, I step over to Quinn.

"Is she okay?" Quinn asks, her voice shaky.

"She's fine," I tell her again, taking her by the shoulders and turning her back in the direction of the trail. "I did some research on the chemo stuff after she told us about it the other night." I step back onto the trail, comforted by the sound of the dirt under my feet. Down below, the lake shimmers under the sun, and the lake house is just barely visible beyond the trees. "The exercise is good for her. It keeps her from having anxiety and from feeling lethargic. She was fine until that last hill. It's a steep one."

She nods and steps onto the trail beside me. She doesn't argue when I keep walking up instead of heading back down. "That all sounds reasonable in theory, but it's so hard to convince your brain of all that when you see someone gasping for air and know they're sick."

Glancing back over my shoulder to make sure there's no way anybody would be able to see us from the lake house—even though the only person left there is Lydia—I reach down and take Quinn's hand. It feels like a miracle, being allowed to touch her whenever I please.

She looks down at our clasped hands and then turns her face away, but I can see the blush traveling along the curves of her ears. I fucked her to within an inch of her life last night, but it's the handholding that makes her blush.

"Did Chase ever tell you about Sabrina being pre-mature?"

Her face turns sharply toward mine. "No. He's never really talked about any of you as babies."

I nod. I figured as much. I can't really imagine Chase taking the time to tell her about me and Sabrina. A man who's been cheating on his wife since the beginning of their relationship is a man who doesn't share any true intimacy with the woman he's married to. On one hand, I'm sad that Quinn has lived with that kind of distance for so long. On the other, I'm glad that's all she's known because when I worship her, when I give her the world, when I share every single part of myself with her, she'll know that's how it's supposed to be.

"All three of us were complicated for our mom," I tell Quinn, guiding her up the slope. We're almost to the very top. "But Sabrina was the hardest. Mom developed this pregnancy complication. I was young, so I don't remember what it was exactly, and Mom isn't one to talk about the past. At least, not the bad stuff. She had to have a c-section, and she almost died."

Quinn's feet skitter, and she almost trips. I tighten my hold on her, keeping her from falling. "Oh, my God. I had no idea."

I smile, holding her hand a little tighter. "That's because my mother looks at something like that as a speck in her past. Almost dying is like a normal Tuesday for her. Sabrina came out healthy and strong, and that's all she cared about. She took her time recovering and then she went back to work because that's who she is. The Unstoppable Madison Lynch."

Quinn grins. "She's amazing."

We crest the top of the hill, and I pull her to a stop. "You're amazing," I tell her, and her face falls. God, I hate that.

"I've never done anything like your mom has. I went to college, abandoned my dreams of the future to get married and be what my husband wanted me to be, and now I'm on the verge of homelessness and I'm lying to the kindest person in the world to get her money."

I sigh. "Come on, it's not that simple, and you know it. You left your home and everything you knew to go away to college. You made sacrifices for a marriage and a man that you trusted and believed in. You came here, not to deceive someone, but to do what you have to in order to take care of yourself. You're resourceful and strong. And you're unstoppable, too."

She turns her face up to me, and it's like a sock to the stomach. Being here, in the place I love, with a woman I love, with things finally falling into place, is more than I could have ever imagined. Her eyes are shining, looking up at me, and I almost blurt it out right then and there. That I love her. That I've loved her for five years. That she owns every part of who I am.

She looks over my shoulder, checking for something, and then she fists her hand into my t-shirt and drags me off the trail and into the woods. I follow her with a smile until she stops, grabs me by both shoulders, and shoves me up against a tree.

Before I have a chance to say a word, she's on her knees in front of me, tugging my shorts down to my knees. My dick pops out, and she immediately wraps her hand around it, running her tongue up the underside.

"Jesus," I hiss, my vision going blurry. How can she be this perfect? How can I want her this much?

She smiles up at me, devious little thing. "Use me," she says. "Fuck my mouth."

I'm shaking so hard I'm afraid I'll shake apart. She wants me to be rough with her. And fuck if I don't want it, too. But I also want to keep her here just like this, in this place where she can be whoever and whatever she wants to be. I want this forever.

"Be a good little slut and open your mouth."

Her eyes immediately lose some of their focus. She makes a tight noise in the back of her throat and her mouth falls open. I step forward, no longer held up by the massive tree trunk, and shove into her mouth. Her lips stretch around me, and I feel like I might die.

"This okay?" I ask, pushing a little further, until she gags and her hands come up to grab hold of my hips, not pushing me away but trying to find leverage.

She gives a little tip of her chin, and I pull back long enough to let her catch her breath before plunging in again. I wrap my hand in her hair and rock into her. She never takes her eyes off me, and I watch her for any signs that I'm going too hard or too deep.

"You're taking it so well," I say, my fingers trailing down her cheek. I know she wants me to be rough, but I'm also so in love with her, it feels like it'll kill me, and that makes me want to praise her and adore her.

When I hold her head against me and feel her gag around me again, I almost lose it. I pull back, falling back against the tree and letting my cock slip from the wet paradise of her mouth.

"I'm not going to last," I gasp. I'm ready to burst, and it's been all of two minutes.

"Don't stop," she says, scooting forward on her knees and swallowing me down again, taking me all the way to the back of her throat.

I lose my grasp on reality. I don't have time to ask her if it's okay that I come in her mouth before my balls are tightening up and I'm spilling down her throat. "Swallow every drop like a good little whore," I manage to grit out.

Her eyes fall closed, and her throat works, swallowing me down. When she finally lets me slide free, I sigh. My whole body is tingling, my nerves all overworked. Over the years, I've imagined having Quinn a million different ways, some of it rough and some of it slow and tender. I want it all with her. But if this is what she wants to do, I'm good with that.

She smiles up at me, running her hands up and down my hips. The feel of it is comforting. Her eyes trace my body, my softening cock, the tattoos on my skin. When she finds the tattoo on my hipbone, my stomach tenses.

She runs her fingertip over it. "I'd never seen this one before this week," she says, and I want to smile because the reason she's never seen it is because it dips below my waistband, most of it covered by clothing. But she knows the rest of them. She's been looking at them all week, every time I take my shirt off. I love that she can't keep her eyes off me.

But now she has her hands on my hip tattoo, a tattoo she probably couldn't make out in the shadowed light we've been fucking in for the last two days. It's in front of her now, at eye level. She traces the lines of the skeleton with her index finger gently enough to almost tickle.

I wait for her to ask. I wait for her to see right through me. I wait for her to understand.

She's quiet as she looks at it, and then, without a word, she puts her hand out and lets me help her to her feet. I pull up my shorts and watch her fix her hair. As soon as she's standing in front of me, I bend down and kiss her. This is the way I imagined our first kiss happening. Somewhere quiet, somewhere we didn't have to hurry or hide. Just her and me, kissing softly at first and then deeper, our mouths opening and our tongues finding each other.

She wraps her arms around me, and I haul her against my body, wanting to get lost in her. She feels perfect in my arms. She feels *right*. She fits me like a puzzle piece. She puts me back together.

We pull apart, gasping into each other's mouths. She puts a finger against my chin in a strangely sweet gesture. "I wish we could make everything else go away," she says, and my heart squeezes.

I know that, for her, this has just been about sex. About coping with this terrible week. About finding herself again after her failed marriage. But maybe, just maybe, it's starting to be about more.

"How many times do you think you've hiked this trail?" Quinn asks me as we walk back down toward the lake house. I feel sick to my stomach at the idea of going back, of having to once again share Quinn with everyone else, of having to once again sneak around and pretend not to be in love with her.

"I've probably hiked it at least twice a year since I was nine or so."

"Until you stopped coming." Her words cut through, slicing guilt into me. When I don't say anything, she tips her chin toward me, curiosity in her eyes.

I'm not ready to tell her the truth. I'm not ready to tell her that I stopped coming to the lake house the summer after she and Chase started seeing each other. The year she started coming out every summer. I couldn't take it. Seeing her and Chase together at family dinners and occasional get-togethers was one thing. We even went on a double date once, an activity that we thankfully never attempted to duplicate. But the idea of spending the week with the two of them was a different thing entirely. I didn't want to have to know they were sharing a bed, watch them in the pool together and at mealtimes. The thought was unbearable.

"Life just got busy," I tell Quinn now, feeling guilty for lying to her. She's opened up to me so completely over the last few days, but I still have all of my secrets. All the things she's not ready to know yet.

When we round the last corner and step back onto the dirt road that leads back to the lake house, Quinn gives a little sigh. "It's been nice not having to pretend," she says quietly as we approach the door. "But here we go again."

I know exactly how she feels.

I hold the door open for her, feeling the relief of the cold air conditioning as soon as I step inside. Sabrina and Mom are in the living room, their voices loud as they speak over each other.

And that's when I realize that it's not just the two of them standing in the center of the sunken living room. There's someone else here. And it's not Chase.

My eyes meet Quinn's. She's figured it out, too, her face falling into a confused scowl.

Because my ex-girlfriend, Amina, is standing in my living room.

"Amina," I say, my voice coming out a croak.

34 REED

5 YEARS AGO

I SIT IN THE MIDDLE OF MY MOM'S LIVING ROOM IN NEW York and watch Quinn on the balcony. She's been out there for twenty minutes, and I've been in here on the couch, trying to decide whether or not to go out there to talk to her. I don't know if she wants to be alone.

I think back to Halloween, just a month ago, when we met. The night I let her think I forgot about. She wanted to be alone then, too, hiding in the hallway like she could disappear. Is that what she wants to do now? Disappear?

"What are you doing?" I turn at the sound of Sabrina's voice. I thought everyone was asleep—well, everyone but Quinn—but she's wide awake, wearing pajamas and clutching her phone in her hand like she just got done making a call. She doesn't even hesitate before coming to sit with me. I must seem like a serial killer or something, sitting in the dark, watching my brother's new girlfriend through a window.

As soon as she's settled, I see her eyes go to the balcony, to Quinn out there in her own pajamas, her hair blowing in the wind. Her eyes slide back to me. "What are you doing?" she asks again, but this time, her tone is different. Suspicious. Confused.

I immediately turn away from the balcony. "Nothing. I just couldn't sleep."

I can tell she doesn't believe me. I've been too obvious. I have to get better at hiding my feelings from her. I lower my head, hoping maybe the shadows will do me some favors.

"She's pretty," Sabrina says.

"Stop," I growl.

"What?" she says, pretending to be innocent. "She is. And she seems to be very nice. Way too nice for the likes of Chase, that's for sure."

I take a deep, steadying breath. "Sabrina. Please stop trying to cause trouble."

I hear the squeak of the leather couch as she stands. And then she drops down on the couch beside me, a whole seat closer, tucking her feet up under her legs. "I'm not trying to start anything," she says. "I'm just saying that it's okay if you have a tiny little crush on Chase's girlfriend. That's entirely normal. You like pretty girls and you like nice girls and just girls in general, so why wouldn't you like her?" She shrugs like it's no big deal, and I'm certainly not going to try to change her mind.

But it's more than that. Yeah, she's pretty, and she's nice.

But what I'm not going to tell Sabrina is that that girl on the balcony made me feel something on Halloween. She made me feel like a real person, something that not a lot of people we go to Suffolk with know how to make someone feel. It was like I'd been walking around, being a mirror for everyone my whole life, and in that hallway, she saw straight through the mirror to the other side. To me.

She didn't just see some kid whose famous mother got him into college. A kid who's never been quite sure how to be the person everyone sees him as. The oldest kid, the quiet kid, the kid that always gets lost in the crowd. The one everyone is always waiting on to fail. Floating around being unextraordinary and disappointing.

She didn't make me feel that way, not even here, with my whole family in the room. She looks at me like I'm something interesting, a treasure that she uncovered and refuses to share with anyone else. Because that's what it feels like. Whatever version of me she found on Halloween, that version of me belongs to her and only her.

So to hear Sabrina call it a crush is insulting at best.

That girl out there? I want her to be mine.

"You should go to bed," I tell her, my eyes traveling back to the balcony. "You've got a big day tomorrow."

I don't know if this is true, but it's a fair assumption. Sabrina has ten times the social life that I do, now that she's modeling in her free time. Seventeen and already following in the Lynch footsteps better than I ever will.

"Okay," she says, her voice small. "But try not to hit on Chase's girlfriend, okay? I don't think he would like it very much." She laughs, like it's a joke. I wish it was a joke. I wish that my life hadn't become something I'm not interested in being a part of over the course of one Thanksgiving meal.

Once Sabrina is gone, I get up and move to the balcony doors. She's still out there, probably freezing her ass off, watching the night pass by, no clue that I'm even here.

I snatch the blanket off the back of the couch and push open the door. "You're going to freeze," I tell her when she gasps and spins around. I shake out the blanket and offer it to her. I want to put it around her shoulders, but if I accidentally brush any of her skin, it might destroy me.

She wraps herself tight but doesn't turn back to the view, the city lights bright beneath us. "You have a lovely family," she says.

I step up beside her and lean against the glass that separates us from thin air. "I'm sure your family is lovely, too."

Her smile falls, her face losing all its color. She looks down at her feet, white in the cold. "My family hasn't been a family for a long time. The second every one of my siblings turned eighteen, they took off. I was the last one standing because I'm the youngest. Home has always felt more like summer camp, where everyone comes and goes." She sighs and covers her face with her hands. "I don't know why I just told you all that."

I reach out and pull one of her hands away, hold her wrist in a gentle grip. She looks up at me, and I think of that girl on Halloween. I was going to kiss her that night when I got back with the drinks. I was going to ask her for her number and walk her to class and ask her out on a date. And Chase did it all first.

Her big eyes stare up at me, until she finally blushes and takes her hand back. "Thanksgiving was never this fun back in Minnesota. This was my first time having cranberry pie."

"Really?" I'm trying to act normal, like I can't taste my pulse in my throat. Like she doesn't look like a dream with the wind blowing through her hair.

"Really. It was delicious. I can't wait to come to your restaurant. If all of your desserts are as heavenly as that pie, you'll be famous within the month." She smiles, her apple cheeks becoming more prominent.

But when I can finally bring myself to look away from her, her words sink into me. I stick my hands in my pockets and lean against the partition. "You really think I can do it?"

She gets a wrinkle between her eyes, her confusion adorable. "You're Madison Lynch's son. You can do anything."

Disappointment settles in my chest. She didn't even know who Mom was a month ago. Maybe even twenty-four hours ago. I don't want her to think I can do it because I'm Madison Lynch's son. That means she thinks I'm going to go to Mom and ask her to buy me a restaurant. Isn't that what super rich kids do? Mom has never been one to hand us money. She gives us what we need and then a little on top to have fun with. She pays for school and there's the stupid thing she's starting to do where she pays us to spend the summer at the lake with her, but it's not like I can ask her for an Aston Martin and expect one to pull up at the curb.

I want her to think I can do it because of who *I* am. A guy who gets good grades and never spends any of the money his mom gives him and never asks for anything. I work a part-time job on the weekends and saved up every penny I made for the bike I'm riding. I want her to believe in *me*, not in my mother's money.

"Anyway," I say, heading back for the door. "I should probably get to bed. Chase, uh, is probably looking for you."

She looks at me without expression. Does she know how jealous I am of him? Does she know how much I wish it was me sharing a bed with her?

She smiles. "Goodnight, Reed."

There's a dagger somewhere in the vicinity of my gut. "Goodnight, Quinn."

"Wʜᴀᴛ ᴛʜᴇ ʜᴇʟʟ ᴡᴇʀᴇ ʏᴏᴜ ᴛʜɪɴᴋɪɴɢ, ʙʀɪɴɢɪɴɢ ʜᴇʀ here?" I try to keep my voice low because even with a closed door and a long hallway between us and everyone else, I don't want them to hear. Not because I'm worried I might hurt Amina's feelings, but because I'm worried about hurting Quinn's.

Mom crosses her arms and levels me with that look of hers. "You don't need to speak to me that way."

I clamp my lips together and take a deep breath. "I think I have every right to be angry with you right now. You invited my ex to come and stay with us."

She shrugs. "The two of you ended on good terms. I didn't think it would be a problem."

I shove my hands into my hair and turn away from her so she doesn't see me lose my shit. I'm not a hot head. I don't get this angry at people, especially not at my mom, but she has to be kidding. That woman out there—Amina—is someone I dated my senior year at Suffolk. Someone who was around for a while, all things considered.

But it ended when I realized I was never going to feel about anyone the way I felt about Quinn. It wasn't so bad at first with Amina. I started seeing her not long after that Thanksgiving when Quinn showed up for the first time, and I figured a relationship would help me forget her.

Except Quinn kept coming around. She kept dating Chase long after I had graduated and Amina had decided that she wanted to live in New York while I wanted to stay in Boston. And seeing as how my feelings for Quinn weren't going anywhere, it made sense to cut ties. Because I knew I was never going to leave Boston as long as Quinn was there. And maybe I was shooting myself in the foot, but I can hardly care about all that now.

"I stayed in touch with her when she moved to the city."

A choking sound bursts out of me. "I'm sorry, what? You stayed in touch with my *ex-girlfriend?*"

My mother sighs. "You're coming at this from the wrong angle, Reed. When you broke it off with Amina, she was a newly-minted college graduate moving to New York City. I helped her find a job. I helped her get on her feet. It wasn't like I was taking her to brunch every other Sunday, okay? So I just need you to calm down."

Oh, there will be no calming down.

"That's all fine and dandy, but it doesn't explain what she's doing *here.*"

She nods, like she knows I've got a point. She has to know. My mother is a very reasonable woman. She can't honestly think this is acceptable. "Amina reached out to me because she was in town with a group of friends. They all rented a little place on the other side of the lake, and she knew we were here because of something Sabrina posted online. I invited her for the party, but her friends were going home, so I told her she could stay here."

I don't know how to respond to any of this. I don't have words for how much she crossed the line with this one. So I don't say anything. I just stand here, hands at my sides, feeling helpless for the way this week has taken a turn. It was already hard enough without throwing my ex into the mix.

When I don't say anything, she goes on. "You dated five years ago. I didn't think it would be a problem—"

"And that's the only reason you brought her here?" I interrupt.

The silence is heavy in the air. She chews on her lip before saying, "I guess I thought it would be nice if the two of you reconnected."

"I knew it," I say, turning away from her. I can't look at her. But once I'm facing the opposite wall, I realize I'm looking at a picture of Chase and Quinn on their wedding day, smiling at the camera like it's the best day of their lives. And I guess it should have been, but we all know it wasn't. I spin back to my mother. "Why me? You didn't bring anyone here to try and crawl into bed with Sabrina."

She sighs at my crude suggestion. "I don't worry about Sabrina the way I worry about you."

"Oh, that's great."

She steps forward, takes me by my upper arms. "I've always felt like you needed someone. A companion. You always seem so lonely. Sabrina is always surrounded by people. But you... you just work so much and then you go home to an empty apartment. I just want you to be happy."

I want to forgive her. I want to sympathize and understand why she's done this. But all I can think about is the fact that Amina is out there with Quinn, the only person on this planet who actually *can* make me happy.

So I slide out of the reach of her arms and swallow the disappointed look on her face. She doesn't get to be disappointed. My whole life, everyone has always been *disappointed* in me. The famous Madison Lynch made her money by commanding board rooms, not by baking cakes. The same woman who convinced me to open a five-star restaurant because we agreed that it would make me *somebody*.

I throw open her bedroom door and storm down the hallway. But before I get to the living room, I press my back to the wall and take a deep breath. This isn't Amina's fault, and I can't take it out on her. I have to find my footing before I go in there.

"Oh, so you and Reed dated for a while then."

I'm trying to keep my cool. We lounge on the couches, Sabrina with her feet in my lap and Amina on the couch opposite ours. She's so pretty it's hard to look at her, with light brown skin and dreadlocked hair that's pulled into a bun. She's dressed all in white, which is something I don't feel like I could pull off in a million years. I'm still in the athletic clothes that I went hiking in, and when I look down, I realize I have dirt on my knees.

Jesus Christ. Hopefully, if no one has noticed by now, they won't notice at all.

"Almost a year," Amina says. "We broke up because I wanted to move to New York and he didn't."

Sabrina stretches, her smooth calves sliding across my thighs. "Yeah, Reed is pretty much married to Boston. That's where his restaurant is."

"Well, *was*," Amina says with a kind smile.

My gut tightens. No. What? Does she know about Aeronaut? Is she about to out Reed? This is not how Sabrina should find out about this. It should be Reed's story to tell.

But if Amina knows, who else does?

"What do you mean?" Sabrina asks, pulling her legs out of my lap just as Reed comes around the corner. Sabrina's eyes immediately go to him, her mouth opening, but before she can say anything, Reed cuts her off.

"Amina," he says, standing at the end of her couch. "Why don't I show you around?"

She smiles up at him, and something sharp hits me in the chest. The two of them were together for a *year*. I remember Amina. She came to a few family things the year after I met Chase, but when Reed graduated, and I stopped seeing him around campus, I never heard about her again.

But here she is. Gorgeous and probably single and now staying in this house just like the rest of us.

"Sure." She puts out her hand, and Reed helps her up off the couch. I don't miss the fact that he's helping her up the same way he helped me up off my knees not even an hour ago. I look down at the floor as they walk out of the room, feeling embarrassed that I'm jealous. This thing with Reed is just sex. He can hold hands with whomever he wants. He can take Amina out to the boat house and fuck her senseless right now, and that's fine.

It's *fine*, right?

I don't care who he sleeps with.

I don't care who he invites to the lake house.

I don't care, I don't care, I don't care.

"What did she mean, his restaurant *was* in Boston?" Sabrina says, now sitting up fully, watching the front door close and Reed and Amina walk by the front windows.

I don't want to lie to her, but I also really don't want to give away what Reed has been keeping from the family. It wouldn't be right. He's keeping my secrets, so I should keep his.

"I'm not sure," I say, but Sabrina narrows her eyes at me, like she knows I'm lying. Her eyes shoot to her cell phone, sitting on the coffee table in front of the couch.

We lunge at the same time, both of us landing with a hand on the phone.

"Let go of it, Quinn," Sabrina growls at me, but I shake my head, adamant.

"You have to let him tell you when he's ready." I know I've already said too much. I know I've given away the fact that I just lied to her and that Reed has been telling me things he's not telling anyone else, but I don't care. Reed deserves to do this on his own time.

Sabrina's eyes widen in shock, but then I feel the muscles in her arm go slack, her shoulders slump. She pulls her hand back from mine, settling back onto the couch.

"Okay," she says and leaves it at that.

Dinner is uncomfortably silent. Everyone is mad at everyone, except for Chase, who's too stupid to know that everyone is mad at everyone.

"It's really great to see you again, Amina," he says, passing her a bowl of pasta salad that Lydia made. "I haven't seen you in, what, four years?"

Across the table, Amina smiles. She doesn't know that everyone is mad at everyone either, but that's because she hasn't been here all week, living with a group of people who are all lying to each other.

At the end of the table, my mother clears her throat and averts her eyes, fully aware of her role in all of this. I still can't believe she thought it would be a good idea to invite my ex here. I mean, who does that?

Madison Lynch does. She's so used to everything going her way, to being able to strong-arm life into doing what she wants it to, that she thought she could use her powers of persuasion on my love life.

And if things were different, if the world had sent us all

down a different path, maybe it would have worked. Amina smells amazing, sitting beside me at the dining table. She smells fresh, like flowers and clean laundry. But she might as well be a ghost because all I can see is Quinn, sitting across the table from me, clearly trying to keep a straight face, even as Chase puts his arm around her shoulders and pulls her close.

"Yeah, just about," Amina says. "And you two are married now." She smiles across the table at them. "I always sort of thought you would be. You were always so cute together."

That brings the silence plunging back as Quinn sends Amina a polite smile and then focuses on spearing broccoli florets with the tip of her fork.

We all turn our attention to our own plates, but when I glance up at Sabrina, it's to find her looking at me like she can't remember who I am. I heard Amina spill it to her that Aeronaut is closing. I didn't want to face it at the time, but I know Sabrina will make me face it soon.

"I'm going to go check on dessert," Mom says, pushing her chair back from the table and turning the corner to go to the kitchen.

The second she's gone, Sabrina leans over to me and hisses, "Why didn't you tell me the restaurant was closing?"

Chase's head pops up. "The restaurant is closing?"

"I'm so sorry," Amina immediately adds, turning in her chair to face me. "I thought they knew."

"How did *you* know?" Chase asks.

Amina shrugs. "I still have friends back in Boston. They've gone by the place and seen that it's empty."

At this, I think Sabrina's head is going to pop off. "*Empty?* How long has this been going on?"

I meet Quinn's eye for comfort. I knew this was going to happen. I knew that everyone was going to freak out the second they found out, and the last thing I need is for the news to get back to Mom. She's definitely not going to be gone much longer.

Quinn sends me a small smile of reassurance.

I have to get it out quick. "I lost the restaurant to some bad business dealings a few months ago."

Chase scoffs and tightens his hold on Quinn. Her right eye twitches almost imperceptibly. "Bad business dealings? Are you kidding?"

I ignore him and keep going. "Look," I say, addressing Sabrina, "you don't need to worry about it. I've got it under control. I didn't want to tell anyone because I didn't want word to make it back to Mom before I got a new place figured out. I've got a guy looking for a new space, and I've got investors lined up. Everything is going to be fine."

"Investors?"

I turn at the sound of Quinn's small voice, and when I find her staring at me, I realize what I've said. I told her Mom's money was going to pay for the new place. I told her I *needed* to be here for that money. Now she knows I lied.

We can't have this conversation here in front of everyone. They don't know the plans in my head or the kinds of things Quinn and I have been talking about all week. They don't understand the confusion on her face or her realization that I'm just as much of a liar as Chase is.

"It's just—" I start, but then Mom appears, taking her place at the table again.

"Dessert is done. I had to beg Reed to let me make it this once." She smiles around the table, clearly expecting a polite laugh, but no one gives it to her. Sabrina is still looking at me with suspicion in her eyes, Quinn's mouth is hanging open in confusion, Chase has clamped his lips shut, clearly not intending to out me to our mom, and I can feel Amina's eyes still on me, probably trying to figure out if I'm mad at her for spilling my secrets.

When she sees that no one is engaging with her, my mother keeps pushing. "I don't think I've gotten to the be the one to prepare desserts in years. Since...wow, I don't know...maybe since Quinn's first Thanksgiving with us."

At that, Quinn's attention is caught. She looks over at my mom, her eyes a little unfocused. "Thanksgiving?"

Mom smiles big, clearly happy that someone at this table is going to have a legitimate conversation with her. "Yes. That would have been, what, five years ago?"

Sabrina, seemingly calmer now, says, "Yeah, that was the first time we all met Quinn."

"Not me." I don't know why I say it. It just bursts out of me, like trying to hold a rabid animal inside an unlatched cage.

All eyes shoot to me, and Sabrina says, "What do you mean? That was the first time you met her. That was the first time we all met her."

I'm already shaking my head, and across the table, Quinn's cheeks have gone pink. "No, Quinn and I met before Thanksgiving. We met at the Halloween party."

Chase's eyebrows furrow and he looks from me to Quinn. "What? The same Halloween party we met at?" He's clearly expecting Quinn to answer, but she's just looking at me. He pulls his arm from around her and leans across the table toward me. "You never said you guys met before that night."

I know I'm not doing this right. I know I'm going to raise questions. But I'm starting to feel desperate. This week is almost over and everything is starting to fall apart, and I want to tell everyone at this table that Quinn is mine.

But instead, I look over at my brother and suffuse my voice with a casual calm. "It slipped my mind. Just remembered recently. I was so drunk that night."

Something has pulled tight between the three of us, stretching and stretching, until my mom's voice breaks in.

"Well, how cool! What are the chances!"

"Yeah," I say, not taking my eyes off Quinn. "What are the chances?"

At this, Quinn finally seems to break. She turns her face toward Chase and I see her arm move under the table, like she's patting his knee. "We just bumped into each other in the hall that night. It was like two seconds. I didn't even recognize him at Thanksgiving. Weird how that happens."

It's almost believable. Quinn has one of those faces, soft and innocent, that makes her seem like she would never lie to you. So, when she says this, everyone believes her, even Chase. The thick air dissipates into something more pleasant, and the storm cloud that was hovering over us seems to burst.

But I know the truth. She remembered me at Thanksgiving. She still thinks about that night outside the Halloween party. I know she does. Because when something like that happens, something that fundamentally changes you forever, you never forget it.

38 REED

CHASE IS DRUNK. LIKE, *DRUNK* DRUNK. THE KIND OF drunk that tells me I'm going to be driving him home. Quinn will have to come get his car in the morning. When I extended the invitation of drinks to Chase last night, I sort of thought he would bring Quinn with him. I *wanted* him to bring Quinn with him. We're celebrating Aeronaut's first Michelin Star. It's pretty pretentious, all things considered, but it brought us a hell of a lot of attention, so I can live with that.

We've been open for two and half years, which seems wild when I think about it. Oscar bought the building, and I set up the restaurant with the money I've been saving up from working since the day I turned sixteen. Sure, some of it was Mom's money, but most of it was mine.

And so, I wanted Quinn here. I wanted her to be proud of me. But when I asked my brother why he hadn't brought her, he said, "God, can't I have a fucking moment of peace?" And to that, I didn't know if he was talking about me or her.

For his sake, I hope he meant me.

Who the hell in their right mind would want a moment of peace from Quinn?

"Gotta break the seal," he says now, practically falling off his stool and stumbling to the bathroom.

This is not the night I imagined. I love my brother, and I wanted to celebrate with him. That's why I called him. But all he's done tonight is complain about work, and I'm about ready to go home. I would prefer to celebrate on my own. I've been perfecting my chocolate chip cookie recipe for Quinn. That would be a hell of a lot more fun than listening to Chase drunkenly grumble about his boss for the fiftieth time tonight.

I start scrolling through my phone, but as I'm about to open Instagram, I find myself suddenly looking at Quinn on my screen. It's a picture of her and Sabrina, their cheeks pressed together and all their teeth showing. It's the picture that I assigned to phone calls from Quinn.

The phone is buzzing in my hands, and I almost drop it. Quinn has only ever called me once, when us and some friends from Suffolk all decided to go to a concert together. We had all exchanged numbers in case we got separated, and Quinn had called me when she went to the bathroom but couldn't find her way back to our seats.

But she's calling now. Is she calling because she can't get a hold of Chase?

His phone is on the table right next to me. As far as I know, she hasn't tried to call him.

My thumb hovers over the answer button. One swipe and this night will be a much better one. One swipe and I could hear her voice under the commotion of this bar that Chase chose because they do two-for-one pints. I want to answer it so bad, but I know I shouldn't. Quinn and Chase are getting serious. They're living together now, so it would be best if I kept my distance.

The phone finally stops vibrating as Chase comes back to the table. He seems to be a little steadier.

When I see his phone start to vibrate on the tabletop, my stomach twists. Quinn is calling him. I can see her face on his screen now, a picture of the two of them smiling. Because he has photos like that with her. Probably a lot of them.

He lets out a sigh, like the last thing he wants in the world is to answer her call. My hands squeeze into fists. He can't even see how fucking lucky he is.

"Answer it," I say, trying to keep the anger out of my voice.

He shakes his head. "She's probably calling to see when I'm coming home."

"So? She's your girlfriend, and she lives with you. You don't think you owe her that much?" I push his phone toward him, but it's already stopped ringing. We both stare at it. All around us, people are talking, laughing, having a good time, but the two pathetic idiots at this table are sitting in solemn silence.

"Call her back," I finally say, much less gentle than before.

And he does. I wave at our waiter and mouth *water* to him. He nods and goes on.

"Baby, what's wrong?"

A chill goes up my spine. I've never heard him call her that before, and I've never heard him speak to her like this, like he's scared and worried. What's going on?

The waiter puts a pitcher of water on the round table, and I pour Chase a glass. Whatever is happening on the other side of that phone, he's going to need it.

Quinn. What's wrong with Quinn?

"I'm coming, baby," he says. "Just hang on. I'm on my way to you."

He hangs up, and I feel sick with not knowing what's happening.

"What happened?" I ask as he throws on his coat and downs several gulps of water.

"Quinn's mom died."

"Jesus." I start searching for my keys immediately, but Chase is already halfway to the door. "You're not driving, asshole!" I shout to him, running after him until I'm close enough that I can latch onto his shoulder and spin him back to face me. "There's no way you're sober enough."

"Then I'll call a cab." To his credit, he seems serious about getting to Quinn. He pushes out onto the sidewalk, past the Saturday night crowd, and I realize too late that I left my credit card at the bar to keep the tab open. I'll have to come back for it in the morning.

"I'll drive you," I say, grabbing onto his sleeve and pulling him down the sidewalk to where I parked the bike. The good thing about riding a motorcycle is that I can pretty much park it anywhere. It's parked now in an alley between a Subway and another bar.

"I'm not getting on that thing," Chase says, and I roll my eyes.

"You don't have a choice. Just don't fall off." I should have asked for a bottle of water to go. I'm really not feeling confident that he's going to be able to stay on the back of the bike with how drunk he is. Luckily, the fresh air will help sober him up.

I give him my spare helmet, and we take off.

We're not far from Chase's apartment, the one he shares with Quinn. It's on a quiet corner uptown, and I park against the sidewalk and let the bike idle so he can get off.

He runs, forgetting until the last minute that he forgot to take off the helmet and running back to hand it to me before turning for the building again. Whatever exasperation he was feeling towards her, it was clearly momentary. He's desperate to get to her, and for that, I'm grateful.

The door shuts behind him, and I sit on my bike, listening to the comforting sound of it idling and wishing I could be up there with her.

39 REED

THE COUCH IN THE BASEMENT IS TOO SMALL FOR ME. That was sort of the whole reason Quinn and I ended up in the bedroom together that first night.

But I'm not crawling into bed with Amina or asking if I can sleep on the floor in there. I would have spent the week sleeping on that floor to get closer to Quinn. But now, I'm considering moving to the couch upstairs. But I know Lydia will be up before the sun, and I'm not very good at waking up to pots and pans banging around. Not to mention sunlight.

All I can think about is what's going on upstairs. Chase and I have always been big fans of the bro code, but it's not like he would know not to make a move on a woman he's been with for five years. And I've seen this film before. People who file for divorce and then go for one last breakup fuck. And sometimes the breakup fuck leads to not breaking up.

But she wouldn't. Right?

The bedroom door creaks open, and I shift to look over at where light is spilling out of the bedroom. And then I hear Amina's quiet voice. "Reed? Could you come here?"

I shoot up to my feet, worried that something might be wrong. We sometimes get snakes in the lake house, though it's been a dry summer, so I haven't seen any. "Amina? You okay?" I ask, pushing the bedroom door open and taking in the scene before me.

Amina in nothing but her underwear, a red lace bra and matching panties, standing beside the bed. She's thrown the covers back in an obvious invitation, but I can't even see her. In my mind, all I see is Quinn, writhing on the bed while I take my tongue to her, shivering with pleasure when I call her filthy names.

"I knew you would probably feel like you couldn't make the first move since it's been a while, so I thought I would do it," Amina says. Before I have a chance to answer, she's up against me, running her hands down my chest. Luckily, I hadn't changed for bed yet, so there was still fabric between her skin and mine.

I grab her wrists, and she puffs out a breath in a way that tells me she thinks I'm about to pin her to the wall or something equally sexy. Instead, I let her go and take a step back. "There's someone..." That's all I can get out.

Her mouth pops open, and then she's rushing back to the bed to yank the covers around herself. I feel satisfied when I realize it's not the same blanket. Lydia changed the sheets, thank God.

"Your mom told me—"

"My mom doesn't know."

Amina's eyebrows raise. "Oh. Wow. Okay. Is it serious?"

I know she's not asking in hopes that maybe it's casual and we can still press forward with her plans. She's just kind and genuinely curious. "Yeah. At least, it is for me."

She sits on the edge of the bed and nods. "So, a hookup is definitely not happening on the trip." It's not a question. It's a statement. And she seems to be speaking more to herself than to me.

"I'm afraid not."

She smiles sadly up at me. "You were never really serious about me. Not even back then. I could tell. There was always… distance."

I sit beside her, making sure there's enough space between us. "It wasn't you. Please don't think that. It was really complicated. And now I have a chance at something real."

"Good. You deserve it." After a beat of silence, she wraps the blanket tighter around herself and says, "Think there will be any hot guys at this party tomorrow?"

I laugh. "I can almost guarantee there will be someone at the party who would be happy to show you a good time."

We look at each other, neither of us really sure where to go from here, and then she leans forward and kisses me. It's not a passionate kiss. It's not even really a romantic kiss. It's more like…a goodbye kiss. Maybe something she's needed for a long time.

After that, I leave the bedroom and shut the door behind me, standing in the dark kitchen, trying to convince myself not to go upstairs and kick down Chase's door. But I want my girl back. I want her in my arms. And not having her here is killing me.

THE HOUSE IS SO STILL, SO QUIET THAT I CAN HEAR STATIC against my ears. I can hear Chase breathing. I'm certain he's still awake. I feel sick to my stomach. All I can think about is what's happening in the basement, the fact that Amina is sleeping in the bed where Reed and I have been having sex for the last three days.

It's not like I think Reed would jump into bed with her because she's *there*, but what if they realize that they still have feelings for each other? What if they realize they're still attracted to each other?

What if Reed remembers that whatever is going on between us can't keep going on once this week is over? There's no way.

Except...

He remembers Halloween. It feels like that changes everything. How could it not? The thing is, I don't know *how* it changes things. Why did he lie about remembering me? Why did he act like he didn't know me when we met in New York?

"Are you still awake?"

My whole body jerks at the sound of Chase's voice. I've been so caught up in my head that I forgot that he was still awake. I roll over to face him and feel a little shocked when he's already turned in my direction. It's strange that I don't feel the way I did when we first got here. All the anger I felt, it sort of just shriveled up and disappeared. Now, I feel...nothing.

"What is it?"

He shrugs. "I don't know. It's sort of nice having you here. It's weird that you've been sleeping in the basement."

"You're usually asleep when I move down there. I didn't think you noticed I was gone."

"I noticed."

His face is awash in blue moonlight, and I think of how many nights I spent lying in bed alone, wondering when he would be home. Never sure if he was working late or out drinking with friends. He would never answer his phone, and I would never complain. Maybe a part of me didn't mind that he was gone. Maybe the loneliness I always felt wasn't for him.

"Did you ever really love me?" I don't know why I ask. None of it matters anymore. But I don't feel like I understand why Chase and I did the things we did to each other. I don't know why I married him when I was so unsure, and I'm not sure why he married me when he knew I wasn't enough for him.

After a long silence, he says, "You fit perfectly into my life. I mean, look how happy my family is to have you here. You and me, we made sense." He stops, blinks at me. "Did you ever really love me?"

There's no reason not to be honest, after all this. "I don't know. Maybe I don't know what love is."

He shakes his head as best he can with his cheek pressed to his pillow. "You're one of the most loving people I know. You're so good with my family, and you were there for your mom when no one else was. You've been taking care of my family all week. You came here to make sure I got the money, even after everything I did to you."

I'm surprised when a tear rolls out of the corner of my eye. "I came here for me, Chase," I say, confidently.

"Sure, but you could have found a way to get that money. You could have blown the whistle on this whole thing. Blown up my whole family. But you haven't. Because you love them."

A sob rises up my throat.

I told Madison I didn't know what I wanted, but it was a lie. I know what I want. I want someone to love me. *Really* love me. Someone who understands me and someone who laughs at my jokes and someone who doesn't sigh when they answer the phone and someone who rushes home because they want to see me so bad.

I don't realize I'm all-out crying until Chase reaches out and sets his hand on my shoulder.

"Don't," I say between sobs. I cough away the lump in my throat and sit up in the bed. "I'm just going to go for a walk."

"Quinn?"

I stop halfway to the door and turn around. He's sitting up in the bed, his hand reached out toward me.

"I'm really sorry I ruined your life."

It feels manipulative, like he wants me to tell him he didn't ruin my life, even though maybe he did. So I don't say anything. I open the door and go out into the hallway.

Down the hall, the light is still on in the living room, but when I get out there, the room is empty. Someone must have left the light on before they went to bed. I'm standing there, trying to figure out what the hell I'm supposed to do next, wiping the tears from my cheeks, when Reed comes out of the hallway leading down to the basement.

For a moment, we just stare at each other. And then Reed

seems to come unfrozen. He stomps toward me, his voice low when he asks, "What's going on? Why are you crying?"

I put a hand over his mouth to get him to be quiet and then drag him toward the front door, where the entryway serves as an alcove for us to hide in.

He has his hands on my face, brushing away the ridiculous tears that I can't seem to stop. "Did Chase do something?" he hisses.

I yank his hands away. "You lied to me."

His hands fall to his sides, and it processes for the first time that he's still dressed in what he was wearing all day. That he doesn't look frazzled at all. He wasn't downstairs having sex with Amina in the bed we've been sharing, that much is obvious.

"You said you needed the money for your new restaurant."

He doesn't say anything for a moment, like he's trying to figure out how to structure his thoughts. "I do."

"You said you already have investors. Surely it can't cost more than half a million to open a restaurant." I'm trying to keep my voice down, but I'm feeling hysterical, and we can both hear it. After that conversation with Chase, I know I can't listen to anymore Lynch men lie to me, especially not Reed. Not when I've opened up to him this week.

His face changes, one eyebrow going up, cockily. "Maybe you shouldn't be so confident in that information."

I want to growl at him. Now is not the time for him to be *cute*. "Reed, what do you need the money for?"

"What?"

"You said you need your mom's money, but you weren't telling me the whole truth. Why do you need it?"

"I never said I needed it. I just let you assume."

I feel like I'm moving through a tunnel of lights and colors. Nothing makes sense. All I want is the whole truth. It doesn't matter if it's important or if it's my business. I don't care. Nothing is what I thought it was when I woke up this morning, and I just want to know what the hell Reed is keeping from me. "Then why are you here?"

All the cute is gone, leaving behind just the serious cut of his jaw. "I'm here because I want to be."

"*Why are you here, Reed?*"

"I'm here because my family is here."

I'm so frustrated that I'm afraid I'm going to start crying again. "Just tell me, Reed. Why are you here? Why do you—" I take a deep breath, force the words out of me. "Why do you have that skeleton tattoo on your hip? Why did you have my picture in your office at Aeronaut? Please, just tell me the truth. Why did you pretend not to know me at that first Thanksgiving?"

He takes a step toward me, using his body to pin me to the wall, his hand coming up to wrap gently around my throat. "Because I needed to pretend that night never happened, Quinn. I needed to pretend I didn't meet the girl of my dreams in that hallway because that was the only way I could handle seeing you with Chase. You know why I'm here, Quinn."

The lump in my throat is so big, I'm afraid I'll choke. I shake my head. "I don't—"

"You *know*, Quinn. I got that tattoo because you were already under my skin. I came here because Chase said you needed the money, and Mom wouldn't give it to you unless I was here. I came here for you. I came here because my idiot of a brother let you go, and I saw an opportunity. I saw the chance that I should have taken five years ago, the chance to make you mine. Because that is all I want in this life, Quinn, for you to be mine. I saw my shot, and I took it. Because I'm in love with you. Because I've always been in love with you. And you're finally mine."

Tears slip down both my cheeks just before he slams his mouth down on mine. I'm immediately wrapped around him, trying to get as close to him as I possibly can. Closer. *Closer.* I want to let him absorb me into his skin.

This can't be real. That's all I can think as he buries his hands in my hair and slips his tongue into my mouth, pushing against me so hard that I can feel the heavy racing of his heart, the thickness of him against my hip.

He loves me. How can he possibly love me?

I should ask more questions. I should get some much-needed clarification. But instead, I hike my leg up onto his hip and let him grind me into the wall with his pelvis. He groans quietly, his hands clutching my jaw and then sliding underneath my hair, holding my scalp like it's something precious.

We have to talk. We have to figure this out.

A loud *thump* sounds from somewhere in the house, and we break apart, fixing our clothes and wiping at our mouths. And then we both just stand there, not moving, not breathing, waiting to see if someone is going to come around the corner and ask us why we're hiding in the entryway.

But nothing ever happens. The house goes back to being quiet and still.

Reed walks slowly to the end of the alcove, looking out both ways before turning back to me. "I should get back to my room," he says quietly, and that feeling in my stomach appears again. He wouldn't touch Amina after all that, right? He wouldn't tell me he's in love with me and then make a move on another woman.

"You and Amina..." I say, crossing my arms.

He stares at me with a blank expression. "You think I would do that to you?"

I know how awful it must seem that I would be suspicious, but considering what I'm going through with Chase, I don't know who I can trust anymore. He opens his mouth to speak, but another loud bump from down the hall catches our attention.

Reed sends me a confused look and then starts to walk down the hallway. I'm not sure whether or not I should follow him. I start down the hallway and see that the light in the guest bathroom is on, but the door isn't closed all the way. Light is spilling into the long hallway. I hear a shuffling from inside and start to worry that maybe Sabrina or Lydia is up and feeling sick. Why else would the door be partially open like that?

Reed stops and nods for me to go ahead of him, probably assuming it's safer for me to look in case one of the girls is inappropriately dressed or something. I push the door open enough to see in the mirror and find myself looking right at Lydia and Sabrina. Sabrina is propped up on the edge of the sink, and Lydia is on her knees in front of her, her face buried between Sabrina's legs.

I gasp, and both girls jerk their heads to the side, their eyes meeting mine in the mirror before I have a chance to close the door. "Oh, my God. I'm sorry. Shit, I'm so sorry."

I turn and grab Reed's hand, pulling him back down the hallway before he can see anything he shouldn't.

"What's happening?" he asks, but I keep moving, feeling like we should be as far away from Lydia and Sabrina's business as we can get right now.

"Wait," I hear Sabrina whisper from behind us. "Please wait, Quinn." I turn to look at her, halfway in the bathroom and halfway out of it. She's buttoning her shorts and then Lydia is rushing out of the bathroom behind her, wiping her mouth with a towel.

I feel the moment Reed realizes what happened, his hand tightening around mine. And then Lydia and Sabrina's eyes fall to where Reed and I are connected, and it's like we've all been struck by lightning. We stand there in shocked silence, none of us able to meet each other's eyes.

Lydia's eyes finally find mine. Her cheeks are flushed, her eyes wide, and I don't think it's because she and Sabrina were just getting hot and heavy. She looks terrified.

Finally, Sabrina lifts a finger to her lips and nods toward the back door, the one leading out to the pool. All four of us move slowly, like we don't want to turn our backs on one another. Once we're outside, the bugs squawking loudly, Reed says, "What the hell is going on?"

Sabrina's abrasive eyes shoot between me and Reed. "I think I should be asking you the same question."

"They've been sleeping together all week."

Reed and I both jump in surprise when Lydia speaks. Her voice is usually so quiet, but she's not being quiet now.

Sabrina spins to face her. "You knew about this?"

Lydia gives her a little expression like she wants to tell Sabrina to calm down. "I'm not a snitch, Sabrina." Lydia focuses her eyes on us, stepping around Sabrina with her hands clasped in front of her. Sabrina must be at least a foot taller than her. "I heard Quinn sneak down to the basement that first night, and then I heard you arrive, Reed. I went down to the basement to see if you needed anything, but when I realized you were both in the bedroom with the door closed, I just left it alone." She shrugs gently, not a hint of judgment in her tone.

Sabrina's tone, however, is so heavy with judgment when she speaks again, it's a wonder she doesn't choke. "So, what, the two of you are going behind Chase's back?" Sabrina waves a hostile hand in my direction. "You're cheating on my brother with my other brother?"

My stomach lurches. "It's not—"

"Hey." Reed steps between us, so all I can see is the jut of his shoulder blades through his thin shirt. "It's not like that, okay? You don't talk to her that way."

"You're one to talk, Reed. You're fucking your brother's wife."

I shove Reed out of the way so that I can see Sabrina. "Chase and I are divorced." Of anyone in the house, I feel confident that Sabrina at least will understand what I'm going through. She knows her brothers. She knows Chase. But there's still a chance that she'll think I'm disgusting or totally fucked up for sleeping with one brother when the other brother, who I was still technically married to when got here, is upstairs the whole time.

Sabrina goes silent, her arms falling down to her sides. Her mouth pulls down into a frown, and her eyes go glassy. "You and Chase got divorced? Why didn't you tell anyone? Why are you here *pretending* like you're still married?"

I sigh. "Chase cheated on me. We didn't tell anyone because I need the money your mother is offering us to help me pay for the house in Boston. I got it in the divorce, but I'm on the verge of losing it because I can't find a job." When I say it all out loud like that, one thing after another, it's practically vomit-inducing. I've pretty much lost everything. Maybe I never had anything to begin with. I glance over my shoulder at Reed, who's watching me with soft eyes.

"God. That's...a lot." Sabrina crosses her arms and looks down at the ground, like she's trying to process.

Beside her, Lydia says, "Maybe I should go inside and let you all talk." She slips quietly back into the house, and as soon as she's gone, Sabrina's eyes drift back over to Reed and me.

"Listen, you guys can't tell Mom about Lydia and me."

"Why?" Reed asks. "Why are the two of you sneaking around?"

Her chin trembles and she lets out a heavy sigh, planting

her hands on her hips. "Because Mom will fire her and Lydia needs this job. You know Mom would never agree to keep employing her kid's girlfriend. But Mom pays her a fortune and Lydia has family to take care of, okay? A mom and a brother, and if I'm the reason they aren't taken care of—"

"Hey," Reed says, stepping forward and grabbing Sabrina by both shoulders. "We're not going to tell Mom anything. I swear."

His words stab me in the gut. I think about how odd and difficult it's been to sneak around with Reed all week. Have they been doing the same thing while we were here? Or have they been doing it back in New York, too? "How long have you two been together?"

"Since I moved back to New York to be with Mom. So like, six months." Her eyes go watery again, and she reaches up to grab onto Reed's wrists. "Please, Reed."

I answer this time. "Sabrina, he said we wouldn't tell, and we mean it."

"We should head back in," Reed says, letting his arms drop. He holds the door open for us and we file back in, trying to stay quiet. Although, apparently, being quiet never did us any good because Lydia was always around the corner, seeing right through us.

Sabrina and I turn for the hallway, but Reed goes the other way, back toward the basement. Our eyes meet across the expanse of the living room, and I know he's thinking exactly what I am. That we need to talk. That he told me he *loves* me, and I have to figure out what the hell I'm going to do with that information.

When we're standing outside Chase's bedroom, Sabrina turns and leans against the wall. So quietly I almost can't hear her, she says, "I'm sorry about Chase."

I shake my head. I'm not sorry about Chase. I'm *free* of Chase. But now I've landed right into a million other problems.

"Are you in love with Lydia?"

She stares back at me. And then she nods.

I smile. "I'm happy for you two."

"I'm happy for you and Reed."

The lie rolls right off my tongue without my even trying. "It's nothing serious. We're just having a good time while we're here. It's not like something permanent would even be an option. Could you imagine trying to explain that to Chase and your mom?"

She grimaces. "Then I guess we'll both just have to take this all to the grave."

41 REED

3 Years Ago

There's a point, I think, in everyone's life when it becomes obvious whether they're going to get to be happy or not. Today, the day my brother is marrying the woman I love, is the day I've realized I'm never going to be truly happy. Things are going well with the restaurant, and I'm pretty comfortable financially and whatnot. But he has her, so for me, happiness is pretty much off the table.

When she came out of that back door earlier, I knew that if I said the right thing, she would call the whole thing off. She would have run, if I had given her permission.

But I could never do that Chase.

I watch them dance now, holding each other tight and smiling, their foreheads pressed together. They're going to be happy. I don't care what the hell I have to do. Even if I'm never happy a day in my life, I need Chase and Quinn to be. They both deserve good lives.

While everyone's eyes are on them, I sneak over to the bar. Mom paid for the wedding, so it's an open bar. I set my glass on the tabletop and tap it with my finger. The bartender nods at me. I don't have to tell him what I'm having because it's the fourth time I've been up here.

As soon as my speech was done, I started in with the gin. Once I no longer had to focus on *not* blurting into the microphone that all I wanted to do was die watching my brother marry the only person on this planet I've ever really wanted, I started to get sloshed.

Drunk is the only way I'm making it through this day.

"That's your last one," the bartender says, and I freeze before taking the glass.

"What do you mean?" I shout to him as the music changes from something gentle and sweet to something with heavy bass. The crowd all cheers and half the room begins to move onto the dancefloor.

"The bride and groom have put a limit on the number of drinks each person can be served. It's for your safety, sir."

I glower at him. He doesn't realize that it's for *everyone's* safety that I be allowed to get blind drunk so I can forget this day ever happened. As if that will help anything. This is the rest of my life. Quinn will be his for the rest of my life.

"Yeah, thanks, man," I say, taking the glass and wandering down the hall leading out of the reception room. I know I have to be a good Best Man and try to stick around as much as possible, but I need to breathe. I need to find some goddamn air.

And then my mother appears before me. It's like she knows. She always does. She pops up out of nowhere, stopping in my tracks, and says, "You need to dance with Quinn."

If I wasn't so numb, I would choke on my own tongue. "What? Why?"

She lifts her chin in the direction of the dancefloor behind me, which I've been very strategically avoiding. When I look over my shoulder, I see that Chase and Sabrina have taken to the floor, dancing close together to a song that's too upbeat to be a slow song but too lazy to be a party song. They're having a conversation, laughing, and off to the side of the dancefloor, Quinn watches quietly, all by herself.

"None of her brothers showed up," my mother hisses to me. "You need to dance with her. You're the only real brother she has."

Bile rises in my throat. *I am not her brother*, I want to growl at my mother, but I've already handed her my gin glass and started to move around the outside of the dancefloor toward Quinn. It doesn't matter how much it hurts, I can't let her stand there alone.

Just like I couldn't let her make a run for it earlier. Nope, I had to convince her to marry my brother. Because what was my other option? Beg her to marry me instead? Convince her to call it off, wait a few months, and then make a play for her myself?

I don't even know when it happened exactly, that moment when I realized I was madly in love with her. Sometime between that first Thanksgiving and her mother's funeral, I guess. I started to realize that every time we were together, I felt *better*. She listened to me. She didn't second-guess everything I did or said. She didn't ask me patronizing questions. She talked to me about stuff that mattered and stuff that didn't. She smiled when she walked into the room and realized I was there. She laughed at my jokes.

And when I would have to leave her, I would feel broken. Lonely. Lost.

I want to be anywhere else. Anywhere that isn't here. That isn't now. That isn't my life. "Care to dance?" I lean down to say into Quinn's ear when I finally reach her. She jumps a little and looks at me over her bare shoulder. I'm trying not to look at her skin, lest I be tempted to caress it.

When Quinn realizes it's me, her eyes go a little shiny and she smiles. "Yes, please."

And when I take her hand in mine, I wonder why I couldn't have chosen to be a terrible person, the kind of person who could see someone's need and look the other way. Because if I had just kept walking, just kept going and walked out the back door, my heart wouldn't be racing at the feel of Quinn's hand in mine. I wouldn't be trying to force down the tremor in my limbs while I place a hand at her back and pull her body close to mine, setting us into a gentle rhythm with the music, a twangy kind of folk song.

She tips her head back, her silver eyeshadow shimmering in the light, and smiles. "Thank you, Reed," she says.

I shake my head. I certainly can't take credit when it was my mom who saw that she was in need instead of me. "I'm sorry that none of your brothers showed up."

Her smile only dims a little bit. She shrugs. "I'm used to it. I knew they wouldn't come. But Chase wanted me to invite them anyway. I think he was hoping our guest count would be a little less lopsided. He pretty much brings everything to the table in this relationship, you know?" She gives a nervous laugh, but I don't join in. How can she think something like that, even as a joke?

"Yeah, lucky you." The bitter words slip out before I can stop them. Behind her, Sabrina and Chase slip past us, and Chase looks over, clearly wondering what we're talking about. I resist the urge to tug Quinn a little closer.

"Are you okay?" she asks, and I want to kick myself. I shouldn't have said that. It was a dick move.

"Yeah. Sorry." I give a fake laugh, trying to reassure her.

"I've just had a lot to drink. But don't worry, the bartender has informed me that I'm officially cut off."

She gives a comical grimace and says, "Yeah, sorry. I invited a lot of people from Suffolk and I didn't want anyone to get sloppy. Especially not in front of your mom."

Is this what's constantly going through her head all the time? Always worrying about making a good impression and what she has to offer everybody? Can't she just...be herself?

"Do you ever just wish everything was different?"

When she looks up at me with a confused tilt to her mouth, I know that I fucked up. I shouldn't be drinking on a day like today. I shouldn't have let myself get so close to her. I shouldn't have said that. I really, really shouldn't have said that.

"What do you mean?" she whispers.

But before I have a chance to explain myself, the song ends and everyone claps. Quinn is still looking up at me, still waiting for an explanation, but I don't give her one. I step away from her and turn for the exit. I have to get out of here.

I have to move on with my life. I can't spend forever pining for a woman I can't have.

42 QUINN

EVERYTHING IS DIFFERENT IN THE LIGHT OF MORNING. IT'S
like in the last twenty-four hours, I've stepped through a portal
into a different dimension. This is not the Lynch family I've
always known. This is not the life I've known for the last five
years.

Reed told me he loved me.

Sabrina is in love with Lydia.

Madison is trying to hook Reed up with his ex.

And Chase is pressed against my side at the breakfast table,
his arm slung over the back of the chair, oblivious to my
distress.

Reed said he *loves* me. That he's *in love with me*. How am I
just supposed to eat some oatmeal and move on with my life?
What the hell are we going to do when it's time to leave? What
the hell does any of this mean for our lives?

Reed sits across the table from me. I can tell he's trying not
to meet my eye, but every few minutes, he does anyway, and I
have to look away quick because it's all just too...*obvious*. If
anyone sees our eyes meet, even for a second, I'm certain they'll

know. They'll know that everything changed between us last night, and that now we can't go back.

"What are the plans for today?" Madison asks. She's clearly trying to break the silence because nobody at the table is speaking. Sabrina has been keeping her head low, and I want to tell her that she can enjoy the rest of her vacation. She has to know by now that we would never tell anyone about her and Lydia, but every time her eyes find mine across the table, they're full of fear. And then she gets Reed in her sights and looks away again. Us and our secrets.

"Jet skis?" Reed says, just as I take a sip from my orange juice.

And then immediately choke on said orange juice. Reed looks over at me, his expression innocent, but I know he remembers asking me about the jet skis when he was fingering me in the hot tub.

Everyone at the table watches me try to catch my breath, and then I say past the constriction of my throat, "Jet skis sound fun."

Madison smiles. "Great. I'm going to run into town with Lydia to get some last-minute things we need before the caterers show up."

"Sounds good," Sabrina immediately pipes in. "Could I come? I need to grab a few things."

"Sure." Madison focuses on cutting into her eggs benedict as the table falls quiet again. That one conversation wasn't enough to undo everything that happened between all of us yesterday.

My eyes meet Reed's again, and I wonder what happened between him and Amina. Did he sleep on the floor the way he did our first night? Did the two of them share the bed with a pillow wall between them?

Like she knows I'm thinking about her, trying to figure out

how much contact she's had with Reed, trying to put out of my mind how many times they probably slept together if they dated for almost a year, Amina looks at Chase and says, "You know who I ran into last week? Carla Clemons. You remember her, right?"

He pulls a contemplative face. "I'm not sure."

"You guys met at that New Year's party in New York, like, four years ago. She talked about it for weeks afterwards. She thought it was so funny that she ran into my boyfriend's brother at some random party."

Silence falls on the table again, but this time, it's stretched tight. My brain begins to run through the facts, all the things that have been laid out before me.

New Year's four years ago. Less than a week after my mother died. I remember Chase leaving to go to New York. He had said he was going to check in on Madison, to spend time with her after my mother's funeral was over because he'd been in Minnesota for a week and was worried about her, was feeling overly sentimental, all things considered.

Madison breaks it, clueless about the chaos in my brain. "New Year's? Chase hasn't spent a New Year's in New York in ages." Her eyes flicker over to us.

Amina's smile falls, and my stomach tightens. "Oh, right. Sorry. I thought I remembered—"

"She must have had you confused for someone else." Reed looks back and forth between the two of us before landing on me. It's like he can't help it. He can't help but lie for his brother, even though his brother is an asshole. Chase doesn't deserve that kindness.

"Maybe...maybe she was wrong. Maybe she meant someone else. It was a long time ago." She can tell this news is distressing, even though she doesn't know why.

Chase leans forward on his elbows. "Yeah, it was definitely

someone else." He glances sideways at me, but I keep my eyes forward, avoiding the eyes of everyone at the table, staring out at the lake over Reed's shoulder.

It shouldn't matter that Chase was clearly cheating on me from the very beginning, lying to me, abandoning me for some fake sentimentality when I needed him most. My mother died the day after Christmas. And five days later, Chase was at a New Year's party in New York, most likely fucking some other woman.

It's not his complete lack of respect that hurts. It's not the fact that he so obviously never loved me.

What hurts is how stupid I was. What hurts is how *blind* I was.

My eyes meet Reed's across the table.

What hurts is all the years I could have been with someone who loved me. And now it's ruined because I chose the wrong guy.

"I remember that New Year's," Madison says, breaking the uncomfortable silence. "Was that the year we were in Aspen, Sabrina?"

Sabrina chimes in with a confirmation and then goes off on a stilted story about skiing, but I can't even make out the words. Everything is an uncomfortable droning in my ears. Reed watches me, and I watch him.

When I feel like enough time has passed that it won't be suspicious, I smile at Madison and say, "I think I'm going to go for a walk, get some sun."

Madison's mouth falls open, a crease of concern forming between her eyebrows, but before she can argue with me, I turn for the hallway. I go to the front patio because I don't have anywhere else to go, and I haven't even made it to the front steps before the door opens behind me and Chase storms out of the house. He gently shuts the door behind him and spins back to me.

"Quinn, look—"

"Were you ever not cheating on me?" I'm surprised by how little anger there is in my voice. I don't have any anger left. I just have exhaustion and surrender and grief.

Chase makes a face, his mouth tightening into a sad line and then pulling into a frown again. "No. I was always cheating."

"You know, I married you because of that week my mom died. You came to Minnesota with me, and you were there for me, and when I wasn't sure if marrying you was the right thing to do, I told myself that you were that man, the one who helped me pack up all her stuff and held me while I cried. But it was all a lie. You waited until I could breathe again and then you ran off to New York to go to some party. Did you fuck someone else there?"

He nods, so matter-of-fact. "Yes, I did."

I scrub my face with my hands, realize when my hands come away wet that I'm crying. "So many fucking wasted years," I whisper.

Chase steps forward and tries to grab onto my shoulders, but I shove him back. He looks surprised, like I punched him, and that's exactly what I want to do. "Quinn..."

"How could you let me marry you, Chase?" I'm trying to keep my voice down because I know if we speak too loudly, everyone at the breakfast table will be able to hear us. "You knew you couldn't be the man I needed you to be, and you still asked me to marry you. You still pretended to be someone I could trust. You still let me give you so many good years."

He sits on one of the rocking chairs on the porch, his shoulders hunched and his head bowed. He shrugs. "I don't know, Quinn. I guess maybe I thought that you would be able to fix me. I guess I thought that if I could find the perfect wife and give her the perfect life that I could someday be the perfect husband."

I don't have a response to that. I don't have any space inside my brain for his self-pity, for his regret.

I have too much of my own.

"I'd like you to leave, please."

He looks at me for a long time, like he thinks I'm going to change my mind, but I need him to not be near me. I need him to go away. I need for this week to be over so that I never have to see him again.

Except, I think as he goes inside, when the week is over, he's not the only one I'll never see again.

43 REED

Quinn doesn't come back inside for a long time. No one really seems to have noticed, or maybe they're trying *not* to notice. I try to play through my head how obvious I think that little show was. Is it clear to my mother now that Chase lied to Quinn? That he's not the person she thinks he is? I think she's trying not to see it.

Mom has decided now is the time to make sure everyone is properly attired for the party tonight, and she's currently got dresses spread across both couches. Sabrina and Lydia are helping her go through them, finding little things that need to be fixed and reasons why most of them can't be worn, all while I watch, feeling dread in my stomach.

Finally, Quinn comes back inside. She looks fine, as put together as she always does, but I know now that Quinn being put together means nothing. It's always been fake.

Guilt whips through me. I didn't know that she didn't know about Chase cheating the whole time. I don't know that I could have been the one to tell her, but I definitely could have figured out a better way for this information to come to light. Chase is such a reckless coward. I certainly didn't know that he lied to her about New Year's four years ago. That would have been days after her mother died, just one day after the funeral, the funeral I had flown to Minnesota to attend. I remember that day so clearly, the way Quinn had clung to Chase and the way he had stepped up to be her support system. All for him to take off and betray her.

He watches her come inside from his spot on the ground beside a pile of shoes that my mother has discarded. He's got his knees up and his arms hanging over them. He looks lost, beat down by life and unsure how to move forward.

It makes me grind my teeth. He acts like he didn't do all of this to his goddamn self. He makes an excuse and leaves out the back door. I see him out by the pool, his hands in his pockets like he's contemplating life. Maybe he should contemplate what a dick he's been.

Quinn goes into the kitchen for a bottle of water, and while everyone else is distracted, I get up and move in there with her, pretending that I need something from the fridge. I stand with my back to the room, my eyes scanning the lit shelves as Quinn leans against the counter beside me, sipping at her water.

"You okay?" I ask her under my breath.

She doesn't look at me, just keeps her eyes forward as she says, "I don't know anymore."

I sigh. I want to take her in my arms. I want to kiss her and tell her that I'll never hurt her the way he did. That she never has to hurt again. But I know it won't undo what's already been done. "You don't have to stay," I tell her. "You don't have to keep putting yourself through this."

She looks down at the floor, the length of her long ponytail falling across her shoulder. "I don't have a choice. I need the money. It's three more days. I'll be fine."

"Quinn, I can take care of you."

Her eyes meet mine, all pretense of us not being in the midst of a conversation gone. "What?"

I shut the fridge and turn to her. It's not like we're not allowed to speak. It's not like everyone in this house doesn't know we're friends and always have been. "Let me take care of you. Once I open my new restaurant—"

"I don't want someone to take care of me, Reed," she whispers, her eyes wide. "I want to be able to take care of myself."

"I know you—"

"Reed," Mom's voice breaks through our conversation, and we both look over at her, all the way on the other side of the living room. "Do you know what you're wearing tonight?"

I shrug. "I've got a few black t-shirts that are clean. I forgot about the party, so I didn't pack—"

Mom waves me off. "I knew you would forget." She nods in Lydia's direction, and Lydia nods back before disappearing down the hallway.

"What the hell was that?" I whisper to Quinn, and she just laughs. Which does something warm to my stomach. I feel like I haven't heard her laugh in days.

Lydia returns with a garment bag attached to a hanger. She lays it across the barstools on the other side of the island and then looks at me. "Everything should fit, but if you wouldn't mind trying it on, that would help. I got it at the shops, so if anything's too small, I can replace it when I go into town today."

She joins my mother, and I step around the island and unzip the garment bag. Inside are a black button-up and black pants, with a black belt and tie. I glance over my shoulder at my mother. She raises an eyebrow at me.

"I'm not wearing a tie," I tell her.

She crosses her arms and gives me that Madison Lynch

look. "You wear a tie at your restaurant all the time. This is a black-tie affair, which means, *black tie.*"

I roll my eyes and turn back to the bag, already undoing my belt with one hand as I pick up the garment bag with the other. I can take it down to the basement to change. I pull my belt off and look up when I hear Quinn make a tiny sound.

Her cheeks are flushed, her mouth hanging open and her eyes on the belt that's dangling from my hand. Her gaze lift to mine, and everything from my waist down goes tight. I raise an eyebrow, silently asking a question that I already know the answer to. She liked seeing me whip this belt off.

Even after everything, this gorgeous girl wants me to do nasty things to her, and I want to give her what she wants. I want to make her forget about all the shit going down in this house. I want her to focus on me, and only me.

"Reed." My mother's voice pulls me away from Quinn again. It's starting to sound like nails on a chalkboard.

I turn to face her, still holding my belt and the garment bag. "Yeah?"

"Don't forget the shoes." She points at a pair of black leather shoes sitting on the step that separates the kitchen from the living room.

"Yeah, thanks." I reach down and use two fingers to snatch up the shoes and go down to the basement. As soon as I get down there though, I drop everything onto the floor and lean against the wall to catch my breath. Three more days. That's all the time I have left to convince Quinn she's mine.

But when she looks at me with those eyes, asks me to do things to her that she's never let anyone do, it convinces me that she already knows. She already knows that we're meant to be together. That the last five years were just a roadblock, and now it's our turn.

I take my time trying on the outfit my mom bought me, like

I'm a kid going to his first middle school dance. It looks great. I stand in the mirror in the bedroom and run my fingers through my short hair. There's nothing to be done for it or the stubble beard that I've become accustomed to, but I don't think Quinn minds. I'm not wearing the tie. Instead, I've got the first two buttons on the shirt undone, the belt firmly in place, the shirt tucked in just so. I even put on the shoes.

When I head back upstairs, Quinn isn't in the kitchen anymore. She's helping Amina and my mother sort through a stack of black dresses that all look exactly the same to me, probably searching for something that Amina can wear.

"It fits," I say, and all of the women turn to look at me.

"Holy shit," Amina says, and it's almost enough to make me feel really fucking good about myself.

But when I see Quinn's face, that's what really does me in. Her cheeks are pink, her eyes running all the way down my body and then back up again. The blush travels across her chest, and I know I need to leave now or embarrass myself by popping a boner.

"All good?" I ask my mother, like I came up here for her approval and not for Quinn's.

"Yes," my mother says, her eyes on Amina.

I turn, and as I head back toward the basement, I hear Quinn say, "Madison, I'm sorry. I think you should count me out on the party shopping. I'm not feeling too great. I think I'm going to go lay down."

44 QUINN

I WAKE TO A WARM HEAT ON MY STOMACH AND OPEN MY eyes to see Reed lick his way up to my breast and take my nipple into his mouth. I gasp, my whole body immediately going taut.

I sink my hands into his hair, and then reality sinks in, and I try to sit up, even with the weight of half his body on me. "Wait. What are you doing?" I ask, trying to shove him away as I look toward the open bedroom door.

Open. As in, anyone could just walk by any minute.

Reed chuckles against my skin. "They're all gone. Everyone went into town, even Chase. We're all alone."

I feel relief first, but then his words really sink in and my skin begins to hum. "Alone?"

He smiles up at me, devious and sexy. "Alone. And I want to make you scream."

My pulse immediately picks up speed. Yes. Yes, I want that, too. I want him to make me scream so loud that I go hoarse. "Please," is all I say before he moves up to kiss me. I don't know how he does it, but when he kisses me, it's almost like I don't need anything else. I love the sex, but the fulfillment I get just from his mouth on mine is almost shocking.

I pull away and turn my head to let him suck at my neck. And that's when I see the belt laying on the bed beside me. The same belt Reed was wearing earlier. The one that made me almost lose myself entirely when he whipped it off in one easy, harsh glide. Just seeing it now, harmlessly beside me like that, has a shiver moving through me. Because I know why Reed brought it in here.

Like he can read my mind, Reed grabs the belt off the bed and then scoops me up in his arms, carrying me out of the room.

"Where are we going?" I ask as we move down the hallway.

He scoffs. "Not even I hate my brother enough to fuck his ex-wife in his bed. I doubt I would even be able to get it up."

Something about the way he says it makes me giggle, even as I can hear the sound of the belt hitting his thigh with every step he takes.

He tosses me onto the couch and immediately starts to take my clothes off, ripping my shirt over my head and undoing my bra. It feels sexy and scary to be doing this in the living room of the Lynch lake house. It feels like anyone could walk in. But I trust Reed. I know he would never put me in that kind of position.

He presses his forehead to mine, breathes heavily against my mouth. "Did you like what you saw earlier?"

I nod, biting my lip. "You looked so delicious, I could have died."

His mouth stretches into a smile. And then his hand fists into my hair and he yanks my head back, making me gasp. Against the skin of my neck, he says, "I'm going to show you you're mine. Are you going to be a good girl and take it?"

My stomach flutters with nerves. "Yes," I say hesitantly.

Reaching down, he slips my shorts and underwear down my legs until I'm bare. And then he says, "Get on your knees on the couch. Hands on the back of it."

I do what he tells me, draping my arms over the back of the couch and settling on my knees, letting my ass stick out. He makes a pleased noise in the back of his throat, and when I look over my shoulder at him, I realize he's rubbing himself through his pants. He's still fully dressed.

"Reed," I whisper, the word coming out needy, and like I shook him out of some kind of trance, he stands up quickly, folds his belt in half, and spanks me with it. I choke a little, my whole body turning into white hot need. It doesn't hurt the way I thought it would. I've never been spanked or paddled or anything during sex, and even though seeing him with that belt in his hand earlier turned me on, I wasn't sure if I was going to like this.

But I do. I like it a lot. It's just enough pain to be startling but not so much that I've immediately crossed into territory I'm not ready for.

When I sigh and set my head against the soft back of the couch, Reed chuckles. "So filthy," he says, running his palm down my ass and the outside of my thigh. "You love it, don't you?" I don't miss the pride in his voice, what it means to him that we're taking this chance together, searching for new parts of ourselves.

I don't answer. Mostly because I want to say yes, but it feels like it makes it a little more exciting if I hide how much I like it. So, I stay quiet as his eyes meet mine, searching. But I feel the smile curling up the corner of my mouth, and when Reed's eyes drop there, I know I've given him his answer. Given him permission.

Snap. The belt hits me again, and I whimper. It's like

there's a direct connection between how hard he hits me and how wet I am.

"Tell me you're mine," he says, and my chest starts to pull tight. Because it's a game but it's not, at the same time. "Tell me you belong to me."

I stare out the back window of the house, my vision full of blue lake and green trees. I have to separate myself from this. I'm terrified that if I let myself feel, I won't be able to undo it. I squeeze my eyes shut, keep my mouth clamped.

Snap.

"Tell me," he growls, his voice more demanding. Are we still playing? Was it ever a game at all? "Tell me who you belong to."

I bury my face in the leather couch cushion. "You," I say, just barely a whisper.

Smack.

"Louder."

"I'm yours," I shout, turned on beyond belief, desperate with need. "I belong to you, Reed."

One of his hands grasps one of my ass cheeks. "Such a good girl," he says. "Do you need a reward for that?"

I nod, feeling wrung out. "Please," I squeak out, all of my emotions taking their toll on me. "Please, give it to me."

He squeezes my hip, and the belt falls to the floor with a *clunk.* "Such a greedy little slut," he says, his mouth touching my hip. He bites down on my skin.

I cry out, squirming, trying to relieve some of the pressure between my legs, rubbing my nipples against the couch like a cat in heat.

"Not yet," he says, his voice gentle. He settles his hand between my shoulder blades, like he's making sure that I keep my upper half against the back of the couch, before sliding it down my spine and then yanking my hips back. And then I feel his tongue between my legs. I moan, immediately moving against him to try and get him to lick inside of me. I feel so empty, and I need something inside me, his tongue, his fingers, his dick, I don't care.

But he just laps at my clit, licking all the way up to my opening and then starting again, like he's trying to make me wet, trying to keep me on the edge, without actually giving me any kind of relief. I set my cheek against the couch, focusing on breathing, on keeping myself calm. I have a feeling the more I beg, the less he's going to give me. I just need to give in.

My muscles relax, now that I'm not straining for him anymore, and Reed seems to sense my surrender because he immediately dips his tongue inside me. My hands ball into fists in the fabric of the couch, and I groan. He spends a second pumping into me and then his tongue slicks up, moving between my cheeks.

My mouth falls open and an inhuman sound escapes my mouth when his tongue prods at my asshole. I've never had anyone do that to me before, and when his tongue pushes past any resistance at the same time his fingers plunge into my pussy, I have to squeeze my eyes shut against the sharp rush of pleasure.

"I'm going to come," I whisper, my mouth flush against the couch.

"What's that, baby?" he pauses just long enough to ask. But then his tongue re-enters me, and I can't repeat myself because an orgasm grips me, my legs shaking and my fingers digging into the fabric beneath me.

When I come back down, Reed moves to sit on the couch beside me, still dressed, only his shorts pushed far enough down to free his cock, pointed directly up at the ceiling. He pats me on the hip, and that's enough to tell me he wants me to climb onto his lap.

We move without speaking, until I'm lowering myself onto his cock. He slips in so easily; my orgasm has left me soaked. We moan together, holding each other's gazes as we start to move, slow at first and then faster and faster.

I didn't know it could feel like this. I didn't know that sex could be something that binds you to a person, that makes you feel like you've somehow melted into one. I don't feel like I belong completely to myself anymore. I know that part of me is his now. I know that no matter what happens, I'll never feel exactly like this ever again.

I wrap my arms around him and bury my face in his neck. "I just feel so—" My voice breaks, and I want to grind my teeth in frustration. I can't cry on him again. I can't do this emotional thing, can't say a bunch of things that will be impossible for me to take back once this trip is over and I never see him again.

But with his arms around me, I can't even explain it. I feel like he's holding me together. Like if he lets me go, I'll shatter, never to be put back together again. His big hands splay across my back, and I want him to dig his nails in, mark me so that I can't convince myself, someday down the line when this is nothing but a distant memory, that it never happened.

"Say it," he says into my ear, his voice a rumble. "Tell me what you need to tell me."

"I feel so safe with you." The words burst out of me in a huff.

His hands drop down to my hips, and I feel him pushing at me, even as we keep moving, keeping thrusting against each other. He tries to put space between us, to unwrap my arms from around his shoulders, but I hold on tight.

"I want to look at you." When he pushes again, I give in, sitting up straight until I can see his eyes. His hands come up to hold my face, and I feel cracked open down the middle.

He holds my gaze that way he does, so fearless and sure,

pressing his forehead to mine as our hips slow, until it's just a gentle rocking. I feel the stubble on his jaw under my fingertips, memorize the feel of it.

Oh, God, please don't do this to me. Please don't make me feel this way.

But I know it's too late. It's far too late.

I'm in love with him. It feels like something starting in my stomach and stretching out inside me until it's all I can feel, not quite pain and not quite pleasure. It's just *wanting*. It's just the need to never let him go. To beg him to never let *me* go.

But I can't. It's not an option. So I kiss him, kiss him and hope that the thing that has stretched itself inside my body will somehow spread to him. Let myself live in a fantasy where we could somehow be more than what has happened here this week.

We kiss as we start to move again, kiss as we grip each other hard, kiss until we both come, shouting into each other's mouths, making as much noise as we can. Just this once.

45 REED

1 Year Ago

I DON'T KNOW WHAT TO DO WITH MYSELF. QUINN IS IN MY restaurant. She came here without Chase, and I know she came here to eat and not to see me but...she's here.

I want to hover around her like a honeybee around a flower, but I don't want to make her uncomfortable. She deserves to have her dinner in peace, but her waiter has told me that she and Brooke are pretty much done eating and are contemplating dessert. I don't want her to leave without me getting one more chance to talk to her, one more chance to see her face, to burn it into my memory because I know it's going to be a long time before I see her again. I've slowly been backing out of family get-togethers since Quinn became a Lynch. I went to Christmas last year, but I don't know if I can do it again. Seeing Quinn slowly lose her glow as the years go on has been like slowly losing my soul. I can't sit across from her again and watch my brother ignore her.

I round the corner and step up to their table. I put them close to the kitchen so that I could keep an eye on them to the best of my ability. They're looking at their menus, having a quiet debate about something. Both of them look very serious.

"Everything to your liking, ladies?"

Quinn slams her menu closed and smiles up at me, like I caught her doing something she wasn't supposed to.

"Of course," she says, polite as ever. "The swordfish was delicious."

"Great. Hey, you wanna come back and meet Oscar?" I don't actually want her to meet Oscar, but I'm not ready to let her leave yet. Mostly I don't want her to meet Oscar because he has a tendency to let his mouth get him in trouble, and I don't want him to say anything that might offend or shock Quinn. There's also the fact that I'm very certain he's been coming to work high.

"Sure."

"Oh, I'm actually going to go use the bathroom. I'll meet you back here for dessert." I whip around to look at Brooke. I sort of forgot that she existed, and I'm fine if she wants to get lost long enough to let me spend a few minutes with Quinn. Maybe I can take her out back and we can talk for a little bit.

In the hall outside the kitchen, Quinn comes to a halt. All the sound from inside has flooded out into the hallway, and I know it can be a little intimidating. I offer her a reassuring smile and a nudge in the direction of the door. I can feel the heat of her through her thin blouse, making my hand sweat.

"Don't worry," I tell her. "It's always like this. It's part of the kitchen experience."

She turns her face up to mine, and I'm stuck for a moment, my eyes hungrily taking her in. She's so beautiful, her eyes rimmed in eyeliner and her lips a pale pink. A light sheen of sweat has settled along her hairline. I'm fairly certain that the sight of her in this moment will be the thing I see when I'm on my death bed.

"Reed, get the fuck out of the way."

I pull Quinn out of the way of Leo, who's coming through with a tray.

"Sorry. These guys don't know how to play nice." I turn and see Oscar, coming up to us with a look on his face like he wants to make trouble.

"Who's this?" he asks. When he looks Quinn up and down like she's something for him to eat, I have to keep myself from lunging at him. He knows what Quinn looks like, and he knows Quinn is Chase's wife, but he still has to turn every single woman he sees into a potential sex partner. Just the thought of it makes my skin crawl.

"This is Quinn."

"Ah. The elusive Quinn. Happy to finally meet you." My stomach rumbles. I don't need Oscar opening his big mouth and making it clear that I talk about Quinn much more than a person should speak about their sister-in-law. Not to mention that Oscar has already met Quinn. He just doesn't remember because he was acting like an ass when I brought my family here before the opening.

"Yeah, that's me," Quinn says pleasantly. "The swordfish was lovely."

The door opens behind us and Romeo sticks his head in. "Mr. Lynch, you're needed up front."

Dammit. This is what it's always like on Saturday nights. I'm running around like crazy, not even overseeing the desserts like I want to be, just flitting from place to place, putting out fires.

"Oh, sure," I tell Romeo and look down at Quinn. Maybe it's for the best. Look at how beautiful she is. Maybe I wouldn't have been able to keep myself from saying something stupid to her or doing something like begging her to leave my brother so that she could be mine instead.

I hold the kitchen door open for her and escort her out. In the hallway, I say, "I'll see you later, Quinn, okay?" before I can do something idiotic, like tell her I've been in love with her for four years. I rush to the front of house, where there was a mix-up in the office with a staff schedule, and when the fire is out, I turn back toward the dining room, hoping to catch Quinn before she's gone.

But when I swing the door open that leads back into the lobby, it's to find Brooke there, standing and looking out the front windows onto the street, like she's waiting for someone.

"Looking for Quinn?" I ask her. She must still be in the back, though what she could be doing back there, I can't imagine. Maybe using the bathroom.

"No," Brooke says, looking up at me. She's a very small person, but her eyes hold a confidence I rarely see. Whatever she's about the say, she's pretty certain of it. "I was waiting for you."

"Oh," I say, putting my hands in the pockets of my slacks. "Is everything okay?"

"No. Everything is not okay."

All I can do is stare at her as an unsettling feeling begins to brew inside me. She clearly has something to say, and I want her to say it before I lose my nerve.

Brooke takes a step toward me, and I realize that my maître d' is listening, that whatever is about to happen here will be all over the staff before the night is out. "I have no idea how Quinn doesn't see right through you, but I do. Everything you're doing, it's so transparent. And while the fact that you're clearly in love with Quinn isn't a problem for me, I have a feeling it would be a problem for your brother."

I will not speak. I will not open my mouth and incriminate myself further than I already have. Which is clearly what Brooke was hoping for because she keeps talking, her chin tipping up and her feet coming closer to mine. "I get it, Reed. Quinn is amazing, and I get why you would be so into her. But..." She looks away from me, her confidence slipping for a moment. When she looks back, it's clearly re-doubled. "But I'm worried that if Quinn knows how you feel about her, it would mess with her head. And she doesn't deserve that. I know you're too good of a guy to try to snatch your brother's wife out from under him, and I think Quinn is too good of a person to let you. But *feelings* can destroy everything. So, I need you to tread carefully."

I open my mouth to argue, feeling like I've already tread pretty carefully here, but Brooke speaks over me.

"You named one of your desserts 'the Quinn,' you idiot."

My eyes go to the floor. I forgot about the stupid cookies. It was an idea that I had that I wouldn't let anyone talk me out of, and at the time, it felt like a friendly gesture. An inside joke between the two of us. But now, through Brooke's eyes, I can see that it's clearly insanity.

There's no getting out of this one, but I can't bear the thought of Brooke being the one to tell Quinn that I have feelings for her. I've worked hard not to let her find out, and I don't want it all shot to shit now.

"Brooke," I say, lowering my voice and taking a step toward her, in hopes that my staff will butt out. "I've loved her for a long time. I've never made a move. I've never tried to...do anything. She doesn't know, and I need it to stay that way. I want her to be happy, and if that means being happy with my brother...well...I've already accepted that, so can we just... drop it?"

She crosses her arms, takes a deep breath. When she

speaks, her voice is much softer. "You're not going to try to ruin her marriage."

I want to laugh. I'm the one that talked her *into* her fucking marriage.

"Never," I finally say.

She taps her foot a few times, glances over my shoulder toward the dining room. When she looks back at me, she's clearly made a decision. "Okay. But if I ever catch a whiff of you trying to charm her away from Chase, I will castrate you myself."

"You would have my blessing."

She nods once and moves around me, heading back toward where I left Quinn.

"And dinner is on me," I call out to her.

"I know," she shoots back over her shoulder at me.

I duck back into the staff room, sitting amongst everyone's bags and jackets while I wait for them to leave. Now that I know I've been so obvious that Quinn's best friend figured me out, I can never be in the same room with Quinn again.

I'VE LOST SIGHT OF QUINN. I CAN'T FIND HER ANYWHERE, and I can't go looking for her because we made a deal that we would do our best not to spend the whole night in each other's orbits. It's one thing to make our family think we're just really good friends by hovering around each other, but it's something else entirely if everyone at the party starts to notice that she's spending more time with me than she is with her own husband.

I glance around the room, trying to see past all of the unfamiliar faces. There are a few I recognize from going into town, and some I recognize from back in the city, people who came all the way out just to say they were at Madison Lynch's 4th of July party. But they're all blank faces to me. Because I'm looking for her.

And then I see her. She's a spot of navy blue over by the kitchen, chatting up a woman I recognize as an old friend of my mother's. Her hair is hanging down around her shoulders in waves, and I have to look away before I start reliving this afternoon in my head, when she rode me to orgasm and then let me put her on her back for round two and fuck her into the couch until she blew out her vocal cords screaming.

Nothing has ever been more perfect. And tonight is the night I'm going to ask her to move in with me. She already knows how I feel about her. Now all I need to do is convince her that when we get back to Boston, she should live with me, and be with me, and spend the rest of her life with me. She won't need the money or the house. We could leave right now.

I think I'll be able to pull it off. This week has been... incredible...and I know she feels it, too. I know that when she was riding me earlier, biting back tears, that she was trying to run from the fact that she's in love with me.

I know she's loved me as long as I've loved her. It's just taken her this long to figure it out.

"Why didn't you tell me?"

My mother has appeared at my side, a glass of champagne in her hand, her face the perfect mask of kind cordiality as she waves at someone across the room.

My stomach protests. Does she know about Quinn and me? I've always been a little suspicious that she had cameras around the lake house, but I don't have any evidence. If I thought my mother was watching, I certainly wouldn't have railed Quinn in the middle of the living room.

"Tell you what?"

She tilts her face up to me. "That your restaurant closed."

Now, this. This I knew was coming. Especially after Sabrina found out. I asked her not to say anything to Mom, but in a room full of socialites, it was just a matter of time. I wish Quinn was here now, standing beside me, keeping me strong while I face the disappointment of my mother.

"I didn't want to upset you. It's temporary. I've got a new place in the works."

"But your business partner was *arrested*. You don't think that's something you should tell me about?"

Someone in a group of people nearby turns their head toward us.

"Mom, this isn't the best time." I turn to face her, needing to get the rest of the people in this room out of my line of sight. I just need to focus on my mother, the woman who's done so much for me. "I just... I didn't want you to be disappointed. So I tried to wait to tell you until I had my next step figured out. I didn't want you to think I failed."

Her eyebrows pull together. "Is that what you think keeps me up at night, Reed? Do you think I pace my bedroom, worrying that your business endeavors won't work out?"

I can't keep myself from looking around the room. I know most of these people are business contacts of my mother's. She's so well-known and successful as a businesswoman that people crawl over each other to be in her sphere of influence. I look back at her.

"I mean, yeah. Pretty much. I know how important it is to you that we—"

"That you be happy."

My words die in my throat. She steps closer to me, reaches up and presses her hand to my cheek. "My dear, darling first-born. You have always been so different from your brother and sister. You've always been a romantic. I know. You got it from your father."

My heart squeezes. My mother almost never speaks about my dad. According to her, there's nothing to say. They met in the wilds of Australia, had a lovely time together, and then chose to go their separate ways. As far as I know, he doesn't even know I exist.

"When you came back from that culinary program in Paris with stars in your eyes, I knew you would choose a different life. I want you to keep choosing a different life." She takes one of my hands in hers, gripping it tight. "I always want you to move passionately in the direction of your dreams, do you understand? Your brother and your sister, they fall so easily into their roles because what they want is security and fame. But you, you want something else. You don't need my blessing, but you always have it."

My eyes slip back to the kitchen, to Quinn, a smile on her face, the most beautiful creature I've ever seen. Mom wants me to go after what I want, but if she really knew, would she still be so accepting?

I bend and kiss her on the cheek. "Thanks, Mom. Believe me, I'm going after what I want. And as soon as I know what's next, I'll let you know."

She smiles back at me. And then her smile fades and she becomes Madison Lynch again. "Fireworks go off at nine. I need to make sure everything is arranged." She gives me a little nudge. "Go have a good time."

As soon as she scampers off, I turn for the kitchen. Maybe enough time has passed that no one will notice if I go and stand by her.

But Quinn is gone. The packed kitchen is full of people who definitely aren't her. I stop in the middle of the room, looking all around but not seeing her. Maybe she needed a breather. I glance down the hall leading to the bedrooms, but there are a lot of people down there. If Quinn was looking for quiet, she definitely didn't go that way. I turn the other way, toward the hall that leads to the master and the basement.

There are people heading for the dining room, but nobody, that I can see, going for the basement. I imagine Quinn down there, in that space that has become ours this week, and I move toward it quickly.

Halfway down the stairs, I come to a halt. I can hear noises, a quiet, soft grunting and a feminine moaning. It must be someone from the party. Sure, these are all very well-to-do professionals, but they're also humans, and sometimes humans like to fuck at parties.

Out of pure curiosity, I silently take the rest of the steps down to the basement and stick my head into the dark. Whoever it is, they're going at it on the love seat. In the moonlight, I can make out the shapes of two people, fucking doggystyle.

I start to back out, but in the time it takes me to move back up a step, my eyes start to adjust, and I can see the faces of the people having sex. They don't even realize I'm here, they're so into each other.

Chase and Amina.

I immediately turn and move up the stairs, my brain trying to erase what I saw. Chase using her, the same way he's used every woman he's ever been with. The way he used Quinn. I expect that shit from him, but I'm surprised that Amina would settle for a man she knows is married when there's a whole house full of unmarried men, ripe for the taking. Chase is just really that manipulative.

Back out in the hall, the anger rises in me. What if I had been Mom? What if someone went down there and saw them together? He's supposed to be pretending to still be married to Quinn. Does he think it doesn't matter anymore now that the week is almost over?

Well, it does matter.

I need to find Quinn before *she* finds *them*.

47 QUINN

I forgot how much I dislike these parties. While the rest of America is having cook-outs in denim shorts and red, white, and blue t-shirts, the Lynches have a black-tie party. Because, of course.

And on top of that, they invite everyone in the New England states that Madison is on a first name basis with, so there has to be over a hundred people squished into the lake house. A lot of them are on the back patio and some still on the front lawn, drinking expensive champagne and looking up at the stars that are visible through the light pollution.

I wander down to the lake, knowing chances are good that nobody from the party will venture this far. I can smell the water, but I can't really see it in the dark. There's no light by the dock because there's never anybody out here this late. But I know exactly where the dock is, having been down here so many times, so I step onto the boards, enjoying the sound of my heels on the wooden slats.

When I reach the end, I let my head fall forward, feeling

the breeze cool the sweat on the back of my neck. I pick my hair up and hold it off my skin to let it dry.

When I hear footsteps on the dock behind me, I spin around. Relief hits me like a tidal wave when I realize it's Reed. I've been trying to keep my distance from him all night. He looks good enough to eat, and I know that if I get too close to him, I'll be tempted to swallow him whole. And here he is, stepping closer to me on the lake, where we're completely alone, with the top two buttons on his shirt open and his sleeves rolled up to his elbows.

Lord save me.

"Trying to find some quiet?" he says, coming to stand beside me and putting his hands in his pockets.

"Yeah. There are a lot of people in there."

He steps closer. "I like finding you outside parties all by yourself."

I laugh, something unpleasant settling in my stomach when I think about the last time he found me outside of a party. I turn my back to him, tilt my face up toward the moon, sparkling down on the water. "It's sort of your specialty. Except this time, if you could refrain from abandoning me to hang out with some other woman, that would be nice." I don't mean for the words to come out bitter, but they do anyway. If he had just come back at the Halloween party, would all of this be different?

He steps up beside me, pushing his way between me and the end of the dock so I'm forced to look at him. "What are you talking about?"

Now that I know he remembers, the memory of that night is even more wrapped in sadness than it always has been. "The Halloween party. You left. You went to hang out with those other girls."

"I didn't leave."

I scoff. Is he really going to tell me I didn't see what I saw? "There were girls—"

"I had friends. And I was at a party, where people sometimes talk to their friends. But I came back."

The world sways a little. No, he didn't. He stood there, talking to those girls for a long time. And then.... And then I left and bumped into Chase. "You came back?" The words come out a whisper. I don't have the strength for anything more than that.

"Yeah. I did. But you were already with Chase."

My stomach riots, and I suddenly can't catch my breath. He saw us that night. He saw me leave with Chase. "I didn't know," I gasp out.

He pushes forward, taking my face in his hands. "I will *always* come back for you, Quinn. Always."

There is no more oxygen left in the world. He's taking up all of it. I shake my head. "You were so perfect. I just didn't understand how you could want me. I think I...I think I was trying to walk away before I got hurt."

"You were *all* I wanted."

I bite my lip, feeling all of the overwhelming emotion that I've been trying to stamp down all day rise up in my throat. "It was too hard to believe that the boy all the girls were after would be interested in me."

He makes a noise in the back of his throat, his hands smoothing down my jaw and gently wrapping around my throat. "Let me make something clear because you obviously don't get it. I'm yours. I've been yours since that night. I belong to you."

I whimper, feeling like he stuck a knife in me, and then his mouth comes down on mine. I've never needed someone's kiss like this, craved it the way I crave oxygen. He wraps himself around me, and I wish, so desperately, that the rest of the world would melt away. That there was no danger in this and that we could walk off this dock and back into the party hand-in-hand.

There has to be a way that this doesn't all end in three days. There has to be.

Because I can't give this up now that I know everything. I can't let him go.

I pull back from him, gasping for air. "Reed, I—"

Over our heads, a firework pops. We both look up, our arms still around each other, watching the colors burst in the inky black sky. The water ripples with rainbows after every explosion. When I look over my shoulder, I see that people are crowding around the pool, trying to get a good vantage point between the trees.

I step back from Reed. "We should probably be a little more careful now that everyone is outside."

He doesn't say anything, just watches me silently.

I don't know if we should head back now and risk being seen coming back from the lake together, or stay here until the crowd goes inside. I turn toward the house, and my eyes catch movement on the trail leading from the house to the boat house. I watch in the moonlight, trying to make out shapes, and realize it's Sabrina and Lydia.

As a spray of red fireworks burst, they stop on the dirt trail and kiss.

"Not getting used to that anytime soon." Reed steps up behind me, his hand curling around my hip and his eyes focused where mine just were. He watches Sabrina and Lydia disappear into the boat house, and then he sighs. "No one in this family is who they claim to be."

I turn to argue, but then I realize he's right. Everyone came to this lake house with secrets, all of them being kept to protect

Madison, and Madison was trying to protect everyone else with her own. A sticky situation, to be sure.

"Now, you know everyone's true selves," I say, feeling confident in the words. All the secrets might not be out in the open, but unless there are going to be anymore revelations, Reed and I at least know everything.

48 REED

When the fireworks are over, the music gets louder. My mother isn't exactly the party hard type, but a lot of the people in the house are closer to our age than hers, so when the older guests start to filter out, what's left is a bunch of horny twenty and thirty-somethings with a lot of champagne in them.

I lean against the kitchen island as pop music plays loudly through the speakers and watch several groups of people in their formal attire dance in the sunken pit that is the living room, including Quinn and Sabrina, who are laughing and dancing with each other. A man steps close, trying to get Sabrina to dance with him, and she turns her back, giving Quinn her full attention.

And Quinn.

Jesus.

She's so sexy, twisting her hips to the beat, the ends of her hair starting to curl from the sweat. I can't wait until this thing is over, and I can find someplace quiet to put my mouth between her legs.

I feel warm. Content.

I feel like, later tonight, when I ask Quinn to be mine when we leave here, she'll say yes. I don't know if she was going to tell me she loved me out there on the dock, but I see it in her eyes every time she looks at me. She's mine.

Chase appears out of nowhere, bumping into my side and grinning into a half-empty glass of clear alcohol. "Great party, huh?"

I look over at him, already annoyed at his existence. "How many have you had?"

He's got a piece of ice in his mouth; he speaks around it. "Not that many." He swallows. "I'm not drunk, if that's what you're thinking. I actually..." He trails off and looks down into his glass, like he's trying to decide what to say next. "I think I'm going to try to get her back."

When I just stare at him, he nods toward the dance floor, and I don't need to look to know who he's gesturing at.

"What the hell are you talking about?" I should stay calm. I should try to be casual. But he has to be kidding, right? He can't actually mean that.

He shrugs, like it's no big deal. Because, to him, it never was. Having Quinn's heart never amounted to much for him. "I don't know. This week has really given us a chance to talk. We stopped doing that, you know, toward the end. And I still really feel like we could fit. I thought, you know, maybe if I asked her out or something, maybe we could find our way back to each other."

All the calm has left my body. All that's left is a boiling rage. "Chase, you just fucked Amina in the basement."

He looks confused but then doesn't ask me how I know. "Well, sure, but that's just sex."

Yeah. That's what he's been telling himself all this time. After everything, he hasn't learned one single goddamn lesson. He wants to go back to the life he had, where he gets to be married to an amazing woman while he fucks every other woman in Boston. He never has to owe Quinn anything. Affection, time, energy, love. He can just use her up and toss her aside.

"That's not gonna happen."

A crease appears between his eyebrows. "You don't think she'd take me back?"

No, I don't think she'd take him back, but that doesn't matter because he's never going to have the chance to try to convince her to. "It's not going to happen because Quinn is mine."

For a moment, I watch as his face stays the same picture of confusion, and then the crease disappears, and anger takes its place in his eyes. "What the fuck did you just say to me?"

I set my glass on the bar beside me, feeling fire burn in my chest. "I said, she's *mine*. She might have been yours once, but you fucked it up, and now she belongs to me, and I'll be damned if you'll ever lay a finger on her again."

Chase is quiet for a long stretch of time, our eyes locked in a battle of wills, here in the middle of this loud party, with everyone around us none the wiser. He takes the smallest step toward me. "Are you telling me you fucked my wife?"

"She's not your wife."

The party is still moving around us, the music still blasting, the guests still dancing. But Chase seems to go still from his head to his toes. His eyes glance back at the dance floor, and whatever dopey optimism was there a moment ago has burned away.

"Fucking *bitch*," he hisses.

I don't remember moving. I don't remember barreling into my brother or how we end up on the floor. I don't remember how many times I punch him before he punches back, before the two of us start kicking and punching and shoving. We end up on our feet again, and then, somehow, we smash into a cock-tail table full of champagne glasses.

"Reed!" I hear her voice, not really sure if it's real or somewhere in my mind. It's like she's shouting to me through a tunnel, but I can't get to her. When I turn my head to find her, Chase uses the opportunity to sock me in the eye.

And then two big arms are wrapping around me, pulling me up and off my brother. I don't even know whose arms they are, but whoever it is, they're strong enough to lift me. When I've got my feet under me, it's like the rest of the world has gone dark, all except Chase, pushing up to his feet, panting.

"What the fuck is your problem?" he growls at me.

"Call her a bitch again and fucking find out."

He wipes away a string of blood pooling out of his lower lip. "I can call her whatever I want. She's my wife."

I fight against the hands holding me, but they're gripping me hard, so hard I'm afraid they're going to snap something. *"She's not your fucking wife."*

The whole world stops moving. My vision opens up, and I begin to process just how many people there are in the room, just how many people heard those words. Exactly what I've *done.*

From somewhere behind me, a small voice says, "What?"

I turn and see my mother, standing in the middle of the room, her hand on her chest and her eyes on me. Her gaze shifts from me to someone beside me, and I realize Quinn is there. Her face is pale. She looks like she's going to throw up.

She looks around the room, and I know she sees what I do. Everybody is looking. Everybody is watching. Everybody *knows.* But it's like she doesn't even see me. Her eyes are glued to my mother.

"I'm so sorry, Madison," she whispers. And because the whole room is silent, her words seem to echo through every corner. "I never meant to cause all...this." She looks over her shoulder at where glass and ice and champagne litter the floor. I can only imagine what a mess I look. Her eyes meet mine, and she shakes her head. The barest of movements. "I'm sorry," she says again.

And then she runs.

She's already halfway to the hall before my mind shakes awake. "Quinn!" I run after her, but she's much smaller than me and trying to get through all the partygoers, standing still like they're guarding her escape, proves impossible. By the time I make it to her room, the door is shut. I try the doorknob, but it's locked.

"Quinn!" I bang on the door, aware now of the murmuring going on behind me. I won't turn and look at all the people at the end of the hallway. It's not about them. It's not about Chase or my mother. It's about Quinn and me. And I'm not going to let her run. "Quinn, come on, don't do this. Talk to me."

Somewhere in the living room, I hear my mother's voice. "Everyone, I apologize, but I believe the party is over. If you'll please allow our family to sort out this mess in private."

I hear the shifting of bodies, the shuffling of feet, the front door opening. I finally turn toward the end of the hallway and see my mother standing there, outlined in the light flowing in from the living room.

"Reed, what's happening?" She sounds like a child in the middle of a thunderstorm.

I sigh. "I—"

Beside me, the bedroom door flies open, and Quinn stands there, the doorknob in one hand and her bag in the other. Her eyes won't meet mine. "Excuse me," she says, but I don't move.

"Quinn, come on. We can figure this out."

She makes a strange, frustrated noise and pushes past me.

It's not as if I can stop her. I'm not going to hold her hostage. But I'm not going to let her leave without a fight.

"Quinn," I say as she stomps down the hallway.

When she gets to my mother, she chokes out, "Madison, I'm sorry. I'll let Chase and Reed explain. Please know that I never meant to hurt anyone."

My mother's eyes are big and full of concern as she watches Quinn continue past her to the front door. It slams behind her, and I'm already moving down the hallway, following her out.

49 QUINN

THERE ARE STILL STRAGGLERS TRYING TO GET OUT OF THE driveway when I reach my car. I'm lucky it's close by; I want to get out of here as quickly as I can.

"Quinn!"

Something inside my chest cracks open. I can't take this. It was bad enough that the shit hit the fan in such a spectacular way without Reed refusing to let me go, too. I toss my bag into the backseat and throw open the driver's side door.

"Quinn, no. You need to talk to me."

I know he's right. I know it's not fair for me to take off like this, but what the hell else am I supposed to do? I can't face him. I can't face any of them.

Before I can get in my car, Reed is there. He reaches out and shuts the door, and like a four-year-old, I stamp my foot. "Reed!" I meet his eye, but I can't read his expression. Angry? Confused? Desperate? Who even knows.

"You can't just leave like this, Quinn. We can figure this out. This thing between us, you know it means something. I'm not just going to let you walk away because you're scared."

A choking noise bursts out of me. "How are we supposed to do this, Reed? You know we can't do this. Your family—"

"I don't care what they think."

"I do!" This finally gets him to close his mouth. All I can see in my head is Chase's bleeding lip. The glass on the floor. Their faces red as they scream at each other. "I can't be the reason anyone in this family hates each other. I won't be the reason this family isn't a family anymore."

When he speaks again, his voice is much quieter. "*Chase* is the reason this family isn't a family anymore. Not you."

He may be right, but there's never going to be any peace in the Lynch family if I stick around. "You had to know this could never work. You had to know this couldn't be real after this week. What, we're supposed to sit across from Chase at Thanksgiving dinner? Show up every summer, having just passed me from one man to the next like hand-me-down clothes?"

His breath bursts out of him. He takes a step closer to me, and I fight not to move away, even though I want to. I don't want him to touch me. My willpower is hanging on by a thread, and if he touches me, I don't know if I'll be strong enough to do what I have to. "Don't say that. That's not what this is."

"This was just sex, Reed." I force the words out, even though I know they're a lie. "This was two people stuck together for a week when they were both vulnerable. This was two people who needed to be touched and trusted each other."

"It wasn't just sex to me, Quinn."

It wasn't just sex to me either, but in this moment, I have to pretend. I have to convince myself because if I can't, I'll shatter. I'll be broken beyond repair. I will never be able to put myself back together again. "I would give *anything* to have my family back, Reed." When I meet his eyes, I see the way they shimmer in the moonlight. I know I'm ripping him apart, but he'll thank me someday. "You owe it to your family to try and heal. And you can't do that with me around."

He watches me for a long time before shaking his head. "I love you, Quinn."

A sob forces its way out of me. *Go,* I tell myself. *Go before it's too late.* "Reed, I can't. I'm sorry."

With one more look over his shoulder at the cabin, I see two figures standing in the doorway, dark silhouettes. But I know who they are. Madison and Sabrina. I feel sick to my stomach.

Reed doesn't try to stop me this time when I get in my car. Without looking at him, I carefully back away from the house and turn out onto the street leading out of town.

I'm halfway to the highway when my phone starts to buzz. Notification after notification comes in, and I glance down in time to see Brooke's name flash across the screen.

Brooke. God, I'm such an awful friend. I forgot all about Brooke, and now I guess I've crossed back into a service area, and all of her texts are coming through, along with social media notifications and emails. I ignore everything and open the texts from Brooke as I crawl down the backroad behind the lake.

What happened last night? Did you kiss Reed again?

Um. Hello! I need an update!

Lady! What the hell is going on??

I can't believe you made out with your ex's brother and now you're not answering any of my texts!

Are you still alive?

Should I call the Lynches?

I STOP READING THE TEXTS AND CALL HER.

The second she picks up, I can't think of anything to say, and instead, I pull off onto the side of the road and cry.

50 REED

I stand outside the lake house for a long time. I wish for Quinn to come back. I contemplate all the ways I ruined everything. Not just tonight, but every single day for the rest of my life. I've ruined my own future.

By the time I turn to back to the lake house, my mother and Sabrina are long gone. I consider not going back in. I could get on my bike right now and drive back to Boston. Whatever reason I had to stay here is gone now, and I don't want to have to face all this.

But Quinn is right. I owe it to my family to at least try.

I shut the door behind me, unsurprised to find Sabrina, my mother, and Chase all in the living room, watching me. I lean back against the door and take a deep breath before joining them. I can't bring myself to sit just yet, so I hover by the kitchen island, trying not to look over at where the table Chase and I broke is still in pieces on the floor, glass surrounding it like a moat. Out of the corner of my eye, I see Lydia retrieving large chunks of broken, green champagne bottle glass from the scene of the crime, stuffing them down into a sturdy trash bag.

Finally, my mother speaks. "Can someone please tell me what's going on?"

There's a long silence as we all wait to see who will speak up first. I don't even know where to begin explaining this to my mother, and there are plenty of details I don't necessarily think she needs to know. But before I have a chance to parse through them and make up my mind, Chase beats me to it.

He speaks from behind the ice pack he has pressed to his face. "Reed has been fucking my wife for the last week."

"She's not your wife," I growl at him. How many fucking times do I need to remind him?

My mother puts her hands up to stop Chase before he can argue. "I don't understand."

I open my mouth to speak, but once again, Chase gets there first. "Reed was so fucking jealous of my life that he had to try and steal it."

"I didn't steal her; you threw her away because you're a fucking idiot."

Mom and Sabrina's eyes settle on me, and Chase finally stops talking. Everyone waits for me to explain. I sigh and sink onto one of the barstools.

"Five years ago, I met Quinn just before Chase did."

My mother looks confused, like I've mentioned two people she's never met before. "Yes, you mentioned that last night. At the Halloween party. Quinn said you bumped into each other." Her voice is so hopeful. I realize how much she wants to believe that nothing has changed. She's grasping at the reality she's known for so long.

"I pretended not to know her when we met at Thanksgiving. I guess I was...embarrassed. I didn't know Chase was going to show up with her. We hit it off at that party, and I sort of thought we were...I don't know, that we were going to hang out. And next thing I know, she and Chase are in a serious relationship. But I've...I've always had feelings for her."

My mother's hand comes up to cover her mouth. "Reed, she's your brother's wife."

I have to clamp my lips together so I don't go off again, and thankfully, someone else pipes in for me. Amina. I forgot she was here. What is she still doing here? "Chase told me that he and Quinn are divorced."

Now my mother looks confused again. Her hand falls from her mouth and her eyes shoot to Chase. "Is that true? Have you been lying to me?" I see the realization cross her face that she's the last one to know. Her expression smooths out. "You've *all* been lying to me?"

During this conversation, Chase's head has been all the way back on the couch, and he's been staring up at the ceiling like it holds the answers to the universe. Now, he looks right at our mother. "You offered us all five times more than usual to come out to the lake house."

My mother sends him an incredulous look. "And, what, you thought I would rescind the offer if I found out you and Quinn were no longer together?"

He shrugs. "Yeah, pretty much."

From the look on Mom's face, she understands his logic about as much as I do. She turns back to me. "Okay, so Quinn and Chase are divorced, but they agreed to come here and pretend to be married anyway to get the money. How do you fit into this?"

I sigh. It sounds awful when I think about saying it out loud. "I've known for a while that Chase and Quinn had split up." I level him with a glare. "I didn't really have contact with Quinn after the fact, but when I heard she was going to be here for one last summer, I saw an opportunity."

"An opportunity to sleep with her."

I shoot up off my stool. "An opportunity to be with the person that I love so much it fucking tears me apart every single day. I was a good brother to you, Chase. I never flirted with her. I never tried to take her away from you. I kept my mouth shut that first Thanksgiving and pretended that night we met never happened. But you fucked up. You didn't fucking deserve her."

"But she *chose* me," he says through gritted teeth.

It's like he's put a knife in my gut. "Yes. I'm very aware of that. But when you decided to cheat on her, she got a chance to choose someone else, and she chose me."

I don't dare say what's going through my mind. After our talk by the lake tonight, I'm certain of it. If I hadn't walked away from her at that Halloween party, she would have chosen me. We would have spent the rest of the party together. We would have gone on a date. We would have kissed, and I would have been the one to take her virginity and move her into my apartment and put a ring on her finger. I'm certain of all of that now.

We're all quiet. None of us is really sure what to do now that all the secrets are out on the table.

My mother's eyes raise to mine. "I would be lying if I said I hadn't been a little suspicious that you might have feelings for Quinn. I've wondered for a long time why it seemed you started to slowly vanish from this family when she came into it, but I convinced myself that it was because of your work." She sighs. "I'm disappointed that you all felt the need to keep this from me. I'm not even sure what to do with the knowledge that you and Quinn have been seeing each other while you've been here."

That, at least, I can understand. Maybe our timing wasn't the best, but I wasn't about to let this chance pass me by. I don't regret it.

She turns to face Chase. "I don't even know what to say to you, Chase. How could you do that to Quinn?"

He doesn't say anything, just stares back at her, his chest rising and falling rapidly, like this conversation is physically demanding for him.

When the silence has settled long enough, Sabrina pipes up. "I don't understand why you needed the money from this trip so bad that you had to drag Quinn into this. You have a well-paying job and you've never needed the money before."

He still doesn't say anything, but his face has changed, moving from angry to anguished. His eyes shoot to me, and I start to feel anxious. I never once asked, but he came to my door to *beg* me to come to the lake house. He *did* drag Quinn into this. Sabrina is right. He needs the money, and he hasn't told anyone why.

I walk toward him, until I've reached the step down into the living room. "Yeah, Chase. What do you need the money for?" I know why Quinn needs the money. She wasn't trying to hide it from me or from Chase. But Chase is a whole other story.

He takes a deep breath. "I got fired from my job, okay? You happy now?"

A beat. "Is that all?" our mother asks. It's the way she asks it that makes me turn to look at her. It's not that she's belittling the fact that he's unemployed. It's that she knows there's more to this story. My skin starts to prickle. I have a very bad feeling about this.

Chase crosses his arms, abandoning his ice pack, and leans back on the couch. At first, I think he's not going to answer, that he's going to be a stubborn asshole. But then he speaks. "I got fired because a woman at work filed a sexual harassment suit against me."

Even I wasn't expecting that one. Sabrina's hand comes up to cover her mouth, and my mother's eyes go wide.

The question lingers over all of us. *What did you do?*

Chase shrugs. "There was a staff party about two months ago. I had a little too much to drink, and I guess I came on a little too strong with one of the accountants. Now she's suing me for $50,000, which I can't pay because I got fired."

"What did you do to her?" Amina asks, her voice thick with horror.

But it doesn't matter because before he can answer, I've stormed my way across the living room and punched him again.

51 QUINN

I'M GASPING FOR AIR, CRYING SO HARD THAT I'VE ALREADY made myself sick once. Chase has been gone all night, and at this point, he could be anywhere. How long has he been lying to me? How long has he been cheating?

I pull the covers up over my head and wish I was dead. The way you want to find out your husband is cheating on you is definitely not by testing positive for chlamydia. I can just imagine all the ways he'll try to wiggle his way out of this. That's what he does. Always trying to find a way to absolve himself. Never the guilty party.

I sure as hell didn't get chlamydia from anyone else.

On the mattress beside me, my phone rings, and I gag. I don't want to speak to him. He doesn't know I know, and if I answer now, I'll call him names. I'll start to scream. I'll cry so hard he won't be able to understand me.

But when I look at the screen, it's not to see Chase's face

looking back at me. I stare at the picture of the three Lynch siblings that I got off Facebook. Reed's name hovers over their faces.

I snatch it up quick. "Reed?"

"Hey!" He sounds exceedingly cheerful, like it's his birthday or something. But no. That's in October. "Sorry to bug you, but I'm trying to get Chase on the phone, and I haven't been able to get through to him. Is he with you?"

I thought I would be able to have a conversation with Reed. Like he would be able to distract me from the situation I currently find myself in. But instead, when I open my mouth, a sob comes out. "No," I say around it. "No, he's not home."

"Quinn? Hey, what's going on? Are you okay?" There was background noise before, but now it's quiet, like he's stepped outside to hear me better. I wonder where he is. Probably at his restaurant. But maybe at a club or something. It's a Saturday night, after all.

"I'm okay. I'm just..." I don't know what to say. It's not right of me to bring him into this. He's Chase's brother. And it's not like we've ever been close. We speak to each other a handful of times a year and see each other even less. But it's Reed. And there's always been something about Reed that made me feel comfortable, like walking into your old family home and recognizing the smell of it. "I'm just having a rough day."

I hear some shuffling, imagine him taking a seat on a curb somewhere in the city. How far is he from where I am right now? Close enough to walk to our house? "Do you want to talk about it?"

I can't. I can't tell him about Chase before I've even spoken to Chase about it first. It's bad enough that Brooke already knows. A week ago, I convinced myself his suspicious behavior was pointing to an affair and then immediately talked myself right back out of it...just for this to happen.

"Not really," I tell Reed.

He doesn't rush me to speak. He doesn't tell me he's busy and has to go. He sighs. "I'm having a rough day, too."

"Do you want to talk about it?"

"Not really." There's a little smile in his voice.

I burrow further under the covers, settling in like I'm about to watch a good movie. "Tell me what's been going on with you."

He makes a humming noise. "Got my wisdom teeth pulled a couple weeks ago."

That makes me smile. "Shouldn't you have done that when you were in high school?"

"Not everybody does. Hang on. I have pictures."

My phone vibrates against my face, and I put it on speaker so I can look at the pictures he sent me. And then I scream with laughter. His cheeks are all puffed up like a chipmunk, and his eyes are half-lidded and purple.

"You look high as fuck."

"Oh, believe me, I was."

I set my phone beside me on the bed.

"What about you? Any interesting updates?"

My stomach clenches. Yeah, your brother is fucking someone else, and I'm going to have to start looking for a divorce lawyer. "Not really. This company I've been volunteering for got this big endowment from the state, so that's about to blow up for them, which is pretty cool."

"Yeah, that's very cool." I hear footsteps on his end, and I realize he's walking. Probably heading home after a long night. "I didn't know you were volunteering with anyone. Chase didn't mention it."

Because Chase would prefer I didn't do it at all. He doesn't want me to have a job so that I can be home waiting for him every day, but about a year ago, I started to feel like a caged animal. I started volunteering, just in the hours when he isn't home. He really thinks I sit at home all day or go to Brooke's place.

"He's probably not all that interested."

"What does the charity do?"

"They assist women who have escaped abusive marriages with putting their lives back together. They hook them up with jobs and financial support for therapy, clothes for their kids. Stuff like that."

"Quinn, that's…" He pauses. "That's really amazing. I had no idea you were doing that."

I put a hand over my mouth, try to decide whether or not to say what I want to. "I don't really talk about it, but I feel guilty, having this money that we don't need." I would donate a bunch of it, but Chase keeps telling me he wants to find a charity together to donate to, only we never do. He's more than content to amass wealth until we die, none of it ever going to any use better than his retirement fund.

"I know what you mean," Reed says, and I find myself smiling. Because of course he does. Reed has always been a lot like me. I always forget it in those stretches of time between meetings.

I close my eyes and try to picture his face. The last time I saw him, his hair was far too long, curling around his ears, and he had a little scruff on his jaw that was never there before. I liked it. It made him look less like someone who would co-own a restaurant and more like that guy I met in a hallway at Suffolk.

"Quinn?"

I suck in a breath. I must have fallen asleep.

"You okay over there?"

I know I should be embarrassed, but I'm not. I feel…calm for the first time since Chase took that phone call outside a week ago that made me suspicious. "I'm okay. Just tired. I think I dozed off."

"Well, hey. I'll let you go. You should get some rest."

"Reed?"

"Yeah?"

I shouldn't ask. I shouldn't do this. He's Chase's brother. But he's also my friend, and I feel better right now than I have in days. And I want to chase that. Just feel it for a little while. Hold onto it. Even if Chase would kill us both if he knew what I was about to ask.

"Could you maybe stay on the phone with me?" I don't say, *while I sleep*, but I know he knows it. I expect him to graciously decline, but a part of me knows that he won't. Because he's Reed.

"Of course I will."

I have to fight back the tears then. These are exhausted tears. Tears for the unknown future. Tears for this man on the other side of the phone who has been kinder to me in the last five years without really knowing me than Chase has been in the three years of our marriage.

"Tell me about your life," I say, and fall asleep to the sound of his voice.

52 QUINN

Brooke stares at me wide-eyed from the other side
of her balcony table. She sets her glass of orange juice down.
"Holy shit. That's the wildest story I've ever heard. I can't
believe Reed hit him."

I stare down at the plants lining the balcony she shares with
Clay just outside of Boston. The second her lease was up, she
moved across the hall, and I have to say, Clay's apartment is
much nicer than Brooke's old place was. "I'm actually really not
surprised," I say. "I think Reed made himself pretty clear, you
know?"

She taps her fingernails against her glass, and even though
I'm not looking at her, I can feel the weight of her stare. "He
did make himself clear, Quinn. So, why are you here talking to
me instead of shacking up with him right now?"

I scrub my hands over my face. The morning heat is starting
to get more intense, and my hands come away sweaty. "It's not
that simple, and you know it. There are too many variables here."
I set my hands flat on the table and study my fingernails. And

then I throw them back up in the air, my body laced with adrenaline and sadness and confusion and frustration that nobody can see reason but me. "I can't just divorce one man and then move on to his brother. That's not how life works. This is not a soap opera. Reed will get over it. I'll get over it. He'll meet someone and I'll…"

I'll what? I think between Chase and Reed, something inside me has been broken beyond repair. I don't know if I can ever see myself being close that way with anyone else again. The risks are too great.

"You never told me it was Reed."

I look up at her, all gold and pink in the morning light. "What?"

"After the Halloween party. I remember it. You told me the next day about the guy that ghosted you. You never told me it was Reed."

I told her about meeting a guy in the hall because she was my best friend, and we told each other everything. But months later, when I discovered that Reed and Chase were brothers, I never mentioned the connection or Reed's identity. "I guess I didn't think it mattered."

She watches me closely, her elbows resting on the table between us. "I don't think that's true. I think you knew it mattered too much."

She's right, of course. It felt like a detail I needed to bury so that nobody would know the situation I had found myself in, so nobody could accuse me of wanting Reed more than Chase, even though it was probably true. "I felt stupid for liking someone that much so quickly. And then felt even more stupid when it turned out to be Reed."

"But you never got any kind of closure. Maybe those feelings never really went away. I know they didn't for him." My eyes meet hers, and I see the knowing in them. "He's always loved you. He told me as much when we saw him at Aeronaut. But it wasn't like I could tell you."

That night at Aeronaut. My picture in his office. I saw it then; I just didn't want to. "My feelings didn't go away either." I can say that confidently now, even though it feels scary to admit it. That truth that I've been hiding inside for so long. "Reed made—makes—me feel like no one else does."

"How does he make you feel?" This is what Brooke does, forces people to confront their feelings for their own good. It's what she's best at.

"Like I matter."

Agony crosses her face. "Of course you matter."

"I just mean, he hears me. And he sees me. My whole life, everyone talked over me and forgot about me and made me feel like a burden they had to shoulder. But Reed...he makes me feel important."

She nods like she understands. "You love him."

"Of course, I love him." There's no use hiding any of it anymore. "But what I need right now is for my life to be less complicated."

She nods. "So you're selling the house."

"So I'm selling the house. I'll take the first job I can get, I'll get the cheapest apartment I can find, and I'll just...take some time to breathe."

At this, she smiles. "Time to breathe sounds like a good idea."

Just then, the balcony door flies open and Clay sticks his head out to smile at us. "I brought croissants."

53 REED

THE CITY IS TOO LOUD AND TOO BRIGHT. I FEEL LIKE THAT guy in *Clockwork Orange* with his eyes pinned open. I want to go back to the lake house, where it was quiet, where the sunshine felt different, where I had *her* with me.

A big hand lands on my shoulder, and I fight not to grimace at the contact.

"What do you think of this place?" Jack asks. "The seating area is way bigger than I thought it was going to be. And those pink walls..."

"I might want to keep the pink walls." My voice sounds hollow. That's what I feel like. Like a suit of armor standing in an empty hallway with nothing inside it.

Jack grins, looking around at the bustling corner we found a good spot on. We're just north of downtown Boston, on a street that's lined with shops. This is going to be a perfect location. Now if only I could feel...*anything*. "Whatever you say, man. So, what do you think? You want to make them an offer?"

"Yeah. Sure." Most of the investors stuck with me after I announced my change of plans, but a few pulled out. Even so,

I've garnered enough trust in the last few years that the investors put in enough money to fund the whole project. Now I have to prove that I can do this without a partner and without tagging onto a five-star restaurant downtown. And maybe I can't, but here goes.

Jack's smile finally falls. I thought he wasn't paying attention to my disposition, but I guess I was wrong. "Hey, we don't have to end the search here. There's no hurry. We can keep looking if you're not feeling this place."

I shake my head. "No. Let's pull the trigger. I want to keep moving forward." I *have* to keep moving forward. If I don't, there will be nothing left of me. I'm afraid I'll waste away.

Jack nods. "Yeah, okay. I'll let them know, and I'll keep you updated." He shakes my hand, and then I'm left there, standing at the edge of the sidewalk, trying to decide what to do now. This is always how it is. When I have the distraction of work, I'm fine. But the second I'm alone, the world goes quiet, and all I'm left with is the glaring realization that I might have to live the rest of my life without Quinn.

Like she knows that I can't handle it right now, Sabrina calls. I stare at the screen, wondering if I should ignore it. She's been calling for days, but the idea of trying to have a conversation with her right now after everything that went down at the lake house feels insane.

But if I don't answer soon, she might come to Boston, and I don't think I could handle that either.

"Hey," I say, putting the phone to my ear.

"Finally!" she shouts, and I realize she's probably standing on a curb in the city too, just in New York instead of Boston. "I know you've been ignoring me, but me and Mom have been really worried about you. How are you? How are things in Boston?"

I feel like an ungrateful asshole for even thinking that

things aren't going well. They are. I'm going to have a running business again soon, and for the most part, life is running pretty smoothly.

But it all feels like it's for nothing because I have a massive hole in my chest.

"Everything's good," I say, but I sound like someone saying their pain level is at an eight while they're bleeding out.

"Reed, come on. You can talk to me. Tell me what's going on in your head. Everything was so quiet by the time we all left the lake. I'm pretty sure Mom is never going to speak to Chase again, which is probably fine, all things considered."

I haven't even thought about Chase. He lifted out of my life so easily. It was a clean break after everything came out. "Is there an update?"

Sabrina sighs. "Mom paid the woman who filed the lawsuit. Not to protect Chase but just so that that poor woman could have some peace. It's all over, but Chase is still out there in the wild, primed to make even more terrible decisions."

Chase is lucky he didn't leave that lake house in a body bag, but I don't say so. "I'm sure Mom is disappointed in all of us."

There's a pause. "Why would she be disappointed in *you*?"

I run a hand over my face. "I don't know, Sabrina. Maybe because Quinn and I lied to her for a week? Maybe because I was sleeping with Quinn under everyone's noses? Maybe because I made a move on my brother's ex?"

"Yeah, keyword being *ex*. Look, I know it probably feels a little backwoods talk show, but it's not your fault that the person for you just happened to also be married to your brother. These things happen. What are you supposed to do, stop loving her because she was your sister-in-law?" There's a beat of silence. "Actually, as that's coming out of my mouth, I realize how weird it sounds."

I groan and turn, pushing back into the empty building on

the corner that's going to be mine very soon. Inside, my voice echoes off the walls. "I love her so fucking much, Sabrina."

"Then why aren't you doing something about it?"

I stare at the shadow on the wall where the last business's name was washed onto it by the sun. "Because she needs space. I made a mistake doing all of this when the ink had barely dried on the divorce papers. I should have taken my time, waited until she had really healed from her marriage. I'm the one who fucked up here."

"You didn't fuck up. You were just...eager. That's hardly a cardinal sin."

I nod, even though she can't see me. "And what about you? Did you tell Mom about Lydia yet?"

"I did, yeah." There's a smile in her voice now, thankfully. "She took it really well. She didn't fire Lydia, but she's making us get a new place so she doesn't accidentally hear us having sex or something."

I smile out into my empty building. "See? I knew she wasn't going to have a problem with it."

She's quiet for a long moment. "It's hard to ever really know what someone would do in this life."

5 Years Ago

THE FIRST TIME I RUN INTO QUINN AFTER THANKSGIVING, she's in the library, with a stack of books at her feet as she scans through the shelves. I consider turning and walking away, letting this be as painless as I can possibly manage to make it. But before I have a chance to make a run for it, she turns, catches sight of me, and smiles so big that she's all teeth and sunshine.

"Reed! Hey. Just the person I wanted to see."

My stomach feels like it's being catapulted out of a sling-shot. "Me?"

She nods and beckons me closer with a motion of her chin. When I'm standing beside her, she says, "Could you grab me that bright red book on the top shelf?" She points up over her head.

I tilt my head back, looking at the book on the top shelf. A glance down the aisle tells me that there are no stools around to assist her. I reach my arm up, snatch the book off the shelf, and hand it to her.

"Thanks," she breathes out in relief. "I've been standing here for at least ten minutes, pretending that I was still looking for something, but this was the last book I needed. I just couldn't figure out how to get it without scaling the shelf."

"Glad I could help."

She drops the book onto the top of her stack and turns to press her shoulders to the shelf behind her. "So, what brings you to these parts? Research paper? Study group?"

I glance down at my cell phone in my hand. Telling her the reason I'm here, in the library, in the middle of the afternoon, doesn't feel like something I want to do. I'm meeting a girl for a hook-up. Both of our roommates are home, so we decided to rent a room at the library for a quickie. But there's no way in hell I'm telling Quinn that.

"Just meeting up with someone."

She nods and crosses her arms. "Yeah. Okay. Well, hey, maybe we could grab some coffee later." She says it so casually, as if she isn't dating my brother. And I realize that, for her, coffee would just be coffee and nothing more. She wants to be friends. She wants to shoot the shit over lattes in the student center as if we didn't almost hook up two months ago.

Because that's what she *should* think. Totally harmless to have coffee with your boyfriend's brother if there are absolutely no feelings involved. Completely innocent.

Except I don't want it to be innocent, I realize. I want her to tell me right now that this thing with Chase is just a fling and that she's way more interested in me. I want her to tell me that she can't stop thinking about me, the way I can't stop thinking about her. Haven't stopped thinking about her for two months.

But instead, she's casually asking me for coffee because she no longer sees me as a romantic prospect. All of her feelings have vanished. Maybe they never existed in the first place.

"Yeah," I find myself saying. "Chase really likes that place right off campus, the one that has the special milk. Has he taken you there? Maybe we could all three go."

Her face shifts. If I wasn't watching her closely, I might not have noticed. Her smile somehow becomes bigger while dimming slightly. Little crinkles appear on the outsides of each eye. "Yes. Chase. Absolutely. He would love that. I'll talk to him and we can find a good time." The offer sounds wooden.

It's like...she wasn't expecting me to bring up Chase. What does that even mean? "Okay, well, I can—"

"Reed?"

I turn. There she is, outlined in sunlight in front of the big library windows. Amina. A girl I met at a party just after Thanksgiving and have been hooking up with ever since. In that month between Halloween and Thanksgiving, I spent a lot of time wandering around campus, hoping to run into Quinn again. But when I didn't, I gave up hope. And then she showed up at Thanksgiving, and I realized I had to get over her.

There's nothing wrong with Amina. She's pretty. She's smart. She makes me laugh. She's really responsive and fun, sexually.

But she's not Quinn. And that's not her fault.

Amina comes to stand beside me, her smile taking up so much of her face as she looks up at me and then over at Quinn. "Hey!" she says, friendly as ever. "I know you. You're in my social sciences class."

Quinn is nodding before Amina is even finished speaking. "Yep. You did that project on that Tinder social experiment."

Amina's eyes light up. "Oh, yeah. That was a lot of fun. I, uh, I don't remember what your project was about."

Quinn makes this little sound in the back of her throat,

something between a laugh and a cough, and tucks her hands into her back pockets, nodding. I've never seen her like this, like she's trying to seem casual. From what I know about Quinn, she doesn't seem to be a very casual person. She seems to really care about things. She's exactly the kind of person who would listen closely to someone's presentation while also not expecting anyone to be listening to hers.

"Oh, it was a market survey on coffee shops and their clientele. Nothing important." She gives a nervous laugh that makes my skin crawl. She's trying to make herself small. She's trying to make herself seem less important than she is. I hate it.

But before I can say anything else, Quinn's phone rings. She looks around, clearly worried she's going to disrupt someone's reading, and presses a button to silence the phone. From where I'm standing, I can see Chase's face on her screen, and I catch the way her shoulders sag in relief, like she was waiting for an excuse to get away.

"I guess Chase is out of class," she says, bending to pick up the massive stack of books from the floor. "I should probably get going."

The stack wobbles in her arms, and I step forward to help her, but she swings the stack out of my grasp and sends me the fakest smile I've ever seen. "I'm good, thanks. I'll see you around, Reed."

She turns away from me as Amina reaches for my hand and gives me a tug in the opposite direction. "Yeah," I say to Quinn's retreating back. "I'll see you around."

Amina, her face lit up in the afternoon sun, pulls me toward the study rooms. "Come on. I don't have a ton of time. Let's do this."

I laugh, following her back down the row of books. But before I round the corner, I glance back over my shoulder and find Quinn down on the other end, her arms full and her eyes on me.

"Give me one second," I say to the figure that has just stepped up to my desk. I know I'm always supposed to stop what I'm doing and greet in-person clients first, but if I don't finish inputting this appointment for my boss, I absolutely will forget and it'll never get done.

"No rush."

My fingers stop on the keyboard. I know that voice. I know that voice the way you know the voice of a family member, the way you can recognize someone's voice over the phone when they call you from a different number and immediately jump into conversation.

I look up to see Madison Lynch on the other side of the reception desk. In the afternoon light streaming in through the windows behind her, she looks like she's glowing, like some kind of guardian angel who landed on my doorstep.

I haven't seen her in six months.

I haven't seen or spoken to any of the Lynches for six months.

I've avoided their names on social media and asked

Brooke not to tell me what's going on with them because the pain of losing the only real family I've ever had has been too much. It was a shock to hear about Chase's sexual harassment suit after the fact. It was the last thing that came across my desk about any of the Lynches before I stopped looking into them.

But now Madison is standing in front of me, and it's clear from the pleased smirk on her face that this is no accidental run-in. She came here to find me.

"Please, finish what you were doing," she says, nodding toward the computer in front of me.

My eyes flash back to the screen. I really do need to input the appointment, so I finish filling in the necessary information, all the while feeling the heat of Madison's gaze on me. When I'm finished, I lay my hands flat on the desk and look up at her, unsure what to say.

She smiles. "Do you have a break coming up by any chance?"

ONCE I'VE GOT MY PHONE SET TO GO STRAIGHT TO voicemail, I meet Madison outside. In the direct sunlight, she's even more beautiful, her silvering blonde hair pulled up into a lose updo and the ruffles on the collar of her perfect white blouse grazing the bottom of her chin.

"What are you doing here?" I ask, because even though not a single day goes by that I don't think about Reed and Madison and Sabrina, I thought it was over. I thought they had washed their hands of me.

She sighs, her eyes still bright. "I came to check up on you. To see how you're doing." Her eyes flit over my head, to the sign on the window that announces the marketing firm where

I've been working since shortly after I came back from New Hampshire. "Are you happy here?"

I shrug. "I don't hate it. It's a paycheck. And it's something to tide me over until I figure out what I want to do."

She nods. "I heard through the grapevine that you sold the house, and I can't say I blame you, not after all that Chase did." She digs in her purse for something. "Well, if you want to stay and work here, that's lovely. But if you don't, this should help." She holds an envelope out to me, and I just stare at it. We're tucked into a corner of the stone courtyard that hides the side door of our offices from the main road. And while I feel pretty confident that no one can see us past the enormous stone sculpture beside us, I flush at the idea that someone might see Madison and me talking. No one here really knows me. Would they start to ask questions? Would they figure out how I'm connected to the Lynch family?

"What is this?" I ask absently as I peer into the envelope. It's a check. And as soon as I realize that, my skin goes hot, even with the cold January wind whipping through the courtyard.

"Your money for coming out to the lake house last summer."

And then I see the amount the check is for. I choke on my own spit, coughing as I say, "This is far too much. I don't deserve any of it, much less..." I lower my voice. "Much less two million."

Madison shrugs. "It's your money, plus everyone else's."

I try to process that, but I can't. I shake my head. "No. I don't mind taking Chase's share, but Reed and Sabrina deserve theirs."

"Sabrina doesn't need hers. She's done well for herself without it. And Reed wanted you to have his." She takes a deep breath, and something about her seems to soften. It's like she shifts from the fierce Madison Lynch that we all know to someone else, just for a second. "I'm sorry it's taken so long for me to get this to you. I knew you had moved out of the city to a smaller place and gotten a job, so I figured I had some time to put some things together. I had Chase to deal with, and my health, of course. I'm in remission."

I breathe out a sigh of relief. One of the many reasons I stopped keeping up with news on the Lynches was my own fear that I would someday hear of Madison's passing. But here she is, healthy and strong and very much alive. "Madison, that's wonderful."

"I'm assuming you've heard about Chase."

My happiness immediately fades. "Just what was on social media."

"I've made sure that he's not homeless and that he's fed. But beyond that, I've unfortunately had to cut ties with him. I love my son very much, but he's chosen a path that I'm not currently able to follow him down."

"I'm sorry." It's strange the way that someone can go from being the most important person in your life to being someone you don't even recognize anymore in the span of less than a year.

Madison nods, knowingly. "I know what everyone thought about this summer, but I didn't bring you all to the lake house as some one-last-time goodbye trip. I brought you all out there as a new beginning. I thought I would give us a fresh start. Spend some time together and repair what seemed to have somehow broken over the years. But I didn't know all the facts, and I couldn't put us back together in the end."

"Madison, I'm so sorry." I choke the words out, clutching the envelope to my chest. "You have no idea how sorry I am."

She scowls, her hair fluttering in the cold wind. She doesn't seem to notice. "For what? For being a good wife to my son, even when he treated you like a commodity? Or for making Reed happier than I've ever seen him?"

Hearing his name come out of her mouth like that makes my throat go tight. "Madison—"

She cuts me off. "I learned this summer that my children are not who I thought they were." She's looking me in the eye now, forcing me to look back. And her eyes are soft and full of wetness. "That I don't know them the way I thought I did. But one thing I do know is that Reed is sick with love for you. Chase has always been everyone's favorite, always gotten exactly what he wanted, but I never saw Reed show a lick of jealousy until the day Chase brought you home. He was different that day. Quieter. I saw it but I didn't understand until now. And he seemed to slowly disappear until this summer. And then he was in full color again."

The tears go cold on my cheeks before I've even had a chance to acknowledge that they're there.

"And I believe that you love him, too. You do, don't you?"

No holding back. "Yes. But we can't—"

She steps toward me, pulling her coat tighter around her thin shoulders. "If they weren't brothers, if the family wasn't involved in any way, would you choose to be with Reed?"

I finally say what I've wanted to say for so long: the truth. "I would have chosen him five years ago." If I had just stayed still that night, waited for him to come back and explain himself to me, it would have been us this whole time. And if they hadn't been brothers and we had found each other again after I started seeing Chase, I would have just broken it off with Chase. But that wasn't an option. The whole world would look different now if they weren't family.

Madison nods. "Then run. Because what's left of this family wants you in it and wants you and Reed to be truly happy. For the past six months, my son has been walking around half-alive, and I can't bear it anymore."

She's handing me something else now, and I know from the size and shape of it what it is before it's in my hands. A business card for a place named *Q*. I stare at that one letter, my stomach doing flips. "He opened his restaurant?"

"He did. I hope to see you again soon, Quinn. None of the other stuff matters. What matters is that, as far as I'm concerned, you're still my daughter, and you're still part of this family."

A sob escapes me then, and Madison steps forward to rub the tears from my cheeks. "I don't know if you know this," I tell her while she's preoccupied with wiping away the mascara, "but you're my hero. All I've ever wanted was to be like you."

She steps back, sniffs and lifts her chin. "Then go after what you want, and don't let anyone stop you."

56 QUINN

I have to take two trains to get to the other side of Boston, where the address on the business card leads me. I find myself in the middle of a bustling corner of shops and restaurants, staring up at the bright gold Q that's shimmering in the evening sun.

It's not a restaurant. I remember the feel of Aeronaut like I was there yesterday. Everything was pristine and white and expensive. This is a bakery the size of a matchbox, painted red and gold, making it look sophisticated but approachable.

As I stand there, a woman and a teenage girl go inside, and the woman glances at me with a question in her eyes. *Should I hold the door for you?*

Even though I'm not ready, I punch forward and take the door, thanking her and then following her inside. And I'm glad they're ahead of me because I need a moment to process this. A huge glass display case, with pastries and goods on the other side of it, silk flowers lining the walls, and several small tables, most of which are filled with people chatting and laughing or typing away at computers.

It looks exactly like I imagined when I told Reed all those months ago that he should open a small bakery instead of a high-end restaurant. Because I was remembering all those weekends that I went with my mother into town and we would buy little cakes and cheap coffee and thrift store clothes, and a part of me was excited about having just a small piece of that again.

And here, Reed has given it all back to me.

"Ma'am?"

I shake awake.

The girl behind the counter, who can't be any older than me, is trying to get my attention. She smiles and speaks to me across the expanse of the bakery. "Can I help you?"

I step up to the display case, my eyes taking in all the colors of the desserts, even though I know that's not what I'm here for.

"Would you like to try an orange bar?" The girl gestures at a tray that's filled with tiny orange cubes on toothpicks sitting atop the display case.

"Um. No. Thanks. I'm actually looking for Reed Lynch." Even as I say it, my eyes travel to the wall beside the case, a long yellow and pink wall that leads to a hallway behind the counter. There are certificates and awards, all beautifully framed. And in the center of it all is a picture of me. The same picture I found in his office at Aeronaut. It's in a silver frame now, and I can't take my eyes off it.

"He's in the back. I'll run and get him for you." Before she goes, she reaches behind her. There's a shelf there, holding a bunch of different boxes, and she picks one up and hands it to me over the case. Pink with a white ribbon around it.

"Oh, I don't—" I start to say, but she interrupts me.

"You're Quinn, right?" she asks, her eyes excited. When I nod, she says, "Reed told us all that if you ever showed up, you were supposed to get a batch of cookies for free."

Before I can respond, she disappears, and I'm left standing in front of the case with the box in my hands. Like a zombie, I walk to an empty table and sit down, robotically opening the box and looking down into it at the chocolate chip cookies. They smell amazing, and they immediately blur behind a cloud of tears.

I'm just sitting there, staring at them, when I hear someone approach my table. I look up at Reed slowly. He still looks the same, his hair buzzed short and dark stubble along his jaw. He's wearing an apron covered in flour over his jeans and t-shirt.

And I love him so much I'm queasy with it.

"Quinn," he says, my name just a breath on his lips. I stand. Tears are pouring down my face now, and I can only imagine what I look like to all of these people trying to enjoy a slice of cake on a Saturday afternoon.

He comes over to the table, his eyes finding the box and then looking back at me while I try to find the right words to start this. But what are the right words when you ran out on someone six months ago, when the two of you are undeniably and eternally linked, when you said no, but now you're ready to say yes?

"Is it too late?" Those are the words that finally come choking out of my mouth.

His mouth parts, his eyebrows curve in, his head begins to shake slowly. "Too late doesn't exist with us, Quinn. What, you think that I just went off and fell in love with someone else? Moved on? That's not possible. I've been living my life, waiting for the minute you would walk back into it. There is no such thing as too late. If it had taken you a hundred years to come back to me, I would have still been here, waiting."

I cover my face with my hands, sobbing into my palms, and feel Reed move into my space. I can practically feel his indecision about whether or not to put his arms around me. All of the wants and unsures buzz around us like an electrical current.

I finally catch my breath and look up at him, aware that everyone in the bakery is watching us and that I'm making a fool of myself, but I don't even care because I have all this fear inside me that has to come out, and it's not waiting any longer. "What happens when you realize that the way you felt about me was just because you couldn't have me?"

He finally touches me. His hands grasp my hands and then my elbows and then my shoulders. "Is that what you think? Quinn, I have never wanted anything in this life other than you. If I lost everything else, it wouldn't mean a damn thing."

"But what about—"

"Stop." He takes my face in his hands and forces me to look at him, those eyes that are the color of chocolate and the earth and everything that's good. "I've spent five years wanting you, trying to get you out of my head, and I just keep coming back to you time and time again. That's not going to change. I love you. Are you...are you here because you love me, too?"

I nod.

He tips my chin up, bends close to me. "Say it, Quinn."

"I love you, Reed. I want to be with you. I want to be yours and only yours."

He smiles. "You always were, skele-girl." And right there in the middle of the bakery, he kisses me.

THIS IS WHAT HAPPINESS LOOKS LIKE: PUTTING A HELMET on the woman you love in the alley behind the bakery you bought for her. Watching her smile nervously because she's never been on a bike before and then waiting for her to swing onto the seat behind you. Feeling her small hands circle your torso and fist into the material of your shirt.

"I promise it's not as scary as it seems," I tell her before starting the bike and pushing up the kickstand with the heel of my boot. "I would never put you in any danger."

She presses her chest to my back, and I'm momentarily distracted by the feel of her breasts against me. I need to get her home so I can rip her clothes off and bury myself inside her. Through our helmets, her muffled voice finds me. "Have you ever fucked anyone on this thing?"

My hand slips off the handlebar, and I have to rub the sweat off my palm before I turn my head. She leans to the side so that our eyes can meet through our helmet visors. "No. You want to be the first?"

Behind the windscreen, I see her smile. She nods, and I

turn back around and slam the bike forward. Behind me, Quinn squeals and holds on tight.

I could go straight to my new apartment, but then the drive would be over too quickly. I want this to last forever, Quinn holding onto me from behind, her palms flat against my chest. There's no better feeling than this, and part of me can't believe it's real. She told me she loves me. She came here for me. She wants to be with me.

She's mine.

I rev up the engine, and we fly down the street. She spent the day with me at the bakery, and now that it's late, the streets aren't as crowded. This part of Boston isn't like being downtown, where the crowds swallow everything. This is a quieter corner, and with the sun down and the streetlights turning on, it looks like magic.

I take a few more turns than I need to, taking her away from my apartment before turning around and going back. As soon as we pull into the parking garage, we both whip our helmets off, pushing against the concrete wall before slamming our mouths together.

"Take me upstairs," she whispers against my mouth. "Now."

I smile. "Whatever you say, baby."

EPILOGUE
QUINN

I WAKE TO THE FEEL OF REED'S FINGERS TRACING DOWN my cheek. I just barely open my eyes, my gaze finding the broad expanse of his chest, dark ink covering half of it. I shift, looking up at him and finding him watching me. He runs his fingertips along my jaw, and he's watching them go like he's never touched me before.

When he speaks, his voice is rough with sleep. "You have no idea how many mornings I spent in bed, wishing I was waking up next to you like this."

My chest pulls tight, and I feel like I'll burst. Have I ever felt so content? So safe? "Oh, yeah? And when you imagined it, what happened next?" I bite my lip and smile up at him, fully expecting to find hunger in his eyes. Morning sex, after all, is our favorite.

But he just smiles, his eyes roving over my face. "Not what you think," he says, scooting closer until I feel his legs tangle with mine. "This is what I imagined." He leans in and kisses me. It isn't a hot, wet, tongue kind of kiss. It's not the claiming I've become so accustomed to. Instead, he kisses me slowly, his hand going into my hair and his body lazily covering mine, no urgency, no pushing.

When we part, he takes my chin in his hand. "Good morning, beautiful," he says, and I inexplicably feel tears gather in the corners of my eyes.

"Good morning, Reed."

"I love you," he says, so matter-of-fact, so casual, the way someone can only be when they've spent six years saying something again and again inside their head.

"I love you, too," I choke out, far less casual. Even six months in, it's still a revelation every time it comes out. I still feel like I wake up in a dream every single morning. I don't know when it will all start to feel real. Maybe never. Maybe that's always what it feels like when you get a second chance at life.

His mouth finds mine again, his dark stubble scraping against my skin as he goes deeper and deeper. Until what was sweet and gentle becomes desperate and needy. I start making noises in the back of my throat and Reed, knowing this script by heart, starts to lift my shirt, slipping his hand under to cup my breast.

"Wait," I gasp. I want it so, so bad. But we have plans. "We have to go or we're going to be late."

He's nibbling at my ear and then across my jaw, making soft little grunting noises as he goes. "Does it really matter if we're on time?"

"Yes," I gasp as he sinks his teeth into my shoulder hard enough to shock me. I never know when he's going to be gentle and when he's going to be rough. It's thrilling.

"Then I guess we better multitask," he says. He slides off

me, and before I have a chance to ask him what he means by that, he's reaching back under the covers and lifting me up into his arms. He carries me into the bathroom and sets me on my feet before reaching into the shower and turning on the water.

He leans against the wall and crosses his arms. "Strip," he says, his voice stern, even as his eyes sparkle with amusement.

I quickly divulge myself of clothing. Reed nods for me to get in the shower, so I do, watching through the foggy glass as he drops his boxer briefs on the floor, his cock jutting out the moment its free. It makes my mouth water.

"Like what you see, filthy little slut?" he asks, stepping into the shower and cornering me against the cold tile. The sting of it on my bare skin is almost too much to stand until he presses his warm body against mine.

He wraps a fist in my hair and yanks my head back. In this position, all I can see is him: the shadow he casts over me, the devilish look in his eyes, the slope of his neck.

"Open your mouth," he says.

I do, and he spits into it. I make a mewling noise and claw at the tiles behind me, so desperate for him now that I feel like I'll catch on fire. I want this to go on forever. I want him to use me and bruise me and show me I'm his.

But we're seriously going to be late.

"That's my good little whore." He jerks me away from the wall and spins me around. With a hand at my neck, he bends me forward. "Hands on the wall."

I do as he says. There are times when Reed wants me to take control. When he wants to slowly move inside me or wants me to climb on top of him and go to town. But other times, times like this, when he's feeling particularly handsy, he pushes me around like a ragdoll, and I love it.

As soon as I'm bent over, he slips two fingers into me, and I go up onto my toes, shocked by the quick invasion.

"You're already wet. Did you know that?" he says. He slips his fingers right back out and replaces them with his dick. "I wish I could take my time with you and your tight little hole, but apparently we're going to be late."

I bite my lip to hold in a dissatisfied reply.

He doesn't go easy on me. As soon as his cock is settled deep inside me, he begins to pump. He grabs my hips hard with both hands and jackhammers into me, until I'm afraid I might slip. A trip to the hospital would definitely be worth it.

"Harder," I say, my head hanging down between my arms. At this angle, I can see his feet between mine, his wet, hairy legs, the heavy swing of his balls.

"You want it harder?" he asks, and I recognize that tone in his voice.

I bring my head up and look over my shoulder, watch as he sticks his thumb into his mouth and sucks on it for a second. I know exactly what's coming. When his thumb finds the tightness of my asshole, I slam my eyes shut and put one of my hands between my legs.

When I start making unintelligible noises, screaming loud and letting it bounce around the shower tiles, Reed chuckles.

"Always gets you there quick, doesn't it?"

I can barely even process his words. There's so much pleasure rocketing through my body that the world goes white.

I come so hard that I lose track of time and space, only coming back to earth when Reed yanks me up, my back flush against his body. He pistons into me hard, using me to get himself off. It's almost enough to send me off one more time.

I know that if we had more time, he would make sure I did.

"Get me there," he whispers in my ear, and I smile up at the ceiling, at the soft light that shines down on us. I reach back to tangle one hand in his hair and push the other flat against the wall for purchase as I start to rock back on him hard. The slap of our skin is loud, and the sound of it shoves me up close against another orgasm.

"Yes," he says against the back of my neck. "That's it. Fuck me."

I squeak, plummeting over the edge again as Reed spills inside me, his warm cum dripping down my leg.

We stand in the shower far longer than we should, panting under the spray of the water before we finally uncoil our bodies and actually scrub ourselves clean.

REED

I CAN TELL WE DIDN'T MAKE IT IN TIME AS SOON AS WE pull up to the lake house. Through the window that peers in at the living room, I can see Mom, Sabrina, and Lydia all sitting around. They've clearly already had lunch and have moved on with their day.

Out of the corner of my eye, I see the way Quinn's shoulders fall. In all fairness, Mom did say to make it here on time or miss out on a hot lunch. She seems to have caught on pretty quickly that Quinn and I have a hard time separating ourselves these days.

I grab our bags out of the backseat as Quinn makes her way up to the door. She raises her hand to knock, but I nudge her aside and throw it open. Quinn still hasn't quite accepted that she's still family.

Hopefully, after tonight, she will.

As soon as the door shuts behind us, I hear footsteps coming down the hall. My mother already has her arms open before she's fully made it into the room.

"Quinn!" she says, wrapping her arms around my girl. I watch Quinn squeeze my mom right back, and I know that as soon as we go to bed tonight, Quinn will cry quietly to herself about how my mother is treating her.

We all know that without the Unstoppable Madison Lynch, Quinn wouldn't be here.

Mom pulls back, her hands on Quinn's shoulders. "How is everything going at work? Do you have enough money? Should I donate a little more?"

Beside me, Sabrina rolls her eyes. "Oh, sure. She wouldn't even give us an allowance as teenagers, but Quinn can have all the money she wants," she says sarcastically.

Just as sarcastically, Mom looks over her shoulder at Sabrina and says, "If you were single-handedly founding a nonprofit for women in need, you could have all the money you wanted, too."

Quinn laughs quietly. "Trust me, I don't need any more money. What you've contributed already has been more than enough."

After everything went down last summer and my mother gave all the lake house money to Quinn, she didn't know what to do with it. She didn't have to pay rent because she immediately moved into my apartment in the city, she had a job that paid well enough for everything else, and she was sitting on a two-million-dollar check.

So, she started her own nonprofit for newly single women who needed financial support. It's been quite a thing to behold.

Quinn and Mom move into the kitchen to speak quietly as Sabrina ducks closer to me, a mischievous smile on her face.

"When are you going to do it?" she asks, and I send her a sideways glance.

"Would you calm down?"

"No." She elbows me in the side. "I planned something

special for the 4th of July party, and I want to make sure you weren't planning to do it then."

I had thought about it, right there under the fireworks. But that felt like a little too much. I don't say as much to Sabrina.

"What if she says no?"

Sabrina scoffs. "Please. She's not going to say no. The two of you are so emotionally attached, they're going to have to surgically separate you to bury you."

I smile. "Maybe they could bury us in one big plot."

She narrows her eyes at me. "You're gross."

"Well, what about you?" I look over her shoulder, down the long hallway, but there's no sign of Lydia. I have no idea how she's so good at disappearing.

Sabrina shrugs, but I know her better than that. She'll pretend to be emotionless but there are enough emotions raging inside her to scare anyone. "We haven't discussed it yet. I don't think Lydia's ready."

"Cool. Take your time." Not everybody can be ready the way I am right now. And I'm only praying that Quinn is.

"Did you know she saw you guys making out in the boat house last summer? You weren't nearly as sneaky as you thought you were."

I whip around to face her. "What, Lydia?"

She scoffs. "You know she sees everything."

All I can do is laugh. Because now, after everything, it just seems funny. At the end of it all, all that work we did amounted to nothing. We tried not to hurt Mom, but she was never going to be hurt by us. We tried not to break up the family, but Chase did it all on his own anyway. We kept ourselves away from each other, but in the end, we still made our back to each other.

"I'm going to take our bags to the room," I call to Quinn, but she doesn't hear me. She's deep in conversation with Mom, and I decide to let her be.

We take the bedroom that was Lydia's last summer. I suggested we stay in the basement, but when I did, Quinn told me that it would feel like hiding all over again.

I just wanted it because the sound of me fucking her senseless was less likely to make its way to my sister, but that's okay. We can be quiet for a week. We have a lot of practice.

I start unpacking our things, surprised at how at home I feel here. For a long time, the lake house was a place that made me feel guilty about my family, but now it feels like the place I finally got Quinn. Digging into the bottom of my duffle bag, I pull out the engagement ring I brought. I know it's soon, but I also know that nothing is going to change, whether I do it this week or wait ten years. I know that Quinn is my future, so why wait?

"Wow."

I shove the ring back down and turn to see Quinn walking slowly into the room, her eyes on the window. When I follow her gaze, I see what she does. The shimmer of the sun on the lake. The trees in the distance, on other side of the water. It's beautiful.

"I always forget," she says, going to stand in front of the window, her arms crossed. "It's like it can't really exist, and then I get here, and there it is, as perfect as it was last summer."

In the reflection of the glass, her eyes move, taking it all in like it's the most beautiful thing she's ever seen. And I know she feels it too, the way the lake house is more than just a lake house. The way everything we've ever been has been cemented inside these walls.

And watching her here, I know I'll never be happier than I am right now, with her by my side and my family in the next room and the future wide open.

I slip my hand back into my bag and take out the ring box. Why fucking wait?

"Quinn?" As I wait for her to turn, I settle onto one knee, the ring box open in my hand.

When she spins around to face me, I see the second it takes her eyes to scan the empty space in front of her and then drop to where I'm crouched. She takes me in, sees the ring, and then immediately starts to cry.

"*Baby*," I say, a laugh in my voice. "I haven't even said anything yet."

She sobs and puts her hands over her face. "I know. I'm sorry. I just love you so much. And it's all a lot to process."

I stand, moving over to her and pulling one of her hands away so I can see her face. It's all wet, her makeup smeared.

"Quinn, it was always you. I know you know that. You were always here..." I take her hand and set it on my chest, feel the way her fingers dig into my shirt with satisfaction. "From the moment I looked over and saw you in that hallway, it was a done deal for me. You ripped my heart out of my chest and you never gave it back. I actually, uh..." I swallow, nervous to tell her this last part. "I actually bought this ring last summer before I came here."

At this, she finally pulls her hands away from her face, her eyes wide. "You did?"

I smile. "I knew I wouldn't use it, but I wanted to have it, just in case. Because I've always been sure that this is what I want. That *you* are what I want. Will you marry me?"

She nods, her wet hands coming up to circle the back of my neck. "Yes, I'll marry you."

She leans in to kiss me as someone says from behind us, "Oh, good."

We both turn and find Sabrina and my mom in the doorway. When I throw my hands up, my mother throws her hands up right back. "You left the door open. I was worried we were going to have to wait all week and keep this a secret."

I stomp toward the door.

"Lydia pulled out lunch leftovers for you," my mother says in a last bid before I slam the door shut and lock it. When I turn back to Quinn, she's grinning, tears still slipping down her face.

"You better get on the bed," I tell her, "so I can make sure you understand that you're mine forever now."

ACKNOWLEDGMENTS

I don't think anyone can understand the impact of the indie romance community until they've been inside it. Since joining this community, I've found so much acceptance and kindness. I've learned things about myself and felt safe to share parts of myself that I always felt others would judge or laugh at me for. So much of that went into Quinn and her fear of being herself. I cannot thank enough everyone who has befriended me, sent me book recommendations, talked about monster peen with me, and just generally been part of this community that has become my home. I love you all so much.

Meghan Logan. Come on, lady. You have to know by now that you're my biggest supporter and that I couldn't do anything without your advice. You help me pick covers, interior images, marketing materials, character names, all of it. You buy and read all the books. You help me talk through outlines. You do write-ins with me. I wouldn't be here if it wasn't for you, bestie.

Jeremy, love of my life, you bust your ass every day so that I can keep making my dream happen. I would never have made it this far without you. Thanks for never being weird about all the monster peen.

Thank you to Christina for my beautiful cover and Gennifer for helping me proofread. You both handled all my jittery nerves with grace.

Big thank you to my ARC team and all my amazing readers and supporters. If you've ever made a social media post, commented, left a review, sent me a message, anything—you make it possible for me to keep going.

ABOUT THE AUTHOR

B. Randall has been a voracious romance reader since she stumbled upon a spicy book at the public library when she was fourteen. She's spent her life falling in love with fictional men and is excited to finally be writing her own. When she's not writing, she's drinking fancy coffee with her friends, listening to the Toni and Ryan Podcast, and watching Formula 1 nonstop. She lives in Dallas with her husband.

ALSO BY B. RANDALL

The Berserkr Gym Series

Come In With The Rain

Make It To Me

Take My Love

Find Me Here

Let Me Fall

Give Your Heart Away

The Vegas Duet

A Man After Midnight

Late Night Talking

Braving the Waves

Writing as Winter Randall

My Best Friend's Mate

The Vamp and I

Five Nights With The Fire Monster

King of the Fire Monsters

Snowed In With The Mountain Monster

Touched by the Shadow Creature

Minotaur Sugar Daddies